Richard William Church, Francis Paget, Mary C Church

Life and Letters of Dean Church

Richard William Church, Francis Paget, Mary C Church

Life and Letters of Dean Church

ISBN/EAN: 9783744704465

Printed in Europe, USA, Canada, Australia, Japan

Cover: Foto ©Raphael Reischuk / pixelio.de

More available books at **www.hansebooks.com**

LIFE AND LETTERS

OF

DEAN CHURCH

EDITED BY HIS DAUGHTER

MARY C. CHURCH

WITH A PREFACE BY

THE DEAN OF CHRIST CHURCH

London

MACMILLAN AND CO.

AND NEW YORK

1894

NOTICE

In putting together this volume of my father's correspondence, it has been my aim to make it a book of
letters rather than in any sense a complete biography.
My father's life, from the time his boyhood ended, fell
naturally into three periods, curiously near to equality
in point of time. Eighteen years were passed at
Oxford; then came nineteen years at Whatley; and
these again were followed by nineteen years at St.
Paul's. These divisions of time I have made use of,
grouping together the series of letters belonging to
each period, and prefixing to each group an introductory sketch, so that the letters might stand with
only such a setting of narrative as is needed to prevent
obscurity in subject or allusion. Only in the Oxford
period, where material was more scanty, has it seemed
necessary to make the narrative rather more continuous
in order that the letters which remain may be fully
intelligible.

It is the defect of such a method that the treatment

of the subjects referred to in the letters is so often slight and fragmentary. As the letters follow each other with their constant and wide variation of allusion and interest, subject after subject seems to rise only to die away without receiving anything like a complete or adequate treatment. But while something of this is doubtless due to a want of skill in editing, it is hard to see how such effect of slightness could to any great extent have been avoided without allowing the volume to grow to the dimensions of a biography, a result which would have defeated the primary object of the book.

I feel that a word of explanation may be needed to account for the large number of letters written from abroad which are included in the volume, and in particular for the series of letters written during a visit to Greece in 1847. It was only after some hesitation, and after finding that they could be included without excluding other letters of general interest, that I decided to give them. The letters of 1847 are so characteristic in themselves, and are so vivid and suggestive in the sketches they contain both of Greek scenery and of the political state of things in Athens at the time of my father's visit, that even at the risk of a certain want of proportion in the volume I have given them almost in their completeness.

Among the many friends whose kindness in lending letters must be acknowledged, my thanks are specially due to Lady Blachford, Mrs. Asa Gray, Miss Mozley, Canon Church, and Dr. Talbot. From my uncle I have also received help in matters concerning my father's family and early life abroad, while without my mother's aid it would have been impossible to put together so fully the sketch of Whatley life. I must also acknowledge Dr. Barrett's kindness in allowing me to reprint his interesting paper of recollections. I cannot conclude without expressing my gratitude to Canon Scott Holland, and to my brother-in-law, the Dean of Christ Church, for contributions to the volume, which have brought out certain aspects of my father's mind and character and influence more clearly and forcibly than they could have been conveyed by the letters alone.

MARY C. CHURCH.

CONTENTS

PREFACE

It is hoped that an attempt may, without impertinence, be here made to put before the reader of these letters some sketch, however slight and faint, of the mind that may be found in them. The letters, with their setting, tell the story of their writer's life : what he was, in the depth of character and personality, must be left untold. But between the outward course of a life and the inner depth (yet interfused with both), there is that broad space in which it is the task of criticism to think out as justly as it can the distinctive notes of a man's mind and work. It is this task that will be here essayed, with the hope of suggesting a few lines of observation, a few points that may be marked in the reading of the book. It must be owned that the case is one in which criticism cannot move without reverence and gratitude attending it. But reverence and gratitude are not a sheer hindrance to criticism in its proper work ; and the intimacy in which they were learnt may countervail,

perhaps, whatever loss of mere impartiality they may
involve.

(i) There was in the mind of the late Dean of St.
Paul's an unusual combination of certain traits and habits
which are generally regarded as characteristic of
separate and special studies; of scholarship, of natural
science, and of history. He had the delicate sense of
appropriateness, the abhorrence of all that was flaunting
and slipshod, the love of neatness and finish, that gave
charm and taught reserve to the scholars of his day.
Nor did he ever drop the pursuits for which these
scholarly gifts enabled him. He loved his classics as
real friends : one volume after another in his library
bears his tidy and discriminating notes, as witnesses to
the width and care with which he read; while the great
authors who were closest to his heart, Homer, Sophocles,
Lucretius, Virgil, went with him on his holidays, and
bear many dates in Switzerland and Italy, with Alpine
flowers between their leaves. Far on in life a tour
through Northern Italy made him think he had never
before done full justice to the *Georgics*, though still he kept
for Lucretius a throne apart. He was working steadily
at the *Ethics* when he was past seventy : he had Homer
by him in his last illness. And thus behind that
scholarly grace and insight which were felt in his essays
on Dante and on Spenser, there was always the sustained interest and work of a true scholar.—He himself

might have laughed if any one had treated him as a real student of natural science. But there was no mistaking the scientific character of his mind, and it can hardly fail to be noticed in his letters. He wrote the article on the discovery of Neptune which caught Le Verrier's attention and first set the *Guardian* in its consistent attitude towards the achievements of natural science. His eager and painstaking interest in botany gave to his friendship with Dr. Asa Gray a peculiar intimacy and delightfulness. His prompt and frank appreciation of Mr. Darwin's great work, at a time when such apprecia- tion was far less general than it is now, was the outcome of a mind that knew at all events what that work meant, and knew enough about it to be neither timorous nor hasty. One feels that such a mind was not likely to blunder about scientific points, nor to imagine that it understood them unless it really did so. It was at least in such sympathy with the distinctive excellences of the man of science as could hardly be attained without some share in them.—But, strong as were the scholarly and scientific elements in the mind, it was in the field of history that its largest and most characteristic and most brilliant powers came to the front. The study of human nature, in its variety, its strangeness, its complexity; the analysis of broad movements into their component forces, or the tracing of them to their many causes ; the severance and appraising of good and bad in the mixed

actions of famous men; the redressing of unjust judgments; the patient observation and description of
great courses of policy or action ;—these were tasks to
which the Dean brought his very keenest interest, on
which he spent his most serious and concentrated work,
in which he seemed to know no weariness. And for
these tasks he had rare gifts—gifts which stood him in
the same stead whether he set them to summon up
and portray the scenes, the struggles, the characters of
St. Anselm's day, or to tell the deeds and sufferings of
that vast drama through which the Ottoman power
moved to its stupendous triumph and the exhausted
Empire to its doom, or to achieve what will surely last
as the most adequate and justly balanced presentation
of the Oxford Movement.

(ii) It was probably through this diversity of gifts
and studies that he gained a peculiar breadth of thought
in deliberation and in judgment. He saw things largely,
with an ample and appreciative survey of their conditions : that which would especially appeal to the scholar
or the man of science, neither displacing nor being
displaced by the dominant interest of the historian.
And, scanning thus the richness of the view, he was apt
to take with him, in judging the affairs and cases of
ordinary life, a broader volume of thought, a greater
multitude of considerations, than most men bear in
mind. He was less likely than most men to forget in

forming a judgment something that should have been
remembered : something that told upon the problem
and might help one towards precisely solving it. One
constantly felt when one was seeking counsel from him
how much his mind was carrying as it did its work. It
carried much, and yet was never cumbered ; partly
because he had a singular habit of disregarding, as if by
set purpose, what was really trivial; never worrying
himself or others over little things, and even, with all
his own exactness, letting harmless, blameless inaccuracy
sometimes go unnoticed ; as though life were too short,
too full, too grave for a man to take every chance of
setting others right. And thus he guarded a certain
simple loftiness, a quiet, unconscious dignity of thought
in the common ways of life ; and when hard cases or
great questions came before him, he seemed instinctively
to know what should be regarded and what let slip.
Statesmanship has always been a rare quality among men;
and it has so often and so disastrously been claimed or
imagined where it was not that its very name is in some
danger of discredit. But it is hard to find another word
which would as well suggest the Dean's way of making
up his mind ; his broad range of thought; his prompt
dismissal of all that was irrelevant or unimportant;
his steady hand in balancing considerations and his
just sense of proportion ; his patient endurance and
frank avowal of uncertainty ; his strong refusal to be

unjust even to his own side ; his undismayed anticipation
of great perils and unexcited contemplation of great
aims ; his equality of courage for self-refraining and for
decisive action.

(iii) In the temperament and disposition of the mind
that was thus endued and trained and used there were
two notes which entered into much that was characteristic of it.   They were its independence and its sense of
humour.   But the note of independence had a peculiar
quality, due in part at least to one great experience in
the Dean's life.   He had been a disciple ; and he had
gone straight on, holding his own unshaken course,
when his master had swerved off and left him.   The
enthusiasm and inspiration which Mr. Newman could
infuse had filled his heart : then came the great loss of
1845 ; and after that he could be no man's disciple ; he
must think for himself, with no dependence on another's
thoughts.   Independent he would anyhow have come
to be, by the necessary bent of his own nature, and as
a matter of duty to himself.   But Mr. Newman's
secession hastened his development in this regard ; and
it gave to the independence of his mind a distinctive
beauty.   For independence, admirable as it is, is apt to
be somewhat unconciliatory and uninviting, apt to dis-
courage the approach of kindness by showing too
plainly the strength if not the pride of self-sufficiency.
In him it was refined and chastened by an undertone of

pathos. He was detached from many things that entangle men; he seemed ready to detach himself from more; and with him peculiarly one felt how the stronghold of a true man's life is not near the frontier, but somewhere far away, remote and lonely and aloft. But that great experience of disappointment which had pressed forward the work of his detachment, the realisation of his independence, was felt in the result: felt through a certain quiet and simple gravity, verging towards sadness, and guarding independence from all touch of hardness or ungentleness or indifference or pride.—It was in his courage of decision that the robust, unhampered energy of an independent mind declared itself most plainly. All his reverence for the rights of others and for the full scope that they should have and use, all his dislike of ill-grounded positiveness, all his insistence on the limitation of our knowledge, all his resolute recollection of our vast uncertainty and ignorance, did not stay him from saying clearly what, so far as he could judge, he clearly saw. So he dealt with the great problems of speculation, with the questions of political and social life, with the difficulties that men come to in their own separate experience. He never forgot the humility that becomes men in this dimly-lighted world, and the determined patience which all true service of mankind demands, where tasks are complex and results are almost sure to be deferred and

mixed and fragmentary : he never trifled with the inde-
feasible right, the inevitable duty of each man ultimately
in matters of conduct to make up his own mind; but
where he had to give advice, or bear his part in controversy or discussion, he saw neither reverence nor
patience nor humility in disguising what he thought or
professing any doubt he did not feel.   He believed that
men were meant to think and judge and choose, as in
God's sight and mindful of their condition : so he did
his best with the faculties he had ; and he frankly said
what he believed.—There was, in his exercise of deliberation and judgment, a rare union of balance and decision,
of reserve and self-committal, of deference and self-
respect, of modesty and boldness.

The sense of humour seldom gets due credit for the
good work it does or helps to do.   Men often mark the
blunders that are made through lack of it; but they
do not generally think of the real excellences of mind
and character into which it enters, and which more or
less depend on it for their preservation and advance-
ment.   It was in the late Dean of St. Paul's a very keen
and delicate sense; it was delightful to tell him a good
story, or to watch him as he saw some ludicrous position,
or recalled some bit of misplaced pompousness : he had
a quick eye for fun, and enjoyed it splendidly.   And
this sense of humour ministered to much that was both
strong and charming in him; it bore a real part in

making him what he was, and enabling him for the especial work he did. Without it he might hardly have been able to sustain the perfect simplicity and lightness of manner which saved him wholly from that suspicion of somehow liking homage, and that annoyance and un-reality in receiving it, to which big people are sometimes liable. It was inconceivable that he should play the great man, or put himself in any attitude, or let any one make a fuss about him, or approach him otherwise than with straightforward plainness, or talk as though there were anything mysterious or unusual about him. He would have seen too vividly the humour of the situation, and might perhaps have conveyed to his visitor very gently whatever sense of it he was able to receive. And so the consciousness of power, the discipline of prominence, the enthusiasm of friends, the praise of strangers never touched with any change his simple, genial enjoyment of all pleasant things that came to him: frankly and naturally he welcomed them: great or small, homely or recondite, rare or common-place, passing or enduring, he found and owned the pleasure in them, delighting if he could help others to be as pleased as he was. But meanwhile all this simplicity and ease and unpretentiousness was making it possible for him, without any risk of mistake in others, minds or in his own, to maintain a singular and natural dignity;—a dignity as clear and obvious as it was unobtrusive; a dignity which others were the more unlikely to forget because he never thought about it. Probably no one ever tried either to flatter him or to take a liberty with him without presently regretting the attempt.

(iv) But all that has hitherto been said stays very far behind what those who knew the Dean will look for in any study of his mind. And as one tries to press on and reach the real secrets of his distinctive strength, the traits which gave his work its singular purity and value, one finds, of course, that it is impossible for criticism to halt at the frontier of personal character : impossible to appraise the gifts and habits of a man's mind without speaking of the forces that ruled his heart and will. If a man is sincere and thoughtful and consistent, if he is trying honestly to live one life, not two or three, his moral qualities and his religious convictions will tell all through his work, in the manner of his thinking, in his instinctive attitude towards all that comes before him, and in the very style of his talking and writing; and on those qualities and convictions his work will depend for its most penetrating and most lasting power. It is certain that if the Dean had been less patient, less strenuous in his effort to be just to all men, he never could have borne the part and left the mark he did. The notes of patience and of justice are on all his work : even as one felt them in the way he

spoke of men, in the weight he gave to the considerations which might fairly weigh with others, in the large
allowance he would always make for the vast diversity
of men's gifts and opportunities, for the inscrutable
depth of every human life, for the unknown hindrances
and difficulties and discouragements through which those
who seem to advance slowly may be winning a heroic
way.—But patient as he was, he could be angry when
need came ; angry with a quiet and self-possessed intensity which made his anger very memorable. The
sight of injustice, of strength or wealth presuming on
its advantages, of insolence—(a word that came from
his lips with a peculiar ring and emphasis),—called out
in him something like the passion that has made men
patriots when their people were oppressed, something
of that temper which will always make tyranny insecure and persecution hazardous. One felt that many
years of quiet and hidden self-control must lie behind
the power of wielding rightly such a weapon as that
anger : an anger that was just and strong and calm.—
But further back in his character than either patience
or the power of anger there was an habitual feeling of
which only those who knew him well, perhaps, became
distinctly conscious, but which, when once it had been
discovered, might be traced in much that he said and
did. It was as though he lived in constant recollection
of something that was awful and even dreadful to him ;

something that bore with searching force on all men's ways and purposes and hopes and fears; something before which he knew himself to be, as it were, continually arraigned; something which it was strange and pathetic to find so little recognised in current views of life. He seemed to bear about with him a certain hidden, isolating, constraining, and ennobling fear, which quenched the dazzling light of many things that attract most men; a fear which would have to be clean got rid of before time-serving or unreality could have a chance with him. Whatever that fear was it told upon his work in many ways; it helped him, probably, in great things to be unworldly; it sustained with an imperious and ever-present sanction his sense and care for perfect justice, in act and word, in his own life and in his verdicts on the past: and it may well have borne part in making his style what it was; for probably few men have ever written so well and stayed so simply anxious to write truly.

(v) It may seem odd that in the attempt which this Preface represents nothing should have been said of the Dean's place and work in the field of theology. The omission is deliberate; and it is not prompted only by the sense of the subtle and manifold difficulty of the subject, and the likelihood and harmfulness of mistakes in dealing with it. That sense seems, indeed, to be deepened as one thinks about the subject, and as one

endeavours to reach anything like thoroughness and
precision in regard to it; and he who would really set
about it might find that it wanted a separate essay for
itself. But there are, further, three reasons to warrant
its omission here.—First, the topic in some of its essential
aspects belongs more naturally to the study of his
life than to the study of his mind.—Secondly, real and
distinctive as his theological power was, its peculiar
character and excellence was derivative rather than
primary;—the general quality and endowments of his
mind, rather than any faculties or characteristics exclusively adapted to theological work, made him what
he was as a theologian. And thus it may be hoped
that, in this volume, not those letters only which con-
cern matters of doctrine and ecclesiastical polity, but
some others also may conspire to give a better idea of
the Dean's bearing in theological study or debate than
could be given at all briefly : an idea which may be
defined, confirmed, enriched by acquaintance with his
books throughout the whole of their wide range. For
in all alike there may appear that union of deference
and independence which probably accounts for much of
his peculiar power as a religious teacher.—And, lastly,
the consideration of his thought and teaching in theology
would, by reason of those demands and opportunities
which make the difference between theology and every
other science, carry this essay deep into the full con-

sideration of traits purely moral and spiritual; and that task has been here disclaimed. It is a task which any one who knew the Dean might at once both long and fear to set about. But there are words of his which effectually reinforce in the present case the instinct of reserve. For not long before his death he wrote thus to the author of this Preface: "I often have a kind of waking dream; up one road, the image of a man decked and adorned as if for a triumph, carried up by rejoicing and exulting friends, who praise his goodness and achievements; and, on the other road, turned back to back to it, there is the very man himself, in sordid and squalid apparel, surrounded not by friends, but by ministers of justice, and going on, while his friends are exulting, to his certain and perhaps awful judgment. That vision rises when I hear, not just and conscientious endeavours to make out a man's character, but when I hear the loose things that are said—often in kindness and love—of those beyond the grave."

F. P.

Christ Church, *August 1st*, 1894.

LIFE & LETTERS OF DEAN CHURCH

PART I

RICHARD WILLIAM CHURCH was born, the eldest of three sons, at Lisbon, the 25th of April 1815. His father, John Dearman Church, was born at Cork in 1781, and was the son of Matthew Church—the head of a merchant-house in that city—and of Ann Dearman, of a Yorkshire family. Both Mr. and Mrs. Matthew Church came of Quaker parentage, and were professing members of the Society of Friends; and there grew up through marriage in the next generation various connections with Backhouses, Gurneys, and other well-known Quaker names. The link which bound the family to the Society did not, however, last longer unbroken, though it would not perhaps be impossible to discern certain distinctive traits of Quaker character, which in some of its members at least survived the outward change. Mr. John Dearman Church was formally "disunited" from the

B

Connection, and was baptized a member of the English Church, at the time of his marriage in 1814. His younger brother Richard, afterwards General Sir Richard Church, broke away earlier, and at sixteen entered the army, where a commission was purchased for him in the 13th Light Infantry; the choice of such a profession in itself involving severance from a community, with which a character, keenly ambitious of military distinction, and marked by a strong natural love of adventure, had very little in common.

In 1810 business affairs in Cork no longer prospering, Mr. J. D. Church went to Portugal and settled in Lisbon, where, since the opening of the war, and the French occupation of Lisbon, which had broken up many of the old mercantile houses, new opportunities for successful ventures in business now offered themselves. Four years later he married Miss Metzener, of an Anglo-German family which had been long resident in Lisbon. The marriage took place in London, and shortly afterwards, Mr. Church returned with his wife to Portugal. An adventure which befell them on their journey thither is a singular example of the dangers to which travellers at that period might be exposed. The passage by mail-packet from Falmouth to Lisbon was made in small armed brigs, and was attended in time of war by a certain amount of risk from the chance of attack by French or American privateers. During their voyage, and when they were some days out to sea, the mail-packet was hailed by an English man-of-war, the *Primrose*, of eighteen guns, commanded by Captain

Phillott. By some strange failure in the reading of the
signals the character of neither vessel was made clear to
the other, and the captain of the *Primrose*, believing the
packet to be an American privateer, opened fire, which
was promptly returned by the brig, and a sharp engagement ensued for half an hour. The misunderstanding was at length cleared up, and each vessel went
her way, but the affair did not close without the loss
of six lives (two of the passengers by the mail-packet
being killed), besides injuries more or less serious to
some twenty of the crew on either side.

The first year of Richard Church's life was spent in
Lisbon. In 1816 his father retired from business, and
with the intention of settling in England, bought a
small property, Ashwick Grove, in Somersetshire. But
threatenings of ill-health rendered an English life un-
desirable, and in 1818 he went to Italy, finally settling
with his family in Florence. Here a house was bought,
the Casa Annalena, in the Via Romana, adjoining the
Boboli Gardens; and this became their home for the
next eight years. Letters of that time, which still
remain, show Mr. and Mrs. Church to have been people
of much quiet reality of religious feeling and open-
hearted affection; possessing a good deal of cultivation
and taste, and taking their part among the English
residents in the social life of Florence, besides seeing
something of the Italian society of the period. The
letters also convey a very pleasant picture of the happy
home-life in Florence, in which the children have plainly
the central place, which was passed amid so much of

brightness and beauty and historic interest, with its yearly changes of scene, and the new experiences brought by each summer's *villeggiatura* at Leghorn or in the hill country about the baths of Lucca. To an English child naturally quick-witted, and readily observant of all that was passing round him, these glimpses into a foreign world, which in many points was in such strange contrast with the life of the little colony in its midst, gave opportunity for ever renewed wonder and inquiry. At five years old Richard went with his parents to the south of Italy to visit his uncle, General Church, who, after a life of varied military adventure during the Napoleonic wars in Egypt, France, and Italy, had entered the service of the King of Naples, and was at this time acting as Viceroy in the two provinces of Apulia, Terra di Bari and Terra d'Otranto. After some years of vigorous administration, General Church had succeeded in restoring order to the provinces under his rule, had stamped out brigandage, and had broken the power of the secret societies which had long been the terror of the country. In 1820 he was residing at Lecce, the capital of the province, in supreme command; enjoying not only the favour of the Bourbon Government, but a wide popularity among the inhabitants of Apulia, both on account of his personal bravery, and for the resolute justice by which he had made possible to them the elements at least of a peaceable and law-abiding life. Some dim memories of this journey, with its strange experiences and changing scenes and picturesque figures, remained in the boy's mind; the one clear im-

pression which survived being the sight of brigands'
heads stuck upon poles, in places along the roadside—
left there as significant tokens of his uncle's authority.
They were still at Naples, on their return from Lecce,
when the city broke out into revolution, and, together
with other foreign residents, they were obliged to take
refuge on board ship in the harbour.   To Mr. and Mrs.
Church it was a time of great anxiety and some peril;
to the child the only recollection that remained was of
being lifted up on deck by the sailors, to watch the
firing from the forts, and the fighting in the streets
and on the Chiaja.

At eleven years old, Richard, who had early shown
signs of unusual intelligence and aptitude for learning,
was sent with his second brother, two years younger
than himself, to a small preparatory school which had
been set up for English boys at Leghorn.   It was during
their stay here that there grew up in both boys that
love for the sea and for everything belonging to it,
which characterised them through life.[1]   In 1826 the
memories of the part played by England in the
Napoleonic wars were still fresh in men's minds, and to
the quick imagination of the elder boy—himself born
only two months before Waterloo—they were brought
home the more vividly, by the share which his uncle
had taken in campaigns in Egypt and Italy, as well as

[1] His brother Bromley eventually entered the merchant service.
In 1852, whilst in command of an East Indiaman bound from Bombay
to China, he was wrecked, and his vessel totally lost, off one of
a group of desolate islands some sixty miles from Sumatra.   With some
of his crew he succeeded in landing upon the island, where he died of
fever after some months of great privation and suffering.

by the foreign scenes and experiences amid which the
life of the family was cast.   But above all, English
naval history, with its stirring narratives of courage
and adventure, woke up all his enthusiastic interest.
Southey's *Life of Nelson* was one of the favourite books
of his boyhood, read and re-read, often and eagerly;
and it is characteristic, that among other early relics
long treasured by the mother, was a card drawn and
painted by him in a childish, irregular hand, with the
words of Nelson's famous signal at Trafalgar.   At
Leghorn the brothers found free scope for their prevail-
ing passion.   Out of school hours all their time was
spent in wandering about the harbour of the little port;
sailing toy boats of their own fashioning in its quiet
waters, or watching the many varieties of foreign
shipping and craft which passed in and out, and learning
to master the differences of their build and rigging.
But this pleasant life was not to be of long duration.
In the beginning of 1828 their father was struck down
by a sudden and fatal illness at Florence; and although
the boys were hastily sent for, they arrived too late to
see him alive.   Some months of great anxiety and sorrow
followed, during which the home in Florence was broken
up, and harassing business arrangements were concluded;
and at length, in May of the same year, Mrs. Church
with her three children left Italy and returned to
England, where they settled in Bath.

So complete a severance of all early surroundings and
associations from those of later years has something
exceptional about it; and it was this perhaps which

helped to give a distinct and enduring freshness to the memory of those years of happy boyhood in Italy which were thus suddenly brought to a close. A charm belonged to them which was never weakened or dispelled. Florence, in the Dean's recollections, always seemed a home, and when he revisited it years after it still wore to him the same home-like and familiar look which he remembered—the one place, it seemed to him, that he never could tire of.

The varied and unusual training of these early years had doubtless secured to the boy much that was of permanent value for mind and character, but it had not been the best preparation for the schooling which was now to follow it, or for the strangeness and isolation of the life of the next few years. The appearance which England presented to the family upon their first arrival from Italy was dreary enough. Mrs. Church had spent the greater part of her life abroad, and had little acquaintance with English ways, and she came to England with scarcely a friend to whom she could turn for counsel or aid. It had been his father's intention that Richard should be sent to Winchester, but his mother's narrower means, and his own health, which at this time was far from strong, prevented this wish from being carried out. He was sent for a term to a school at Exeter, where his first experience of English school life was brought to an abrupt conclusion by the sudden disappearance of the master, the boys being sent back to their several homes. He was then sent to Redlands, near Bristol, a school of a pronounced Evangelical type,

under the headmastership of Dr. Swete, where the teaching was careful and accurate, but with little apparently
of power or inspiration about it.   No letters of this date
remain, but a few pages of recollections written long
after recall the character of school and college training.
Whatever were the defects in the teaching at Redlands,
he quickly learnt there to work well and steadily.   " I
suppose I sapped," he writes, "and was made to learn
rules carefully.   But as to any spirit in our lessons, or
examples of scholarship or scholarly tastes, there was
none.   The grind was the thing, and not a bad thing.
It saved time afterwards."   Great stress was laid on
Evangelical principles, which coloured all the religious
teaching of the school, and the boys were encouraged,
side by side with their classical work, to write out
sermon notes, and to find texts in defence of Justifica-
tion by Faith, Sanctification, Total Depravity, Election,
and Final Perseverance.   "I remember," he writes,
"questions arising in my thoughts as to whether we
really could be so cocksure about the absolute truth of
the Evangelical formulæ, as was commonly taken for
granted.   One of the great watchwords was the right
of private judgment: and we used on Sundays to have
to find texts to prove it.   And it used to occur to me,
how then can we condemn the Socinians, who go wrongly
by using it—they with the Roman Catholics being the
special type of heretics whom we thought of, and looked
at when we saw them, with a kind of awful curiosity
and dismay.   And the question, what is the proof of the
Bible and of its inspiration was one of those uneasy

ones, on which I did not feel that I had a solid ground,
though I never doubted that there was one." It was
the time of Catholic Emancipation, and men's minds,
especially among • the Evangelicals, were full of the
dangers and evils of Popery. There was a Reformation
Society, to the meetings and debates of which the elder
boys of the school were allowed to go—" where a certain
Rev. N. Armstrong used to pour forth wonderful de-
clamations on the 'Sacrifice of the Mass,' 'Tradition,'
etc., with glib quotations from the Council of Trent and
the Breviary. I remember," the recollections continue,
" buying a 'Council of Trent' that I might emulate him
in finding passages to confound possible Popish controversialists, who at that time were in the softening
and minimising mood. I used to think Mr. Armstrong
the height of eloquence. I once heard Robert Hall, and
thought how pale and subdued his preaching was, compared with Mr. Armstrong's highly-spiced tropes and
elaborate similes." Teaching of this kind could scarcely
fail to have its effect on a boy's mind ; and in recalling
the character of his religious convictions at this period
he speaks of having taken in the religious colour of the
place too much for any healthy sincerity. For the rest,
whilst on good terms, both with schoolfellows and masters,
he went very much his own way, a reserved, serious,
studious boy, loving books and already beginning to
collect them ; and with an eye to editions, which he
used to search for among the second-hand book shops in
Bristol.

But school life did not pass altogether devoid of incident and excitement of a more secular kind :—" The great event, while I was at Redlands, was the Bristol Riots, and the burning of the gaols, the Bishop's Palace, and Queen Square, in October 1831. We were going to church on Sunday, when we heard shots fired in the direction of Bristol. We knew that Bristol was excited about Sir Charles Wetherell, who had had to escape from the mob over the roofs of houses; but we knew nothing more. In the evening I went out of the school-room into the playground, and there was half the horizon lighted up with vast conflagrations. Of course the excitement was tremendous. No news had come out, and next morning the news was that the mob were in possession."

To the boys, of course, it seemed as if attack on the school were imminent :—"It was a question whether any of us had a pistol among his contraband treasures. I cannot remember how we passed the night, but I think we must have gone to bed. However, we heard in the course of the day that the yeomanry and some of the cavalry had come back, and cleared the streets, and slain some of the mob. There were after-tragedies—the court-martial, and Colonel Brereton's suicide, and the hanging of the rioters. But I don't think it made much impression on us, except to make us think Reform and · Radicalism very abominable things."

Mr. Church remained at Redlands until 1833, when he went up to Oxford, and went into residence at Wadham. "I was sent to Wadham," he writes, "because B. P. Symons and Thomas Griffiths and Vores, the tutors, were of Evangelical principles, and it was a college where some men worked. It had always been settled in Florence days that I was to go to Oxford. After matriculation I went back to school, till I went into residence at the Easter Term, 1833. I did not hear much about Oxford in the interval. I became acquainted in the interval with Keble's *Christian Year*. But I was warned by some Evangelical clergyman that it was not quite 'sound' about 'vital religion.' Also I heard two names, but only heard them, Michell of Lincoln, a great tutor, and Charles Marriott. I forget from whom I heard of Marriott. He was spoken of as very clever, but in danger of being influenced by ' un-evangelical doctrines.' "

An event which indirectly had considerable influence on Mr. Church's career at Oxford arose out of his mother's second marriage, which had taken place in 1833, to Mr. Crokat, a widower with a grown-up family. This was followed a year later by the marriage of one of his step-sisters to George Moberly, who was then Fellow and Tutor of Balliol, and who subsequently be-came Headmaster of Winchester and Bishop of Salis-bury. For one who had gone up to Oxford, as Mr. Church had gone, shy and diffident, with few acquaint-ances and no University connections, the friendship which was thus brought about with a man of unusual distinction and of high standing in the University was the help and stimulus he most needed. He owed to it his first insight into a new world, wider both intellectu-

ally and morally than any he had yet known. After
the narrow sympathies and commonplace teaching of
Redlands, the force and keenness and suggestiveness of
Mr. Moberly's talk, combined with his fine scholarship
and literary taste, came upon the younger man with the
awakening power of a revelation.

At first starting Mr. Church's life at Wadham was
a solitary one. "When I went up after Easter in
1833," he writes, "I knew no one in Oxford; I had an
introduction to R. Michell of Lincoln, who was ever
very kind to me, but at that time could not do much
for a freshman, beyond asking him to breakfast." A
contemporary letter to his mother confirms these recollections :—

WADHAM, 2nd June 1833.

I suppose you are very anxious to know what I think of
Oxford. I must answer you as I have done all my corre-
spondents whom I have favoured with a letter : " pretty
well," or " I do not know." " Oh, I forgot, I like it very
well." You must excuse all the nonsense I write, for the
heat, I believe, has sublimated my head; and if I was to
attempt to write gravely, my head would begin to ache.
My greatest bore here is not knowing men. I am a freshman as yet, and of course everybody is shy. However, I
hope to be better off in time. Indeed I have hardly anything to tell you of. My life here is quite as monotonous
as it was at school. I have had no adventures as yet, and I
have only been proctorised once, for not having my gown on.
People leave me alone, and I leave them alone, and so it
goes on. " Pleasant life ! " you will say. " Very pleasant,"
I answer.

But, by degrees, as he became more at home in his new life, he began to extend the range of his acquaintance. " There was a very clever set at Wadham," the recollections continue : " Brancker from Shrewsbury had just got the Ireland over older men like R. Scott, and was rather set up by it. Lloyd and E. Massie were also Shrewsbury men ; and O. H. B. Hyman, afterwards Ireland Scholar, and C. Badham from Eton, who might have been anything he pleased, and is now Professor of Greek in the University of Sydney, and one of the first Greek scholars going, and C. B. Dalton, who had just taken his degree, were all men far above the ordinary rank. . . . I shrank from the very pronounced Evangelical men ; my friends were mostly men of no special colour, quiet, well-behaved, sensible, not likely to make a noise in the University or the world. . . . But all sets touched more or less ; the quiet set had relations with the fast set, and met occasionally at wine parties and breakfasts. . . . The only out-college man of any mark, except Moberly, that I knew much of while I was at Wadham, was Charles Marriott. He called on me the first term. He had got his Oriel Fellowship, and I thought it an immense honour to be noticed by such a swell. I don't suppose I saw very much of him, but he never lost sight of me. His kindness and affection grew and never faltered to the day of his death. He was the earliest friend to whose undeniable superiority I could look up : others had been more or less my equals. . . . No man, I suppose, was more smiled at in Oxford, both for his words and his silence. But no

man, that I ever heard of, had such strange influence,
the influence arising from sheer respect, in turbulent
Oxford scenes among the undergraduates, as in the rows
at the Union.[1] No one was so listened to, as if men
believed in his sincerity and truth of purpose, and
entire absence of indirect motives. . . . I passed my
Little-go in the October Term of 1833, and then had to
go home ill. Little-go was the first public exhibition I
had made of myself, and so was a serious affair to me :
but a Wadham tutor, Harding, wanted, I think, to show
me off to his colleague, Peter Hansell of University, and
besides the regular work, which was quite easy, asked
me to do a bit of Greek prose, as a work of supererogation. I think this was the first thing that made me
think I might perhaps read for honours. And when I
came back I settled regularly to read."

In a letter to his mother, dated the 6th July 1835,
occurs the first mention of the names of Newman and
Keble :—

I dined the other day at Oriel, and was introduced to
Newman, and to Keble, the author of the *Christian Year;*
both of them men to whom I have looked up with great
interest and veneration. I had a conversation with our
Warden. Among other things, he said that he hoped I had
no idle sisters at home to interrupt my reading ; and
cautioned me against them—pray tell this to Louisa.

"I do not remember," the recollections continue,

[1] Mr. Church was elected a member of the Union in February
1834.

"when I first heard Newman preach. I did not for some time much care to go to St. Mary's to the four o'clock service, because I thought it rather a fashion of a set who talked a kind of religious philosophy— Evangelico-Coleridgian, and claimed at once to admire Newman, whom the common set decried, and to admire with reserve. It was said that the dinner hour at Wadham was set to make it inconvenient. But whether it was the first sermon or not, I remember the first sermon that impressed me : the sermon on St. Andrew's Day, 'The World's Benefactors.' It seemed to me so entirely out of the beaten track of sermons, waking up recollections of πολλὰ τὰ δεινὰ, and the Prometheus. But I don't think I went frequently till later : till after my degree. I was now in earnest reading for the schools. Moberly helped me, and in my last term R. Michell very kindly let me come to him gratis, he being in high request as a private tutor. I used to go to him with Mules of B. N. C. (afterwards of Exeter), and sometimes when he was shaving ; and he used to cross-question us in Rhetoric and Ethics. I went into the schools (at the end of the October Term of 1836) with no great hope. . . . I was deeply disgusted with the logic paper, and not much better pleased with the succeeding ones. Marriott comforted me, saying that a third was a very good class, and that classes were altogether not of much account. And under that impression I went in for *vivâ voce*. The examiners were F. Oakeley, H. B. Wilson, T. Twiss, and T. L. Claughton. I did not expect to shine in *vivâ voce*, and I didn't.

Claughton took me in 'science,' Twiss in history, Wilson in translation, and I don't think I did anything well. But I was thanked for my papers — 'science,' essay, history, Latin — and that of course meant that my first was safe. In due time the list came out. It was a great surprise to me: and to the University I was a dark horse. But it was more than a surprise. It opened to me a new prospect: I had never thought much of remaining at Oxford after my degree. From most fellowships I was shut out, from having been born abroad. But now I might think of going in for one at Balliol or Oriel. And for this I made my account, taking pupils in the meantime. And now I could dine at high tables and go into Common rooms. From this time, from the leisure following the schools, began my closer connection with the men of the Movement — first through Marriott, and men to whom he introduced me, and then in time through Newman himself. There was a year and a half between my degree (November 1836– April 1838) and going to Oriel as Fellow. I had pupils, and an exhibition at Wadham, which enabled me to stay up at Oxford: I was reading with a view to the Oriel Fellowship, and in Common rooms, etc., making new out-college acquaintance, mainly of the Exeter and Oriel men. I wrote for the English essay, on Mahomet, which P. C. Claughton got: mine was a lumbering affair, overweighted with information which I had not the skill to use; but I was disappointed at not getting it. But what indicated the company into which I was passing was my work on the translation of St. Cyril of

Jerusalem, on which I was employed through 1837, and which was published in the autumn of 1838. It was edited and prepared for press by J. H. N., who dated his preface St. Matthew's Day, 1838. It was the second of the series—St. Augustine's *Confessions* having been the first. Looking back at it now I see the marks of hurry. It is shamefully full of errata, his fault as much as mine. And for its importance I don't think it was adequately done. Indeed I never properly liked the work, and did it rather as a task. I don't think I knew enough to estimate its importance, and translating, unless you have some enthusiasm, is flat work."

At this point the recollections end. Mr. Church's note-books show that he was reading hard for the Fellowship, and that his reading was taking a wider range. Two entries in them are worth recording, for the evidence they afford of some of the influences by which his mind was now being moulded. "It is a great wish of mine," he notes down, "to be properly acquainted with Butler, to lay the foundations of my own mind amid his works—to have him ever facing me and imbuing me with his spirit;" and a little later, "there is something in Maurice, and his master Coleridge, which wakens thought in me more than any other writings almost: with all their imputed mysticism they seem to me to say plain things as often as most people." From the time he took his degree he became a regular attendant at St. Mary's. Mr. Newman's sermon, "Ventures of Faith," or as it was called when first published, "Make Ventures for Christ's Sake," had already, in 1836, made a deep impression upon his mind, seeming to come to him as a direct call to a deeper and more searching reality in his religious life. It inspired his first great practical effort at self-denial. It seemed to him, as he looked back, to have been in some sort the turning point of his life.

In April of 1838 Mr. Church stood for and gained his Oriel Fellowship. The late Rector of Lincoln, himself a candidate at Oriel at this election, speaks in his Autobiography with generous appreciation of his rival's success:[1]—"The successful candidates were Church of Wadham, now Dean of St. Paul's, and J. C. Prichard of Trinity. . . . I presume that Church was Newman's candidate, though so accomplished a scholar as the Dean need not have required any party push. I have always looked upon Church as the type of the Oriel Fellow; Richard Michell said, at the time of the election : 'there is such a moral beauty about Church, that they could not help taking him !'"

In a letter written in 1885 to Dr. Liddon,[2] the Dean describes the character which the examination took in his day, and the forms which belonged to it :—"I will try and put down what I remember of the Oriel Fellowship examinations in the old time. They never advertised vacancies in those days. The Provost held his head high, and said if persons wanted to know if there were any Fellowships to be filled up they could come and inquire ; and it was only late in my residence that some

---

[1] Pattison's *Memoirs*, p. 163.
[2] *Life of Dr. Pusey*, vol. i. p. 66.

of the younger and more practical men carried the point about advertising. Besides, in the older time, Oriel and Balliol Fellowships were things that every one was keen about, and every one knew without advertising how many were to be tried for. The first thing was to call on the Provost, and ask his leave to stand. He would ask you what your plans were, and whether you knew any of the Fellows, and what your family was, and what your means were; for independent means were held to exclude a man. . . . If the Provost gave leave, he told you that you were to write a Latin letter to each of the Fellows, stating the grounds on which you desired election, and on which you thought you might be entitled to do so. This was not a mere formal application, and in some cases it was a lengthy affair : it was meant to test a man's power of putting his own personal case and wishes and intentions into Latin : some of these letters were very good and characteristic. You were also to call and present yourself to the Dean, and some one or other of the Fellows, or else the Dean asked you to dine and go to Common room, where of course you were more or less trotted out and observed upon.

"The examination was always in Easter week, and lasted four days, from Monday to Thursday. I received a card (I am speaking of 1838) from the Dean, W. J. Copleston, telling me to be in hall at ten on Monday, and bring with me a certain volume of the *Spectator*. On Monday accordingly we all met in the hall. We were told we might have as long as we liked

for our papers till it got too dark to see, but we should
not have candles : that the papers would be given us
together, which we might work at as we pleased ; but
that we must remain in the hall till we had done them,
or till we went out for good.   There was to be no
break in the middle of the day to go out. Copleston
then told us what we were to do. We had a longish
passage from our *Spectator* to turn into Latin, and an
English essay to write on a passage of Bacon. And
then he left us to make what use of the time we liked.
Most of us worked on till about five. I remember
being bored at not knowing which paper to attack first.
It used to be said that when James Mozley was in for
the Fellowship he kept on till the last, and when it got
dark lay down by the fire and wrote by firelight, and
produced an essay of about ten lines, but the ten lines
were such as no other man in Oxford could have
written. On Tuesday it was the same thing, the papers
being a Latin essay and, I think, a bit of English to be
translated into Greek. On Wednesday a bit of Greek
to be translated into English, and a paper of so called
philosophical questions.   But the work was mainly
composition and translation.   The questions were very
general, not involving directly much knowledge, but
trying how a man could treat ordinary questions which
interest cultivated men.   It was altogether a trial, not
of how much men knew, but of how they knew, and
what they could do.   The last two days were varied by
excursions to the ' Tower ' for *vivâ voce*, which was made
a good deal of.   One of the Fellows called you out of

the hall, and led you up a winding cork-screw staircase,
at the top of which a door opened, and let you into the
presence of the assembled Fellows seated round a table
with pen and paper before them. You were placed
before a desk, on which were Latin and Greek texts.
You were given one of these, and told to look over a
given passage for two minutes or one minute, or to read
it off at sight and translate it. This you did in perfect
silence round you—the only thing heard, besides your
own voice, being the scratching of a dozen pens at the
table. You bungled through it without remark, and
another book was given you, and then another—the
last being perhaps some unintelligible passage from
Plutarch about the moon or the like. When you had
done the Provost thanked you, and another Junior
Fellow took charge of you, conversing pleasantly with
you in your stupified condition, and escorted you to the
Common room, where you remained for the rest of the
time. The next and last day *vivâ voce* again, in the
same way, not quite so bad, because you were more
accustomed to it, but still very horrible ; and then you
went home. If you were elected, the Provost's servant
called on you the next day, with the Provost's compliments, and requested your presence at the scene of
your late torture, the Tower ; and you went and received
the congratulations of the Provost and Fellows; and
later, you were admitted probationer Fellow in chapel.
You were introduced after service by one of the Junior
Fellows, who led you to the Provost's stall, and the
Provost, as if much surprised, asked you 'Domine, quid

petis ?' to which you answered, Peto beneficium
hujusce collegii in annum,' which the Provost graciously
conceded to you, and you were conducted to your
place."

With Mr. Church's success at Oriel new thoughts
and new prospects opened upon him. If he had looked
forward before, it had been to taking orders when he
left Oxford, and settling down to a quiet scholar's life
in some country parish, where he might have plenty
of leisure for thought and reading. But at Oriel he
found himself at once brought into contact with new
and powerful influences. In 1838, the Oxford Movement was already preparing to pass out of its earlier
stages and on towards its stormy conclusion, and Mr.
Church took his place in its ranks, where he soon
became connected, in different degrees of intimacy,
with the group of younger men round Newman, who
were to affect the character of its later development.
Two friendships, in particular, both of them lasting unbroken through life, date from this period. One of
them was with Mr., afterwards Sir Frederic Rogers,
who became Lord Blachford—a former pupil of Hurrell
Froude's and an intimate friend of Mr. Newman's—
himself a Fellow of Oriel. The other was with James
Mozley. But above all, Mr. Church was brought by
his residence at Oriel into personal intimacy with Mr.
Newman himself; and to the influence which the
sermons at St. Mary's had already exerted, was now
added that of a daily companionship, which soon grew
into a friendship of the closest and most familiar kind.

The letters of the next seven years deal very incom-
pletely, alike with the Tractarian Movement at Oxford
and with Mr. Church's share in it. Up to 1845 his
intimate friends were for the most part, like himself,
resident in Oxford, and constant intercourse took the
place of letter-writing. Some letters remain which were
written to Mr. Rogers after he had left Oriel for London ;
but his only regular correspondent was his mother, who
knew little of Oxford, and who was still deeply attached
to the Evangelical teaching of her youth. This, though
it could not disturb the confidence and affection which
existed between them, made it natural that Mr. Church
in his letters to her should dwell rather on the personal
aspects of his life at Oxford, than on the varying phases
of the Movement in which he was taking his share.

Mr. Church's ordination took place at Christmas, 1839,
in St. Mary's, in company, among others, with A. P.
Stanley, whose contemporary he was. "I shall read,"
he writes after it to his mother, "for the first time in
St. Mary's on Sunday in the afternoon at four o'clock.
It is trying, as it is rather a large church, and difficult
to read in. But it is the custom for the Fellows of
Oriel to read there for the first time." The two following years saw him fairly settled in his new life. Within
the year which followed his election to the Fellowship
he found himself obliged, reluctantly enough, to take a
vacant tutorship at Oriel. The work was not in its
nature congenial to him, and it interfered beyond all
anticipation with his schemes for reading. "Oh the
weight of this tutorship," he sighs, "instead of quiet

reading." But he found time, in addition to his work with his pupils, and his own reading, for pushing on his studies in new directions.

To his Mother.

Oriel, 11th March 1839.

I have just been attending a course of lectures on anatomy, which have not had the effect usually ascribed to them of making people valetudinarians. I cannot say that my equanimity either was or is much disturbed. I am afraid I am very hard-hearted, for I neither found it requisite to turn pale when others did, nor did the reflection that I had seen strange sights interfere with my dinner or sleep. However, I cannot say I should like a doctor's business; it is one thing to see things where there can be no pain, and another to operate oneself on a living man. . . . My vacation will be a short and broken one, I am sorry to say. I shall have to be back here again by Easter Sunday to be admitted actual Fellow, but I shall return to you after that I hope. It seems so strange to think that it was but a year ago that I was trembling and shrinking on the verge of my examination. I did not dream then of being tutor here on the next anniversary.

Of his work as tutor he writes again, in half-humorous complaint, to his mother, who was then living at Burnham :—

Oriel, 5th May 1839.

Oxford is very pleasant : the gardens are looking very beautiful in this fine weather. But I miss the liberty of Burnham. Instead of lounging out at my pleasure, or looking through the Beeches at the sky, I am tied all the morning, and can only see how fine it is out of doors through the windows : and my chief objects of contemplation are the impudent faces, gay waistcoats, sparkling breast-pins, tattered gowns and unread books of my "young friends," the undergraduates,—dear creatures, who come in steaming and perfuming my room with every possible combination of tobacco smoke, scents, and pomatum.   However, I am rather hard on them ; they don't all smoke, and scent themselves, and look impudent, but I had a strong contrast in my mind between them and the Beeches, which none of them look impudent.

A few weeks of the Long Vacation of 1839 were spent abroad in company with Stanley and Frederick Faber, exploring Belgian cities, seeing Treves and Cologne, and wandering about the valley of the Moselle. The summer following found him boating off the Isle of Wight with Charles Marriott and J. A. Froude. A considerable portion of the vacations, however, from this time onwards was spent at Oxford.   Residence at Oxford especially during the leisure of Long Vacations, for the sake of quiet study, had been a point often and strongly insisted upon by Mr. Newman, for himself and for his brother Fellows, and it became more and more a habit with Mr. Church as years went on.   A letter to his mother during the Long Vacation of 1840 shows that it was already not without its charm for him :—

ORIEL, 21*st July* 1840.

I write a line to say that I am quite well, and hope that you do not think I am so exceedingly desolate and solitary that I shall end with hanging myself.   Really if folks knew

how pleasant Oxford is in the Long Vacation I think that
they would spoil the quiet by coming up here.   There are
not very many people in residence, but of those who are
here, one sees so much more than at other times that if they
are a decent lot of people, the quality makes up for the
diminution of quantity in the article of society.   Newman,
Rogers, and myself compose the residents at Oriel now, and
we have it very cosily to ourselves, seeing the five or six
out-college friends, who are up, whenever we please. . . .
Just now I am very busy, and can hardly spare a morning.
I may, however, run down on Saturday for the day, but I
must return in the evening, as I have work here on Sunday.

But this succession of work and quiet reading was
not destined to go on long undisturbed.   The following
letter gives a budget of Oxford news, and shows in its
sketch of the little knot of men meeting in the tower
over Exeter gateway to "talk strong," as the phrase
was, that already some of the elements of danger were
not wanting.   A few months later, in February of
1841,[1] Mr. Newman brought out No. 90 of the Tracts

---

[1] In his dedication, in 1871, to Dean Church, of a new edition of
his volume of University sermons, Dr. Newman himself recalls the
close and intimate friendship which existed between them at this time.
"For you were one of those dear friends resident in Oxford . . .
who in those trying five years, from 1841 to 1845, in the course of
which this volume was given to the world, did so much to comfort and
uphold me by their patient, tender kindness, and their zealous services
in my behalf.   I cannot forget how, in the February of 1841, you
suffered me day after day to open to you my anxieties and plans, as
events successively elicited them ; and much less can I lose the
memory of your great act of friendship, as well as of justice and courage,
in the February of 1845, your Proctor's year, when you, with another
now departed, shielded me from the ' civium ardor prava jubentium '
by the interposition of a prerogative belonging to your academical
position."

for the Times, and with its appearance began the storm
of controversy which was to last with little abatement
until the final break-up of the Tractarian party in 1845.

To FREDERIC ROGERS, ESQ.

ORIEL, *In Vigil. Fest. Omn. SS.*, 1840.

MY DEAR ROGERS—. . . . Now I suppose I must send you
some gossip, which, I fear, is the unprofitable stuffing of most
of my epistles.   I wish you had waited to hear Sewell make
ἐπιδείξεις about Ireland.   He is chock-full up to the throat
about it, and whoever he comes across is sure to have a
quantity of " little traits," and " illustrations," and " striking
little facts," poured out for his edification.   He had got up
a great scheme for converting the Irish by means of scripture
readers, who should make shoes and mend kettles half the
day, and controvert the rest : but he was snubbed by Pusey
and J. H. N., each in his own way, which has made him
melancholy and out of sorts.   He is quite Irish-mad : thinks
Popery there " diabolical," and the Irish clergy a noble set of
fellows, who are improving fast. . . .   What do you think of
the Bishop of Chichester offering the Principalship (of the
Theological College) to Golightly ?   It was intended to be
done quietly, but Golightly told Eden, and Eden told it me
across the table at dinner, and then recollected it was a
secret.   G., on mature deliberation, refused, alleging that
people here would not send him any disciples ; and he walks
about looking as pleased as if he had refused a piece of preferment.   Pugin has been staying with Bloxam. . . .   The
only specimens of Oxford that Pugin saw must have edified
him.   Jack Morris had invited the rest of the " Mountain "
(Newman's name for them), *i.e.* Ward, Bloxam, and Bowyer,

to dine with him in the Tower and "talk strong": and to their delight Bloxam brought Pugin as his *umbra*. Ward is said to have repeatedly jumped up and almost screamed in ecstasy at what was said, and Bowyer and Pugin had a fight about Gothic and Italian architecture; but what else took place I know not. Morris is not pleased with Pugin, however: I wonder if he has humbugged Bloxam. Do you know Bowyer? I wish he would not come here so much; his line is to defend what everybody else gives up, and he took the side of O'Connell and his friends against Pugin. These theological συμπόσια up in the Tower, where they "talk strong," as Morris says, and laugh till their heads are dizzy, are ticklish things. I met Gooch up there yesterday, and had to defend myself for thinking Hooker not merely a respectable person, but a Catholic divine, and entitled to be looked up to as a teacher. . . .—Ever yours affectionately,

R. W. CHURCH.

Writing to Mr. Rogers, who was at the time in Italy, just before the appearance of No. 90, Mr. Church had said:—"J. H. N. is just publishing a new tract about the Articles: he thinks it will make no row. Ward thinks it will." A second letter, a month later, describes the storm which had now broken in earnest:—

To FREDERIC ROGERS, ESQ.

ORIEL, 14th March 1841.

MY DEAR ROGERS—I quite dread to begin a letter to you, not from lack but from abundance of matter. Don't, however, prick up your ears too high, else you may be disappointed: people on the spot can scarcely tell what is great

and what little; yet I think that curious things have
happened since I wrote last.   I think I told you that the
Times had been letting in letters signed Catholicus, against
Sir R. Peel, criticising an address delivered by him to the
Tamworth Reading-Room, in which he took Lord Brougham's
scientific natural-theology line ; and not only had let them
in, but puffed them in its leading article, without, however,
giving up Peel.   These said letters, signed Catholicus, with
one or two others of the same sort on duelling, etc., were
thought to smack strongly of Puseyism, and brought out
furious attacks on the said Puseyites in the *Globe;* expostula-
tions and remonstrances, on political and theological grounds,
from the poor old *Standard;* and a triumphant Macaulayism
in the *Morning Chronicle,* in which the writer, with great
cleverness, drew a picture of the alliance between effete,
plausible, hollow Toryism, with Puseyism, which he described
as a principle which for earnestness and strength had had no
parallel since the Reformers and Puritans, and rejoiced greatly
over the prospect that Puseyism must soon blow Toryism to
shivers.   And the *Globe* admitted that people were most
egregiously out in supposing that this same Puseyism was an
affair of vestments and ceremonies ; that it was, on the
contrary, something far deeper and more dangerous.   Such
was the state of things out of doors last month.   Meanwhile,
about the beginning of this month, a debate took place in the
House of Commons about Maynooth, in which Lord Morpeth
made a savage attack on Oxford, as being a place where
people, who were paid for teaching Protestantism, were doing
all they could to bring things nearer and nearer to Rome, and
suggested that this would be a fitter subject for parliamentary
inquiry than Maynooth.   Sir R. Inglis, of course, said that
the University was not responsible for the Tracts for the

Times, and so on ; and O'Connell said that the Puseyites
were breaking their oaths. This brought a strong article in
the *Times*, in which, without identifying itself with us here
theologically, it stoutly defended the Tract writers from being
ill-affected to the Church of England, fully entered into their
dislike of the word "Protestant," and ended by saying that
it had said so much because it had been "misled some time
ago by the authority quoted by Lord Morpeth" (*The Church
of England Quarterly*), "to speak of them in terms of harsh-
ness which it now regretted." This, of course, was called
"ominous" by the Conservatives and Whigs together, and
the *Times* was accused of Puseyism. This led to a second
article in the *Times*, in which, carefully guarding against
identifying themselves, they gave a very good sketch of the
history of things from the meeting at Rose's house, written
as accurately and in as good a spirit as any one could wish,
and went on to puff the strength and importance of the party,
the great good it had done, and the strictness, high principle,
and so on, of the people up here. This astonished people
not a little ; but in spite of wondering letters and remonstrances, the *Times* kept its ground in a third article, still
not professing to be able to enter into the merits of the theological controversy, but maintaining that these Oxford people
were the only people who had done, or were likely to do,
any good in the Church ; that they had stopped the attacks
on the Liturgy and Articles which had been made, or most
weakly met, by Conservatives and Evangelicals, and that, let
people say what they please, they were making way fast.

Three days before this article in the *Times*, Newman
published a new Tract, No. 90, the object of which was to
show *how* patient the Articles are of a Catholic interpretation,
on certain points where they have been usually taken to

pronounce an unqualified condemnation of Catholic doctrines
or opinions, or to maintain Protestant ones; *e.g.* that the
article on *Masses* did not condemn the Sacrifice of the Mass,
or that on Purgatory, *all* Catholic opinions on the subject,
but only that "Romanensium," assuming that to be meant
which is spoken of in the Homilies. The chief points were,
of course, Scripture, the Church, General Councils, Justi-
fication, Purgatory, Invocation of Saints, Masses, Homilies,
Celibacy of Clergy, and the Pope : on all these points
speaking pretty freely, and putting out explicitly what of
course many must have felt more or less for a long time.
He must have the credit of having taken some pains to find
out beforehand whether it was likely to make much row.
He did not think it would be more attacked than others,
nor did Keble or H. Wilberforce. Ward, however, pro-
phesied from the first that it would be hotly received, and
so it proved. It came out at an unlucky time, just when
people here were frightened to death and puzzled by the
tone of the papers, and galled by Lord Morpeth's and
·O'Connell's attacks. Tait of Balliol first began to talk
fiercely ; he had thought himself secure behind the Articles,
and found his entrenchments suddenly turned. But he was,
after all, merely a skirmisher set on to rouse people by
Golightly, whose genius and activity have contributed in
the greatest degree to raise and direct the storm. He saw
his advantage from the first, and has used it well. He first
puffed the tract all over Oxford as the greatest "curiosity"
that had been seen for some time ; his diligence and activity
were unwearied. He then turned his attention to the
country, became a purchaser of No. 90 to such an amount
that Parker could hardly supply him, and sent copies to all
the bishops, etc. In the course of a week he had got the

agitation into a satisfactory state, and his efforts were re-
doubled. He then made an application to the Rector of
Exeter to be allowed to come and state the case to him, with
the view of his heading a movement ; but he was politely
refused admittance. He had better success with the Warden
of Wadham. It was determined, in the first instance, to
move the tutors ; and accordingly last Monday came a letter
to the editor of the Tracts, attacking No. 90, as removing all
fences against Rome, and calling on the said editor to give
up the name of the writer. This was signed by four senior
tutors, Churton, B.N.C. ; Wilson, St. John's ; Griffiths,
Wadham ; and Tait—gentlemen who had scarcely the
happiness of each other's acquaintance till Golightly's skill
harnessed them together. He fought hard to get Eden, but
failed ; as also in his attempts on Johnson of Queen's, and
Twiss, and Hansell, and Hussey, etc. etc. This absurd
move merely brought an acknowledgment of their note
from the editor, and they printed their letter, and so this
matter ended. But it soon became known that the Heads
were furious, and meant to move ; driven frantic by G. and
the *Standard,* they met, full of mischief ; but it was judged
expedient to separate ἄπρακτοι, partly from the press of
business, and especially because it appeared that *many had
not read No. 90.*

At their second meeting all present were for proceeding,
except the Rector of Exeter and the Exeter Proctor, Dayman ;
but all the Board did not come. The new Warden of New
College seized the opportunity to take an airing instead of
disputing about difficult points. The matter was referred to
a committee, and we are now waiting their decision. It
seems, however, certain that they are afraid to try Convocation ; this would be their game, and they would carry it I

think, but they will not venture on the risk. Meanwhile
Newman is very much relieved by having got a load off his
back, and has been pretty cheerful ; the thought of Convocation harassed him and Keble very much. He is
writing an explanation, but he thinks that his Tract-writing
is done for. He is pretty confident about the Bishop of
Oxford, and he has been very kindly backed up. W.
Palmer of Worcester, as soon as the row began, wrote him
a very kind letter, speaking of No. 90 as the *most valuable*
that had appeared, as likely to break down traditionary
interpretations, and lead to greater agreement on essentials,
and toleration of Catholic opinions. A. Perceval also wrote
to much the same effect. Keble wrote to the Vice-Chancellor,
taking an equal share of responsibility in the Tracts. Pusey
has also written, but he is very much cast down about the
turn things have taken,—thinks the game up, and, *inter nos*,
does not agree with Newman's view of the Articles, though
he softens down.

The row, which has been prodigious, they say, has made
Golightly a great man. He now ventures to patronise the
Provost, who even condescended to lose his breakfast t'other
day to hear G. prose. He has received letters of thanks for
his great and indefatigable exertions, from four bishops,
London, Chester, Chichester, and Winton. It is supposed
that a niche will be left for him among the great Reformers,
in the Memorial, and that his life will be put in Biographi-
cal Dictionaries. Newman talks of him as a future "great
man." I shall finish in a day or two. You will be sorry
to hear that Sam Wilberforce has lost his wife. His Bamptons are given up.

21*st March.*—As soon as it became known that the Heads
meant to fall upon No. 90, Newman began writing a short

D

pamphlet to explain its statements and objects, and let the Heads know that it was coming, through Pusey and the Provost. However, they thought it undignified or awkward to wait, and on Monday last they "resolved" that "No. 90 suggested a mode of interpreting the Articles which evaded rather than explained" them, and "which defeated the object, and was inconsistent with the observance of the statutes," about them. All agreed except Routh and Richards and Dayman, who protested strongly.

As soon as this was published, Newman wrote a short letter to the Vice-Chancellor avowing the authorship, and, without giving up the principle of the Tract, taking their sentence with a calm and lofty meekness, that must have let in a new light into those excellent old gentlemen. Newman making an apology to Fox, Grayson, and Company ! This softened many people ; even the Provost, who is very strong, thought it necessary to butter a little about "excellent spirit under trying circumstances," etc. And soon after came out Newman's explanation in a letter to Jelf : his point being to defend himself against the charges (1) of dishonesty and evasion, and (2) of wantonness. This has rather staggered people, i.e. as to the immediate move. I think they feel that he has shown they did not take quite time enough to understand his meaning, and he has brought together for their benefit, in a short compass, and in a pamphlet that everybody is sure to read, some disagreeable facts and statements from our Divines. And the Heads show that they feel it rather a floor for the present, by affecting to consider it, which it is not in the least (judice Ward), a retractation or reconsideration, as our Provost said to Newman. So the matter has ended here, as far as public measures go. On one side we have escaped the bore and defeat of Convocation, and the Heads are loudly condemned on all hands for an arbitrary and hasty act, by which they have usurped the powers of Convocation, of which they are supposed to be afraid. Newman, personally, has appeared to great advantage, has made argumentatively a very strong case, which has checked and baffled them for the time, and weakened the effect of their authority by showing that they did not know who or what they were dealing with. And Newman himself feels that he may now breathe and speak more freely. On the other hand, they have at last been able to deal a hard slap from authority, and the mass of the people in the country will be humbugged into thinking this a formal act of the University. Great exertions have been made both in England and Ireland to frighten people, and, I should think, have been very successful.

And then it remains to be seen what the Bishops will do. They were at first very much disgusted, and we heard all sorts of rumours about meetings in London, and attempts to stir up the Bishop of Oxford. But whatever their first impulse may have been, they have this week seen reason to think that their best course is to keep things quiet as far as they possibly can. Last week the Bishop of Oxford wrote to Pusey, expressing the pain he felt at the Tract, and enclosing a letter to Newman, which contained a proposal to Newman to do something which he hoped he would not refuse. Newman's anxiety was not a little relieved when he found, on opening the letter, that what the Bishop wished was that he would undertake not to discuss the Articles any more in the Tracts. Newman wrote back offering to do anything the Bishop wished,—suppress No. 90, or stop the Tracts, or give up St. Mary's ; which brought back a most kind letter, expressing his " great satisfaction " (almost as if

it was more than he expected), and saying that in anything
he might say hereafter he (Newman) and his friends need
fear nothing disagreeable or painful. And in his letter to
Pusey he quite disconnects himself from the charges brought
by the Tutors and Heads of evasion. Newman was encouraged by this to open his heart rather freely to the
Bishop, and is now waiting the answer. So far, things look
well. . . .

People in the country have in general backed up man-
fully and heartily. Newman has had most kind letters of
approval and concurrence from W. Palmer of Worcester, A.
Perceval, Hook, Todd, and Moberly. B. Harrison is shocked
rather. But Pusey, I fear, has been much annoyed. He
scarcely agrees with Newman's view, and though he is very
kind, I think there is no doubt he much regrets the publication ; indeed, there is a false report, which yet indicates
something, that he is working against Newman. A great
difficulty with him and with the Bishop is that Newman has
committed himself to leaving "Ora pro nobis" an open
question.

The Moral Philosophy Professor [Sewell] has seized the
opportunity to publish a letter, nominally to Pusey, but
really to Messrs. Magee and the Irish peculiars, in which he
deeply laments the Tract, as incautious, tending to unsettle
and shake people's faith in the English Church, and leading
men to receive *paradoxes and therefore errors* (good—*vide*
Sewell's *Christian Ethics*), and after feelingly reminding
Pusey of his own services once on a time in the *Quarterly
Review*, strongly disclaims any connection with the Tracts
and their authors, recommending that they should cease.
"Longum, formose, vale, vale,—Iolla."

The papers have been full of the row, which has stirred

up London itself in no common manner ; 2500 copies sold off in less than a fortnight. . . . The *Times* has "confessed it knew not what to do, both parties were so learned and good ;" so it has contented itself with criticising the *style* of the Four Tutors, reprehending those who could substitute authority for argument, admiring the dignified way in which the controversy has been carried on, and puffing Dr. Jelf, to whom Newman addressed his letter. One hardly knows how things are at this moment. They say Arnold is going to write against Newman.

I have no more room, so good-bye. Just received your letter from Naples. Many thanks.—Ever yours affection-ately,   R. W. C.

In a postscript to the letter, follow a few lines from Mr. Newman himself :—

Carissime—Church has told you the scrape I have got into. Yet, though my own infirmity mixes with everything I do, I trust you would approve of my *position* much. I now am in my right place, which I have long wished to be in, which I did not know how to attain, and which has been brought about without my intention, I hope I may say providentially, though I am perfectly aware, at the same time, that it is a rebuke and punishment for my secret pride and sloth. I do not think, indeed I know I have not had one misgiving about what I have done, though I have done it in imperfection ;—and, so be it, all will turn out well. I cannot anticipate what will be the result of it in this place or elsewhere as regards *myself*. Somehow I do not fear for the *cause*. . . .—Ever yours affectionately,   J. H. N.

A year later, Dr. Arnold, as Professor of Modern

History, was delivering his famous series of lectures. The following letter, whilst it records the impression made by the lectures in Oxford, shows the keen interest with which Mr. Church already entered into all branches of history :—

To FREDERIC ROGERS, ESQ.

ORIEL, *February* 1842.

MY DEAR ROGERS— . . . The great lion at present is Arnold and his lectures, which have created a great stir in the exalted, the literary, and the fashionable world of Oxford. He is here with his whole family ; and people look forward to his lecture in the theatre, day after day, as they might to a play. He will be quite missed when he goes. Almost every Head goes with his wife and daughters, if he has any ; and so powerful is Arnold's eloquence, that the Master of Balliol was on one occasion quite overcome, and fairly went—not quite into hysterics, but into tears— upon which the Provost remarked, at a large party, that " he supposed it was the gout."

However, they are very striking lectures. . . . He is working out his inaugural. Everything he does, he does with life and force ; and I cannot help liking his manly and open way, and the great reality which he throws about such things as descriptions of country, military laws and operations, and such-like low concerns. He has exercised, on the whole, a generous forbearance towards us, and let us off with a few angular points about Priesthood and the Puritans in one lecture ; while he has been immensely liberal in some other ways, and, I should think, not to the taste of the Capitular body ; *e.g.* puffing with all his might the magnificent age

and intensely interesting contests of Innocent III.; and
allowing any one to believe, without any suspicion of super-
stition, a very great many of Bede's miracles, and some others
besides. . . .—Yours ever affectionately,   R. W. C.

The publication of Tract 90 was not long without
its personal bearings on Mr. Church's position at Oriel.
His connection with the Movement, emphasised through
his intimacy with Mr. Newman, brought on him the
suspicion, common at the time, of disloyalty to the
English Church. He belonged to a college whose Head
was one of the most active opponents to the Tractarian
party in Oxford; and upon the appearance of the Tract
he wrote stating to the Provost, Dr. Hawkins, his general
agreement with the line taken by it in regard to the
Articles, and offering to resign his tutorship. After
some hesitation the offer was accepted.

To DR. MOBERLY.

ORIEL, 26th June 1842.

MY DEAR G.—The Provost himself has settled things. I
have kept quiet, and meant to do so, as you advised me,
though both Newman and Rogers were for bringing matters
to an issue now. However, yesterday the Provost sent for
me, and said that if I was still of the same mind as when I
wrote to him, he did not see how he could consistently continue me as tutor. He was very kind, offered me to take
my time to reconsider matters (of course not lecturing on the
Articles), and regretted much having to take this course.
This, however, I declined; it would not be honest to talk of
reconsidering, or to hold out hopes of changing one's mind;

nor, of course, should I like to hold the tutorship, giving up myself, and throwing on others, the responsibility which is particularly annexed to the Statutes.   He then proposed a reference to the Vice-Chancellor without mentioning names, but this also, for very obvious reasons, I have since declined. I am now, therefore, expecting to hear from him finally.

The Provost is playing a bold game.   Daman and Prichard are both going to be married this summer, and have given up their tutorships, so that of the four, there are three vacant ; and one of the three juniors is somewhat (and not a little) stronger than I am.   I am, I confess, anxious to let the Provost know somehow or other, without seeming to be patronising, that I am quite willing to do anything I can consistently to help him, in the way of continuing lectures. He is rather a trying person to have to deal with.   With all his candour, he has no notion of putting another case fairly before him, though I believe he tries often to do it. Of course one who agreed with No. 90 would not quite lecture on the Articles as the Provost would approve ; but he is not content with this, but goes on caricaturing his supposed lecture, representing one as intending to make No. 90 and its bare, unqualified, negative statements one's text-book and model for teaching undergraduates, who have forgotten their Catechism.

The Provost was again at his distinction between *principles* and *modes of arguing*, which, unluckily, always fails, like Dr. Daubeny's experiments, when tried in detail.   It tries one's muscles, too, to be told that the Board "were not to be supposed to be acquainted with Newman's other writings ;" "could not know that No. 90 was his,"—and could only look at it as an isolated anonymous publication.—Yours affection-ately,   R. W. CHURCH.

To the Rev. J. H. Newman.

26th June.

My dear Newman—I did not see the Provost to speak to, after I left you, so I sent him a note, saying that I had rather that the matter should not be referred to the Vice-Chancellor, and that it would be absurd in me to ask for time to reconsider. So things stand. He is puzzled about our own Divines. He asked whether Andrewes, Bull, etc., would agree with No. 90. I said I did not know whether every one would agree with every word of the Tract, but that I thought they would strongly condemn and repudiate the censure of the Heads of Houses. I have written to Moberly : I don't know which of us, the Provost or myself, will vex him most.—Yours affectionately,

R. W. Church.

The year 1842 saw the introduction, by Sir Robert Peel, of the Income-tax. To Mr. Church, who had become Treasurer of his college, the new and unfamiliar regulations which accompanied its working brought a good deal of additional labour. He writes to his mother : "Term ends in about three weeks, but I am such a great man that I cannot move without putting the college in a fidget—Provost, Fellows, tenants, masons, carpenters, and painters all having such an intense interest in me, and attachment to me, that they cannot bear me out of their sight." And again a little earlier in the term :—

Oriel, *17th October* 1842.

I am just getting out of the horrors of audit, and write a line home, as one takes in a breath of fresh air. . . . For four mortal days have we been at it, living on accounts (and sandwiches) from ten till near six, with nothing but ledgers and account books, big, middling, and little, old and new, red, green, and white, meeting one's eye—nothing to amuse one but corn rents and money rents, consols and reduced annuities, sums in long addition and long division, practice, and interest—all of us shut up in a queer old tower, turned into men of business for the nonce, writing and cyphering away like mad, all in our gowns, and all our work a good part in Latin. One gets into such a habit of dealing with figures, that one can scarcely help their coming out "all promiscuously," as the phrase is, from the end of one's pen ; one almost forgets that there is anything else in the world. . . . Well, there is enough nonsense scribbled to enable me to go through another day of audit, over which the blank, mysterious spectre of Income-tax hangs menacingly, inexplicable by men and lawyers.

23rd October.

I forget when I wrote to you last—I think it was when I was in the middle of audit. That is happily now over, and I escaped without any serious mistakes proved against me. But oh ! the miseries entailed upon unhappy Treasurers of colleges by the Income-tax, especially if they are unlucky enough to have Provosts to do business with,-who like making the most of whatever business falls in their way, and spin it out as long as it will last. First comes the question how the return is to be made. Now the Act not being over-clear, and the affairs of a college, with a large rental and large expenditure coming in and going out in all sorts of ways, not having been especially provided for, there is room left for a variety of small perplexities and difficulties such as the Provost loves. . . . The process is as follows :—At one o'clock

I wait on the Provost. We get our books and papers, and
the blank form to fill up. Something is to be put down.
The Provost starts a difficulty ; I hold my tongue while he
hunts it down. When he has caught it and settled it, he
catches sight of a second ; so to despatch this more deliberately,
he leaves the books and draws his chair to the fire, puts his
feet on the fender, and begins disputing most vigorously the
pros and cons of the new puzzle—all with himself, just like
a dog running round after his own tail. At last he grabs
it, gives it a hard bite, and then perhaps returns to the table
again, much gratified, but not much the wiser for his exercise,
whilst poor I have been standing patiently by while this
amusement has been going on. And so things go on, with
much talk and little done, till four o'clock. And much of
the same fun is still to come. I should like to roast Sir R.
Peel with all the returns made about his Tax.

A letter written during the same term refers to Mr.
Church's first venture in original literary work on any
considerable scale. The essays on Anselm and William
Rufus, and Anselm and Henry I., were republished in
1853 in his volume of *Essays and Reviews.*

To his Mother.

ORIEL, 12*th November* 1842.

I am hard at work on an article for the *British Critic,* on
the life of a certain Archbishop of Canterbury, named Anselm,
who was a very great man in the eyes of people a long while
ago, but has been shelved a good while now, for having had
the misfortune to be a monk and a papist. He lived in the
days of a certain unspeakable scamp of a king called William

Rufus, a sort of combination of Lords * * *, * * *, and
* * *, with a good spice of peculiar wickedness of his own
to boot; and he and Anselm, as was natural, could not quite,
as it is called, "hit it off together," or live on the best of
terms.   So accordingly in my presumption, my article in-
tends, if it is admitted within the purple covers, to record to
the nineteenth century the sort of cat-and-dog-life of an
Archbishop of Canterbury in the eleventh. . . .—Your
affectionate son,   R. W. C.

The scene of confusion and uproar which signalised
the Commemoration of 1843 was long remembered by
those who witnessed it. It was an occasion (following as
it did closely upon Dr. Pusey's suspension) which marked
a further stage in the steadily growing antagonism
between the University authorities and the Tractarian
party.

To FREDERIC ROGERS, ESQ.

ORIEL, 28th June 1843.

Certainly there is no denying the irresistible tendency to
self-suspension on the part of our respected Heads and
Governors. What do you think of a diversion, in both
senses, got up by them to-day—an extemporaneous row,
whereby they have brought the hornets of Convocation about
their cars, in fine style. The whole business is so ludicrous
to me, that though there were disagreeables mixed up with
it, it has quite for the time put out of my head all the despairing thoughts with which I left London. With such
people to help us we may yet get on.

Everybody got up this morning with the full belief that
Jelf would be awfully hissed in the theatre, and most sober-
minded persons with the conviction that they would be able

to find better employment for their time than hearing the
said hissing. It was also known (a notice to that effect having been sent out yesterday) that Mr. Everett, the American
minister, would be proposed for an honorary degree. But
soon after the town and University were stirring, Lewis and
Morris were seen flitting about from college to college, with
the intelligence that Mr. Everett was a Socinian. Stern,
unflinching, untiring men, with their hard features, and
strong fire within,—they had sounded the tocsin to some
effect by nine o'clock, and every one was on the *qui vive.*
Poor, innocent Mr. Everett meanwhile—I do pity him—was
breakfasting unconsciously at Buckland's, showing that he
was an accomplished, intelligent, refined man, — enjoying
Oxford society, and Buckland's jokes, and the prospect of
plaudits and a red gown in the theatre. Heads of Houses
also were breakfasting, unconscious that Lewis and Morris
were *not* breakfasting, it being St. Peter's Eve. But breakfast and unconsciousness must come to an end, the clock
must strike, and the resolute Welshman is at the V.-C.'s
door with a letter. "Is Mr. Everett known to the V.-C. to
be a Socinian?" Other Heads are "just going to shave"
and dress for the theatre; they are stopped by the anxious
question, "Can they contradict the assertion that Mr. E. is
a Socinian?" The V.-C. sends for the Welshman—does not
deny that Mr. E. is a Unitarian, but in England he conforms.
Besides, honorary degrees have no reference to theological
opinions, only to moral conduct—witness Dr. Dalton. The
Welshman is inexorable. He has not come to argue with
the V.-C., only to learn a fact; but thinks it a curious time
to make light of theological differences. V.-C. tries to come
over him still—tries the civil and the patriotic—"Would he
blow up a war between England and America?" The

Welshman cannot help consequences. Jelf, who is by, looks fierce, and is rude, all but insults the Welshman : " he never was so treated by any one before." But bullying and coaxing are no good ; the Welshman comes away, after giving notice of an opposition, thinking himself ill-treated, and with the fact in his pocket that the V.-C. cannot deny Mr. E.'s heterodoxy. Eden also tries his luck with the same great functionary—also writes a letter—sentences well poised and turned, constructions and words exquisite—but coming to this, that unless V.-C. will deny the assertion, " he (Eden) must act on the best information he can get." V.-C. only will say that Mr. E. " goes to church " in England ; it is also said that he will sign the Apostles' Creed. *Dominus Propositus* " can give no information," but met him at Buckland's and liked him, and saw nothing in his conversation to show Socinianism. Various other efforts were made to get a disclaimer from the Heads and Mr. Everett, but it only came to this, that he did not call himself a Socinian, and went to church when he was in England ; but there was no denying that he was an " American Unitarian."

All this passed in the space of two hours. The theatre meanwhile was opened and filled. Mr. E.'s degree would be *non-placetted* considerably. Every one felt it a very great bore, but it could not be let pass. But there was another row gathering up in the gallery, which was destined to mingle with, and finally swamp the magisterial one. From the moment Jelf came into the theatre, an uninterrupted, unslackening storm of groans began (rendered more furious and loud by the counter-cheering), which lasted literally, without a break, till after three-quarters of an hour, when the V.-C. was obliged to break up the Convocation without the prizes having been read. I never heard anything so kept

up. They say that men had bound themselves not to stop
till they drove Jelf out. It will cause the expulsion of some
three or four men—among others a man who has just got a
double first : they richly deserve it.

Meanwhile, under the cover of this cannonade, important
events were going on below. I was in the body of the room,
and I could see the V.-C. get up, and gesticulate, and then sit
down as if in despair ; but every one about me thought that
he was waiting till he could be heard. But he knew a trick
worth two of that. Why should he want to be heard, or to
hear ? So, in course of time, why or wherefore having been
concealed by the crowd, up emerges Mr. Everett in red
gown, and by the helping hand of the V.-C. is comfortably
installed among the D.C.L.'s.

Such was the scene from a distance ; but round the foot
of the V.-C.'s tribunal another storm had been raging. There
it was perceived that Dr. Bliss, in spite of the gallery fire,
was presenting Mr. Everett ; that the V.-C. was asking the
sense of Convocation, that the proctors were taking off their
caps ; there, accordingly, Marriott got upon a form, and was
seen moving his lips, and gesticulating to the V.-C. He
affirms, and it is believed, that he made a Latin speech,
which he has since put into writing. There also were frantic
and furious struggles made to draw the V.-C.'s attention ;
wild yells of "*non placet*" and "*peto scrutinium*" were distinguished by the bystanders very plainly. At last the
V.-C. heard them ; but "after he had sent the bedels to
conduct Mr. Everett to him." Those were moments of most
intense and agonising excitement. Woollcombe of Balliol
all but flew at Cox the poker to throttle him for telling
Woollcombe that his *non placet* was too late. However, too
late it was to prevent Mr. Everett from being a Doctor at

least *de facto*. So were the *non placets* floored, and the V.-C. sat down triumphing—blessing, if he had any gratitude, his stars and the undergraduates, the powers above. But nowadays M.A.'s, when they are snubbed, wax fierce and warm. So forth poured a stream of malcontents from the theatre, leaving Messrs. V.-C. and Everett, and the Creweian oration as it issued from the lips of Garbett, to the protection of the gallery, to assemble in Exeter Common Room and deliberate. All sorts collected, all in the most explosive condition; all Balliol, as usual, furious; Sewell as indignant as his turn for pathos would allow; Eden lofty, thoughtful, and ominous; Lewis and Morris faint from their toils of the morning. At once half a dozen men rushed to the table, and were at work, not sitting but kneeling at it, writing protests. They began in English, and doubtless a dozen men would have followed their example, when some one luckily suggested that, as the notion was to deliver the protest to the V.-C. before he left the theatre, it ought to be in Latin, which checked the ardour of the protest-writers. In the course of a quarter of an hour Seager and Spranger had their rival protests ready in fair statutable Latin; they were being discussed when Sewell appeared with one of his own devising, put into more like classical Latin, which at once commanded all votes. It was just being sent off, when news was brought that the V.-C. had been obliged, by the perseverance of his late allies, to put an end, an untimely end, to the Convocation, and the fond, long-cherished dreams of the young prize poets about bright eyes and white handkerchiefs. The gallery gave three cheers for "their victory," and descended; and so finished Commemoration 1843.

But I shall miss the post with all this stuff; so, to be brief, a deputation waited on Mr. Everett to assure him that nothing personal was intended, etc. etc., which went off with mutual civility, and is to be followed by a written address to the same effect. A deputation also waited on the V.-C. with a protest against the validity of the degree, on which Convocation was prevented from expressing its sense ; which the V.-C. answers by saying that " he did not hear the *non placets* " till after he had sent the bedels to inform Mr. Everett that Convocation had granted the degree, and it would have been informal to have recalled it. This answer, however, is voted by all parties, part of the original job ; and a committee of five is to be appointed to carry the thing on, and to get the degree annulled.

The V.-C. *has* made a mess of it ; first, by proposing Mr. Everett, and then by smuggling his degree through in this barefaced way ; a measure which shifts the ground of opposition from the obnoxious theological one, to the privileges of Convocation. We shall see what will come of it. Meanwhile our good friends have attracted to themselves *quant. suff.* of odium, and have again made people act together when they were falling apart.

Unluckily the credit of the University will not rise in all this. I never saw such a disgraceful scene altogether as the theatre this morning. . . .—Yours ever, R. W. C.

In spite, however, of the momentary amusement which such a scene as that described in the last letter might excite, the direction that matters were taking in the University was becoming an increasingly anxious one.[1] The attack on Dr. Pusey, which had ended in his suspension for two years from preaching in the University pulpit, had taken place in June 1843 ; and this

[1] See also *The Oxford Movement*, chap. xvi. The Three Defeats.

was followed by Mr. Newman's resignation of St. Mary's in the September of the same year. Both these were events of ominous significance; and in addition to them, to friends who like Mr. Church and Mr. James Mozley were in Mr. Newman's confidence, there were other warnings of an even more discouraging sort. Some words of Mozley's at this time give expression to the feeling that changes were preparing. "Things are looking melancholy now, my dear Church; and you and I, and all of us who can act together, must be bestirring ourselves. I feel as if a new stage in the drama were beginning, in which we shall have to do the uncomfortable thing, and take rather higher parts than we have done hitherto, or at any rate we must try our best."

And along with the pressure of these anxieties there were besides private fears to be met, and questions to be answered, such as could scarcely rise without pain. Mr. Church's own position and outlook had become uncertain. He had been warned by the Head of his college that in the event of his applying for testimonials for priest's orders, they might in the present condition of affairs be refused him. And this was a consideration which opened afresh the whole question as to his future. In answer to his mother's anxious inquiries as to his own position, he writes :—

To his Mother.

Oriel, 1st November 1843.

As to the other part of your letter I hardly know what to say. It is most natural that you should feel alarm, and should express it, and yet I do not know how to dispel it effectually. All I can do is to beg of you earnestly not to suspect me, for as far as I can know and answer for myself, I am not in any danger. All that I could say on the subject would simply come to this, that I believe myself in no danger. I am afraid that I could scarcely make you understand my reasons for thinking so, when the question is asked ; perhaps the most practical that I could give is, that I never felt a temptation to move. After this, I hope that you will not think that I am annoyed—for your fears are most natural, and I do not the least complain—if I ask one favour, that you will kindly not put the idea before me, unless you have strong reasons from anything you should hear, or that I should do or say, to fear. For it does one harm to be doubted. Please remember that I do not say this as complaining—it is merely with regard to the future. . . .

As to those who have gone over, I may as well say, that though I have known two or three of them more or less— for my acquaintance used to be rather large—I was intimate with none of them. A large circle, and a large party, takes in all kinds of people.

As to what is coming, I can say nothing, because I know nothing. As far as I can see, we must be content to be suspected for the present—there is no help for it ; there is no way of stopping the popular outcry just now without abandoning what seems true. We must be content to live, and perhaps die, suspected. In some cases perhaps, the outcry, as often happens, will verify itself ; but it will not be so with the great body ; and perhaps the next generation may profit by what they have done towards breaking down unchristian prejudices.

Meantime the game is not up.   This distrust and unpopularity may blow over ;—in spite of the Heads we have a great deal of power here, and we may still be able, notwithstanding their violence, to gain a hold on the Church, and show that there is much of that good which Rome claims as her own which belongs to us as well and as really.   There is no use despairing till the last chance is lost, which is not yet by a good deal.

Please excuse this hasty note.   I hope you will not think any of it unkind : it was written in a great hurry.— Your affectionate son,   R. W. C.

To his Mother.

Oriel, 21*st* *November* 1843.

Oxford, I think, is more foggy and murky than it usually is at this season, which is saying a good deal. . . . But we are very quiet for the present.   Our great men are a little fatigued just now with their late gigantic efforts, and are taking an interval of repose, so we breakfast and dine with an appetite ; there are no threatening sounds of a storm approaching, and there is nothing to break the dull rumble of the great University, as it jolts and jostles and rolls along from week to week, but now and then an explosion of fire-works in a college quadrangle, which the *Times* grossly exaggerates into a sort of little gunpowder-plot.   It is very odd how difficult people find it to help lying.—Your affectionate son,   R. W. C.

In 1844 Mr. Church was elected to serve as proctor his companion in the office being Mr. Guillemard of Trinity.   At this time the control of the police was in the hands of the University authorities, and accordingly

among the duties falling to the proctors were those of
police supervision and inspection. He writes to his
mother of his first experience :—

ORIEL, 13*th April* 1844.

I began work to-day, and so now I am fairly in for a
year's employment in keeping the peace, with its various
rubs and amusements. I have only had experience of the
latter as yet, *e.g.* I have every other week to post the police
in various parts of the town, and to receive their report of
the previous day. One goes at nine at night to a vaulted
room underground, as dreary looking and grim as a melo-
drama would require ;—table with pen and ink, feeble
lamp, and sundry cutlasses disposed round the walls. One
sits down in great dignity at a table, and then the police
are marched in by batches of six. They enter like robbers
or conspirators in a play, all belted and great-coated, looking
fierce. "All quiet last night ?" passes your lips. All
their heads begin to bob, as if they were hung on springs,
and without any stopping for three or four minutes, all
their voices commence repeating, "All quiet, sir," as fast as
they can ; and when they have lost their breath, *exeunt* all
bobbing. The first time I was present I fairly lost my
gravity, as I should think most of my predecessors must
have done before me.

A few weeks of the Long Vacation spent in Brittany
with his friend Mr. Rogers, came as a welcome break
to the strain of events in Oxford. The essay on
Brittany, which appeared next year in the *Christian
Remembrancer*, grew out of the impressions received
during this visit.

To C. M. Church, Esq.[1]

St. Pol de Leon, 30th August 1844.

My dear Charles—I cannot possibly give you a journal of our proceedings; you shall see my jottings when I get home if you choose. You may thank this place for this note, for I want to preserve my impressions while they are fresh by writing them down. To see where we are, look at the N.W. corner of Brittany, and on a rugged point of land fringed with rocks and islands you will see the name of this place. It was the old ecclesiastical capital of this part, and an Archbishop's see. Brittany is a strange wild place, where the historical associations are a mixture of Celtic, romantic, and feudal,—the Druids, King Arthur, and the Dukes of Brittany; it is quite different from the rest of France, with a different language, and a rude, severe, old-fashioned people. This was sufficiently impressed on us all along our road, so we were prepared for a queer place at St. Pol de Leon. We had a beautiful hot day to-day, travelling in a country cabriolet from Lannion, through Morlaix— quaint, grotesque, feudal towns, with such street architecture that Rogers' pencil has never ceased going all day; but still busy, stirring towns in beautiful valleys, with fine tidal rivers, or arms of the sea, running through them. Towards the end of our day we came on higher ground out of a green valley, with a stream running through it. The country began to run in straight horizontal lines—a moor-like tableland with furze and broom. On turning a corner we caught sight of the sea on our right, and before us rose a tall single spire, and near it, a pile with two lower spires of the same kind, which continued in sight, growing larger

---

[1] Mr. Church's youngest brother, then an undergraduate at Oriel.

till we finished our journey. The day was now cool, and
the sun set just as we got into the place. It is a stern,
hard, rugged town, people and houses clean, but small and
stern—houses all granite, even to the least, and very plain,
and there are no very large ones—a great contrast to the
fantastic wooden ones of the towns we had seen. The
single spire is the most beautiful thing of its sort I have
seen for a long time ; like everything else here there is a
severe cast about it. It is granite, and there are many
square forms about it, but it quite shoots up from the dreary,
desolate, silent place. Just as we went out the bells of
two or three churches rang the " Angelus."

A short way from the spire we came to the cemetery.
An avenue of trees ran up to an extraordinary looking
church, another to a calvary. At intervals, on the outside
wall, were arched places in which were placed sculls and
bones,—the sculls sometimes in a sort of box with the name
of the person on it. On each side of the avenue to the
calvary were shrines with a representation—large wooden
or earthenware figures—of a scene of the Passion ; and at
the end there was a circle, in the midst of which a large
crucifix rose against the sky, with two large columns on
each side, and two shrines with representations of the taking
down from the cross, and the burial. In front was a large
space paved with gravestones. I never saw any representation of this kind which struck me so much. It is no use
being sentimental, but the effect of these "stations" among
the tombs in a cool evening, following a hot day, and among
these wild sad people, with their gloomy customs respecting
the dead, was something unlike anything I ever felt. From
this place we looked down on a bay ; it was quite dusk,
the sea a black blue, and the hills a deep blue grey. The

moon rose behind them, first a deep red, then burning copper, then with a strange yellow brilliance all round, reflected dimly on the bay.

Everything is in keeping about this place, everything still and severe, and everything rude and melancholy, except the spires of the churches, and even they, with the architecture generally, are stern though they are so very beautiful. At the inn our supper was clean and good, and so was the table, but it had no table-cloth. We asked the servant girl about the cemetery, and she did not like to talk about it, and at last went out of the room. Next year this strange cemetery is to be done up new in the Père la Chaise style.

We have had beautiful days all the time. Our line has been Dinan, St. Brieuc, Paimpol, through Tréguier to Lannion, through Morlaix to St. Pol ;—to-morrow Landerneau, then Brest, Quimper, Vannes, to the middle of Brittany, which they call Cornuaille (Cornwall). We have had a cabriolet from St. Brieuc, and so had things in our own hands. Hitherto it has been very beautiful and very strange. I shall send all my friends to Brittany ; and, for their comfort, the dirt is very much exaggerated, and the inns are very cheap. . . . I wish you would call at the Post-Office at Southampton for a letter which Rogers expected from Gladstone, with an introduction to a person here.—-Yours affectionately, R. W. C.

To his Mother.

LANDERNEAU, 4th September 1844.

We have an idle day to-day, so you shall hear a little about our doings and plans. . . . We stopped Sunday here, and in the afternoon walked out into the country to see a "Pardon," as they call it—a sort of wake, or gathering at a church, on some particular day. A very hot walk of five

miles brought us to the place—a church called La Forêt, as
its name implies, among woods, on the banks of a river, with
a fine ridge of rock and heath on the opposite side of the
valley. The churchyard and the roads about were full of
people, who could not get into the church—men and women
in separate bodies—the women sitting or standing by the
churchyard wall, or the banks round it, the men clustered
round the church itself—as picturesque groups as could be
wished. They are a fine-looking set these Bretons, though
with a strong dash of the savage about them too; severe,
thoughtful-looking fellows, with deeply-marked features,
and, most of them, with long black or dark-brown hair,
falling down their backs: in huge broad-brimmed hats
with a band of silver lace, or blue or red and white chenille,
or black velvet with a buckle round them, and black jacket
and trousers. Black is the predominating colour in the
dress of men and women: the women wear a gown of coarse
black cloth, with a large apron and small shawl, of different
colours—and these colours are very well combined. Their
head-dress is a cap, with a worked handkerchief made up
into a kind of flattened roll on the top of the head. You
cannot conceive how beautiful these groups of women looked:
the black ground of the gown setting off the combined
colours of the shawl and apron—very varied, but without
any gaudiness—there was not a bit of yellow to be seen—
and topped by the quaint, beautifully white head-dresses.
All the men and women were very clean, and all seemed to
be of the same rank.

When we got there the people in the church were
singing—in a wild kind of way, but most lustily; those
outside—the men at least, near the church, kneeling down
with their hats off. Then came the sermon, in Breton,

during which the women in the church sat on the ground,
the men standing.   Then came a procession round the
churchyard, crowds joining in it, walking round and singing
—but great numbers also kneeling on the ground as it
passed round, and three or four boys ringing the bells from
the roof of the church with all their might.   It was a
magnificent sight to see these people pass by in deep crowded
masses, with a bright sun shining on them—the men all
together, stern and serious, with their long black hair and
black dresses, and the women following, or kneeling round.
After this was over they dispersed, with some difficulty, for
the road was almost choked up.   There was to be a dance in
the evening, but they said that not many would stop for it.

On Monday we went to Brest, and took a steamer to a
place on the other side of the Rade de Brest, as fine a place
for a navy to lie in as can well be imagined—a broad sheet
of sea completely shut in except by one narrow passage, on
which they can bring four hundred guns to bear at once.
At the place where we stopped we had a narrow escape.
Our inn was about a mile off, and a diligence passed by it,
by which we meant to get to it.   But the diligence, which
was just starting, was full, so we could only send our bags,
and we set out walking.   We stood for a little while looking
at a Breton dance which was going on in the " Place ; " this
kept us a few minutes, and showed us what followed.   The
diligence started with a drunken driver and troublesome
leader—it dashed round a corner and was overturned.   The
people inside were very much cut and bruised, and one of
them, an old Frenchman with whom we had made acquaintance on board the steamer, had his arm broken.   I never
saw a thing come down with such a crash. . . .—Your
affectionate son,   R. W. C.

Mr. Church's term of office as proctor coincided with
the last stormy year of the Movement at Oxford. In
the University feeling on both sides was running high,
and an opportunity for its expression presented itself in
the nomination to the Vice-Chancellorship, which took
place immediately before the October term of 1844. In
its ordinary course the office would have passed from
the President of St. John's, Dr. Wynter, whose term
had expired, to Dr. Symons, Warden of Wadham, Mr.
Church's old college. Dr. Symons was well known as a
man of extreme opinions, who had strongly expressed
condemnation of the Tractarian party, and it was determined by the Tractarians, although against the judgment of the wiser heads among them, to challenge his
nomination. In the result the nomination was confirmed
by 883 votes to 183.

To his Mother.

Oriel, 12th October 1844.

You will have seen in the *Times* an account of all the
doings up here. It has been a stormy end of the Long
Vacation ; and the beginning of the term, instead of seeming,
as it usually does, the commencement of stir and bustle here,
is quite flat and dull after the great gathering of last Tuesday
—a mere settling down of routine. But I am afraid we
shall have some more squalls before it is over. We proctors
now have double duty—to look after Heads of Houses and
undergraduates.

Strange twists come about. I certainly did not expect,
when I used at Wadham to stand before the old Warden in
immense awe of his bigness and deep voice, that I should be

presiding over his election and sitting in dignity next to him. We keep pretty good friends however. But unless this lesson may have given him a hint, he will make a queer Vice-Chancellor.

Proctorial work did not get pleasanter as the winter advanced. "My winter campaigning," he writes, "is beginning, not quite so active as in the summer, but more disagreeable when in the field—dark nights and sloppy streets." And in addition to these labours, his official position required his presence at the meetings of the Hebdomadal Board, where, among the old-fashioned and elderly Heads of Houses, he half laughingly declares to his mother that he finds himself looked on "with a mixture of horror and contempt, as a semi-papist and a young man."

Even at the risk of repeating what has been often told, it may be well at this point to recall briefly the situation as it took shape towards the close of 1844. In July of that year Mr. Ward had published his famous book, the *Ideal of a Christian Church*, in which he claimed for himself, as a member of the English Church, the right to hold, whilst subscribing to the Articles, "the whole cycle of Roman doctrine." Such a claim necessarily raised the Roman question in its most pressing and practical form. Among the Tractarians themselves it was felt as the expression, brought out at length into clearness, of a severance in principle which had been gradually growing up within the party; and to the University authorities such outspoken language offered a fair opportunity for taking decisive measures. In the beginning of December the Hebdomadal Board announced that it proposed to submit to Convocation three measures : (1) the condemnation of Mr. Ward's book; (2) his degradation, by depriving him of his University degrees; (3) and the institution of a new test, by which the Vice-Chancellor should have power at any time to require a member of the University, in order to prove his orthodoxy, to subscribe the Articles in the sense in which "they were both first published and were now imposed." A penalty of expulsion was attached to the refusal, three times repeated, of such subscription. The third proposition excited at once general and wide-spread displeasure; and it was in the end withdrawn, its place being taken by a censure of Mr. Newman's Tract No. 90, proposed in the language of condemnation used by the Board at its appearance four years before. Such a measure, brought forward as it was within ten days of the meeting of Convocation, aroused the indigna-tion of Mr. Newman's friends, as well as of all fair-minded men. "The interval before the Convocation was short, but it was long enough for decisive opinions on the proposal of the Board to be formed and expressed. Leading men in London, Mr. Gladstone among them, were clear that it was an occasion for the exercise of the joint veto with which the proctors were invested. . . . The feeling of the younger Liberals, Mr. Stanley, Mr. Donkin, Mr. Jowett, Dr. Greenhill, was in the same direc-tion. On the 10th of February the proctors announced to the Board their intention to veto the third proposal."[1]

[1] *The Oxford Movement*, p. 381.

Canon Buckle of Wells, who, in 1845, was a junior Fellow of Oriel, and cognisant of what was passing then in Oxford, writing of Mr. Church's part in this unusual course, touches a characteristic note. "It was the Dean's way," he writes, "then as always, to be an invisible force—not conspicuously acting or speaking himself, but influencing others who did speak and act."

The following letter to Mr. Newman tells Mr. Church's purpose in his own words :—

My dear Newman—I had made up my mind to veto from the first, and I have little doubt that Guillemard will agree to it. But it need not be talked about more than is necessary. . . . Gladstone has written to the Provost against this move, and asking for delay. We shall hear the letter on Monday. I am only afraid of their delaying it, though as yet they have shown no symptoms of shrinking. It would not be very respectable to change their minds again, but I think it would be their best game. . . .—Ever yours affectionately,   R. W. C.

The day for the meeting of Convocation was fixed for the 13th of February, "St. Valentine's Eve." The excitement and fever of expectation in the University had risen by this time extraordinarily high. On the day itself, Oxford was thronged with members of Convocation, who had come up from London and the country to record their vote ; and even the snow and sleet which fell heavily through the day could not daunt the spirits of the undergraduates, who, although denied entrance to the theatre, gathered about its approaches, eager to

be as near as possible to the scene of action. Mr. Church's
youngest brother, then an undergraduate at Oriel, a
college which for obvious reasons was keenly interested
on this occasion, had stationed himself at a window in
Broad Street, in order better to view the proceedings;
and he recalls the excitement of the moment—the sight
of the crowd, which still, after the procession had entered,
lingered round the railings that enclose the theatre—
the dull roar of the shouting which could be heard at
intervals from within the building itself—and at last
the appearance of the assemblage streaming out through
the snow, the big figure of Ward emerging among the
earliest, with his papers under his arm, to be greeted
with shouts and cheers, which passed into laughter as
in his hurry he slipped and fell headlong in the snow,
his papers flying in every direction.

The spectacle within the Sheldonian, crowded from
end to end with voters, was always spoken of by those
present as a very memorable one. "I was introduced,"
writes Canon Buckle, "into the famous Convocation
by Church, under the shelter of his velvet sleeves, not
having the right of entry myself, being only a B.A. It
was a highly exciting scene—Ward being allowed the
novelty of speaking in English, and making point after
point that elicited cheers and howls; and it culminated
in the great sensation when, on the proposal of the
censure, the two proctors rose, and the senior, Guillemard, pronounced the veto—'*Nobis procuratoribus non
placet*'"—words which, except upon the occasion of the
Hampden conflict in 1836, no one then living had heard

spoken in Convocation. "Guillemard, the senior proctor," writes James Mozley, "delivered his veto with immense effect. A shout of 'Non' was raised, and resounded through the whole building, and 'Placets' from the other side, over which Guillemard's '*Nobis procuratoribus non placet*' was heard like a trumpet, and cheered enormously. The Dean of Chichester threw himself out of his doctor's seat and shook both proctors violently by the hand." For the time proceedings were at an end. "Without any formal dissolution, indeed without a word more being spoken, as if such an interposition (as the proctors' veto) stopped all business, the Vice-Chancellor tucked up his gown, and hurried down the steps that led from the throne into the area, and hurried out of the theatre ; and in five minutes the whole scene of action was cleared."[1] Ward and the proctors were warmly received when they appeared, and a cry went up, "Cheers for the proctors" from among the throng of undergraduates as they made their way out ; whilst, as if to add point to their reception, the Vice-Chancellor was met by hisses, and even, it was said, by snow-balls, thrown by some of the more audacious spirits among the crowd. On the same evening Mr. Church wrote to his mother :—

You will probably have seen the result of to-day's proceedings in the *Times* before you receive this. They have been painful proceedings, and the University has committed itself to measures which, whatever Ward has said, are

[1] *Edinburgh Review*, April 1845, p. 394. See also *Ibid.*, April 1881, p. 381.

flagrantly disproportionate to his offence, and to the punishment which has been inflicted on much greater offenders—
if they have been visited at all.

The only thing to relieve the day has been the extreme
satisfaction I had in helping to veto the third iniquitous
measure against Newman. It was worth while being proctor
to have had the unmixed pleasure of doing this.

On another aspect of the matter he wrote a little later
to Mr. Stanley :—

To THE REV. A. P. STANLEY.

February 1845.

MY DEAR STANLEY—You will not, I am sure, accuse me
of fishing for thanks ; it is quite sufficient for me to have
helped in staving off an insult from Newman, even if nothing
else at all came of the move.

But with a view to the future, I cannot help thinking
very strongly that you must not lose or throw away this
move. The Heads must not be allowed, uncontradicted, to
represent themselves as aggrieved by an act of power on the
part of two party men. Courtesy will not touch them, if
this their natural feeling is allowed to gain strength, or
become confirmed, by the veto passing off unnoticed. It is
most important, in order to bring them to reason, that they
should distinctly feel that it is *they* who have made the
mistake. Even with the consciousness this forces on them,
I doubt whether they will be very practicable ; but they will
be much less so if suffered to persuade themselves that they
have been defeated by a technicality. Unless the veto is
fully and publicly sanctioned, I fear it will be but a respite,
and that with respect to further measures, as soon as its

F

immediate effect ceases, it will be of unmixed advantage to them.

It is a critical time : if the Board is allowed to think that the confidence of the University in them is still unimpaired, I think that, however people may ask for peace, the Board will still trust that they shall not forfeit confidence, even though, with the best wishes for peace, they themselves see reason to act vigorously. However, do as you think best. If our moderate friends cannot screw themselves up to " play off " the veto, they must take their chance of the Board turning tender-hearted next term.

Night thoughts are not very clear, so please excuse this scrawl.—Ever yours,   R. W. C.

As you saw Mozley in my room, I may as well say that I have not talked to him at all about the matter.

The letter was returned by Dean Stanley in 1876, and was thus acknowledged :—" Thank you for sending me the enclosed. It brings back a very generous, as well as wise, action on your part and that of the men who joined with you. And it was a very bold thing too at the time. For all your friends did not think with you on that matter."

An address, signed by over five hundred members of the University, of widely different shades of opinion, was presented to the proctors, thanking them for their exercise of the veto, and Mr. Newman himself wrote privately to acknowledge their service to him. In April their year of office was at an end ; but the veto had done its work, and no further attack on Mr. Newman was attempted. The year passed quietly on, although it was now well known that Mr. Newman's secession could not be much longer delayed. Much of the Long Vacation was spent by Mr. Church in Oxford.

To HIS MOTHER.

ORIEL, 1st August 1845.

I wish I could persuade you that Oxford is a very enjoyable place in the Long Vacation. One is very quiet with one other Fellow, one cat, one dog, and one jackdaw with clipped wings, for one's companions in College ; and when I am in the sulks, I can go to a friend who lives just out of the town, and all but in the country, at the Observatory, and smoke a cigar with him, and look at Jupiter and Saturn through his telescopes.

In October he heard from Mr. Newman that the decisive step was taken, and he writes again :—

You will be distressed to hear what I have just this moment heard from himself, that Newman has left us, and joined the Church of Rome. It is a matter on which I can say little at present. I will ask you to pardon me once for all for my reserve on these points. It is so intensely painful to me to talk of them with those who do not know the whole case, and who, naturally, from distance, cannot have it put before them, that it has seemed better to abstain from it altogether. I will only say that about myself personally you need not make yourself unhappy.—Ever your affectionate son, R. W. C.

Thus ended, to use a phrase of Keble's, "the desolating anxiety of the past two years." Mr. Newman

stayed on at Littlemore, still seeing something of some
of his friends, until February of the following year,
when he finally left Oxford; but the unreserve and
openness of the past could scarcely be kept up.　Mr.
Church was one of the friends, as Mr. Newman records
in the *Apologia*, who went to bid him good-bye at the
Observatory, where he passed his last night at Oxford.
It was felt at the time on both sides to be a parting
of more than ordinary significance.　A friendship which
had been so close, and which had been bound up with
the hopes and enthusiasm of a great enterprise, could
scarcely at once withdraw itself within the limits of
mere friendly intercourse.　Time was needed for its re-
adjustment to new and strange conditions; and much
had to happen before the old companionship could be
resumed, as it was at length, on almost the old terms of
freedom and confidence and affection, to last with no
further interruption till the end of life.　In the interval,
however, the separation was strangely and pathetically
complete.　After the parting at the Observatory fourteen
years elapsed, during which no direct communication
by word or letter passed between them.

Within a few weeks of Mr. Newman's secession, a
private sorrow came upon Mr. Church in the sudden
death of his mother, to whom he was deeply attached;
and the year which to him, as to many, had been one
of peculiar trial and sadness, closed with a deepened
sense of change and loss.

No letters of 1846 have been preserved.　In Oxford,
University life was resumed under its ordinary con-

ditions, and men went back to their various occupations;
the Tractarians who had not followed Mr. Newman in
his final step having to meet as best they might the tide
of angry suspicion and condemnation which was still
running against them.[1] But in spite of inevitable dis-
couragement they refused to regard their cause as a lost
one. As a distinctively Oxford enterprise the Movement was at an end, and it was in London and the
country that the fresh development of its power, under
Pusey and Keble as its chiefs, was henceforward to show
itself. But it was a time of new ventures, in which
men, whose general principle and aim were the same,
struck out their own line, and chose the work which
was naturally most congenial to them. Such a venture
was the starting of the *Guardian* newspaper, which was
to carry on, although with no official link with the
High Church party, many of the distinctive principles

[1] The following letter is interesting as a contemporary record of
the state of things in Oxford after 1845 :—

ORIEL, 23rd March 1846.

MY DEAR MOBERLY— . . . The present state of things must, I suppose,
resolve a little before long. At this moment one really does not see what to
make of it or where to attach any one who wants hold. I sometimes feel half
angry with myself for declining the Bishop of New Zealand's offer of his
College, though at the time I had certainly no prospect of being able to undertake such a labour, and though I had then distinctly before me the present
crisis with the exception of one point, that I thought Newman would have
stayed with us. The extremity of distrust, proscription, and inquisition was
before me, and I felt it my duty to stay here and fight it out; but I did expect
to have his counsel and sympathy to fall back upon. One takes comfort now
in thinking that if one does right it is sure not to be wasted, but the immediate
prospect is dreary enough. Bright spots, however, there are, and one must
strive on and be thankful for so much. I can hardly see what hope we have
of things in general, except in persecution. Yet one fears that for the many.
One does long for some spot where those who ought to be guardians and
helpers are not playing the wolf. Here, the way in which one sees men
worried out of our Church is enough to stir up no little bitterness. And yet
the only way to do good is, I believe, to be quiet, and wait one's time. I am
not telling you news, but only opening one side of my feelings about what has
lately passed and is passing. . . . But I run on too long.—Believe me ever
yours most sincerely,   C. MARRIOTT.

of the Movement itself. It was the undertaking of a little knot of friends, of whom Mr. Church was one, who were intimate together, and who had shared in various degrees Mr. Newman's friendship. The notion of a newspaper which should take among weekly papers the position held by the *British Critic*, and afterwards by the *Christian Remembrancer* among quarterlies, had been already thought of in 1845; and in January 1846 the *Guardian* appeared, the day of its first issue coinciding with that of the *Daily News*.

Some notes from a MS. autobiography of Lord Blachford's describe some of the difficulties and risks which attended the first steps of the undertaking. "The idea was taken up," he writes, "by the knot to which I belonged, embracing James Mozley and Thomas Haddan, who with myself had written not unsuccessfully for the *Times*, and Church and Bernard, who had signalised themselves in reviews. We, I think, comprised the substantial staff of the undertaking; that is, we tried to collect contributors and cash, but made ourselves responsible to each other for finding what was wanting in writing and capital. We expected to succeed in doing good to the cause—for it was something to shake out a standard and seem not discouraged. But though, through Keble and Pusey and others, we could command a good deal of Tractarian support, we were totally inexperienced in the handling of a newspaper, or in the conduct of business. . . . We made an agreement with some printers, still existing, in Little Pulteney Street, and hired a room opposite the printing establishment in

the shop of a baker, where we could attend or meet to
see what was going on, and where some of us spent the
greater part of every Tuesday night, correcting proofs,
rejecting or inserting matter, writing articles on the last
subjects which had turned up, giving last touches, and
generally editing. Bernard, Haddan, and I being in
London, must I suppose have done most of this work,
but Church and Mozley used to take their share, making use of a bedroom in my lodgings in Queen Street,
Mayfair. To these we used sometimes to return at four
or five o'clock in the morning—sometimes perhaps later
—for I connect some of these returns home with the smell
of hot bread from the oven, on which I think we sometimes made our breakfast."

To Mr. Church fell, in great part, the review department of the paper, and reviews by him of Carlyle's
Cromwell, d'Aubigné's *History of the Reformation*, Keble's
Lyra Innocentium, appeared among its first numbers.
Two early successes which brought the *Guardian* into
wider notice were also due to Mr. Church's pen : one of
them, a review of Lyell's *Vestiges of Creation*, which
attracted the notice and commendation of the late Sir
Richard Owen; whilst the other, an article describing the
method and character of Le Verrier's discovery of the
planet Neptune, gained for the paper a communication
from the great astronomer himself. Mr. Church writes
of this, with great satisfaction, to James Mozley, in
October 1846 :—" Sharpe and Rogers too are in great
force about the *Guardian*. At last we have got quoted
in a morning paper, the *Daily News*, by help of Le

Verrier's letter.   We may be caught out in some 'floor,'
but if we are not, I shall be very proud of the planet all
my life long."

The greater part of 1847 was spent by Mr. Church
abroad.   He inherited a full share of the family love
of travel and foreign scenes; and such a break after the
strain of the past few years offered the change both to
body and mind which he was most in need of, and there
were no longer any ties in England to interfere with a
prolonged absence.   His uncle, Sir Richard Church, who
in 1826 had been chosen by the Greek Assembly to
command the Greek armies during the war of independence, was now living in Athens, and this determined the
direction of Mr. Church's journey.   He left England
towards the end of January, crossing the Bay of Biscay
in very heavy weather, and after touching at Gibraltar
and Malta went direct to Athens.   The next four months
were spent in Greece.   At Athens he found himself,
whilst staying with his uncle, who was at that time one
of the leading members of the Opposition party, in the
centre of hot political discussions, which contrasted
strangely enough with the history and associations of
the past.   An excursion into Attica, and a month's
wandering on horseback through the Morea, completed
his Greek travels.   His further plans had included an
expedition into Asia Minor and a visit to Palestine,
but this part of his tour had finally to be relinquished,
though he succeeded in pushing on as far as to Constantinople.   He returned to Athens to bid farewell to
his uncle, and then turned homewards, spending a week

at Corfu as the guest of Lord Seaton, at that time Lord
High Commissioner of the Ionian Islands, and passing
on thence into Italy. The following letters, giving the
account of his travels at length, show the zest and enjoyment with which he threw himself into the new and
varied experiences of his year's holiday :—

To C. M. CHURCH, ESQ.

ON BOARD THE *RIPON*, 27*th January* 1847.

Here we are, off the coast of Portugal, knocking about at
a grand rate. I write in pencil, because ink is a dangerous
material, when one finds oneself every five minutes making
the most extraordinary angles with the horizon ; and scarcely
a quarter of an hour passes without the most horrifying
crashes of plates and glasses and tables and chairs. I used
to wish to see the Bay of Biscay doing its best, and I have
had my wish pretty fully. I am quite satisfied that the said
Bay is a potentate of great dignity and power, and—here
goes a great roll—now keeping a very vivid recollection of
him, I do not wish to see any more of him. We have had,
by way of luck, one of the worst passages known for some
time back. The wind changed on Wednesday to W. and
S.W., and has kept us at bay ever since, and always with a
good vigorous gale ;—on Monday, with what I have the
authority of one of the sailor people on board for calling a
hurricane, and to-day with a resolute obstinate southwester,
with a heavy sea, clouds without a break, and continuous
spitting drizzle ; so that we, who were to have been at
Gibraltar on Monday, think ourselves lucky that we have
perhaps passed Vigo. I have been congratulating myself half
a dozen times a day (beg pardon, great thump on the bows !)

that Coleridge [1] did not come : he would have been half dead with ennui if not with sea-sickness. Though I am pretty well seasoned now, I must confess to have been fairly vanquished. However, I got over it after a couple of days so as not to be sick, and in a couple more so as to be able to eat, and get up without feeling squeamish, in the thick of a gale of wind, with everything flying about one's head or one's heels ; and now I am writing, as you see, in an awful toss—but I do not stand on my character as an undisturbed sailor any more.

One of the most trying pieces of business was reading service on Sunday, having to balance myself with one hand and keep my book from tumbling off with the other. I never was so dizzy in my life as I was at the end. Except as a thorough good specimen of what sea weather can be, our voyage has been as uninteresting as could well be. Passengers, mostly freshmen for India—very schoolboyish, apt to talk of how their trunks are fastened, and where they bought their outfit; a few semi-invisible ladies, and a half-dozen of commonplace gentlemen. . . .

29th January.—Off coast of Portugal, no land in sight. To proceed. To-day, as you see, ink is useable, though still with due precaution, and seas still thump every now and then at our bows and paddle-boxes. But we have at last, and for the first time, a wind which does not actually head us, and are running along under fore and main trysails, seven or eight knots. Hitherto we have done little more than from two to four knots, drifting away before a broken swell from N.W., crossed by strong wind from S.W. You cannot imagine, or, on the other hand, I dare say you can, the sickening feeling of finding our first point to be reached

---

[1] Henry James Coleridge, Fellow of Oriel.

put off day after day, and then to be disappointed when the time comes, and to be told that we were only, it may be, twenty miles from where we were twenty-four hours back. However, now our main troubles are, I hope, pretty well over.   We saw the coast of Spain early on Tuesday, somewhere between Corunna and Finisterre.   It was very striking and solemn to come on deck, and over the wild, tumbling, indigo black sea, to see the strongly marked outline of the hills through the mist.   They are quite what the ocean coast of Europe ought to be ; something of the Apennine outline on a larger scale.   The utter solitude of the morning made it more solemn ; not a fishing boat or a bird between us and the mountains, nothing but the waves break-ing here and there into crests—or, what is still more wild—*manes* of white foam.   Alas ! we did not see the Cape Finis-terre for which we had been longing so much ; we had to get away from the land as hard as we could, for we had drifted twenty miles to the eastward of our course, and the fate of the great *Liverpool* is still fresh in every one's memory on board.   Since Tuesday morning we have seen no land.   It is still doubtful whether we shall have to go into Lisbon for coals.   We are now (11 A.M.) somewhere between Oporto and Lisbon—nearer the former—no chance of Gibraltar till Saturday.

The *Ripon* is unlucky.   She will hardly get credit for this voyage, because it has been so long and bad ; but people say, who know what they are talking about, that it might have gone hard with us on Monday if she had not been a very good ship.   She is very slow : the strength of her 450 horses is not enough to get her through a head sea more than four or five miles an hour, and she gets well abused for being so slow.   But it was quite a grand sight to see her at

work in the storm. She rose to the frightful looking seas as
if she had a huge spring which shot her bows up out of the
deep trough of the waves, and not one of them rolled into
her, though they hung over her as high almost as her
chimney-tops. I had quite got over all my squeamishness by
that time, and could look on the process without any
physical discomfort. And now that it is over, it is quite a
sight to see once in one's life. It is not merely the storm,
but the battling between the ship and the storm. You can,
without any strong stretch of imagination, fancy life in both
of them, each wave taking its blow as it passes, sometimes
successfully, sometimes parried, but always with a single
wild effort, spent altogether when done ; and the continuous
sustained strength of the ship, never exhausted, and directed
with a mixture of calmness and anxiety — the idea of
the man at the wheel — seems to pass into the whole
machine.

I am comfortably housed—a cabin to myself, which I
fancy I enjoy in solitude, because it is quite aft, and kicks
about a good deal, and you have a chance of being *sprung*
out of bed now and then. But it is a comfort of comforts to
be by oneself. They feed us like luxury loving Englishmen
—hot rolls for breakfast and champagne for dinner, and by
this time people have learnt to eat them.

8 P.M.—We are going on still very slowly. Just now we
are about forty miles from Lisbon, with two intermitting
lights appearing and disappearing on the invisible Portuguese
coast, and some rocky islands, like the Holms of the Bristol
Channel, showing a dark outline in the moonlight. I am
afraid that we shall not go into Lisbon, and that we shall
not be at Gibraltar till Saturday, and Malta till Thursday
or Friday. So that I shall not have saved much by avoiding

France, in point of time. (Excuse bad writing, but we are rolling grandly with a long N.W. swell.)

This has been a different day from any before it. It has been quiet as to weather, and people are for the first time finding themselves at home, and making acquaintance. . . .

Friday morning.—All the wind in the world will be spent if it goes on wasting itself upon us in this fashion. Last night another "splendid breeze," or "heavy gale," which knocked sleep out of most heads. Just fancy for four days now a huge regular swell from one quarter crossing our course, and an obstinate gale from the other, settling accounts between themselves in their very magnificent fashion, and kicking us small people about without remorse in their battle. We have to sneak and slide along between them, ploughing most warily and humbly between the two grand contending parties, most insolently thumped and kicked out of the way of the swells, and receiving the most meagre pittance of help from the wind, which just deigns to keep our miserable trysails from shaking. They are really very strong great people, this wind and sea, and the *Ripon*, which looked so big in Southampton docks, and seemed as if nothing in the world but herself could move her, has had the shine completely taken out of her, and been made to look most inconceivably small. Really, comparing my imagination of what she was, and the present look of her, she seems dwindled to the size of a mere Jersey packet. The bright, clear moon, with two or three bright stars, over the wild sea this morning, about 2 A.M., was most glorious. The sea has sights as well as the land most undoubtedly.

Saturday, 30th January.—We have been disappointed in all our land sights. We were to have seen Cape St. Vincent close—the " sacred promontory " of the old world, of which

Strabo recounts many mysterious things; but in our great caution we gave the land so wide a berth that we almost missed it. All eyes strained themselves in vain, for several hours, expecting to see it peer up; at last a small jet of light, about nine o'clock, shot up from the horizon, showed itself, and disappeared,—" there's the Cape !" We saw the light two or three times more, and that was all we saw of it. All we can console ourselves with is, that probably the ground over which we were passing is strewed with Nelson's and Jervis's stray cannon shot, in a state of corrosion. To-night we shall pass over that strewn with the remains of Trafalgar, and reach Gibraltar, where I shall post this : though we are so late that probably Malta letters will reach you with or before this. To-day is delightful—smooth water, and every one looking jolly, and writing away as hard as their pens can carry them.

1 P.M.—I am going to shut up now. We have a beautiful day, with, at last, clear green and blue sea. We are now in sight of Cape Trafalgar and the shore of Africa : Cape Spartel with the entrance of the straits open ; Cape Trafalgar, a long low cape with a bluff end, and white chalky - looking cliffs. Africa and the opposite Spanish mountains are very grand looking masses, looking like crouching wild beasts gazing at one another across the sea. . . .

Just in Gibraltar Bay, by moonlight : nothing can be more beautiful and glorious, such a moon and sky, like summer. I can scarcely believe that we have been knocking about as we have. I feel quite in the South.

. . . We had a short but very pleasant Sunday at Gibraltar—a magnificent spring day, enough to revive the most miserable among the sea-sick. Of course, there was a rush on shore, and woe that day to every horse, mule, and jackass let for hire in the town of Gibraltar. Our young Indians formed a body of irregular cavalry, and made furious foray into the Spanish territory; the array would have astonished any other place but Gibraltar, but it is probably accustomed to these cavalcades; and besides, it is such a place of strange people, that if men were to come there with two heads they would hardly be looked at. The Barbary Moors are very queer looking fellows; and it requires an effort to feel quite comfortable within their reach. It is astonishing how much there is in dress in making one feel at ease as to a man's tameness. These Moors, with their huge bare legs and coarse rough capote of brown and white stripes, approach most disagreeably to the character of wild animals, and even in Gibraltar they grin and scowl on the Christian passers-by, and they lounge about and stand at their doors, and lie in the sun on the ramparts like so many savage dogs with nothing to do. Close by the bare legs and stripes of the Moors are seen also the bare legs and tartan stripes of the 79th Highlanders, as if even the Horse Guards took a pleasure in adding to the grotesque contrasts of the Rock.

It is certainly a place to be seen, both in itself and its surrounding landscape. The mountains round are exceedingly fine, and on the other side of the straits, and as it were closing the bay, is the African shore, rising into a great pyramid of a mountain, which is dignified by the name of Ape's Hill. On shore it was like spring. They have managed to get gardens on the Rock, and there you have the same mixture of north and south as in the town—huge aloes, and prickly pears, and orange trees with fruit on them; and, quite scenting the air, borders of geraniums and roses in flower, and periwinkles in great abundance, and the

freshest green on the grass and trees. I suppose this must
be the best time at Gibraltar ; it must be frightful in summer.
It is, of course, crammed with soldiers—five regiments, and
a battalion of artillery, and all the regulations are of the
most un-English strictness ; all in commerce are scrutinised
and catechised most jealously as to their being British subjects. I don't know how foreigners get in. Our occupation
certainly is a remarkable piece of coolness on the part of
England towards her friend Spain. The outline of the Rock
is itself suggestive of our position towards Spain ; it is just
like a great beast—if you like, the British lion (by no
means caricatured), crouching down watchfully with its nose
on the ground and eyeing the neutral ground and the
Spanish posts. We left the bay at about five o'clock, with
its opposite hills over Algesiras of a rich purple, with misty
sunlight filling the spaces between the near and more
distant ones, and long rays of light shooting down from the
clouds above upon their faces.

And now we are once more at sea, our deck in shadow
from the sails ; with a bright space under the foot of the
foresail, and our bow and bowsprit pointing up to the full
moon, and over the bright greenish-yellow rolling waves
which stretch on to the eastern horizon.

MALTA, *6th February* 1847.

Here we are at Malta after a five days' run (very delightful) from Gibraltar. We got in yesterday at 1.30, and have
been lionising since. This is a most wonderful and beautiful
place, quite the perfection of street architecture. The first
thought that strikes one is that the whole town must have
been built yesterday ; it looks as if only just out of the
stonemasons' hands. Fancy the richest and warmest free-

stone (much warmer and richer than even the Bolsover stone) employed with the greatest profusion, and cut into the most picturesque doorways, windows, galleries, and balconies, and set off with green woodwork in the balconies—streets of this stone seen from end to end, looking like streets of palaces for size and ornament, and seen in all kinds of curious perspective from the varied rise and fall of the ground ; and further, these magnificent streets are the cleanest I ever saw. As a city, taking it as a whole, and seen by walking through its streets, I have never seen anything which struck me so much —I do not expect to be more struck with Venice. Then the separate *Auberges* of the different nations or " languages " of the Order, are as grand as they can be, all of the sixteenth century : a rich, and somewhat heavy and barbaric Italian or Palladian, but of very noble proportions.

The great church here, St. John's, the chapel of the Grand Master, and now called the Cathedral, is in the same style, heavy Italian piers and arches, and waggon vault ; but the pillars are cased with verde antico, or with richly carved and gilded woodwork, and the floor is made up of the grave-stones of the knights, all of the richest mosaic, and the roof painted in fresco. Valetta is quite worth a voyage to see ; I had no idea that it was such a sight in itself.

Then there is the magnificent harbour and fortifications ; and such a population, such strange half European, half Oriental creatures, who quarrel more gloriously than even the Gibraltar boatmen. Excuse this short note, I only write to say how much I am delighted with Malta.

MALTA, 14*th February* 1847.

I told you all about Valetta before, I think, except that the streets are narrow, and even this is in character. I still

G

think it one of the most striking specimens of architecture I have seen ; and it is populated by a race of men, horses, and carriages, which keeps it in perpetual life, and makes the carnival, which is now going on, seem a most tame and stupid business. The real masquerade is daily in the Strada Reale. A great addition has lately been made to the live curiosities of the place by the arrival of two large ships, *Rodney* and *Albion*, whose heroic crews come ashore in shoals, and besides walking on their own legs in the peculiar fashion of the sea, take to bestriding donkeys at a very large angle, exciting the mirth of the Maltese and Italians, and the grave disdain of the sober, dry, bare-legged Scotchmen of the 42nd —tall, upright fellows, who step out with quite a tragic tread. If ever you come travelling to Italy, don't miss Malta if you can help it.

Outside Valetta the country looks as if the people spent their time in nothing but building big stone walls across their land. But in spite of this extremely unpromising similitude, it is anything but commonplace and uninteresting. It is in reality made a great deal of, these walls being a sort of buttresses to prevent the light soil being washed away by the rains ; and the narrow fields are now brilliantly green between their dreary grey boundaries, with wheat, barley, and clover. The trees are very few—scattered, black, shrubby carobas (or locust-bean) are the most numerous over the fields ; fig-trees, and here and there a single palm ; and in one direction an olive plantation, in another a garden with dark Turkish looking cypresses—all Oriental. And the Oriental look is increased by a number of square, flat-roofed buildings, with few windows, either cottages or cattle sheds. The whole of the country round Valetta is densely populated —the people collected in large villages or *Casals*—so large

that they look at a distance like great towns, most of them
containing some striking looking houses in narrow winding
lanes, and all of them a fine Italian church with its piazza,
and its towers and central dome, whose outlines quite crowd
the horizon, and stand out most picturesquely along the line
of hills which enclose Valetta.   On one of the highest points
stands the old capital, Città-Vecchia, fortified and looking
down from a precipitous ridge, over plain and sea, and
crowned by a grand church, Τηλεφανής, where tradition
places the residence of the "chief man of the island," and
where they show strange catacombs, and a cave said to have
been inhabited by St. Paul.   Not far off is the bay where he
is said to have been shipwrecked.   We talk of riding there
to-morrow.   I came in for the festival of the shipwreck, the
10th of February.   The Church of St. Paul in Valetta was
decked out with much rude magnificence with lights and
damask hangings, and for several days was thronged from
morning to night.   On the evening of the day itself a great
statue of St. Paul was carried in procession through the city.
From my window, in the Strada S. Paolo, where the church
is, I had a full view of it ; a fine specimen in its way of the
religion of the crowd—very coarse and unrefined and mixed,
but in its way hearty and warm.   The street is straight, like
all in Valetta, and rises very steep at one end : toward the
other end is the church to which the procession, which had
issued from it, was to return after a round.   I got to my
window, just as the head of it had reached the church, about
5.30 in the evening.   The street was illuminated : along the
cornices of the church pots of fire were burning and smoking
away, and at the top of the façade was a cross of yellow
lamps ; lamps were hung from poles all along the street, and
at the top of the steep end was a fine arch of yellow lamps

closely ranged. The sky was still bright, and gave a
peculiarly soft effect to the illumination, as well as giving
full colour to the red and yellow hangings of the windows.
The procession moved in two lines, and the tapers which
each person carried glimmered up the hill ; and on each side
the street was lined by a dense crowd of the motley throng
of Malta — Greeks, Turks, grey - coated and patent - leather
belted policemen, Maltese fishermen and calesse - drivers,
bare-legged Highlanders, smoking *farouche* looking Frenchmen in beards and pointed boots, and groups of women
—looking all alike in the black veil and gown, which is the
national dress of the island. As the procession came up,
the members—religious confraternities and clergy—halted
and ranged along the street ; there was a row of rough
Capucines drawn up opposite my window, and next them the
cleanest and neatest of monks, the Dominicans, with their
smooth faces and white robes, and light stockings and well-
polished shoes. After some delay, for the procession was
very long, we heard a great huzzaing. All eyes were bent
up to the arch of lamps ; the huzzas became nearer and
louder ; a cloud of boys turned into the street, waving hats
and handkerchiefs, and then we saw beneath the illuminated
arch at the head of the street, standing out against the clear
evening sky, the figure of the Apostle, a bold large statue
with outstretched hand, as it were looking down on the
crowds below, among whom every face was turned up
towards it. The effect was theatrical, but still very striking.
The statue remained there a few minutes and then moved
down the street, escorted by the mob of shouting boys, dirty,
ragged little urchins, who, in spite of priests and police,
continued cheering St. Paul till the statue was lodged in the
church. Whilst these fellows were shouting, the clergy

were chanting. I could not make out whether the Host
was carried : something very sacred was, by the way in
which the priest who carried it was supported, but there was
no canopy, and it might have been relics ; but it made no
difference to the shouting and skirmishing of the boys. I
suppose it is simply a mistake to look for and expect reverence of manner in these people ; it is not one of the ways in
which their faith shows itself, though there are many others :
certainly, as far as look went, the pageant or national festival
seemed to overpower the religious ceremony. But of course
all displays of popular religion, however imposing, must be
grotesque also. Certainly this was. . . . I propose to leave
on Wednesday, the 17th, direct for the Piræus.

TÉLÉMAQUE, GULF OF LACONIA,
19*th February*, 7 P.M.

I begin a letter which I hope to finish at Athens.
Here we are sailing across the Gulf of Laconia, under the
clearest of skies and on the smoothest of seas, with the
bright crescent new moon over Tænarus, the great Bear over
the hills of Helos, Orion and Sirius blazing over Cythera,
and a bright star (Canopus ?) just showing itself over the
south-eastern horizon. To-day has been one of great enjoyment. We left Malta on the 17th at six in the evening, and
had a good run across yesterday. This morning, on coming
on deck at eight, there was Navarino and the Messenian
coast before us, and towering high over everything else,
Taygetus, with his two peaks covered with snow, and at 70
miles off, showing that peculiarly soft and creamy whiteness
which I have noticed in all the snowy mountains I have
seen here, all of them seen across great distances, and with
the sun full and bright upon them—the Sierra Nevada,

Etna, and Taygetus. We had him in view all day till four
o'clock, changing in some degree, but not much, as we
crossed the Gulf of Kalamata or Coron, and ran close along
the mountains of Maina. Old Laconia was meant to be a
fortress, at least on this side. Nothing can exceed the stern
hardness of the coast. The hills here, viewed from the Gulf
of Kalamata, run in a rounded outline, very often into cones,
and sweep down steeply to the sea in ravines divided by
sharp edges of rock—hog-backs or ῥαχίδες, is not that the
word? They look utterly bare, and without trees or earth,
except that here and there a village appeared at the bottom
of a gully surrounded with an olive plantation, and there is
an ambiguous green tint blending with the grey and red of
the limestone, which a telescope detects to be some kind of
heath or gorse. As we ran on and the day declined, the
tints upon this, without being brilliant, were very striking,
from the delicate grey and blue of the more distant hills of
Messenia to the reddish brown, mixed with dull green, of
the nearer ones of Maina, softened by a delicate yellow haze
between us and the land, which melted above and below
equally imperceptibly into the blue of the sea and the sky.

A whole fleet of small brigs and schooners, which had
been wind-bound till to-day, were pressing round the cape.
I have not seen so many ships at sea since I left England ;
we must have passed some thirty or forty, and their white
sails, and the white houses and towers which dotted the
mountain sides, gave a summery look to the whole view. It
was difficult to give up gazing on these old hills, and still
more difficult to make myself believe that here I was within
a few miles of Laconia. About half-past four we passed
Cape Matapan—rugged and strange in form, a sort of peninsula running out under the brow of a loftier mountain. All

along this coast the sea is extremely deep—30 fathoms close to the shore, and 150, 200, 300, a little way out. The evening at sunset was as beautiful as the day ; the purple of the hills became deeper and richer, and the blood-red and orange of the sky was gorgeous ; and now we are running across the bay of Laconia under a moon which, though only four or five days old, gives a most brilliant light.

9 P.M.—Just round Cape Malea, a sort of double cape with a bay between its horns. We were close in shore, and the moonlight was bright enough to give a clear view of the outline, while the filling up of crag and cavern and gully was half shown and half confused in the dim light and dark shadow. A single light glimmered upon it as we passed from some boat on the shore. It is a far finer cape, as far as could be seen in the moonlight, than Cape Matapan : a peak to the west, and round and bluff to the east, not very high, but with sufficient size to look very great and massive as we steered over the deep waters at its base, within a stone's throw of the hermit's cell upon it, who lives there all through the year, and is greatly reverenced by the Greek sailors who pass the cape. The moon sunk below it as we rounded it, and left us under its shadow ; and it gradually drew out into the outline of a wild beast couchant, which is not uncommon in some of the finest headlands, *e.g.* Gibraltar and Monte Circello. The spray dashing up against our bows, and the long swell from the N.E., told us that we were in comparatively open sea again after having had it as smooth as a lake hitherto ; and now we have our head pointed almost straight for the Piræus, where we are told that we shall be to-morrow morning at six ; so that I suppose I shall be dining with the General to-morrow ; and by this time then I shall have been along the Long Walls, and looked up at the Acropolis,

and by way of preface, squabbled with Greek douaniers and cabmen.

Athens, 20th.—We got here this morning. I turned out at five, as we were running along the smooth water, with Ægina and the low coast of Attica in sight, in the dim light of the morning. There, verily, were the places themselves. You may suppose I stayed on deck. As the day broke the scene came out more distinctly. Ægina, two miles from us, and a vista of capes and islands retiring behind one another, and opening out in their different shades of grey and purple all along the Argolic side, and the gulf ; before us, for a long time very grey and dim, the mountains of Attica, Parnes (I believe) with snow on its top, and Hymettus. The morning was most beautifully clear, and when the sun rose over Sunium, as it did by way of a treat, the delicacy and richness of the tints, the pale green of the sea, the rich red-brown of Ægina, and the various purples, and blues, and greys of the other distances, taken together with the noble forms of the mountains, made a most wonderful scene. The places, too, seemed so strangely familiar, and yet the whole feeling of this morning was as if I was looking at something quite unreal. . . .

At the Piræus the interest altered, at least a new element came in ;—a French line-of-battle ship with band playing, and queer looking fellows in red caps and white kilts paddling about, and a modern Greek frigate, with her equally modern name, in Greek letters, upon her stern, brought the present world into the old one in a very strange way. Then came the ride to Athens, passing in a rickety *calèche*, driven by a moustached fellow in petticoats, over the line of the Long Walls with the Acropolis in sight, and with a vulgar fellow-traveller at my side, who observed that the grazing along the roadside was not equal to that of England. And this is the sort of queer incongruity in which the day passes. It is a different thing from the feeling I have had in visiting other ruined places. There is an activity and life going on here, claiming close kindred and connection with the classical past —so brilliant and refined and highly wrought, so full of solemnity and greatness—and quite unconscious of the contrast between its own vulgarity and bustle, and the utter death-like quiet which hangs over the scenes and ruins among which it works, and which, it seems to fancy, belong to it, in the same way as they did to the Athens of Pericles and Demosthenes.

To FREDERIC ROGERS, ESQ.

26th February 1847.

I have been living for the last few days in the General's house, in a complete whirl of modern Greek politics, which are the engrossing subjects of Athenian conversation. I will describe our abode and general day's work. The house is reached through a labyrinth of narrow and not very clean streets, as most houses are in Athens; it stands, like its brethren, in something between a court and a garden, surrounded by a wall, and built in the irregular way which is the fashion here—with two or three bits of old sculpture, found in digging the foundations, and built into the outer walls just anyhow. Domestic architecture in Athens has not yet attained the rank of an ornamental art; it is of a temporary or make-shift character, and takes anything that comes to hand, and when it has covered a man, thinks it has done quite enough for him. All the houses nearly are new, for the Turks and Greeks, between them, knocked down the old town—a miserable collection of hovels—and left the

space clear for a new one, which has sprung up in spite of
attempts at straight streets at right angles to one another
("Places d'Othon and de Louis," and so on, and the example
of a most exactly square white palace of the King's), much
according to the fashion of its predecessor, in glorious contempt of straight lines. Our particular house is situated, as
I said, in one of these meandering streets (lanes we should
call them in England), which wanders at its own sweet will
all round the town from one end to the other, and is trying
to get itself the name—though the nation steadily ignores it
—of the street of Hadrian. Here is one part of its course,
and some one who, instead of building in solitary state, as
many people build in Athens, wished to have a next neighbour, fenced in with a wall a bit of ground next to what had
been last built upon and commenced work. Perhaps he was
the more tempted by the shell in good preservation of a stout
Turkish tower, which had not been knocked down, and
which saved him a good bit of building ; so he added on an
elbow (two storeys) to the Turkish tower, and thus he had a
pleasing irregular house occupying the two sides of the square
of ground, with a rough wall on the street side, and with
windows opening into the court. The staircase is on the outside to the second storey of the new building, in which are the
drawing and dining rooms, fair rooms, and inside comfortable
enough. . . . The romantic part of the business is that in these
troublesome times, when parties run so high, my uncle considers it necessary to have his house capable of sustaining an
assault, in case of any sudden disturbance ; so that things
are arranged for defence, and he has friends and old retainers
living in the neighbourhood to whom his house would be a
rendezvous in case of a row. I hope he deceives himself into
thinking there is more insecurity than is really the case ;

but, certainly, the idea of being prepared for a skirmish pleases him. Parties run very high here, and the English party call the French party (none of whom, of course, I have seen) all sorts of names—brigand, assassin, and so forth, with the greatest profusion of aggravating and horrifying epithets. But as regards actual security of the person, in Athens, or in the country, at least to strangers, other Englishmen are much less alarming than my uncle, so you need not be frightened ; I only mention our fortifications as a part of the grotesque world in which I am living. . . .

The house is a regular trysting-place for the members of the Opposition. First comes one of the old captains of the war, a rugged old gentleman from the mountains of the west, in a great white woollen sort of capote, like a sheepskin with the wool inside, with the white petticoat or fustanella, and then leggings and slippers ; probably he only talks modern Greek, but he is introduced to me, and we have a great deal of mute but smiling bowing, and shaking of hands, and so on ; presently in comes one of the white-kilted servants, and with a humble inclination of body, and placing his hand on his heart, offers a long pipe to my friend, who commences puffing. Of course the conversation is not very intelligible ; but it always consists in abusing Coletti and King Otho. Presently in comes another gentleman ; he may be dressed in the extreme of the Parisian fashion, tight boots and lemon-coloured kid gloves ; he is sure to talk French and Italian with the greatest fluency, perhaps also English. The pipe is brought in and offered, probably he declines it. Then comes a dandy of another cut, one who sticks to the native dress and wears it (an extremely handsome one anyhow, when the white kilt is clean) in its greatest elegance : a cloth jacket of red, or blue, or olive, richly embroidered with black lace,

with loose sleeves opened all down the arm, and just fastened
round it in two or three places ; over this a waistcoat without
sleeves still more richly embroidered, shirt and kilt of snowy
whiteness, a rich shawl girdle, and red or blue leggings—and
just nourishing a small moustache which contrasts strongly
with the huge grizzle which twists up under the hooked nose
of our shaggy friend ; and so the session goes on, enlarging
as people drop in one after another, in all sorts of dresses; and
as each comes in, he is soon followed by a long pipe, which
none but the more exquisite or the invalids refuse.   There
they sit in a circle, talking very loud Greek, Italian, and
French, abusing the ministry and the present state of things,
for two hours.

For the last weeks I have been living among people who
form the most grotesque contrasts to all that I have been
accustomed to.   The difference of scene and dress is very
soon got over, and the views of the Acropolis, and the rickety
cabs driven below them by fierce moustached coachmen in
red caps and white petticoats, do not move me more than St.
Mary's and a Vice-Chancellor and pokers would do.   But
the company that I keep—quite, I assure you, the *élite* of
Athens—is very different from all your people at Oxford.
First, all my friends are strong Liberals, and I hear nothing
but Liberalism all day long.   No one here has any notion
that an Englishman can be other than a Liberal ; if he was
not, he would be a sort of unintelligible contradictory monster,
who by some accident had come to be bred in the great
country of enlightened constitutionalism.   Of course all our
governments have acted more or less so as to foster the idea,
and the English who come to live here, besides the strong
temptations of a foreign residence to become real Liberals,
can hardly help appearing to be so, unless they take the line

of talking against England and English policy and proceedings. *Primâ facie*, it is taken for granted that an
Englishman abhors Jesuits and despotism as the two greatest
of evils, and would die—or at least give a good deal of money
—to provide constitutions for all nations wanting them ; and
it is difficult to make the natives understand that one is quite
content with one's freedom at home from thumb-screws and
black-holes without violently sympathising with all the
insurrectionists in Europe. The confusion of ideas is quite
grotesque ; they get their notions of liberalism from French
radical papers, the only ones which are read by the Greeks ;
then they say England is liberal, and so father all the
French radical doctrines on England, who is supposed to
patronise and enforce them against France, which here at
least is supposed to back up despotism, and to work against
"the Constitution." So that viewed as a Greek would
represent it, the battle here between England and France is
a sort of endless pursuing of their own tails. Next, I find
myself in the focus of a political row, which my Oxford
experience helps me to understand, but which is still more
ferocious than even the onslaught of * * * and * * *.
There is first the open public row in the Chamber, between
the Ministry and the Opposition, who have been for the last
three years fighting in a most Homeric manner, which is
remembered not so much by this or that motion lost or won,
but by the skill and success on particular occasions of this or
that πρόμαχος, how energetically Diomedes slew his opponent,
and how Lysander and Lycurgus struck terror into the hosts
of the Moschomangi—which is the nickname (I don't understand it) of the Ministerialists. Their House of Commons is
a striking sight in its way : the half military, half country
gentleman look of the moustachioed members, the mixture

of showy Greek with sad - coloured, sombre European
dresses, and the faces and airs of a number of the members,
not unlike the pictures of the burly soldiers and flash
courtiers of the time of Charles I., always puts me in mind
of his House of Commons. And those of the Opposition
Greeks who are learned enough in Western history to have
heard anything about the parliamentary struggles before our
civil war, like to draw a parallel between them and their
own battle with King Otho and his pet Minister Coletti.
Then, when the public battle is over, succeeds an endless
series of visitings and gatherings where they speculate, and
abuse their enemies, and bring and receive news—what new
votes the Minister has bought, and how much national
property he has granted away for them, what new sneaking,
sharp practice the King has employed to silence one witness,
and what sort of poison was used to get another out of the
way, how many English ships are coming, and how terrible
they will be to the corrupt court. There is no intercourse
between the two parties; each thinks the other fit for
nothing but to be food for the crows, and would not be
sorry for a favourable opportunity of preparing the dish for
them. The things that are spoken of as likely or desirable,
and still more those that are alluded to, are quite horrifying
to my quiet English proprieties. I have certainly got a
clearer notion than I used to have of a political fight as it
used to be two hundred years ago.

In all this political row between the Moschomangi people
and the Opposition ecclesiastical matters are not very prominent. The Roman Catholic King is practical head of the
Church, which, in the Constitution, is made to profess entire
independence of Constantinople, though united with it in
doctrine. He nominates the bishops, and out of the bishops

he also appoints the five who form the governing synod.
Meanwhile, as a power in the State, the Church as yet makes
very little show ; the Liberals on both sides are, of course,
for cutting down, suppressing monasteries, paying the clergy
by the State, and having as few bishops as possible ; and
probably they will carry out their wishes, though at present
they are too busy with other things.   The Church party, the
" Phil-orthodox," who are patronised by Russia, are now in
close league with the Liberals of the Opposition against the
Liberals of the Ministry, and so do not say very much about
their differences, but they are said to be people of very strong
opinions (" bigoted, fanatical," are the words applied to them
by my friends), who are exceedingly disgusted with the
Liberal ways of proceeding with Church property, and with
the position of the Greek Church, as laid down in the Constitution, against the Patriarch of Constantinople ; and as
they have some clever fellows among them, and have Russia
to back them, they will probably be heard of in time.   The
bulk of the population appear to be completely under the
influence of the Church ; of course everything is very rude,
churches, priests, service and congregation, as you would
naturally expect a popular religion, kept up and followed, in
a very rude people, to be.

ATHENS, 4th March.

I have dropped down here at a good moment, at least a
curious one.   The Minister is a certain M. Coletti, an ex-
secretary or quack doctor, I forget which, of Ali Pacha, and
said to have been made good use of by that respectable old
gentleman ; but in due time he became a patriot, and white-
washed and polished himself up by a six years' residence in
Paris as Minister.   He is personally a favourite of the King's,
and hand in glove with M. Piscatory, the Minister, and with

the French party. I saw him the other day in the Senate,
the γερουσία or Upper House. This body, consisting of
members for life (about forty), is supposed to be made up of
the most distinguished people of the country ; and here the
English party is generally the strongest. Coletti came as
Minister, to give explanations about a bill. He marched in
with extreme pomp : a big, broad-shouldered man in Greek
costume of red cap, and white kilt, and embroidered leggings,
seeming almost smothered in the rich fur on his jacket. His
appearance was not in his favour ; he sat in a moody sort of
way, seldom looking up, and never looking any one in the
face, and acting the great man out of humour in a grotesque
sort of way. This M. Coletti, the Opposition says, is doing
all he can to subvert the Constitution, and bring in a
despotism such as the King would like ; and he does this by
making the Government go on as badly as possible, and
speciatim by privately encouraging all sorts of bad characters
and brigandism, so that he may drive the nation at last to
lay the blame of all their troubles on the Constitution, and
ask, " What good has this Constitution done us ? " This has
been going on for nearly three years. People abuse one
another so furiously that it is hard to believe all that is said ;
but I should think that there is little doubt that M. Coletti
is no better than he should be. He is at present, however,
apparently at the end of his ministry ; at least he is involved
in some half dozen extremely awkward scrapes, and if the
King persist in keeping him, I should really think that there
will be fighting. He has persisted all along in bearing on
his own broad shoulders the weight of four out of the seven
" responsible Ministerships " appointed by the Constitution,
—Interior, Justice, Education and Ecclesiastical Affairs, and
Foreign Affairs,—an arrangement which, of course, has many

advantages, but increases also a man's chances of scrapes, which, with arrears, are said to be considerable in these several departments. The number of displaced functionaries —displaced by their own account on political grounds only —police magistrates, professors, and "judges of Areopagus," whom I have met here is pretty well ; and these fellows are turned loose to write newspapers, which are numerous and warmly supported by their party, and eagerly read. (There are some twenty at least in Athens, the largest part being Opposition papers.) Then he is beginning to break with some of his friends. Two of the most effective were two sworn brothers in arms, named Grivas and Grizzotis—two inseparables, who are always to be seen together in the streets, or in the Chamber, dressed in the richest style of Greek military costume, and carrying it off with a swagger which is not uncommon with the wearers of the native dress. Grivas looks very like a theatrical captain of banditti ; and Grizzotis like a theatrical grey-haired Parliamentarian in *I Puritani.* Both these gentlemen would require some soap and water to wash them clean—Grivas requiring considerably the larger quantity. They used to walk about with the most terrifying "tails" of palicari (bravi is just the Italian for them), which they were wont to switch most uncomfortably in the faces of the Opposition members. However, Grivas quarrelled with the King about a dinner, and Grizzotis, his friend, about something else ; and now they have turned steady men, disinterested citizens, who have resigned their preferments, and are ready to serve their country, and have become quiet and almost respectable characters, having cut off and laid aside their "tails," at least for the present. They are now holding out hands to the Opposition ; and among other things they have taken to worrying the unlucky

Coletti with the most determined ferocity in the Chamber of
Deputies; and he, like a great offended owl, not knowing
how to maintain his dignity, instead of facing them runs
away, which does not raise his character. Just at this crisis
he has contrived to get into a quarrel with the Turks, and to
get caught out in a piece of financial sharp practice, which
there is no denying, and which has brought the Chambers
upon him. The King turned his back at one of his own
balls on the Turkish Minister for refusing a passport, which
he had been expressly ordered by his own Government not
to give, and then Coletti insulted the Ambassador further,
by telling him that it was just like him, and that the King
had served him right; whereupon the Ambassador wrote to
Constantinople, and the Turk now, who certainly has behaved
with great dignity and diplomatic propriety, tells Coletti that
satisfaction must be given within thirty days, or all intercourse will be broken off. The man to whom the passport
was refused tried quite lately to get up an insurrection in
Macedonia, and is now one of the King's aides-de-camp. I
have read the letters of all parties, and the comments of the
different Greek papers, and Coletti and the King certainly
seem to have very little to say for themselves. When this
took place there was a good deal of vapouring about war with
Turkey, and approaching marriages and christenings were to
be celebrated in Santa Sophia; but this seems to have gone
off, the Opposition warriors, who are some of the most distinguished, not being at present in the humour to fight with
the Turks; and the Ministers at Constantinople, except the
French, siding very strongly with the Turkish Ambassador.
The home affair is only the discovery of a system of falsifica-
tion of the official corn averages by which the duty on corn (a
sliding scale) is fixed, of which the Finance Minister bearing

the inauspicious name of " Poneropoulos " (—" poulos " being
equivalent to our son) has as yet given an extremely lame
account, and which an energetic commission of the Chamber
of Deputies is now diligently engaged in hunting out to the
bottom.   Of the fact there is no doubt, and the Minister
throws himself on the mercy of the Chamber by pleading
guilty to lâches ; he had so much to do ; but the Chamber,
with perfect propriety, are not disposed to acquit him of any
negligence ; and as Coletti's signature is also to the averages,
and he besides is such an atlas of administration, he will be
in for whatever his subordinate catches from the commission.
To add to his distress, England wants some of her money,
and he is daily in expectation of three line-of-battle ships off
the Piræus, by way of hint ; he has been already allowed
400,000 drachmae in his budgets of '45 and '46, which have
disappeared in some other way, and he is now trying to
smuggle an irregular bill to authorise a credit for the payment, without putting it in the budget.   Unlucky gentleman !   He certainly appears to be got to the edge ; but they
say the King will not let him go, and the Opposition, who
are undoubtedly gaining every day, make no scruple of
saying, that whoever else goes with him, Coletti shall go,
and if not by fair means, still in some way. . . . If he is
turned out I do not see who there is to take his place,
for the Opposition people are so much out with the King
personally, that I cannot imagine their getting on with him.
How they would do I don't know.   They would certainly
be under honester influences than I think Coletti is, and one
of their leading men was expatiating the other day on the
lesson which the corruption and profligate waste of public
property by this Ministry had given to the Opposition,
against the time when they should come into power.   It

would make them mind their proprieties, and be a warning to them to keep from picking and stealing,—they would be forced to keep up "une administration austère."

The Chamber of Deputies appears to offer a good field for a Minister to operate upon. They tell me that not one man in ten has enough to maintain himself on in Athens, and accordingly, places are most acceptable, and promises are the great engines of government; and not a tenth can be fulfilled, yet, with a sanguine people like this, the principle of a lottery is said to work well, and to keep votes with the Ministers. The interest which the Athenian public take in politics seems to be absorbing; there are nearly a score of newspapers published twice a week to satisfy their cravings; but they like to hear and to tell, rather than to read. The uncertainty of any news is a curious feature of this part of the world. Every one, even leading people, seem quite content with it as a report, and to trouble themselves very little to ascertain on what authority it rests; it is quite sufficient for them in its unauthenticated oral shape, and by the time that a cautious Englishman, who is deprived of the *Times*, feels clear that it is true, it has become quite out of date and stale. It is to me one of the most curious contrasts between the half civilisation here and our own state. of society; the circulation and verification of intelligence goes on still, mainly by the same imperfect means as it did in the days of Thucydides, and is practically to the nation and even the city as precarious and difficult. France is in the way to get hold of the political training of these people; for the only foreign newspapers they look at are the French —*Siècle, National, Débats*, and *Presse*. I should doubt, were it not so improbable à *priori*, whether a *Times* ever reaches Athens: I have not seen or heard of one (yes—

there is one at the English reading-room). And the course of opinion is decidedly French, even among the English party who detest the French Government because it is upholding the German Court notions and policy of the King ; they look for material help to Lord Palmerston and his three-deckers, but for intellectual direction, they take ideas and formulæ from their oracles, the French Liberal press and M. Thiers.   It is curious though to see France viewed as backing up the old notions of Royal power, and England simply as the representative of Liberalism and all that sort of thing.   And one cannot help looking at it oneself in a great measure with Greek spectacles ; it appears curiously different seen at a distance or close.   It is uncommonly difficult to get hold of anything that one can entirely under-stand and believe ; partly from one's own want of quickness, and partly because it is necessary to pass the day in a sceptical state of mind when in company with these lively Greeks.   Truth-telling, however, is highly prized here, one of them told me, " Quando in Grecia un uomo dice la verità, veramente l'adorano " ; it was meant, as one naturally takes it, as an ambiguous compliment to his countrymen.   Of their " sharpness " there can be no doubt ; the schools (Government chiefly) are crowded, and there are a great number in Athens of poor scholars, who come here and take service in order to go to the schools at the same time— regular servitors.   I wish I had room to give you a full account of the means taken by a friend of mine, who was Governor somewhere, to make the old people take to his schools—those who hung back from sending their children, " gli ho perseguitato "—" l'uno io metteva in arresto," and so on ; while he coaxed and favoured those who sent their children (a most grotesque story, told with the utmost εὐήθεια),

so that there is no danger of the young Greeks not being
fond of some sort or other of illumination ; but it will be of
a curious sort.   At present they are a curious mixture of
sharpness and simplicity ; living in a kind of dreamland, in
which Greece is the central point, and the great " Protecting
Powers" are strange mysterious divinities, fighting among
themselves for the exclusive control of its fate.   Their
curiosity and quickness and mistakes are amusing, like those
of children ; and like children, it is impossible to put them
up to the complicated state of things in the West.   I cannot
tell what hold the Church has on them : a great number of
the leading men are, I should think, highly Liberal, and the
course of legislation is to clip Church revenues and power ;
but the churches are full morning and afternoon, and the
strong religious feeling at present of the nation at large is
undoubted.   I was edified by an old weather-beaten soldier
from the mountains of Western Greece, one of the heroes of
the late war, who keeps Lent with a strictness most disagreeable to some of his more enlightened fellow-partisans, who
are afraid to drink milk with their tea for fear of scandalis-
ing him.   The old gentleman is a fine specimen in his way,
and would obviously like nothing better than a good time of
war again, for which it really looks as if he would not have
to wait long.   The parish clergy are said to be ignorant, but
good sort of people.   The King being a Roman Catholic is
an anomalous sort of thing, which does not add to his chance
of being well with the nation.   He has great power in
ecclesiastical matters (nominating bishops, and selecting the
five who form the governing synod).   On the other hand,
he being a very strong Roman Catholic, (1) is married to a
Protestant ; (2) is bound by the Constitution to bring up his
children as members of the Greek Church ; and (3) has to

attend the Greek services on certain days, for which he is said to receive absolution as soon as he returns to the palace. It is a strange arrangement. One of my friends tells me continually that we (England) should send the Greeks three things, and that then they would get on grandly, viz.— Engineers to make Artesian wells ; People to teach the Greeks not to waste and spoil their grapes ; Capital. "Acqua ci manca, danari ci mancano, ed il vino nostro guastiamo noi."

To C. M. CHURCH, ESQ.

TURKISH TOWER, UNDER THE N. E. ANGLE
OF THE ACROPOLIS, 8th March 1847.

I am weather-bound here, waiting for the weather to say one or the other, whether it will be fine or not, before I begin an expedition round Attica. My route is—1st day, a village near Sunium ; 2nd day, Sunium, Thoricus, and Prasiæ ; 3rd day, Marathon ; 4th day, by Rhamnus to Oropus ; 5th day, by Deceleia, or else by Phylæ to Athens; or perhaps turn off to Eleusis first, which will make another day. Travelling is slow on horseback with baggage horses. My companion is a Greek friend of the General's, an employé in the "Woods and Forests," who knows all the country, and who takes with him some of his men as a guard against klephts. He is a sharp little man, with moustachios, named Vilaeti, who speaks Italian not much better, but more fluently than I do, and, I daresay, will be a good guide. I hope to have a grand dispatch to send you by the post after this.

I have been inactive for the last fortnight, but I could not well do otherwise ; it would not have done to run off into the country, and to have left the General at once ; but I hope now my campaigning will begin. I have lost some time by not getting up better my work before I came. I have had to be reading when I ought to have been looking about me, or learning modern Greek, which is a great puzzle from the way in which familiar words are disguised by their *accentual* pronunciation. However, by this time I know Athens pretty nearly as well as I know Winchester, and I don't think I shall easily forget it. I have at last been to the Acropolis, which I left to the last. It is certainly most magnificent. The size of the Parthenon is much greater than the view of it from the town leads you to expect, and when you get up to the platform of the rock, it spreads out its colonnade, broken as it is, with a mixture of calm solemnity and brightness, which calls up the idea of a beautiful human face such as you see in Greek sculpture, as if that was the expression which the architect, by his own method, meant to suggest to the beholder. It is remarkable what extreme attention these Greek architects paid to the effect of their buildings. There is a young architect here, a Mr. Penrose, who is taking all the measurements with the utmost accuracy ; and the results as to the contrivances employed to give the fullest optical effect to the building are very curious. For instance, there is not a single column which is perpendicular ; they all lean inwards to a definite degree. Then, he says, there is scarcely a straight line in the building ; all, except some few straight lines, are mathematical curves, sections of the cone which agree with the *calculated* curves exactly, and are such as just would give the fullest effect to the lights and shadows.

There are also some French architects at work, one of whom has just discovered what he supposes to be the mark of Neptune's trident (v. Herod. 8. 55 ; Pausanias, 26. 6 ; Wordsworth's *Athens*, 133). In excavating under the

northern wing of the Erechtheum he came to a walled
chamber, in the rocky floor of which are three natural holes
in a straight line, not quite equidistant, but near enough to
convey the idea of the σημεῖον ; and near it, channels as if
for water cut in the rock.   There seems no reason why it
should not be what it is taken for.   These things bring back
the past with a sort of thrill, and the Acropolis is full of
these mementos.   The impression of the votive shield on the
east end of the Parthenon — the marks of the wheels of
chariots in the rocky entrance under the Propylæa — the
architect's lines and circles, still left in the unfinished basement of the columns of the Propylæa, left unfinished from
the breaking out of the Peloponnesian war ;—the finished
rustic work of the basement of the old temple which the
Persians destroyed, left as part of the foundation of the more
magnificent Parthenon, the new part of the foundation of
which is continued on from it with rough blocks, to the
requisite length—and the fragments of columns and triglyphs
belonging to the same temple built into the northern wall of
the Acropolis, in the hurry of the repairs under Themistocles
—have a different effect from that of mere repairs ; they
bring back the sort of private history and the everyday
business of those times ; it is like catching a glimpse of the
men themselves ; it in some measure peoples the scene.

And now to our private life.   The day passes generally
as I described in my last : solitary breakfast, day to myself,
partie carrée at dinner, pipes and coffee after, and the company of the old chieftain Demo Chelio, with his deep laugh,
and white woollen capote, whence he derives the name of
Ἄσπρο διάβολο, *i.e.* white devil.   There are not many
English.   I have dined once or twice at Sir E. Lyons', and
at Mr. Hill's the chaplain. . . . I have not met with any

chance of a companion, and I do not much expect one.   I
shall try hard to get on to Delphi.   My next plan after that
is Ægina, Epidaurus, the plain of Argos, if possible, Nemea,
and the Stymphalian country, Corinth, and home.   I am
afraid I must give up Sparta ; the General will not hear
of it.

FROM THE HOUSE OF THE EX-DEMARCH.
KERATIA, 10th March 1847.

I begin a sort of journal letter of my expedition.   If you
want to know where I am, look in a good map of Attica,
e.g. Leake or Wordsworth, about 15 miles to the north of
Sunium, and you may, perhaps, find the out-of-the-way place
where I am writing, much to the astonishment of all my
companions and the inmates of my domicile.   We have just
done dinner in a large upper room in one of the chief houses
of this village, which, though something like a good large
barn in England, is by no means a bad resting-place after a
day's ride.   Imagine, then, a large barn, with a good blazing
fire of cedar brushwood, smelling very aromatic.   My companions are, first, a chief ranger in the Greek " Woods and
Forests," who is my guide and cicerone ; secondly, two of his
men, fine-looking fellows, of the Albanian cut, armed up to
the teeth with Turkish sabre, silver-mounted pistol and
dagger and long gun, in the fashionable white kilt and red
cap, and sheepskin " floccata " or cape—uncommonly warlike
gentry, who, if they were not allowed to wear arms in the
service of the Government as keepers of the woods and
forests, would probably wear them on their own account, and
guard the woods and forests for themselves ; thirdly, the
sons of the demarch, or rather the ex-demarch, an authority
equivalent to our mayor, who have just come in from the
plough, and appear to be honest sort of labourers.   These

arc all assembled in one big room, smoking and looking on
with much curiosity at my proceedings (one of the boys has
just come without any shyness, but without any forwardness
either, simply to look over my shoulder, to see what operation was going on while I was writing). We have just
dined—first myself and M. Vilacti my companion, at a
table, on "pillaw" of rice and butter, boiled fish, and cold
lamb, finishing off with pipes (in which I am quite an adept)
and coffee; then, on a mat spread on the floor, the guards
and the demarch's family, who, as it is Lent (which these
wild soldiers observe in their way most strictly), have re-
stricted themselves to olives, and a sort of caviare. They
would not eat our "pillaw" because there was butter in it,
and now they are marching about the room talking, and one
of them preparing tea. My "guardia boschi" I have really
quite taken a fancy to, in spite of their somewhat roughish
looks; there is a curious simplicity and natural civility
mixed up with the military dandyism and conceit which
marks their whole tribe, which gives a good deal of zest to
the intercourse which I carry on with them, partly in bad
Italian and worse Greek, and partly by signs. But I must
give you a sketch of our line of march.

We started from Athens at half-past eight this morning,
myself and M. Vilacti on horseback, the two "guardia
boschi" exalted high on the backs of two mules laden with
carpet-bags and baskets of provisions, with their long guns
in front of them and across their knees, and the muleteer on
foot, armed with a long gun also, and a couple of pipes for
us, stuck like pistols in his belt. We rode through the
narrow plain, between Hymettus and Lycabettus, a red stony
flat, covered with wild thyme and dwarf shrubs of the
prickly oak. It was a beautiful morning, and the three

great mountains—Hymettus, grey and silvery, on our right ;
Parnes, with its black patches of forest scattered over its
bare, craggy sides, on our left ; and Pentelicus in front, a
beautiful rich purple pyramid, rising straight from the plain
—made a glorious scene.   Travelling in this fashion, we go
at a foot's pace, about three miles an hour, and so have
plenty of time to look about us.   We wound round the
northern spur of Hymettus, and then doubled it, moving
along its eastern base.   Here we got into the Mesogœa, a
series of small flat plains, winding in and out, as the great
ranges open or close on them, and with a number of small
hills rising over them, some broken and craggy, where the
rock has broken through the soil, and others round and
conical.   The mountains are covered with brushwood, cedar,
tamarisk, the prickly oak, and the " Pinus maritima "—
πεῦκος—which often grows to a large tree ; but the shepherds who wander about the country with their flocks, and
find but very little to feed them with, are in the habit of
setting fire to the woods, to make a clearing and produce
pasture-tracks,—a habit which it is the chief office of my
companion to restrain.   Every now and then we came to a
grove of olives, often in a recess in the hills, a regular
ἄλσος, which generally showed a church half-appearing
through the grey foliage and grotesquely twisted trunks ; but
through all the country, except a solitary church, not a
building was to be seen except in the villages.   The people
live together, and go out and work in the district belonging
to their village at the corn-lands and vineyards ; but they
do not live in single farmhouses.   This gives a solitary look
to the country, such as one sees only in downs in England ;
but in spite of great quantities of stony and uncultivated
land, it is not dreary.   The flowers are coming out ; here

and there among the brushwood a bright red anemone, and other sorts less brilliant, white, violet, and blue ; the yellow broom, too, is coming out on the hills ; and the olive has to me an extremely pleasing effect. We dined at a place you will probably look for in vain, Koroupia, just under the base of one of the spurs of Hymettus, and after a beautiful afternoon's ride of three hours, got to this place, under the shadow of a noble mountain, which they call here Elympo, or Olympo. To-morrow we start for Sunium and Thoricus.

My Greek guards are immense fun with the mackintosh air-bed which I have with me. They have taken it into their special care, and are just like children with it, racing one against another, which shall fill a compartment first with the bellows, or with their mouth. They consider it a wonder of art, and intend to floor their friends at Athens with riddles about a man whom they have seen, who sleeps on wind. They are capital attendants, and quite watch every want which they fancy I may have. It is very curious to be among these wild people with their pistols and daggers and scimitars, mounted with silver ; the passion for ornamental arms is quite a ruling one with them ; and Government indulges it by allowing the irregular troops, and the police, etc. (besides some not very creditable retainers of the great men), to dress as they like, and to sport all sorts of dangerous weapons.

11th March.—To-day we have had a long, but most delightful ride to Sunium. We started at seven, and rode through a very noble mountain pass, down to Thoricus : a great part of the road was high on the mountain side, over-looking a deep, gloomy ravine ; we looked down on a wide chasm in the limestone rocks, which were of all colours,— green, red, yellow, and purple,—through which the winter torrents must rush along in fine style, and this ended in a dell thickly wooded with evergreens of this country, with their varied shades. The view at the end of this was very fine ; the channel of Euboea, like a broad river, with two long islands, one behind the other, the water of the deepest blue, and the beautiful purples of the various distances contrasting with all the greens and reds of the mountains which opened out upon the shore. Every now and then we came to long tracts of scoriæ. These are from the now exhausted mines of Laurium, and all over the wooded hills of this extremity of Attica one comes to places where the smelting was carried on. The ride to Sunium along the face of the hills, with the sea glistening and just crisped by the wind, was delicious ; it had the zest, too, of being thought a little dangerous, and we rode in military order, one of our guards riding in front as our advanced guard, perched up on the top of a mule, with his long gun across his knees, ourselves in the centre, and the other bringing up the rear. However, no klephts appeared, and we rode up the steepest hill that I can conceive a horse carrying a man up, to the temple. You know generally how it stands ; fourteen or sixteen white marble Doric columns on the top of a cape 400 feet high, which stretches far out into the sea, and looks up the Gulf of Ægina in one direction, and the Euboean Channel in the other, and in front commands a vista of the islands, as they run out one beyond another, from Makronisi to (they say, but ?) Melos.

MARATHON, 12*th March.*

I must give you a line from this place, though I was too sleepy to finish my work last night, and have had eleven hours on horseback to-day. We have come from Keratia, passing by the old Prasiæ (Porto Raphti), a beautiful bay,

where a lot of very ruffian-looking Greek irregulars were
breakfasting. We dined under a hot June sun, which quite
burnt my hands, near the old Brauron, and rode along the
outside of the hills, between them and the sea, through the
woods. About five the weather changed, and the clouds
gathered very thick over Pentelicus and its spurs ; and at
six we rode into the plain of Marathon, with a wild and
gloomy sky, the evening sunlight just catching the distant
headlands of Euboea, and throwing a white sickly gleam
upon them. I am glad to have seen Marathon as I have
done—late in the evening, the time of day of the battle
itself, under a dark, stern, stormy sky, which, without con-
cealing the features of the scene, gave them a great solemnity.
The plain, as flat as the sea itself, is one of the gulfs of land
which run in here among the mountains. Entering it from
the south, it is bounded by rounded down-like hills of considerable height, while behind rise — steep, craggy, and
pointed—the last spurs of Pentelicus ; over these last the
clouds hung low and rolled together, just leaving in the
south-west an opening of light, which gave additional depth
and shade to the outline of hills along which it was spread.
The one conspicuous object in this wide flat of about six
miles is the Tumulus of the 192 Athenians. There are
great differences of opinion about the position of the armies ;
but by the consent of all the critics, we were allowed to
believe, on this wild evening, as it closed on us in the
solitary field, that here had been the brunt of the battle,
and that we were riding across ground where Europe and
Asia first fairly met and tried their strength. It was
impossible to have seen the place under a better light ; one
which so well suited the strange, mysterious character of the
old victory, which, even to the Greeks themselves, had

something in it of the supernatural.   We were benighted on
the field, with the wind rising, and the sea breaking on the
beach near us, where the Persian ships with Hippias had
moored.   With some trouble, and amid the furious onslaught
of shepherds' dogs, we found our way, in the thick, dusky
evening, to the demarch's house at Marathona; and here we
were very hospitably and civilly received by the Greek
family.   The lady came in, after the first compliments had
passed, with a tray of sweetmeats and a glass of some sort of
liqueur, and offered it gracefully as a kind of welcome.
They are like the last demarch, plain, farmer sort of people,
who live chiefly in their kitchen, but they have a big room
besides, which has served for our dining-room, and will
serve for our bedroom.   But I must prepare to make use
of it in this latter character.

MARATHONA, 13th March.

I did my hosts injustice, for they gave me a room to
myself, and a very comfortable, though somewhat rude bed,
without fleas, which indeed I have not met with yet.   I
make myself at home, squat on a mat with the rest before
the kitchen fire, and smoke : and so I am treated with much
favour.   To-day, instead of going on to Oropus, I have made
my headquarters here, and rode in the morning to Rhamnus,
and in the afternoon had a gallop over the field, and looked
at Vraná, which is said to have been the ancient Marathon
(<i>vide</i> Leake).   For Rhamnus I refer you to the same, or else
to Wordsworth.   The temple of the awful goddess of the
Persian war vies with that of Athenæ of the Acropolis and of
Sunium, in the grandeur of its situation.   It stood, a Doric
marble hexastyle like the Theseium, at the head of a steep
gorge, looking down over a fortified cape with walls of huge
blocks of marble, which runs out from the ends of the

ravine, upon the river-like Eubœan Channel, down which
the Persian ships sailed to Marathon. And as Minerva at
Sunium seemed to place herself in front of her own land,
and on the Acropolis, to watch over her city, its denizen, its
champion, and unsullied object of worship—πολιάς, πρόμαχος, παρθένος—so on the other side of Attica those ships
who approached it, as they looked up from the water to the
white front of the temple of Nemesis, standing out against
its dark background of wood, and facing Asia, must have
been reminded of the power which had once protected
Athens so signally, and might have foreseen that the same
power, ἡ θεῶν μάλιστα ἀνθρώποις ὑβρισταῖς ἀπαραίτητος,
would one day punish her as signally. The temple was a
monument against themselves.

SCALA D'OROPO, 14th March.

I have been travelling all to-day. We left Marathona
by a very fine mountain-path, like all those which we have
passed,—one which would make an English horse open his
eyes wide, but which these horses step up and down with
the greatest possible coolness. This expedition has taught
me that there is no place, not absolutely perpendicular, up
and down which a horse will not go : sheets of slippery rock,
tracks of loose and broken stones, steps or sharp crags or
deep holes—it is all one to them : they walk coolly over
everything, at any angle at which a man could stand. I
have long ceased to be nervous, though our road to-day has
been up and down a succession of deep gorges, or along their
faces, looking down their steep sides. We have travelled
to-day through the Diacria, a country of ravines, some of
them very magnificent ones, cut deeply into the soft soil,
with a torrent-bed at the bottom, but with a want of wood,
owing to the perpetual burning which goes on here.

I

Kapandriti, Kalamo, Marcopoulo, and this place, will give you our route. The Oropia is a flat plain along the sea, reaching up from the Asopus to the wall of moorlands, which are the ending of Attica proper. We had our first rain to-day, but it did not do us much harm ; but it will be a bore if it keeps us here to-morrow. The views of Euboea and the channel are very fine all along the road we have been to-day. There is a great mountain just over against us behind Eretria (Dirphys in ancient maps), of which we have not yet seen the summit. It is not sketching weather, however, and I am sorry to say that I have come away without anything of Marathon, though there is at least one very striking view : the great hill which overhangs the plain and battle-ground to the south was tempting me all the time I was there ; but it was too cold at the only times I could spare for sketching.

ATHENS, 19th March.

The weather was so unpromising at Scala d'Oropo on Monday morning, that we resolved to give up Mount Parnes, and get back to Athens as quick as we could. We came through the same sort of moorland hills that we had passed the day before, and through the pass between Pentelicus and the lower ridges which connect it with Parnes ; you will find in Leake's map the pass of Katifori. It was a gusty, showery day, and the snowstorms which covered Parnes even as low down as the peak of Deceleia showed that we had been prudent.

We dined at a small village, Kapandriti, where we tried for the first time a clay floor, and the company of horses and fowls eating in the same room with us. It was the house of the chief magistrate, πάρεδρος, he is called (*i.e.* deputy to the demarch of the larger district). The dignitary himself was

out at work, most honestly getting his bread. His house was
divided lengthways by two arches, shiny and black with
smoke, as were also the rafters of the roof which they supported, and in which was a hole for the smoke, and divers
accidental holes for the refrigeration and humefaction of the
inhabitants. Across ran a rail, on the one side the beasts in
the dark,—on the other, the human creatures, by the light
of the fire and door, and the fowls were everywhere. When
we came in, the daughter was kneading bread, the mother
spinning and watching the pot on the fire, the children crying,
the husband of the daughter standing about doing nothing.
M. Vilaeti said that they were very good people, and that the
πάρεδρος never sent away a poor man or a traveller from his
door. We did not put them out much. Ghiorghi simply
put some wood on, and made a better fire, without saying
by your leave, and took possession of one side of it for his
cooking business, while the old lady went on with hers at
the other. A carpet was spread on the floor, and we squatted
down close to the fire, which was very acceptable that day,
and smoked till our dinner was ready to warm us better.
We dined very well, off a horse-sieve for a table ; our
attendants and the son-in-law dining on a mess of rice next
to us, and the ladies eating by snatches out of a pipkin, of
some kind of broth or pottage on the other side of the fire.
Our ride through the valley below Kapandriti, which ends
the highlands of North-Eastern Attica or Diacria, was pretty,
and the weather mended. The pass itself is striking, an
easy ascent winding up a red hill with pines, and between
deep banks of red earth, overhung with shrubs and trees ;
a place once, and I believe even now, famous for klephts,
"signorini"—or ἔμποροι as they are still called—whose
occasionally chivalrous way of doing business commanded

a share even of M. Vilaeti's admiration. However, we saw
no more of them here than we had at Sunium, and got home
without the smallest adventure to boast of.

To C. M. CHURCH, ESQ.

ATHENS, *8th April* 1847.

I begin a letter, though I have not much to write that is
new since my last date. Easter here has been, as might be
expected, more noisy and hurried than is pleasant. But it
was a satisfaction on Easter Sunday to have some faces at
church which brought back St. Mary's early service and St.
Peter's-in-the-East, viz. Watson, and Mildmay of Merton, who
have been here all the week. The last week was observed
by the Greeks in a curious way ;—strict and severe fasting ;
long services very early in the morning and late at night ;
and in the middle of the day they were hurrying and bustling
about preparing for Easter, and the streets were full of stalls
decked out with evergreens and bad prints of the king and
queen, saints, and heroes of the war. I went to one or two
of their services, *i.e.* those at the Russian Church, where there
was less crowd. There seemed to be both more reverence
and attention and more levity than in an English congregation. I don't profess to understand their way of behaving.
The sort of orderly inattention and stealthy gossip that goes
on with us you never see here. They are either attending
in earnest, or not pretending to attend at all ; and they seem
to pass abruptly, and without any hesitation or concealment,
from devotion to mutual salutations and smiles. This was
the case among the Russians, who all belong to the embassy ;
the Greeks proper, I should think, are much the same, except
that the service on the part of the clergy is more slovenly,
which it was not at all at the Russian Church. All Saturday

was devoted to killing lambs ; the shepherds came down from the mountains with their flocks, and were to be seen going about everywhere with their lambs on their shoulders —just Overbeck's " Pastor Bonus " ; and at every corner of the streets the butchering was going on in public, and one was in danger of stepping into a stream of blood. Easter begins at twelve o'clock on Saturday night with a great service, at which the King and Queen are present (one being a Roman Catholic, the other a Lutheran), and all Athens crowds there, partly as a religious duty, partly for the spectacle. After this is over (it lasts three hours), all return home and begin eating roast lamb with a greediness which is not creditable to the moral effect of their previous abstinence. But, of course, there are two sides to all holiday-keeping. Here they seem, most of them, to go half mad. Among other things, they keep up all night and all day long a never-ceasing fire from their guns and pistols, which has slackened but not stopped yet ; and they think it no fun unless they load with ball. This, as half of them are drunk, interferes with the satisfaction of walking in the streets or looking out of window. Then, yesterday, by way of variety, they had a Jew riot. They have been accustomed other years to burn a Jew in effigy on Easter Sunday, which the police stopped : so by way of making amends a mob of, they say, between 2000 and 3000 (but ?) collected and attacked the house of one of the few Jews here [1]—pillaged, gutted, and all but demolished it ; and were with difficulty prevented from demolishing the unhappy Jew himself. This is the disgusting side of their way of keeping Easter ; on the

---

[1] This was the noted Don Pacifico, an Ionian Jew, for whose losses Lord Palmerston demanded redress from the Greek Government in 1849.

other hand, the extreme pre-eminence which they seem to give it above all other festivals, seems to me very striking. It seems to be to them what Christmas is with us—the household and family festival. They can't bear not to keep it at home. The old salutation continues ; Χριστὸς ἀνέστη, answered by ἀληθῶς ἀνέστη, is the regular form for forty days ; and on Easter Day, when friends meet in the street, it is exchanged with a kiss. The day really seemed to bring out all their friendliness, and several times the heartiness and affectionateness with which the kiss was given was very pleasant : it seemed to be done, too, with a kind of serious- ness. However, I do not wish to spend another Easter here ; though I have no reason to complain on the whole. Of course we had full service in our chapel, and a new organ which they have got out from England was opened yesterday.

NAUPLIA, 13*th April* 1847.

As I have some time to-day I send you a report from here of so much of our Peloponnesian expedition. We started from Piraeus last Friday night in a Greek boat of a curious fashion, not very unlike in its hull to those paper boats which are produced in some mysterious way by folding and pulling out a square sheet of paper, which I remember used to please me much in ancient times. There was a small cabin at the stern, with a picture of St. George, and a lamp burning ; but the fleas, who never hurt me, drove Penrose out of it to lie on the ballast. The Piraeus has four line-of-battle ships in it now, besides no end of brigs and schooners. We left on a beautiful still night, music playing, and lights glancing about on board our *Albion*, and the echoes of the evening guns rolling and thundering among the hills of Salamis. We were close to Ægina when I

crawled out of my den at four next morning, its cliffs and
peaks beginning to look tawny and brown in the grey of the
dawn. We soon got on shore, and saw the sun rise on our
way to the temple—whether of Jupiter Panhellenius, or
Minerva. I don't know whether I don't like it better than
Sunium. The nearer scenery of Ægina itself is wilder than
that near Sunium, and though you have not the grand
precipice towering above the sea to stand on, you have sea
on each side of you, and the outlines of Gerancia, Cithæron,
and those of the plain of Athens. But it is no use
describing, you won't be the wiser. When we had done
with the old grey limestone temple, we sailed round the
north of the island to the town, which is on the edge of a
flat plain, which lies like a sort of quay at the foot of the
mountain. Of the fierce and spirited little Dorian Athens
there remains a scathed Doric column of one of its temples,
and in the sea the ruined but still serviceable moles which
formed (I think) three square basins of considerable size.
Its houses now chiefly straggle in a long line along the quay,
and there were two brigs building. Opposite to it rises
a dark jagged volcanic peninsula, Methana, which looked
quite black and awful against a rather wild western sky,
and between it and a number of larger and smaller islands
appeared the hills of Epidaurus, whither we were bound.
We started again in the evening, but the wind was first
against us, and then dropped altogether.

All Sunday morning till eleven we were slowly creeping
along, but the sight was glorious all round ; the mountains
were all round us—behind, but in clear outline, Hymettus
and Pentelicus running on to those of the isthmus on our
right : in front we were gradually approaching those of
Epidaurus, magnificent fellows, running down with a steep

slope into the sea, and with the sun full on them, and
bringing out all their features ; and the rest of the panorama
was completed by the still more picturesque outlines of
Methana and Ægina. Our church was rather a low one
this Sunday, between the shingle ballast and the deck of our
boat, where we could only crouch down. Epidaurus,
however, we reached at last : nothing to see there but the
exceedingly beautiful site of the place. From here we
were to ride across to Nauplia, taking the sacred valley of
Æsculapius on the way ; so we exchanged our Greek boat
for Greek saddles, not a change to perfect bliss, but not so
intolerable as I expected. The road from the sea to the
valley is through a green glen between noble mountains.
The nightingales were in full song, and we got to the sacred
valley in high spirits. It is a curious place, an ancient
watering-place for idlers and invalids ; with remains, on an
equally magnificent scale, of a theatre, hospital, and baths ;
and the secluded valley itself having the look of a great
pleasure park, a sort of Rasselas happy valley run to waste
and disorder. The theatre, which drove Pausanias into
raptures, is cut in the side of a hill facing the grey summit
of Mount Arachne, and gave him for the first time the idea
of what a Greek theatre must have been, at least in its
landscape, and in the crowds which it would hold. But a
theatre is a melancholy place, like a field of battle.

From the Hieron, a road, the broadest I have seen in
this country, leads through heath-like valleys, and over a
succession of low hills, to Nauplia. We were caught among
them, not by a storm, but by the evening, and as the gates
of Nauplia are shut at eight or nine, we did not know
which, we were in the comfortable state of wishing to ride
fast, and of having strongly impressed upon our minds, by

occasional stumbles, the great probability of getting our necks broken if we did. But at last our Greek servant made up his mind, and, riding behind us, kept up a continual bastinado on our horses and his own, and so we proceeded for nearly an hour, jogging and jolting awfully down hill, with the lights of Nauplia twinkling before us with a most tantalising sameness of look, and seeing nothing on each side of us but a black, huge, undefined outline, which might be a bank or a plain. Just as we got to the suburb, we heard the drums beating and a bell going in a very shut-up sort of way, and just at this agonising moment, our horses, mine at least, remembered some suburban stable, and thought he might as well go there as elsewhere ; and as we had nothing but halters to ride with, there was some difficulty in persuading his ill-disposed mind to give up the preposterous idea. Sure enough, when we got to the gates they were shut. However, in consideration of our close shave, and a Greek officer being late also, they let us in without our horses ; and I shall never think of the gates of Nauplia without lively sensations of satisfaction. A close shave, in retrospect, is one of the most delightful of recollections.

You would think me wild if I went on to expatiate on the plain of Argos. This is our third day at Nauplia, and we are not tired yet. It is very different from that of Athens. At Athens, though there is no luxuriance, and there is the usual severity of a Greek landscape, there is a grace and brightness which never fails. Here everything, though strikingly beautiful, has a stern solemnity, even in the bright mornings we have had here. The broad, flat, tawny plain, spread out between the magnificent mountains, much higher all round and more massed together than those

of Attica,—in one corner, the Larissa of Argos, like a huge
tumulus with the trees and houses of the city lying in lines
below it ; at the other, the red rocky Palamidi of Nauplia,
a great isolated cliff, on the top of which is perched a modern
fortress with its winding walls, a costly relic of the Venetian
conquests ; in the plain itself, among a number of island-
like hills and rocks, the low flattened ruined Acropolis of
Tiryns, half hidden behind a clump of white poplars ; at
the most distant edge of the plain, not Mycenæ itself, for it
is hidden, but the grey hard mountains which enclose and
overhang it ; and piercing into the plain, the thin blue line
of sea, unbroken, or broken only by a solitary boat,—make
up a picture which corresponds singularly with the stern
history which belongs to it. At Mycenæ this character is
exhibited in the highest degree. It lies between two great
bare mountains in a recess of the plain, on a ridge equally
bare and grey as the mountains, rising up to the citadel,
where it slopes down steep on one side, and, on the other,
is broken down into a sheer dark precipice. All is grey,
except the reddish lines of walls formed of enormous blocks
which run round most part of it. They are vast and rude
enough to be the walls of the heroes ; they crown the slopes
on one side, and hang over the deep precipice on the other.
The gate of the Lions is one of the most solemn spots I ever
was in. It faces the north, and is generally in shadow ; it
lies at the end of a sort of passage or court formed by the
huge walls to the right and left ; over it the strange-looking
animals stand out from their black slab of basalt as clear as
when they were first carved, and in its sides and threshold
are still visible the holes for the bars and bolts which
fastened its folding doors, and the ruts worn by the chariot
wheels which entered it. The whole scene is one of gaunt,

grim desolation. It does not so much recall Homer as
Æschylus. Argos with its peaked Larissa and grand theatre
hewn out of the rock, and facing the whole landscape of the
plain, is very Greek in its way, and the proud old churlish
Dorian democracy has left its character to its modern inhabitants. To-morrow we start off again on our travels.

We cross the gulf to Astros, and then ride across to
Sparta—then to Kalamata, Ithome, Bassæ, Olympia. The
rough work has to begin now ; hitherto it has been comparatively plain sailing. Henceforward we shall have to
sleep with the pigs. When I get back to Athens I shall
settle about my future movements.

KALAMATA, 20th April 1847.

I wrote to you from Nauplia five days ago, not expecting
to have another opportunity of writing so soon ; but a wet
day has curtailed our travelling. We have done a great
deal since then. We started by water from Nauplia on
Thursday to Astros (in the Thyreatis), where we had settled
to meet our horses and muleteers from Argos. We arrived,
admired, and waited for many hours, but no muleteers came,
and our combinations for the day were cruelly spoilt. At
last, just as we had given them up in despair, and had
resolved on proceeding on foot to a monastery near, they
made their appearance, coolly made no sort of excuse, but
trusted to our necessity (since there was but one horse in
Astros to be hired) to plead in their favour. We and our
servant scolded, but were glad enough to get them.

We spent the night in the said monastery—a beautiful
spot among the mountains, reached by a road over the plain
of Astros, which that evening gave us some of the most
beautiful views that I ever saw ; a rich plain illuminated by

the evening sun, the headland and peninsula of Astros, the
Gulf of Argolis, and the grand mountain of Arachne falling
into the hills of Epidaurus, and faced by a lower line of
cliffs in front : all this seen out of a deep wooded gorge, full
of rich greens and browns, kept down and mellowed, but
not yet darkened, by the shadows of the overhanging
mountains. The monastery lies out of the beaten track.
The monks received us with all hospitality, and though it
must be said that the fleas were equally glad to see us and
attentive, we passed a night there which we have several
times looked back to with much longing. The people
seemed a nicer set than those that I had seen in Attica.
Their employments are chiefly agricultural, though they
have some books. At two hours before dawn their big bell
echoes through the valleys, and they get up to prayers ; and
they have service also in the afternoon. I can't tell you
more now of our route from there to Sparta, than that we
passed by Agios Petros, Arachova and Vourlia, and got to
Sparta the middle of the second day. Our first view of
Taygetus was very imposing. It is a long ridge ending
towards the south in huge snowy peaks. We have had him
before our eyes in one shape and another for four days, and
have made up our minds that he is worth coming to Greece
to see.

. . . We spent a few hours at Sparta, the evening and
night at Mistra, came right through the mountain yesterday
from Mistra to a village called Lada, and to-day, through
continued rain, the first I have seen in Greece, to this place,
where the English consul, a Greek, receives us. Sparta,
where a new town has been built, and is being *forced* by the
modern system, which tries to revive old names and associations, is striking from its desolation. The quantity of tiles

and brick, and fragments of walls, show where a great city has been, but all that can be identified with the Sparta of the Peloponnesian war is Taygetus and the Eurotas. The river still flows, a shallow stream, now a little broader than the Cherwell, in the midst of a wide gravelly bed, where it expatiates in winter. On one side run a range of low, round, red hills, on the other a gradation of flattened heights, like platforms, low cliffs to the river, and smoothed away into the vale of Sparta. Here stood the city, and two or three miles across the plain Taygetus rises straight out of it. The look of the mountain is very remarkable ; a series of hills from 1000 to 6000 feet, separated by deep dark gorges, seem to have been cut clean down from top to bottom with a singular evenness, so as to present a succession of high cliffs, each the section of a hill, of which the rounded top rises above it. These hills are like outworks to the main mass of the mountain, which rises magnificently behind into snowy peaks, the last and highest of which falls steep down for a long way, and thus isolates the mountain. Like other Greek mountains, it springs sheer, and by itself, from the plain, and you have the whole height at once before you. It certainly far exceeded even what I had expected.

We stopped the night at Mistra. It is on a great rock, which is detached from the mass of Taygetus by magnificent gorges. At the foot of the hill is the modern town, and on the side the ruins of a Frank town, built by some of the crusading gentlemen who thought it better worth their while to conquer the Morea than the Holy Sepulchre. (I shall find out the name when I get to Athens.) These ruins are of great extent, and the walls of the houses, and of a church and palace, which reminded one of the West, are little injured.   I shall have much to tell you of our host, a sort of laird or feudal chief, with his tail of forty hangers-on, and poor relations, living daily at his expense.   But the grandest thing we have had yet was the road from Mistra to this place.   It is the direct tract through Taygetus, and is looked upon as rather formidable.   Most people go by Londari and turn the mountain.   We took our horses with us, but we had to walk more than nine-tenths of the way ; and, as it was, I cannot understand how our horses did not break their legs fifty times over.   Even the Greeks call it a bad road, and not fit for horses.   But I never saw anything grander than the pass for the greater part of the way.   I know little about mountain scenery, but Penrose, who knows the Apennines well, and also the Swiss passes, was enthusiastic in his admiration, and thought that the pass would quite bear comparison with the latter.   I am surprised that so little is said of it.   The difficulty of the road, which is very considerable, and the fear of klephts, which is not altogether unfounded, but a good deal greater than necessary, has, I suppose, kept travellers out of it; but no one can say he has seen Greece without seeing this.   It ought to be done on foot, with a mule carrying luggage, and not with horses, as we did it.   They kept us back, and we could not mount them.   It can also be done on mule-back.   Our Mistra host sent his *name* to a village on the road, which produced a guard of five wild fellows, who scampered about the rocks, and fired off their long guns, as if they were mad.   I have not time to write more now.   We are just starting for Ithome.   We hope to be at Athens in about ten days.   Our lodgings have sometimes been quaint enough.   Here we are in the consul's house, an Ionian Greek.

To Frederic Rogers, Esq.

7th May.

My expedition into Peloponnesus has been very satisfactory—only, we were robbed. We were riding up the
mountain side of a beautiful lake—that of Phoniá, under
Cyllene, admiring it as it deserves, when three or four *pro-
tégés* of Mercury astonished us by starting out of the wood by
the roadside, and levelling their long guns at us, with orders
to surrender at once and dismount.

We had an escort, the best we could get, by means of a
very large and positive order, signed by the Minister M.
Coletti, viz. an asthmatic peasant, with a very rickety old
gun. Our escort did not think twice about the matter, but
wisely laid down his gun ; and as we had no weapons but
what nature had given us to oppose three or four guns and
pistols and Turkish scimitars (except some stones which
Penrose always carried to fight dogs with), we dismounted,
and submitted to be marched up a ravine, where, when we
were out of sight of the road, the enemy took possession of
watches, purses, knives, and everything, in short, of metal ;
and tied our arms, and left us to examine our luggage which
they pulled about unceremoniously, and from which they
abstracted about ten pounds sterling, in money, and some
small things. They left us under orders not to move till
they should come to unloose us in the evening ; but they
had tied us so loosely that we could easily free ourselves,
which, after waiting for some time, we did, though our
muleteer and escort were extremely alarmed, and wished us
to remain. But of course we saw nothing more of them, and
finished the remaining few days of our journey—they had
luckily visited us at the end and not the beginning—without
any trouble, except that of having to beg now and then,

which was not pleasant. The rest of our journey was, but for the weather now and then, very pleasant.

To C. M. Church, Esq.

Athens, 6th May 1847.

I got back this morning from the Morea, after nearly a month's wandering. . . . In spite of the robbers, and some very bad weather, the expedition has been a very pleasant one, and has fully repaid a good deal of roughing ; and I shall, for the future, exult considerably over people who do not venture there.   I think I dilated before on the stern grandeur of the plain of Argos, and the magnificence of Taygetus and the plain of Sparta.   Nothing can beat Taygetus, but some things which we have seen in Arcadia and Messenia are quite as striking in their way.

I don't wonder at the Spartans coveting the plain of Messenia.   It lies spread out in most tempting richness under the western spurs of the long range of Taygetus ; one can almost fancy the hungry invaders seated like wolves on the grim grey rocks which fall abruptly into vineyards and corn-fields, and devising schemes for getting possession of the rich prize with ingenuity and patience, which nothing could beat. Opposite to the great Spartan mountain, with his peaks and snows, rises on the other side of the plain Mount Ithome, standing out separate from the ridges behind it, conspicuous and distinct in every part of the plain, especially from the north, where it rises in the shape of an altar, with flat sum-mit and rapid sides, but without the look of isolation which a mountain has which rises in the middle of a plain.   Ithome, standing on the edge of the plain, and backed by other moun-tains which appear to support it, without taking away from

its separate importance, rivals in dignity even the giant
mountain which towers far above it. It is one of the most
striking sites I ever saw—a place made for a history.

I shall remember Ithome for many things : for itself, for
the view from it, for the magnificent walls and gateway of
Messene under it (one of Epaminondas' bridles for Sparta—
Megalopolis was the other), for a desperate scramble down
its sides, and for a complete drenching which we got beneath
its shadow. From Ithome we made our way across the upper
Messenian plain, Stenyclarus, across the mountains and the
valley of the Neda (very beautiful) to Andritzena, a curious
place, consisting of four distinct villages—as, I think, they
say that Sparta was built—where we were to have our headquarters, while Penrose worked on the temple at Bassæ. We
were there four days, but the weather would not let us do
anything but look at the ruin, and shiver while Penrose was
at work at the temple. I was to have gone to Olympia, but
I had to give it up. The distant view of the country was
striking from Andritzena, a foreground of mountainous
broken country, then a long even line, like a long bank,
marking the valley of the Alpheus, backed at first by the
snowy mountains of Olonos, and afterwards running out
sharp against the sky, with one very distant ridge in
Northern Greece coming up above it as above a sea-line.
We made our way straight through Arcadia from Andritzena
to Kalavryta by Karitena, Dimitzana, and the site of Clitor
—all extremely beautiful country. We had got into the
land of waters and springs ever since crossing Parnon and
coming down into the valley of the Eurotas ; but here the
streams were delicious. I never saw anything so beautiful
in the way of running water as a spring which we came
upon one fine evening, near Karitena : the source gushing

out full and strong under some huge rocks at the head of a
valley, under the shade of noble plane-trees ; beyond them,
and seen through them, were grassy slopes lit up by the sun ;
and then the mountains rose at once, closing the head of the
valley, covered a long way up with woods of the richest
brown and green, with the top of Lycæus looking over them.
The gorges of the Alpheus at Karitena, and of the Gortynius
between Karitena and Dimitzana, must be of the finest order
of scenery, both for outline, colour, and scale.   They have
their traditions, like most of the passes in Greece, of the
days of Braimi, as they call Ibrahim Pasha, and the cliffs
of the Gortynius are *hung* with monasteries, built apparently
against their sides, which, in the war, were turned into
fastnesses.   The great monastery of Megaspelion, near
Kalavryta, is one of these strange sort of buildings : a great
cavern has been built up with a wall of great thickness,
varying from four to eight or nine storeys, so that the
monastery seems applied and fastened to the face of the
perpendicular rock.   At Megaspelion the rock and buildings
are both on a very large scale ; and a long way down below
the monastery there are terraces of gardens, with here and
there a tall black cypress, which are very beautiful.   From
Kalavryta our line was by the valley of the Styx, the lake of
Phoniá, plain of Stymphalus, Nemea, and on to Corinth.
The valley of the Styx was suggested by some talk of
Stanley's, who, I remember, once spoke of it as a place that
he wished to see.   It is a remarkable place.   We travelled
from Kalavryta over a very high mountain plain, where the
snow was still lying about in patches, and the crocuses were
just flowering and pushing themselves through the snow.   A
line of stone pillars, surmounted by wooden crosses, marked
the road along this plain, which in winter, in the deep snow,

is a perilous place ; it had still a most dreary and wintry
look even when we crossed. When we reached the last of
these pillars the view was one of the strangest I ever saw ;
it quite took away my breath for a moment. At the brink
of the plain the mountain sides broke down abruptly to a
great depth, and there lay before us a dark deep circular
valley, made of the bare grey limestone precipices of Mount
Khelmos, with a strange looking smooth mountain, of a kind
of ghastly yellow, in the middle of it. The Styx lay some
distance off at the head of the valley, and we scrambled
away, with a guide, to get to it. It is a mineral spring,
which falls down a face of rock, high up on the side of one
of the loftiest and most precipitous summits of Khelmos.
When we saw it, it was mixed probably with snow water,
and fell in a stream which appeared to us to vary in quantity
from time to time ; but in summer it merely trickles down
the rock, which is discoloured on each side of it. The rock
looks as if eaten away or poisoned by it. The scene is
certainly as sombre and awful as the Styx ought to be,
though very different from what I had expected. The vast
height of the bare dark mountain, and the vast height at
which the water is seen issuing from its side, form a very
strange, mysterious scene ; and all round there is the same
gloom about the grey precipices, and black fir-trees, thrown
out by patches of snow, and the mountain torrent below,
which complete the picture. I can quite fancy it impressing
strongly the imagination of the wild madman Cleomenes, if
it is to this that Herodotus alludes (vi. 74). After the Styx
came the beautiful lake of Phoniá and that of Stymphalus,
which, as a lake, is at present a failure, though it would be
very fine as a *full* lake or a completely dry plain. On the
borders of the lake of Phoniá, just beyond a place marked in

Leake's map, Tricrena, we had our interview with the robbers. Penrose attributes our misfortune to the anger of Mercury, whose mountain Cyllene, on the side of which it happened, we had just been abusing, and had also been laughing at his being washed, as Pausanias says he was, after he was born, in the "Three fountains," Tricrena.

This is a poor account of our proceedings, but I am writing in a hurry, to save the post.

. . . I shall pass Cholderton with great regret. If I had been in England, I dare say I should have gone there, for I want to get to something less desultory than my present college life. But I should not do so without talking the matter over, and there is no time for that now.

To his Stepsister Miss Crokat.

Constantinople, 25th May 1847.

I believe I am in your debt, so you must be receiver of news for my friends in general this time. I have come up here because I found that a great piece of work was made about my travelling in Greece; there were elections going on, and part of the electioneering business is carried on, so they say, by the klephts,—who might mistake me for a Greek elector, and canvass me. A good deal of this is political talk, I think, but after having been caught once, I am not so well able to argue against it. So here I am, outside Christendom for the first time in my life, seeing with my own eyes people prostrating themselves towards Mecca, and crying out from the minarets. This, of course, forces itself upon you; you can satisfy yourself as much as you please that you are a unit among tens of thousands of unbelievers; but I am twenty years too late for Constantinople. The barbaric state and ancient caprice and extravagance of Eastern power have given way to a semi-European regularity and decorum ; they don't ̈cut off Pachas' heads now for a whim, and stick them up at the gate of the Seraglio ; there is a sort of respectable ministry, and I don't believe that there is any danger of their being strangled, should they be turned out. The troops, even the cavalry, alas ! are all like awkward Prussian or French soldiers, except that they have red caps ; and veritable *peelers*, blue policemen, though without glazed hats, keep the peace in the streets of Constantinople.   Imagine, as we were coming up the Sea of Marmora, straining our eyes for a first sight of Santa Sophia, the first objects which presented themselves were two or three tall factory chimneys of the perfect Birmingham or London breed, streaming away with black coal smoke, just as if they were comfortably doing their business at home instead of on the Bosphorus. Nothing of the kind, steam-driven flourmill or sawmill, has ventured yet into Greece.   Another strange sight occurred as I rowed up the Golden Horn yesterday to the Sweet Waters. We passed a meadow where the horses of part of the Sultan's cavalry were turned out to grass ; the men were with them, and their green tents pitched by the water-side.   It was about four o'clock when I passed, and about 150 of the men were performing their devotions, drawn up in regular line with their faces turned towards Mecca, and their backs to the river, rising, bowing, and prostrating themselves, all at the same moment.   If they had been in turbans and loose trousers the sight would have been natural enough ; but they were all in cavalry foraging jackets and white European military trousers, and this gave an indescribable anomaly and grotesqueness to the whole scene ; it looked like a very queer sort of military exercise.

However, in spite of the barbarisms of the West, there is
still something to see here which is primitive and Turkish—
the basking, masterless dogs ("sono tutti liberi i cani quì,"
said my guide) who sleep about the streets by day, and prowl
and scavenger by night ; the black, solemn cemeteries with
their cypresses and scattered turbaned stones, and the veiled
women, looking like the *Misericordia* in Italy.   Nor have
the truculent turban and beard, and stately bagging trousers,
disappeared, except among the employés of Government and
the respectable gentlemen.   Fires, too, that very characteristic feature of Constantinople, have not ceased to be frequent,
and, though I have only been twenty-four hours here, I have
already heard the fire-watch going his rounds, and beating with
a stick on the ground, or at the doors of the houses, while
he gives notice of a fire.   And in the course of time, no
doubt, I shall see a little more ; I have not yet been into the
genuine Turkish quarter.

They have begun to use horse carriages, and very properly
have begun at the beginning.   Not like the hasty Greeks of
Athens, who have built on the model of the modern German
calesse or French cabriolet ; the Turkish coachbuilders have
drawn their ideas, if not from the very earliest era of coach-
building, at least from the venerable days when the Lord
Mayor's coach was a new-fangled invention.   The form is of
unexceptionable seventeenth - century shape ; and gilding
outside and plain boards within give the coach its due
grandeur and discomfort.   Besides these, which I should
think are parts of the European civilisation which has begun
to invade ancient Turkey, there are other conveyances, covered
waggons drawn by oxen, of untainted Eastern fashion.   It
was a fine sight yesterday (Whit-Monday, a great holiday
with the Christian population, and with the Jews in con-

sequence, because they can make holiday under shelter of the Greeks and Armenians, without being snubbed by the Turks ; so at least I was told) to see these arabàs rolling sonorously along the road to the Sweet Waters,—the Richmond or Greenwich Park of Constantinople,—their grave dun oxen stepping along as majestically as if they were human Turks, each with an elastic arch of fringe and tassels of red and gold, rising and shaking over their backs (being fastened in front to the yoke and behind to their tails), the ponderous waggon itself stuffed with cushions, and fat Greek women, or sometimes smoking Greek men,—who had to descend from their vehicle by steps like those of the old coaching days in England, by which outside passengers, especially if they were lady passengers, came down so tremulously by help of the gallantry of coachmen and ostlers. The Sweet Waters were pretty yesterday. The banks of the stream are shaded by fine trees, and spread into narrow green meadows between low hills ; and under the trees were numerous parties " performing picnic," as my guide accurately expressed it, squatted on mats and carpets on the river-side, half-veiled Armenians, and crested Jewesses, and bare-headed or French bonneted Greeks, with a due proportion of boys and men of less characteristic dress, a few Turks smoking or lazily fishing, singers and guitar-players making a noise not unpleasant at a distance, a company of Bulgarians offering to dance to their bagpipes, and some gipsies and sellers of refreshments, one of whom earnestly recommended to my notice, as a genuine antique, a well-worn French sou of the Republic. These Sweet Waters are very famous, and were one of the scenes of Constantinople which I expected a great deal from : perhaps because I was by myself, I did not think them more than I have said, pretty, in their way.

26th May.—I am under the hard necessity of lionising by
myself under the pilotage of a *valet-de-place;* and so I lionise
rather in the sulks, feeling all the time that I am seeing
only the outside of things,—the *valetian* mind not being
accustomed to anything else, and not comprehending any
questions of an abstruse kind.   For instance, I followed the
travelling world yesterday to see the dancing dervishes.   These
people assemble in an octagonal room, in their high white
felt caps and clokes of blue and brown, and after performing their devotions for the hour of the day, all in silence,
threw off their clokes, and after walking three times in
procession round the room, began spinning round and round
with arms extended, and eyes half closed, to a monotonous
chant, accompanied with drum and pipe, and going on with
this exercise, never showing the least sign of giddiness or
even touching one another with their extended arms, for
nearly a quarter of an hour, beginning again after a short
interval—their long petticoats flying out in the shape of a
bell or cone round them.   It is a strange sight to see, but
anything beyond the sight I find very difficult to get at ; and
why the dervishes spin round with such great solemnity and
apparent religious abstraction and devotion, I have not been
able to find out.   There are others who, instead of dancing,
howl, *i.e.* repeat the profession of faith in a wild yell, for an
hour together, but this is not so strange to me as the dancing,
which realised to me the rites of ancient heathenism more
than anything I expected to find among Mussulmen.

Yesterday I crossed over into Constantinople proper, the
south side of the Golden Horn.   The bridge, a broad wooden
one, across the Horn, strange to say, strongly suggested
London Bridge ; what produced this effect was, not so much
the broad stream, lined on each bank first with innumerable

masts, and beyond them with innumerable houses, both
above and below the bridge—as the number of steamers,
big and little, getting their steam up or on the move, just as
you see them at London Bridge. They are nearly all of
them Turkish steamers (engineered by Englishmen), with
their names written in all the twisting intricacy of Arabic
letters. Such is another of the queer contrasts of this
place—steamers sending their black smoke among the thick
trees and sacred mansions of the very Seraglio.

The interior of Constantinople has been calumniated, at
least the part that I was through yesterday. There is
nothing fine about the streets certainly, but neither are they
so mean, or so filthy, or so ill-paved, as I expected to find
them—far more respectable than Athens, newly built under
the auspices of enlightened Bavarians from classical Munich.
There are still a few remains which recall the city of the
Greek Emperors ;—huge cisterns with roofs of brick supported by rows of columns, all underground, and now used
by silk and thread spinners from Trebizond ; the site of the
Hippodrome with two obelisks still bearing the pompous
inscriptions cut into their bases by the Greek Emperors, and
with another monument of still greater interest, if it is what
it is said to be, the triple brazen serpent which supported
the offering made by the Greeks at Delphi, from the Persian
spoils after the battle of Platæa ; and the old walls of the
city, which are said to be, in a great measure, those of
Constantine. Effete and miserable as that old Greek
Empire was in its policy and doings, it was not without
its romance and magnificence, and it is satisfactory to find
any vestiges of it ; for, on the whole, the Turkish city has
entirely overrun and trodden out the old Greek city. Many
of the mosques were Christian churches ; but the minarets

so entirely give them a Mahomedan character, that even
Santa Sophia does not suggest the notion of its ever having
been the great cathedral of the East.   I was not so much
struck by the mosques in Constantinople as by the tombs of
the Sultans.   As you go along the streets you come every
now and then to a marble octagon, with large windows
glazed and with ornamental bars.   Behind is generally a
garden.   You can look into the room from the street, and
you see in the centre a high tomb covered with a rich pall,
with a turban or red cap placed at the head, and around
the principal tomb a number of lower ones, some with
turbans on them and some without—the sons and daughters
of the Sultan who lie around him.   Attached to these tombs
is generally another marble building of the same sort, enclosing a fountain ; and in the windows are placed rows of
brazen cups with water, for the benefit of passers-by ; and
from some of them soup and bread are served out to the
poor twice a day.   Yesterday we passed three of these
tombs : they do not give you the notion of tombs so much
as halls where the dead Sultans lie in state perpetually.

To C. M. CHURCH, Esq.

CONSTANTINOPLE, 1st June 1847.

You owe this letter to a cold, which keeps me in my
room, and has prevented me from starting this morning to
Brusa, which I particularly wished to see, and which now I
fear I shall not see.   I went last Saturday to spend Sunday
with a friend of the General's, a German officer, who, after
having fought against the Turks in Greece with the General,
and against the Carlists in Spain with General Evans, went
and fought with the Turks in Syria against Ibrahim Pacha,

and has ended in a Christian Pacha of two tails, enjoying himself on a handsome salary, in a pretty village on the Bosphorus. You see I come across strange cattle now and then. . . .

The village where I stopped is one of the prettiest points —a long row of quaint-looking, wooden houses, sweeping round a bay backed by hills covered with gardens and trees, the bright rich greens of spring mixed with the perpetual black of the cypress. The immense quantity of shipping passing up and down, anchoring or setting sail in the bay, as the wind changes about, gives great liveliness to the place. I spent Trinity Sunday morning there quietly and pleasantly, living at the hotel, and dining with the German Pacha. In the afternoon we had a gallop round the neighbourhood to get a view of the Black Sea. I had the satisfaction of seeing it fiercely black. There was a pitchy, solid thunder-cloud all round the horizon to seaward, and, under its shadow, the old sea looked as terrible and stormy as could be wished. The rain overtook us in a pine forest, in which are the reservoirs of water which supply Constantinople, imperial · works in their way, valleys dammed up, and made into small lakes by great marble dams built across them, from which the water is carried underground, or across aqueducts for some 17 or 18 miles. The price of our very pleasant ride was a good soaking, for which I was not in the least prepared, and it has left me with the cold which, as I said, has produced this letter, and prevented my expedition to Brusa. . . .

We returned in regular Gravesend fashion early in the morning by steamer to Constantinople, and had a dull, hard day's work of sight-seeing, the first unmitigated treadmill day that I have had since I have been out. But to see the

Seraglio and the mosques, it is necessary, or, at least, highly
expedient to get a firman, which costs a good deal of money,
and so people club together and make up a party. We
were twenty-seven, and, of course, had to proceed by word
of command and forced marches. It was unsatisfactory
work, for there was no one who knew much about what we
were seeing, as far as the history of it went. We were
shown first over parts of the Seraglio—I suppose what
answer to State apartments—large matted rooms, for a
palace coarsely decorated (*inter alia*, with rat-traps for the
rats who come to feed on the mattresses), marble bathing-
rooms, and long galleries adorned merely with coloured
French prints of the meanest kind—the only striking thing
being some of the ceilings, if they had been in good order.
Then the gardens, regular and shabby ; then the stables ;
and then (what was characteristic, and would have been
interesting if explained) the older courts and gates and
reception-rooms of the palace ; a queer old library standing
in the middle of a sort of cloister, about which lounged a lot
of lazy pages of the Sultan ; the old great throne-room, a
dark solemn chamber, not very large, with iron-grated
windows, and walls inlaid with rich porcelain and, I think,
marble ; and with the throne—a great four-post bedstead,
with silver-gilt posts adorned with jewels true and false, in one
corner underneath which the old Selims and Soleymans and
Murads used to squat when they gave audience—and finally,
the great gate of the Seraglio, which used to be adorned with
the heads of disobedient or unlucky Viziers and Pachas. The
armoury has some curious relics—the mace of Mahomed II.,
and, among a variety of terrible-looking sword blades, the
broad, straight, two-edged sword of Eyoub (or Job), the
standard - bearer of the Prophet. Then we were marched

over the three great mosques, Aia Sophia, that of Sultan
Achmet, and that of Sultan Soleyman the Magnificent, and
also over a smaller one, together with the mausoleums of
Achmet, Soleyman, and the late Sultan. You can find all
these described in books, and I shall not trouble myself with
them. It is curious how the Mussulmen have copied, as far
as I saw, absolutely, the Christian type which they found
here, S. Sophia. In one instance they have struck out a
noble building, the mosque of Soleyman—lighter and more
symmetrical than the original, but though nearly as large,
without the imposing vastness which Aia Sophia certainly
has inside. Aia Sophia is under repair, but still its greatness is visible : the effect of it and of the mosques is of an
enormous court covered in, and surrounded with cloisters
and galleries. Your eye is not carried up to the roof, and
even the mosaic-covered dome of S. Sophia is not of that
importance in the general effect that I should have expected.
The mosques are matted and quiet and kept clean ; lighted,
when necessary, with wide circles—concentric, I think—of
small oil lamps intermingled with ostrich eggs and tinsel.
We had the choice of taking off our shoes, or putting slippers
over them. The Turks looked disgusted at our being
allowed to poke about at our pleasure, but did not say anything to us : those at their devotions went on without
taking notice, those who had finished gathered round and
looked at us, or scowled at a distance. The boys ran about
without much ceremony, and offered bits of the mosaic of
S. Sophia for sale, and in one or two there were pigeons
flying about. . . .

As far as sight-seeing goes I have been doing my duty.
I think, perhaps, the most interesting business I have done
in that way was a perambulation and pernavigation of the

walls. They are, I believe, in the main, the work of the Byzantine emperors, in some few places repaired, but in most left to crumble, by the Turks. A paved road follows their line towards the land. There was a triple line of them, with a ditch, which now supplies Constantinople with vegetables, and the road for a long way is flanked towards the country with a thick cypress grove with tombs. They are, at least, remains of the old Christian city, and have looked strange enemies in the face. I wish for a Gibbon twenty times a day. I think that Constantinople will be very great in remembrance. I rather feel conscious that there is something strangely striking and grand before my eyes every time that I get a sight of it, and yet that I do not acknowledge really its grandeur to myself, as I was struck in Greece with Athens and Taygetus.

To Frederic Rogers, Esq.

CONSTANTINOPLE, *4th June.*

I can hardly tell you what I feel about this strange place ; a queer mixture of feelings, the general effect of which at present is disagreeable, tending towards disgust. In the first place, the place itself is undoubtedly very grand. I don't know that it is what I should call beauty that strikes me in the views I have had of it, so much as the imperial magnificence of its position and appearance ; the spread of the city and its suburbs in all directions, over the swell of the hills, and along their summits, and along the shore of the sea wherever you look ; its apparently endless extent, with the great quantity of it which can be seen at once ; the profusion of verdure within it, bright greens, set off by the black cypress groves of the cemeteries ; and the majestic

outline of the main city, produced very much by some three
or four great mosques, with their minarets and great low
domes, which crown the highest point of ground in it. Then
there is the sea all round, and in various shapes—a magnificent port in the Golden Horn—a broad winding river in
the Bosphorus—and again, with its islands and capes, and
open horizon, the Sea of Marmora, covered with ships of all
sizes, and showing the greatest variety of flags I have ever
seen. In its beauty I think I was disappointed; but not
in its grandeur. Then, when you get into it, there is still
plenty of Oriental life to be seen; there are crowds, partly in
a state of the most perfect quiescence and meditative repose,
partly in a state of violent action—pushing, jostling, and
especially screaming and yelling, with confounding energy;
there are veiled women, shovelling and sliding along in their
yellow boots; there are turbans, and kalpacs, and fezzes;
there is also the great estate of the dogs, the free and independent dogs, who never get out of the way for man or horse.
But, as you know, the Turks have been Europeanised of late,
and there is a stupid mongrel air about these crowds; and
with the exception of some old-fashioned, grave, proud-look-
ing, green and white turbans, who disdain to show their
remarkably ugly legs in tight white pantaloons and straps,
the Turks look like people who hardly know whether they
are standing on their heads or their heels, and this, I believe,
is pretty much the case with them. They seem to me like
people who are put out of their way and don't know how to
behave themselves, as if Stamboul was transported bodily
into Regent Street or the Rue de Rivoli, and they feel in
their own city the sort of awkwardness and *soggezione* that
they would feel in the West. One used to think that a
Turkish gentleman was, under all circumstances, the very

model of quiet, grave dignity; those that I have fallen in
with have shown nothing of it. I went up yesterday with
the embassy here to see them take possession of some ground
on the Bosphorus, which the Sultan had made them a present of to build a summer palace ; and a Turkish colonel
came with us to deliver the key, as it were. He wore a
stuffed and padded and braided military frock-coat and white
trousers, slippers and spurs, and red fez, *i.e.* full uniform.
He was made quite at home ; the *attachés* talked Turkish to
him, and he "performed picnic" with us ; he was not shy,
and he appeared to enjoy himself, and drank as much sherry
and claret and champagne as any Frank of the party ; but
there was a good-natured, smiling awkwardness that would
have suited a Greek or Italian, but which was contrary to
one's notions of a Turk in authority. I thought I saw the
same kind of thing among a number of them who were
collected together waiting to attend the Sultan to mosque.
They were, I was told, an assembly of Pachas, most of them
men of fatness and respectable age, all dressed in the European
dress, with various military decorations, sitting, not squatting,
in a circle under the trees, near a quay on the Bosphorus.
There they smoked, chatted, and drank coffee. Most of
them, as I said, were fat, and so pompous ; and there was a
good deal of ceremony, especially when a Pacha of a larger
number of tails, and more developed double chin, straddled
into the conclave ; but it was an awkward mixture of European
military ceremony and behaviour, such as they might have
seen in the European officers in their service, and the Turkish
gesticulations of courtesy ; and there was certainly, in appearance, the awkwardness of men who are not yet accustomed
to the part which they are to play before the public. Their
servants were in the same costume, beginning with the red

scull-cap, and passing on to the blue frock-coat and white
duck trousers, till these ended in a woful pair of slippered
feet ; and they waited on their masters, bearing in one hand
their master's sabre, in the other his pipe-case ; and the
hurry was amusing, when the Sultan appeared, of servants
receiving pipes and putting them in their covers, and Pachas
buckling on their scimitars. Of course this is only the outside of things, and a partial outside ; of the inside I know
nothing ; but this outside is unnatural and disagreeable to
see. The general song here is that the Turks are improving.
I cannot help fancying that the meaning of this is, that they
have been bemystified into wearing tight trousers contrary to
the nature of their legs, and drinking wine contrary to their
religion ; that they have been partly persuaded and partly
frightened into moderation in the use of the bowstring and
scimitar, which, of course, is a good thing ; that their Oriental
admiration of the effects of machinery has very much overcome their jealousy of foreigners, and that the peace which
is kept in the East by the West has enabled them to indulge
their taste this way to a considerable extent. They say here
that the revenue is flourishing, well managed, well spent,
and collected without oppression—*chi lo sa ?*—but very likely
it is so. One ancient fashion, meantime, is still preserved ;
when the public of Constantinople is dissatisfied with ministerial measures, they set fire to the city, and go on from
night to night till they are satisfied—so they did last February, I am told, until Reschid Pacha, the grand vizier, who
is disliked as a Frankist, had to give way. There is no
doubt a strong fanatic Mussulman element in the population ;
but I do not suppose that it has much power, though I dare
say the encroachments of Liberalism will yet provoke some
fierce outbreaks. It must be a sore trial to ancient Mussul-

men to see pert, curious, hatted Franks allowed to poke
about the mosques, by force of a firman, which is given for
the asking, and to see them swagger through the streets of
the capital with none of their former awe and reverence,
confident of protection from cuff or spitting from an impartial set of peelers who parade the streets and keep every
one in order but the dogs—the only inhabitants who are at
liberty, if they like, to molest strangers.

To C. M. CHURCH, ESQ.

PERICLES, OFF PIRÆUS, 10*th June.*

I send this just to say that I have left Constantinople,
and am now sailing under the yellow flag, and awaiting a
week of imprisonment.   We have had a pleasant voyage as
to weather, and seen some bits of interesting coast well : the
Troad again, Lesbos green and pretty, Chios much bolder,
with a noble peak, and my old friend Cape Sunium, for the
third time, in the grey of this morning.

PIRÆUS, 10*th June* 1847.

I dispatched a letter of this date written on board the
French steamer, now I am going to send you my first views
and impressions of quarantine life and manners.   Our prison
is a large set of buildings, like a set of warehouses, on the
water's edge, on the southern side of the harbour, where we
were received by a cautious gentleman, pen in hand, who
looked at our boatful with the same sort of look as a butcher
contemplates a flock of sheep brought for him to buy.   He
determined finally on the purchase, and we were walked out
of a kind of pen where we stood by the water-side, to a
room.   There our position was, for a moment, perplexing:

whichever way we turned we were met by exclamations and
warnings in fierce Greek and Italian,—"not there"—"keep
off here"—"move off to that place"—"no, don't touch that";
—all uttered with the energy of five or six persons afraid of
the plague. At last, when we had found out where we
might stand without peril to the health of others, or our
own safety, our names were taken down by a gruff gentleman,
who appeared to have no wish to be more in our society
than he could help. Our party was, it must be confessed,
not a pleasant one ; myself and an Austrian gentleman, I
believe a Jew, with certainly a Hebrew bearded servant,
were the respectabilities of the party, the rest consisted of
some ten or fifteen uncomfortable-looking Greeks, with much
greasy luggage, among whom, we were informed, was a
famous *chef de voleurs*, with some three or four of his crew.
To do the gruff gentleman credit, as soon as he heard my
name, his gruffness changed into the blandest politeness ;
the General had kindly spoken a word to him in my favour,
and the director immediately professed the greatest desire to
make me comfortable, and to let me have everything I could
want, except the relaxation of my sentence of condemnation
to eight days' imprisonment. However, I was shown to a
room opening on a gravel walk, which I was told to consider
my own. It had nothing in it, but was clean and fairly
large, and presently became furnished with an iron bedstead
and mattress, which I forbore to examine too closely (the
sheets were clean), and a deal table, and chair, and washing
apparatus,—and thus I am set up for my week. We are
supplied with food by a restaurateur ; how he manages to
escape being "compromised" I don't know. He came to
receive his orders, and looked as frightened as every other
person not in quarantine does at those who are. I am writ-

ing with my door open, and my "guardian" sitting on the
step.   He watches me with the most tender interest, never
allowing me out of his sight.   I am thinking of spending
this week in making him teach me modern Greek.   The
Lazaretto is very full.   There is a long room overhead, filled
with a lot of awkward sort of companions, some seventy
Arabs, pilgrims from Mecca, who were shipwrecked somewhere and brought here to be purified, black, wild looking,
ourang-outang looking creatures, in their white cloaks, unpleasant to come in contact with.   But they seem to keep
the poor wretches in safe custody. . . .

My friends from the Ἄστυ have paid me a visit to-day.
We were allowed to meet in a room, the General sitting at
one end, I at the other, and a guard to see that I did not
infect him ; this was much less humiliating than talking
through a grating like a prisoner for debt : and except that
one had to repress one's instinctive tendency to shake hands,
there was nothing particular to remind one of one's situation.
But if I have to receive anything from some member of the
sane part of the public, the rules of quarantine start into
instant vigour.   A friend brought me yesterday a packet of
letters.   I was going, in my ignorance, to take them from
his hand, when one of the guards, with horror depicted on
his countenance, snatched the packet from my friend's hand
and threw it at my feet, just as one throws something to a
dog, who, you are afraid, may bite your fingers in his anxiety
to secure what you offer him.   To-day time has not hung
very heavy.   My watch is, as you know, telling the time—
unless it has been wound up the wrong way—on the sides
of Cyllene to a Greek klepht, so that I have no temptation
to count hours, and breakfast, dinner, and the evening gun
of the French man-of-war are my only marks of time ; but

I have involved myself in a brisk attack on Gibbon and the
Iliad, which will last at least my eight days. This evening
I was amused by our Greek fellow-prisoners, who set to
work to pass their time in a variety of games—modern
editions of the heroic ones, but which did considerable credit
to their athletic powers. There was wrestling, leaping, and
throwing χερμάδια; and no doubt if there was a sufficient
stadium, we should have had running. . . . All this went
on with great energy and noise, to our amusement, and the
apparent astonishment of the Bedouins, in the room upstairs,
who presented a contrast, sitting in silence at the windows,
black, grim faces, and shapeless figures shrouded in their
white burnouses, to the capering, tumbling, laughing, and
yelling Greeks down on whom they gazed. . . .

15th June.—One day more, and then hip, hip, hurra.
Yesterday evening we had a rare entertainment, which has
almost made up for the imprisonment. Our Greeks were
amusing themselves with one of their games, the gist of
which consisted in one of the party, who was tethered to a
stake, trying to touch with his foot some of the rest who
skirmished round him, licking him unmercifully whenever
they could safely, with their girdles twisted hard into
instruments of severe punishment. The Bedouins at their
windows were looking on as usual, when suddenly the desire
of play seized them, and almost the whole body came
tumbling down a steep wooden staircase which led, from
outside, up to their apartment—very difficult to ascend or
descend in loose slippers—into the back court of the
Lazaretto. The whole Christian population rushed to look
at them, and great was the trepidation and loud the cries of
the *guardiani* to prevent any number of one crowd touching
any one of the other. The Bedouins were certainly a queer

assembly, tall, lanky, dark brown faces, legs, and arms, scarcely human looking, with long shirts and great white cloaks muffling them up, and tied round their heads. They always remind me, even in point of colour and expression, of Sebastian del Piombo's *Lazarus* in the National Gallery: they have that pinched, sharp look, and mummy-like hue. They had changed from their usual still quiescence into a state of great animation, and they began their form of the Greek game I have mentioned. They stripped off their burnouses, and rolled and tied them up into a great bundle, and these bundles were laid together at the feet of the man who was tethered ; then the rest of the players were to try and snatch away each his bundle, without being kicked by the bundle-keeper, and pelt him with it, and whoever he touched took his place. It was a most extraordinary sight, some twenty or thirty of these wild black fellows dancing about, in nothing but their shirts, and the rest squatted against the wall, looking on, and showing their white teeth as they grinned, quite in a beast-like way. The man who was tethered kept the bundles between his feet, and kept jumping and hopping round them, every now and then kicking vigorously with his black wiry shanks ; while the rest of the party surrounded him, and came on in a sort of crouching attitude, giving a sort of suppressed hiss or short jerking " hah ! " at each jump, as they tried to snatch away their bundles. There was a sort of tiger-like activity about them, a curious contrast to the human activity of the Greeks. It was kept up with great spirit, when, in the midst of a most energetic contest, some great visitors were announced. It was the French Admiral with several of his officers, who had come to see the Bedouins, and fairly caught them romping. He desired to have them mustered, and they were all drawn up before him and us, one of them acting as interpreter. On one side were sixty of the wildest looking creatures out of Africa, standing in a long row, muffled up in ragged white cloaks ; facing them was the little, squat, dapper French Admiral with his hand on his walking-stick, backed by three or four officers in epaulettes and aiguillettes, standing in the attitude in which aides-de-camp are usually drawn behind their chief, *i.e.* leg stretched out, hand resting on the hip, face smiling and scornful. The Admiral made a speech to them, telling them that they were to be let out of quarantine to-morrow, that the French Government felt most kindly disposed to them, that they should be shipped on board the man-of-war (introducing, at the same time, the swell-looking captain to the savages), and that every care should be taken of them till they got back to Algiers. The speech made very little impression, as far as appeared ; the white burnouses shambled off without expressing thanks or pleasure, and retired up the difficult staircase to their long room. It struck me that the Frenchman hoped to get a " Vive la France " out of them, as he made a great point with the interpreter of explaining his speech at once, and on the spot, to the whole body, which the interpreter obstinately would not do, but only interpreted to some of the headmen round him.

To C. M. CHURCH, Esq.

ATHENS, 17th *July* 1847.

I must beg you to excuse a hasty letter, and my past idleness in letter-writing. In Athens itself the heat makes one intolerably lazy, and when I am out of it I am on horse-back (or asleep) the whole day, and have not much time, and in the sort of lodgings with which one gets acquainted and contented in the course of Greek travelling, not much opportunity. And now I am preparing to take my leave of Greece, very glad to exchange Athenian life, which at this season is very heavy work, for something more varied, and yet with a good deal of regret at leaving Greece,—more than I expected to feel. I may congratulate myself, however, on having got leave to go at all.

I am just back from a pilgrimage to Delphi. My route was Thebes, Lebadeia, Charoneia, Daulis, Arachova, Kastri, and back by the southern side of Helicon, Stiri, Thisbe, Leuctra, Thespiæ, to Thebes ; then by Platæa across Cithæron to Megara, and across Salamis to Athens. I went with my former *compagnon de voyage* Vilacti, with his two δασοφύλακες, Ghiorghi, my old friend, and another queer old Bulgarian, an old soldier of the Greek War. As far as Lebadeia we went in a carriage, which was a great help ; the rest on horseback, starting, if possible before daybreak, halting at nine or ten, and starting again about three or four. Once or twice we were caught by the sun, and pretty well broiled ; but on the whole, considering the time of year, we escaped very well. But the heat interrupted sight-seeing in the middle of the day, and, as usual, I have some two or three points on my traveller's conscience, as having been carelessly seen. But on the whole my nine days' work was satisfactory. The Bœotian plains are very striking. As we came down from Cithæron on the way from Eleusis, they lay before us, the low rolling downs intersected by watercourses of Platæa, rising beyond the Asopus into reddish gentle heights, which hide Thebes itself : then the plain of Thebes, flat as a table, to the foot of its bounding mountain, with round mounds rising out of it, parched and yellow with fallows and stubble fields ; then on the left, the great flat of

Orchomenus, half swamp, half meadow, its lines of dark and light green, and occasional clumps of willows or poplars, finishing in the dim blue of water, the water of the lake Copais, which retreats within narrow limits in the summer, and contrasting remarkably with the dry brown plain of Thebes, which is separated only by a low ridge. And round this expanse of level is thrown a noble girdle of mountains, the two summits of Cithæron rising immediately over Platæa, and spreading and falling right and left of it. Then Helicon, a grey, distant summit, and a more wooded and near peak, and then the remarkable serrated crags of green and grey Libethrus, which border the south side of the plain of Orchomenus ; over them the dim huge majestic mass of Parnassus, then the fine Phocian, Locrian, and northern Bœotian ranges, beyond which appear the noble outlines of the mountains of Eubœa. It is one of the grandest of the many grand and characteristic combinations of plain and mountain which are to be found in Greece.

LUTRAKI, 19th July.

At last I am off, and have taken final leave of Athens. In spite of some disagreeables, I had become attached to the place, and I have been something like unhappy all the morning at saying good-bye, not only to my uncle, but to several of his Greek friends, whom I have come to like very much, with all their imperfections. They have, many of them at least, the virtue of strong devotion to a person, in-volving their goodwill and services to the best of their power to all his belongings. From being my headquarters, Athens had come to feel something like a home, and I dare say that I shall sulk a little now that I shall be alone for some time. I go from here to Corfu. I don't think that I shall stay longer than the time which the steamer stays, as otherwise I should have to wait a week or even a fortnight for another steamer. I hope, however, to see Lord Seaton, for whom I am overwhelmed with letters. From Corfu I purpose going on to Ancona, then Bologna, Ravenna (if not absolutely dangerous on account of the heat), Venice, Milan, Genoa, Leghorn, and there I hope to meet you about the end of August.

From this point in his journey the continuous series of letters is broken. After a week spent with Lord Seaton at Corfu, Mr. Church went on into Italy—in spite of summer heats, seeing Venice, Ravenna, and Bologna. Two letters written from the two latter cities remain, but beyond them, little or nothing of his correspondence during the rest of his tour has been preserved.

To FREDERIC ROGERS, ESQ.

BOLOGNA, 15th August 1847.

I came here from Ravenna yesterday. I wish I could express to you how much Ravenna has struck me. It is, indeed, a place worth coming to, even at this time of the year. As I approached it in the evening, over the vast swamp which spreads for miles and miles round, fringed with rows of poplars, and bounded on one side by the jagged strange-looking ridge of the distant Apennines, and on the other by the Pineta, a pine forest which skirts the seashore for twenty-five miles—and saw the churches of Ravenna standing out against the sky from the open horizon of the plain, I was reminded first of Oxford and then of St. Pol de Leon. Not that it is like either, but its position and associa-

tions, and visibly ecclesiastical appearance, form the link of
association. It is a solemn place, desolate and melancholy
now, with its empty streets, and fine palaces all shut up, and
its historical interest, which is finished before the Middle
Ages begin, and its churches built and restored in the fifth
and sixth centuries. The Middle Ages, which have given all
their character to the other Italian cities, have almost left
Ravenna untouched; it remains among them, recalling the
times of Theodosius and Justinian, and bringing one very
near to those of St. Athanasius and St. Chrysostom. The
churches, most of them of the age of Justinian, retain, though
in very various degrees, traces and remains of that time, the
mosaics in some are very perfect, and the effect sometimes is
quite gorgeous.

This place is a contrast : Ravenna, with its basilicas, and
old baptisteries, and mosaics, and Christian tombs, is a sort of
Pompeii of the early ages, with grass growing in its streets.
Bologna has all the bustle and stir of a modern capital. Its
streets, full of people, and its churches and ancient public
buildings, recall the days of Italian republicanism or tyranny.
I have only got a glimpse of it yet, and of its magnificent
piazza, where the saucy old populace dragged down and
smashed M. Angelo's statue of Julius, and sold the cross to
be turned into a cannon. There is a vast unfinished church
on one side, where Charles V. was crowned Emperor, and
the various public buildings of different dates, from the
thirteenth to the sixteenth centuries, on the other side, form
the most striking monument I have yet seen of the turbulent,
but very interesting Middle Ages of Italy. And the population is still in character. Their enthusiasm for Pio Nono is
quite mediæval ; they can talk nothing else ; " Viva Pio
Nono " was written up over almost every other door in the

little towns that I passed through—and there is no title too grand for him in the various inscriptions to his honour, from the placard at the street corner to the lofty Latin compositions in San Petronio ; these last very striking in their way. I came in this morning for the end of a grand *funzione* at San Petronio ; the aisles were filled with soldiers under arms, and the nave, an immense place, thronged with people,—the main body of the mass profoundly attentive, but, on the outskirts of it, those free and easy ways, and that rapid transition from devotion to what we should call irreverence, which these people have inherited from their Middle Age forefathers. After the service was over they streamed out most grandly down the steps into the piazza, which was filled with vendors, ambulatory and stationary, of all sorts of things eatable and wearable. But the great attractions were two quacks, one of high, and the other of low degree, who had taken post at each end of the piazza waiting for the exit of the crowd. The gentleman quack was in his carriage, quite a grand turn-out, with servants, liveries, and cockades ; himself a portly man in black, with a magnificent gold chain across his waistcoat ; and round the carriage were arranged trays and drawers, with surgical and dentist instruments, and various quack paraphernalia. He stood in his carriage and harangued the crowd. The cad quack was more curious still ; he had taken his stand by the grand fountain in the piazza, and was a complete mob orator. He had in his hand a box, which, he said, contained crucifixes, which were a safeguard against all kinds of evils—earthquake, lightning, pestilence, and every sort of danger. These he was going to make presents of to his friends, and they could give him, to be sure, something for his trouble in bringing them, but " mezzo paola è niente "—for the sake of the crosses—" e non credete,

Signori, che siamo di stagno ; sono di metallo bianco di
Corinte ;" and, besides this, he would give with each cross a
little packet "della radica di S. Apollinare," which would at
once stop toothache ; "and now, Signorini, I am going to
show you the crosses, so take off your hats : " and every hat
was off in a moment as he showed the rows of crosses round.
The people looked eagerly—men, women, and children.   It
was curious to watch the buyers as they walked away with
their purchase ; some looking very grave and putting it safely
away—others, half incredulous, and obviously with strong
suspicion that they had made fools of themselves.   The
quack's impudence and gravity were superb, and so was his
Italian, which is unusual.   Pio Nono is at present at the top
of the wall, at least to judge from appearance.   The *Fuorusciti*,
who have taken advantage of the amnesty, and are successively
coming back to their several cities, keep alive the enthusiasm ;
each refugee who returns and is fêted, makes a fresh stir in his
town.   And now the creation of this civic guard, and the
discovery of " la Congiura di Roma," have given fresh impulse
to the popular feeling.   It is in the towns that this feeling
is so strong.   The priests in the country are said to be of the
old party, and though the townspeople say that the Pope's
popularity is equally great in the country, their admission
about the priests makes it doubtful.   I received as I came
along the most horrible accounts of what the Congiura di
Roma was to have produced : sack of Rome, a sort of Jac-
querie in the provinces, deposition or murder of the Pope,
and election of Lambruschini at Naples.   This is the popular
idea, and the townspeople are savage.   The new civic guard,
though hardly organised yet, is beginning to distinguish itself
by its activity in making arrests, and they say that it is time
now for the Pope to be severe—" Bisogna tagliar qualche

teste, è una soddisfazione dovuta al popolo,"—and I suppose Ciceruacchio will make him do it. At one of the inns on the road the innkeeper brought me a translation of a paragraph in the *Morning Chronicle* about Rothschild's election, in which Pio IX. is called the "most enlightened sovereign of the age." The fat old gentleman was much delighted by this English testimony to the greatness of the Pope, and was very anxious to know what part England would take in the struggle which all here think inevitable between the Pope and Austria. What strikes one a good deal in the people whom I have talked to is, in spite of their enthusiasm, the hopelessness that lies at the bottom of it. They all seem to think that success and prosperity are not for them—that all this is too good to last—that it will end in failure and disappointment. The Pope will be poisoned, or Austria will pull it all down, and the other Powers will stand by. It is the experiment alone which interests them ; they become gloomy and desponding as soon as they begin to look forward to its result. And, as far as I know Italian history, this seems almost ingrained. They are in a great rage with the French papers for saying that the conspiracy is a fancy—"un sogn." The impudence, they say, of making light of it. The whole country is looking out for "il gran processo" and in a state of daily fear of "i nimici," as they call the old Pope's party, whom the Liberals look upon with that sort of mingled suspicion, contempt, and fear which the Whigs felt towards the Jacobites. The occupation of the city of Ferrara by the Austrians on the 18th has puzzled them. Certainly the Roman states, if they are let alone, bid fair to be a nucleus of anti-Austrian feeling, which the wise old Prince,—"quel vecchio infame," as my political innkeeper called him, may think prudent to nip at once.

Mr. Church was still wandering in Italy, when he was called to Lyons to nurse the brother to whom the Greek letters had been addressed, who had been taken dangerously ill there whilst on his way to Athens and the East. Upon his recovery they returned together to Italy, where they revisited Florence, which they had not seen since their father's death in 1828. Turning homewards at length, at the end of the year Mr. Church went to Genoa, crossing thence by steamer to Marseilles ; and after watching the peaks of the Carrara mountains, " magnificent that evening, pink with the last sunset of 1847," and experiencing the force and keenness of a mistral, which was blowing furiously at Marseilles on the first day of the new year, he crossed France in bitter wintry weather, and arrived in England in the second week of January after a year's absence.

Little record remains of the few years which had still to elapse of Mr. Church's Oxford life. On his return from abroad he resumed his customary life at Oriel, reading widely, both on theological and historical subjects, and writing regularly for the *Guardian* and the *Christian Remembrancer.* He turned to good account the knowledge he had gained during his year's wandering, in essays and articles which gather up the results of his own observation on foreign politics, and his study of the foreign political writers of the time—Rosmini, Gioberti, d'Azeglio, Louis Blanc. His articles on Farini's *Roman State*, and on the French Revolution of 1848, both of them afterwards reprinted in his volume of *Essays and Reviews*, are examples of this combination. The latter

article, in particular, whilst it is one of the most masterly
in the collection, has plainly gained vividness from
touches suggested to him by what he had seen and heard
at Lyons, as he waited there, during the autumn of
1847, detained by his brother's illness, as well as from
the impression made on him by Paris, which he had
passed through only a few weeks before the Revolution
of February.   Dante had been an unfailing companion,
never out of reach during his Italian journeys and the
long days of *retturino* travelling, as the brothers drove
together from Lyons to Marseilles, and along the Cornice
Road to Genoa on their way to Florence.   The little
well-worn volume of the *Divina Commedia*, which had
been laid on Dante's tomb at Ravenna, is filled with
marginal notes and jottings, bearing witness to its constant use, and to the associations which had grown up
during the journey round numberless passages of the
poem, the last entry at the closing canto of the *Paradiso*
bearing the date, "Florence, Christmas Day, 1847."
The essay on Dante, which two years later was the outcome of this diligent study, as well as the essay on
Church and State,[1] which had been occasioned by the
Gorham judgment of 1850, both of them made their

---

[1] See Mozley's *Letters*, p. 203.   "Church's article [on Church and
State] is very good, and will, I hope, have the effect of quieting some
minds who think so fearfully of our Reformation Erastianism.   It had
the effect upon me, as if one whole side of the truth, which had been
completely suppressed throughout this controversy, and all the controversy of the last twenty years, had now fairly come out.   Of course
we shall displease our ultra friends who are eager for a convulsion.
I confess I am not.   Nor do I see anything in the temper of those
who are which attracts me."

first appearance in the *Christian Remembrancer* of
1850.

But he was beginning to feel the need of more
definite and permanent occupation than his life at
Oxford now offered. A tutor's life had never been very
much to his mind, and his inclinations turned more and
more towards pastoral work in some country parish.
His engagement in 1850 to Miss Bennett, the daughter
of a Somersetshire squire and parson, and a niece of
Dr. Moberly, gave a fresh impulse to his wish to settle
and make a home. Whilst waiting for a benefice, he
took up again for a short time the tutorship at Oriel.
"There is no one to take the tutorship," he writes to
James Mozley, " * * * and * * * for various reasons
not being wished for. So Chretien opened his troubles
to me about the college being in a bad way, and his
having no one to work with—and would I take it if
the Provost offered it me. And after some negotiation,
it has ended in my being stop-gap again for a time, and
I shall have the satisfaction of ending my Oxford life as
a tutor." In November of 1852 he made one of a
deputation which was sent up by the University to
attend the funeral of the Duke of Wellington in St.
Paul's. The letter describing the ceremony gives Mr.
Church's first experience of St. Paul's on a great public
occasion; his last formal act in connection with the
University thus constituting, as it were, a link between
the life he was leaving and that which was awaiting
him in the distant future :—

M

ORIEL, 21*st November* 1852.

The funeral was really a great solemnity, and I should
think as real and genuine a one as such a thing can ever be.
It was, of course, as much of a triumph as a funeral; but
there was both feeling and self-restraint shown on a wonderful scale, for a mere crowd; and the ecclesiastical part of the
ceremonial was not unworthy of the rest. The procession of
clergy in surplices, and the distinctness and clearness of the
chanting, were much beyond what I ever expected: the
burial service was not lost, as I half feared, in the spectacle,
but had its full prominence. To the last he seemed to carry
with him his good success.

In the autumn of 1852 Mr. Church was offered and
accepted the living of Whatley, a small parish in
Somersetshire, in the gift of Mr. Horner of Mells. He
was ordained priest at the Christmas ordination of the
same year, and in the following January he left Oxford
finally for his country parish, spending a solitary six
months there before his marriage, which took place in
July. He carried with him from Oxford the warm
affection and regret both of friends and colleagues.
And from the Head of his college came the expression
of regard, in words which gain an added value in the
light of former differences:—"No one," wrote the
Provost of Oriel, "regrets our losing you from Oxford
more than myself."

It was long indeed before Mr. Church himself became
fully reconciled to the separation; no other place,
however dear, ever had the peculiar position in his

heart held by Oxford. To the eighteen years he had passed there—years which had brought great happiness, even if at times great anxieties—he felt that he owed all that had most enriched and deepened his life, of knowledge, of friendships, of experience. "Oxford has been a glorious place for me," he wrote, "so one must not complain of changes."

PART II

IT would be hard to imagine a more complete contrast than that which awaited Mr. Church when he exchanged his life at Oxford for the care of a country parish. Whatley was a little village of two hundred people, wholly agricultural in its occupations, lying in the midst of the rich Somersetshire pasture country, twelve miles from Wells, and three miles from Frome, its nearest market town. For many years the parish had been without a resident rector; both church and rectory were out of repair; and the people of the place, unused to and suspicious of strangers, lived, as such small and isolated communities are apt to do, almost exclusively within the range of their own little local occupations and interests and feuds. To Mr. Church, who had had no training in parochial work, and no experience beyond what he had gained when helping some clerical friend during the leisure of Oxford vacations, there was a good deal in the life awaiting him that was at first unfamiliar and irksome. The separation from friends, which his

position, single-handed in his parish, entailed, as well as
the loss of the freedom and the variety of interests to
which Oxford had accustomed him, told heavily at first
upon his spirits. "I am tired of telling my friends
how badly I do without them," he writes to Mrs.
Johnson at the Observatory, in May 1853, during the
solitary months which had to elapse before his marriage.
"I am sure it is very kind of them to think of me ; but
I can assure them that they cannot miss me as much as
I miss them. . . . I see nobody, and feel no great wish
for acquaintances. And two sermons a Sunday is not
after my mind. I suppose I am being punished for my
antipathy in former days. . . . The weather is very
fine, and the country looking very pretty ; but it does
not reconcile me to my transplanting. I think all day
long of Shotover, and the bowls at the Observatory, and
my den, cold and dirty as it was, at Oriel."

But though he thus wrote, he took up his work with
his usual thoroughness and strength of purpose, and
before many years were passed he had begun to strike
deep root in his new home. As time went on, and his
experience grew, he formed a parochial method of his
own, which, simple and unambitious as it was, suited
well the circumstances of his parish. His earliest efforts
were directed towards his schools—to the parish school,
where he went daily, to the Sunday school, and in the
winter to the night school, where, with his wife, he
gathered the men and elder lads of the place for instruc-
tion on two or three evenings of each week. With the
children of the village his relations out of school hours

were always full of pleasant freedom. Paper chases for the boys (an amusement unheard of before at Whatley) became an institution of the place, and one in which he might be counted on to take a foremost part; and with the elder children there were long country walks in summer, when they were encouraged to search for wild flowers to be looked at afterwards with Mr. Church's microscope. It was not long before throughout the place the hesitating welcome which had awaited him as a stranger passed into a loyal and affectionate confidence. Although his work at Whatley was not untouched by those disappointments which every parish priest must know, the relationship which thus grew up between him and his people was never disturbed or weakened. They turned to him unquestioningly as their friend, as one on whose counsel they could rely, who could understand their perplexities, and who could be trusted to keep their secrets. They could not mistake the presence of a sympathy which honestly and naturally entered into the familiar and homely details of their everyday life, and into all that concerned them,—their work, their children, their gardens,—and which could be interested, as they said themselves, even in their pigs. "He were such a gentleman, and he cared for us so," was the phrase by which an old woman described the considerateness and the ready, genuine courtesy which won the hearts of the poorest and most ignorant. By the old, and by the sick and dying, his visits were eagerly looked for. It was no uncommon request that he would come and sit by the bedside of the sick, watching with them until the dreaded "turn of the night" had passed; and in any case of sudden or urgent illness, or to a dying person, he would be summoned in haste—roused, it might be, at night by the sound of pebbles thrown up against his window—for they longed not to pass away without the help of his presence and his prayers. And among the men of the village his influence was not less remarkable. The roughest and most turbulent of them did not question his authority, or refuse a respect which was never forgotten even in the free and frank intercourse which had grown up in the night schools or the cricket-field. No one took liberties with him, and men were quick to recognise a power which on occasion could flash out in prompt and stern rebuke of faults of conduct, in a way that was all the more impressive by its contrast with the gentleness of his usual manner. It used to be a saying during the early days of his work at Whatley that "a man durstn't any longer beat his wife, else the parson would be down on him;" and in any drunken brawl it was he who was sent for to stop the dispute with his straightforward resoluteness, and if need were, to step in to part the combatants. An occasion of this kind was long remembered in the village, when, after being sent for late at night to stop a fight between two men, both very drunk, and both fiercely quarrelsome, Mr. Church laid hold of the more dangerous of the two and walked with him up and down the road, not letting him go,· until at last the man, sobered and quieted, turned and shook his hand, saying, "Well, sir, I think now I'll go to bed."

And the qualities by which he won his peculiar power over his people were those which made themselves felt in church and in his sermons. One who was for many years a parishioner recalls the impression made by his manner in church. "The first thing that impressed us all was the extreme solemnity and devotion with which Mr. Church celebrated the Holy Communion. We had heard nothing then about the Eastward position, but I can see now his slight figure bent in lowly reverence before the altar, giving the whole service a new and higher and holier meaning by his bearing and entire absorption in the act of worship." His sermons, short and clear and practical, carefully written so as to avoid the use of long or difficult words, or of any lengthened thread of argument, had the same simple reality and directness of purpose about them. None could mistake his meaning; but simple as his words were, they had a force and sincerity which made their way to the hearts and consciences of all those who gathered weekly to listen to him in the little village church.

Side by side with his pastoral work went the pleasant country life, with its quietness and freedom, its varied interests and occupations, and its home happiness. It gave command of leisure for reading, and for a great deal of regular writing, much of the latter, for many years, taking the shape of articles and reviews written weekly for the *Guardian* and the *Saturday Review*. In his near neighbour and dear friend, Mr. Horner of Mells, with whom he was in almost daily intercourse, he had a companion who shared his interests in scientific and

literary matters. Almost insensibly the charm of the
life grew upon him as years went on. So dear had it
at last become, that when, in nineteen years' time, the
call to leave it came, it seemed at first as if there could
be no compensations in the work that awaited him
which could adequately meet the loss of all that he was
giving up.

Among the friendships of his later life none was
more valued by Mr. Church than that with Dr. Asa
Gray, the distinguished American botanist, whose acquaintance he had made some years before at Oxford.
The following letters are among the first in a correspondence which continued unbroken until Dr. Gray's
death in 1888 :—

TO DR. ASA GRAY.

WHATLEY, 3rd April 1854.

MY DEAR DR. GRAY—I am almost ashamed to venture to
reply to your kind letter of last year (the date I am ashamed
to add), but I hope you will let me do so, though so late.
It has been on my conscience for a very long while. But in
truth I have been very long settling, and even now am not
so settled as I should wish to be. And all through last year,
till quite the end of it, I found time and thoughts occupied
with a variety of details, domestic and other, which were
quite new to me, and not at all to my taste. And such en-
gagements are a great damper to letter-writing.

But now I have put an old house in a habitable state of
repair, and I am married, and I am getting to know something about my parishioners, and I am more broken in to a
new mode of life than I was this time last year. I am set

down in a rather interesting bit of country, on the borders of Somerset and Wilts, on the edge of the Somerset coalfield, where the mountain lime has been thrown up and broken through so as to form some really beautiful rocky valleys and woody hollows, with streams running through them. Whatley itself has not much to boast of, except a rather late spire to its church, which is conspicuous in a wide landscape, which, as you approach from the London side, seems spread out at the foot of the hills. The church I cannot boast of, either for its antiquity or its beauty; it was rebuilt some thirty years ago, and must remain a monument of the taste and economy of that time.

But it is a part of England where the Romans seem to have settled a good deal; and all round us we are meeting from time to time with remains of Roman villas, hypocausts, and tesselated pavements, and so forth. What brought them here I don't know, except that the neighbouring Mendip Hills contain various ores, which possibly were worked in Roman times. Not very far off, for those who have a carriage, are Wells and Glastonbury on one side, and Salisbury, with its plain, and Stonehenge on the other. But I have not found my way there yet. I find myself getting very like a mussel stuck to his rock; and with the exception of an occasional railway flight to Oxford on business, I have hardly stirred out of my parish since I have been here. . . .

I have taken the liberty of forwarding to you a volume of *Essays and Reviews*,[1] which some kind friends of mine have been at the trouble of reprinting from periodicals.

---

[1] A collection of essays and articles contributed by Mr. Church to the *British Critic* and *Christian Remembrancer*. It was published under the same title as the famous volume which appeared six years later.

I should not have republished them myself, but as it has
been done, the volume may remind you of Oxford, and I
send it to you.

I hope to hear, one of these days, that you are setting
your face Eastward again, and that I may have a chance again
of shaking hands with you. My hopes of getting to the
West are infinitely small, unless it be as an immigrant ; for
what an independent Fellow of a college might do, is effectually barred to a country parson with a small living. But
my travelling inclinations do not grow weaker, and I should
be only too glad to make acquaintance with a country which
becomes every day more interesting to Englishmen. . . .—
Believe me, yours most sincerely,   R. W. CHURCH.

Another letter, somewhat earlier in date, contains
the mention of a name which has a singular power of
arousing interest :—

Have you met a friend of mine, formerly a Fellow of my
college, Clough, who has been in your neighbourhood lately ?
He is a noble-minded and most able fellow, who has sacrificed
a good deal—on very high principles, if not wisely.

Writing again to Dr. Gray after the conclusion of
the first Oxford University Commission :—

WHATLEY, 24th August 1854.

Well, you see, we have been reformed, if not revolution-
ised, at least on paper. It will be a curious, and also an
anxious thing, to see how the changes will work. I imagine
that very few people can have any very good conjectures.
For though the reform has been prepared by careful and
friendly thinkers, and though there is a general wish among

the residents for some such reform, yet when a great body
of alterations comes in a lump, suddenly, and from without,
on a body with ancient and complicated organisation, with
considerable mental training, and various and subtle sympathies, and traditional ways of thinking and feeling, which
are ever changing in themselves, yet are very incomprehen-
sible to the big public outside, it is very hard to say how
the new will fit with the old, and become incorporated with
it. I have been, on the whole, a well-wisher to the changes
—to most, though not to all. But I do feel nervous to see
them at work. Say what people will, Oxford has turned
out more highly-cultivated thought, thought which acts with
greater power on the country, both in the purely intellectual,
and in the practical order of life, than any other English
body ; and if it should be spoilt by clumsy doctoring ——!

I am so glad to hear that there is a good chance of your
having to pay us another visit. I hope, if you do come, you
will try to spare us a few days, and Mrs. Gray too.—Yours
most sincerely,   R. W. CHURCH.

To MANUEL JOHNSON, ESQ.

WHATLEY, 28th November 1854.

DEAR JOHNSON— . . . I have not moved since you last
heard of me. I should like to get a holiday, but war prices,
and increased expenses, and double income-tax, are strong
dissuasives, and I shall hearken to them as long as I am not
driven away by actual want of holiday. . . . However, I
feel ashamed of complaining when people are fighting for us
at Sebastopol. It is getting to look very ugly, and seemingly for want of foresight, and from thinking ourselves
such great people that we could do without reserves and

reinforcements. I have the Athenians and Syracuse perpetually in my thoughts. It will go hard with Master
Newcastle and his fellows if any disaster happens. . . .

What is the new Council doing? I see they have put
forth an edict against pigeon-shooting : anything more ?

WHATLEY, *2nd January* 1855.

Mozley's book[1] will no doubt make a great row, and
accomplish the break-up that J. H. N. began. I am very
sorry for the result, yet it need not have come, if our friends
had not stuck up for so much dogmatic certainty, and drawn
so narrowly the limits of liberty of thinking. In the
Middle Ages, and much more in the early times of the
Church, there was infinitely more free speculation than
seems compatible with Church views now. I think it must
be we who are wrong. The nature of things seems more in
favour of the old way than of ours.

I have been busy lately with a sketch of early Turkish
history[2] for the *Christian Remembrancer*. But my labour—
and it has been a good deal, and not very convenient—has
been thrown away, because Scott has managed so that, at
the last moment, there was no room for me, being as usual
somewhat bulky. I am in a rage with him, because he
pressed me very hard to write for this number, and that in
spite of my telling him that I should be long.

. . . I still, you see, hanker after scribbling. I have
been thinking lately over an old idea of mine, an account of
the times just before the Reformation and Renaissance ;
the councils of Basle, etc., and John Gerson : not with any

---

[1] *The Primitive Doctrine of Baptismal Regeneration.*
[2] Reprinted, under the title of *The Early Ottomans*, in vol i. of the
Dean's Miscellaneous Works. Macmillan, 1888.

controversial purpose, but simply as a curious period of history. But it would require much hunting into books to do it in a proper way, and perhaps some travelling, and that is a great obstacle nowadays. I am now, I am glad to say, able to turn my German to account—not with the same facility as French or Italian, but still usefully. . . . —Ever yours affectionately,   R. W. C.

To Mr. Mozley himself he writes, later in the year :—

I congratulate you on the conclusion of your book. I have followed it, with great interest, sheet by sheet. It seems to me to have brought out very clearly the fact of the double and parallel lines of ideas, and to have confronted them with great distinctness and power. The subject is one which, I suppose, is not likely to tempt lazy readers. But you have not written for them. It makes one feel how one goes on, taking things for granted, both as principles and explanations, and as facts. I am very glad you worked the point well about our ignorance. I never should be a metaphysician ; but the way in which assumptions excite no question, and people go on spinning arguments, as if the whole of the invisible world was as easy to be understood as the theory of the steam-engine, has long been one of my standing wonders. . . . I am glad that you have brought out so strongly the two-sided character of all our means of knowing, and the fact that what we know in religious matters is but the tendency to know. The idea of perfect and absolute knowledge, which is involved in so much of what is said and taught on all sides, becomes daily more and more unendurable to me.—Ever yours affectionately,   R. W. C.

To the Rev. J. B. Mozley.

WHATLEY, 6th August 1855.

MY DEAR MOZLEY—I should think Malvern must be a mild kind of purgatory at best. But as you have been manful enough to go through with it, I can quite suppose that it may be just what you want, the proper mixture of enforced idleness and bracing treatment.

. . . I was in Oxford about three weeks ago for a day or two. I went up to see poor Marriott, or at least to hear on the spot about him. I was only allowed to see him once for a few minutes, and there was nothing to be done for him, but to leave him quiet to the nurse and one or two people who used to come and read Layard's *Nineveh* to him. His mind did not seem at all touched—only astonished, as it were, and not able to realise the extent of the blow and its consequences. The doctors had good hope of his coming round in the end, but said that it would be a very long business, and that it would be many weeks before any change was perceptible. What an end to all his plans! The great difficulty will be to convince him that he must really give them up. He was wanting to write and make arrangements about his Hall, as if he should be well and about again in a month.

. . . Rogers is anxious about his artillery brother, who has had to leave the camp with the fever, and is in hospital at Scutari. Only think of poor Stowe venturing out there, and just getting in time to see a battle and describe it, and then being carried off.

I am afraid I have written but a valetudinarian letter. I wish you were here to eat our currants. Can't you come at the end of the Long ?—Ever yours affectionately,

R. W. CHURCH.

To the Rev. W. J. Copeland.

Whatley, 26*th December* 1856.

My dear Copeland—. . . These judgments, in *re* St. Paul's,[1] are very trying to one's temper. It is a bad time when people get to feel that they really cannot get justice and fair-play. I confess for myself, it is not so much for the questions involved that I care for them. I have my likings and beliefs and opinions on them; but if so be that the Prayer-Book *had* really said, "You must not have a cross on the altar, or an embroidered cloth, or lighted candles," I might have thought it a pity, but it would not have made much difference as to what I felt otherwise about the Prayer-Book. But it is this determination, in courts of justice, to find a meaning and a direction where there is none, and to close questions which at the least are open ones, which is enough to drive fair and quiet men into savage thoughts and feelings. One knows how points have been and would be stretched on the other side, while on ours a meaning is *found* by judges where, by their own confession, there was none discernible before.—Ever yours affectionately,   R. W. C.

To Sir Frederic Rogers.

Whatley, 26*th January* 1857.

My dear Rogers—. . . I have just been reading a book which I advise you to look into if it falls in your way : the memoirs and letters of a certain Frederic Perthes, a German bookseller, which I have been much struck with. He was a man who made his trade a great work, and

---

[1] St. Paul's, Knightsbridge. See Westerton case, *Guardian*, 24th December 1856.

followed it in the highest spirit ; a thoroughly fine fellow, overflowing with energy, and cleverness, and kindliness, and affectionateness of all kinds, an enthusiastic German, nearly getting hanged by Davoust for stirring up the Hamburghers against the French in 1813, and full of all kinds of interests —political, religious, social, scientific—a remarkable mixture of unceasing activity of mind and body, both in his business and in all that concerned public questions, with a most genuine and increasing depth of religious feeling.   The curious thing is, how he is an instance showing how those Germans contrive to show deep religious earnestness—and what certainly has all the look of New Testament religion —without Church or any fixed creed, and with a most unrestrained intercourse with men of the most clashing opinions, Roman Catholics, rationalists, sceptics, and every-thing.   His business and his very high character brought him into acquaintance and intimacy with a vast number of great German names—Niebuhr, Stolberg, Neander, Schleier-macher, Jacobi, and a hundred others, and their and his letters are given.   And the book lets one into the real feelings and workings of all those wild German thinkers, whose proceedings startle and astonish us so much.   It shows us their domestic and undress side, and certainly, to my mind, abates the strong dislike and condemnation which we have been taught is the right thing to feel towards them. I don't mean that it reconciles me to their way of going on ; but it does make one feel how very much without real knowledge has been a great deal of the broad abuse of Germanism that goes on ; and how much real goodness, and often strong religious feeling there has been in quarters among them, where it has been à priori assumed to be incompatible with their speculative opinions. . . .

N

It is a book which seems to have made me, in a sort of way, personally acquainted with a set of people who have been soundly abused without our knowing much about them ; and to have shown that whatever there was unsatisfactory among them, it was certainly accompanied with a real height, and nobleness, and goodness, for which we have given them sparing credit.   I should like to hear the impression the book made on you, though I fear it is too long, and in parts too prosy to suit you.

17th February 1857.

I have been reading Helps' *Conquest* on your recommendation.   It is a curiously told story—as if it was being *told* with all the narrator's little private ways of allusion or remark—but very interesting.   There is something very dreadful in the apparent inevitableness of the catastrophe to the poor Indians.   And what a curious double development of the Spanish character in such people as the Governor Ovando, and the Dominican monk Antonio, who broke into the king's presence to plead for the Indians, and abused his Franciscan rival into coming over to his side.

I quite feel with you about this horrid Chinese business. It seems perfectly incredible, on the face of what we know, that such things should have been allowed to go on, as this bombardment of Canton.   One cannot help doubting whether we can know the whole case ; and yet if there was more to be said I suppose it would have appeared.   I have no doubt that the Chinese are very provoking gentry, and I suppose that the original cause of quarrel will soon be entirely out of sight ; but what a case it is of a war on "false pretences."

So your Board is to be broken up.   Well, I suppose that you feel that it is a euthanasia, and you have the special satisfaction of coming to an end after work well done, only because there is no more of it for you to do. All Boards do not end so flourishingly nowadays.

I wish I could send the medicine you ask about for an anti-talking-to-poor-people diathesis. After four years' trial I find it as strong in myself as ever, i.e. I know as little how to go about it satisfactorily, and still read with wonder and admiration any small book which describes the easy-going, glib, persuasive way in which the typical parson is painted talking to the members of his flock. To me they seem to live in impenetrable shells of their own; now and then you seem to pinch them or please them, but I can never find out the rule that either goes by. I think sometimes whether one ought not to give up reading, and all communication with the world one has been accustomed to, in order to try and get accustomed to theirs—but this does not seem a promising plan either. I hope that something tells, though one does not see the way how.—Ever yours affectionately,

R. W. C.

To Manuel Johnson, Esq.

Whatley, 15th March 1858.

Dear Observer—I wish I could have run up to-day, if only to see Le Verrier, for perhaps I should not have seen the eclipse [1] better than we did here. Here it was a bad failure. The morning promised fairly—a lot of cirro-stratus clouds about, but the sun shining in and out of them nicely. But at eleven a thick layer of cumulo-stratus began to come over, covering up most of the sky, with a rapid scud under-neath; still this was sufficiently broken from time to time to see the sun. I observed the first contact at 11.32, as far

---

[1] A total eclipse of the sun which took place on the 15th March 1858.

as I could judge, but our clocks are not very trustworthy. The sun was visible in and out, with scud rapidly flying across, till about 12.15, when the clouds thickened, became more continuous, and seemed lowering, and there were no breaks.   At 12.30 I just caught sight of the sun for a moment three-fourths covered ; but there was no perceptible darkening, more than would seem natural with such a clouded sky ; at 12.35 the cloud was of a uniform texture, dark grey, especially in the north.   Then there came on a thickish damp mist, and the wind increased, as if rain was coming ; but none came, only it felt very cold and damp. There was a kind of grey dimness like evening ; I did not notice the stillness that is talked of—perhaps, however, because the wind was freshening.   But the rooks seemed puzzled, and to be thinking of going home to Mells Park. There was a slightly lighter patch in the cloud where the sun was.   Just about one o'clock there seemed to pass through the rooms and the house a rapidly-increasing darkness ; my wife, sitting in a north room, had to leave off writing ; and it came on so suddenly, that it suggested the idea of some startling change being impending, quite different from anything which seemed to have been preparing outside. But it was not more than a minute.   Just after, about 1.2 the sun was again visible through the scud, about three-quarters of a ring, but the upper and left-hand portion was gone.   It appeared and disappeared for a few minutes, and then the grey uniform cloud covered it up again ; and before 1.15 everything had got back to the grey misty look which it had just before the short burst of gloom, which, however, at its deepest was not deeper than I have seen caused by a summer thunderstorm.   About 1.45 the mist disappeared, and it became merely grey stratus, with scud flying rapidly across its face. Then the stratus began to break up and give patches of lighter colour, and at 2.7 I caught the sun again, and watched the disappearance of the moon's limb. It seemed to leave the sun at 2.11. Thus there was no opportunity of seeing any of the sights which Mr. Hind and Airy had set us on looking out for ; of observing the change of colour in the sky, for no sky was visible during the whole time, the sun being seen only through thin clouds ; or of noting the effect in bringing the horizon near, for there was a thick mist apparently all round the distance, and slightly even near. After all my lecturing to my school children out of Mr. Hind I am afraid they must have thought me a humbug ; for though the effect was striking, it was not more so than the closing in of evening, except just in that rapid darkening which came on for a minute and then went off again. . . .—Ever yours affectionately, R. W. C.

An amusing sequel to the disappointment caused on the day of the eclipse by the overclouded sky is given in a letter to Dr. Gray :—" In our neighbouring country town some one sent the common crier round to announce that, in consequence of the disappointment, the eclipse would be repeated next day. I don't know what effect the announcement had, I only know that the bellman took the fee, and very solemnly went round the town to cry the intelligence."

To Dr. Asa Gray.

DENNIL HILL, CHEPSTOW, *5th July* 1859.

MY DEAR PROFESSOR GRAY—I have received the extracts from the Proceedings of the American Academy of Arts and

Sciences, containing an abstract of your discussion with
Agassiz on the distribution of species.   A layman like
myself, very destitute of facts, can only follow such a discussion in a kind of hypothetical way.   But the interest it
excites is enough to make me wish that I had time to know
more about it.   What a world it carries one back to !—and
to what an inconceivable condition of things, compared with
all that we are familiar with, when we come to speculate on
the laws and phenomena which prevailed in the creative
periods of time.   It certainly strikes me that your view, as
a theory to be tried, is the one to take, instead of Agassiz's,
which simply amounts to taking species as they are found,
without any inquiry as to their possible previous history.
With the indications of affinities and vicissitudes in the
history of species which there are, it is more philosophical
to see if they will bear being traced out into a simple connection with each other.   But the strangeness of creation,
whether in many distant centres or one, whether by an
individual or pair, or by a whole family at once, seems
equally overwhelming to our present faculties and thoughts.
And I am not quite sure that I feel the probability of
Maupertuis' law of economy of power.   The *waste* of nature
seems to me at least as striking ; apparent waste, I ought to
have said, like that, *e.g.* of seeds or of unimpregnated ova,
which do not seem to fulfil their *direct* purpose, though of
course they may some other.   But I am rambling on, and
talking about what I know nothing of.   You must please
excuse it, for it has been suggested by your paper, which has
stirred up my wish to know what I don't know.

You will see by my address that I am not in my usual
abode.   I am enjoying a three months' holiday from my
parish work, and am here with my family, in a place made

for a delightful summer idleness. We live in a house perched up on the cliffs which overhang the Wye, just opposite the Wyndcliff; and with a glorious view of the meeting of the Severn and the Wye among grey rocks and densely wooded banks, with the river twisting about in all kinds of curious bends, and within reach of fine ruins like Tintern, Chepstow Castle, and Raglan. I have not had a holiday since I have been at Whatley, some six years; and last year I was very much out of health and condition. But I am fast mending now, and I hope to be set up quite for such work as I have at home ; not hard work, certainly, but with a good deal of quiet sameness and monotony about it, which, to my shame be it spoken, seems to have the same exhausting effect after a time as a downright spell of fagging. . . .

The other day at Oxford I saw your handwriting in a letter to the widow of my very dear friend, Manuel Johnson,[1] of the Radcliffe Observatory. I was very much gratified at seeing how much he was appreciated among you ; he did indeed deserve it. A nobler mind, a larger heart, I never knew.

WHATLEY, 12th March 1860.

I have to thank you for some very interesting papers. I have received two abstracts of papers on the distribution of plants in North-East Asia and America ; and, lately, your review of Darwin.[2] And I have also received your note accompanying the review.

I thought of you when Darwin's book came out. . . . I am particularly pleased to see that it has engaged your attention, and to be able to read your views about it. I

---

[1] Mr. Johnson's death had taken place in February 1859.
[2] Darwin's *Origin of Species*.

have not had time yet to do more than glance at the book itself. But, of course, it would be impossible to read the papers, and hear people talk, without knowing, in general, the line he takes, and the nature of his argument. I believe I must confess that I owe my first interest in the subject to the once famous *Vestiges;* and I remember thinking at the time it came out, that the line taken against it was un-philosophical and unsatisfactory ; and that people wrote against it in much too great a fright, as to the consequences of the theory, and answered him often more like old ladies than philosophers. Mr. Darwin's book, partly from the greater gravity and power of the writer, and partly from, I think, a little more wisdom in the public, has not made such an outcry. Perhaps it is not so popular in style, and so widely read ; but I should think that it is *the* book of science which has produced most impression here of any that has appeared for many years. As far as I have any right to judge, I entirely concur with the line of your criticism. I mean, that to a bystander, whose notions of the probabilities and the evidence of the difficult and complicated case are most vague and imperfect, it is most refreshing to see it so calmly and wisely examined, both in respect to the strong points of the theory, and its still more (at present) formidable difficulties. And you seem to me to have stated with the happiest precision and fairness just exactly what is true to say of its bearing on theology. One wishes such a book to be more explicit. But it is wonderful "shortness of thought" to treat the theory itself as incompatible with the ideas of a higher and spiritual order.

The idea of cross-fertilisation is new to me, and very curious, and, as you say, brings us a new step nearer to the understanding of that economy of nature, which yet, however,

after all, has such a large margin of apparent prodigality.
The spring always brings back this thought to me—or rather,
the *combination* of such extreme regularity, delicacy, and
economy, with what seems the roughest and coarsest methods
—a continual creation out of ruins.

I am very glad you have had the grand opportunity of
carrying further your comparisons of geographical botany.
The fact you have got out of it is very remarkable. The
line of investigation you have entered on must be singularly
attractive, with all the promise of large discovery looming
through it. I think that that condition of investigation
must be a great inducement to physical studies. It hardly
exists, or at least is accompanied with much heavier risks and
drawbacks in the more exclusively mental ones.—Yours very
sincerely,   R. W. CHURCH.

In 1860 appeared the famous volume of *Essays and
Reviews ;* and the storm about it was already gathering,
though the full vehemence of the outbreak did not come
till somewhat later. The following letter refers to a
general criticism upon the book, which Dr. Moberly
proposed prefixing to a volume of sermons he was about
to bring out :—

To DR. MOBERLY.

WHATLEY, *14th September* 1860.

I have read your Preface with great interest, but with
divided feelings as to the expediency of publishing it. I
should like it to be published for the sake of many things in
it. On the other hand, it does not go fully enough into
others to satisfy people who will be looking out for satisfaction ; and in noticing a book of this kind it is a question

whether anything but a tolerably complete answer does not give advantage to the other side.

It seems to me that this is a book for a point-blank answer : I mean that it is not enough to point out, as you truly do, the way in which it shakes to pieces the faith of ordinary Christians ; but for any effect to be produced, the main things said must be met face to face, and their real value and significance duly measured.

The guerilla way in which these men write, each man fighting for his own hand, though with a common purpose, or, at least, result, makes a fair point-blank answer doubly difficult ; but I think it is the only one that will tell, and so the only one worth making.

What is the human element in Scripture ? What is its real amount ? How is it to be viewed ? How is it to be distinguished from the Divine element ? These men treat it so as to exclude the Divine almost entirely ; but I see no way of stopping them, except by meeting the question they have raised, as far as the bounds of our knowledge enable us to do so. Of course there are other questions raised (among them, and very painfully handled, the question of the *necessity of having any truth*, at least any historical truth, *to believe in at all) ;* but the main thing seems to me, that we must meet them on a ground which has become inevitable almost, that of actual historical criticism ; and that their power lies in their being left alone in possession of it.

The upshot, as far as I know my own opinion, is, that I should like to have many things in your Preface published : —your general criticism on their design and way of putting out difficulties (though perhaps I should feel obliged to be more merciful in my own speech about them, and the amount of religious feeling which, in spite of all, I believe most of

them to have at bottom); your criticism on Jowett's crude
and one-sided canon of interpretation; and the particular
arguments, *e.g.* that on Infant Baptism at the end of the
Preface. And also, I quite feel the importance of people of
weight not shrinking from speaking out their disapproval,
even though they do not feel called on to enter the lists
themselves. But, on the other hand, I had rather that, if
you do attack them controversially, it should be in a more
deliberate and less perfunctory manner than can be done in a
Preface.

I hope I have not been very impertinent. I feel in
writing about these great and, as yet, almost unsounded
questions, that a person with my want of clearness of head,
and of readiness of memory—not to say, also, scanty and
piecemeal knowledge—is almost like a landsman giving
advice on board a ship in a storm. Certainly every age has
its fiery trials of faith. . . .—Ever yours affectionately,

R. W. C.

To Dr. Asa Gray.

Whatley, *28th March* 1861.

I have had it on my mind for a long time that I have
never thanked you for the last paper you sent me about
Darwin. I don't know why it should seem a more formidable
undertaking to sit down and write a letter which is to go
across the Atlantic than one which is to go to London. But
imagination certainly does invest the work with a kind of
gravity, as if it required some peculiar preparation and effort
of mind; and imagination is a powerful disposer of the
actions of life. To-day, however, I have at length got the
better of the tyrant, and now I don't find that there is any
good reason to allege for my having been so dilatory. I read

your paper with very great interest, as indeed I have done all that you have written upon the subject. The more I think of it, the more I feel persuaded of the "shortness of thought" which would make out what is in itself a purely physical hypothesis on the mode of creation or origination (in which it seems to me very difficult at present to imagine our *knowing* anything), to be incompatible with moral and religious ideas of an entirely different order. But I am afraid that this is the general way of thinking among our religious people; and so the theory does not get fair discussion, either for or against, because there is on both sides an irresistible tacit reference to other interests in the minds of disputants. You seem to me to have cleared the way for a fair discussion of it on its merits and evidence. The book, I have no doubt, would be the subject still of a great row, if there were not a much greater row going on about *Essays and Reviews*. It is not wonderful that this book should have caused much consternation. It seems to me, with many good and true things in it, to be a reckless book; and several of the writers have not got their thoughts and theories into such order and consistency as to warrant their coming before the world with such revolutionary views. But there has been a great deal of unwise panic, and unjust and hasty abuse; and people who have not an inkling of the difficulties which beset the questions, are for settling them in a summary way, which is perilous for every one. However, I hope the time of protest and condemnation is now passing away; and the time of examination and discussion in a quieter tone beginning.

The great subject of my thoughts and interest for the last four months has been the course of events among yourselves. To my mind, it quite throws into the shade the nearer, and, at first sight, more striking events in Italy. It seems to touch an Englishman's feelings as a quarrel between North and South in England. As it has come to this, I am inclined to be an optimist about it, and to think that it is a case where separation, when once accepted, may make both parts greater, though there are very formidable necessities involved in the fundamental conditions under which the South begins its new development.

Pray remember me very kindly to Mrs. Gray. In hope still to see you some day here, I am yours very sincerely,

R. W. CHURCH.

In the summer of 1861 occurred the first step, after the long silence of fifteen years, towards a renewal of intercourse with Dr. Newman :—

To THE REV. W. J. COPELAND.

WHATLEY, *2nd August* 1861.

I should have answered your letter before, but I have been away from home, and going away always involves a little more to do on coming back. I wish you gave a better account of yourself. . . . Don't you think you could spare a few days and run down here ? I should be very glad to see you, and it would be very pleasant to have some talk about old days. I, too, am getting to feel old, and almost something of a survivor, but this is nothing, I suppose, to what one must look forward to, if one lives long enough.

I have had just the same sort of little passing remembrances from Newman. He sent me a book belonging to W. H. Scott ; and then a letter or so passed, very like his old self, with not much of his present position. To be sure the world has not been grateful among our Roman brethren any more than among ourselves. I often wish, as you say, that I had Boswellised. But unhappily, or happily, I didn't. And I often think with wonder, how much I should be puzzled if I were called on to draw up a sketch of those times and doings. Seeing things too close is almost as much an impediment to taking them in altogether, as seeing them too far off. They have left their stamp and general impression. But I mourn over the utterly faded details.

A foreign holiday, the first for fifteen years—spent partly in and about Grenoble, and partly in Paris—revived the old delight in travelling, a delight which found expression in the descriptions of his letters home:—

To his Wife.

GRENOBLE, 11th May 1862.

Grenoble is a great success. The railway branching off from the Rhone at a place called St. Rambert brings one by a surprise into the heart of the mountains, and rushes, twisting about and going down most unrailway-like descents, till it brings you into a rich green flat valley plain, with high sharp tooth-like crags all round it, and the snowy summits beyond them,—so far only half disclosed through the trooping clouds which cling to them, or slowly float along them. This valley is of the shape of a Y : down one horn comes twisting about in a snake-like fashion the Isère ; down the other, much straighter, the Drac, and they join just below Grenoble. The feature of the country is the mixture of rich green luxuriance with the ragged rocky mountain outlines, and the snowy tops in the background.

The lower mountain buttresses come down straight into the plain; they are formed of strata turned up at a very high angle, and so their edges are ragged and jagged in the most picturesque manner. They are detached also for the most part from one another, and so form a series of ever-changing forms as you change your point of view. It is a glorious place certainly. There is a kind of rocky citadel on one of these shoulders of rock, commanding the town, and I went up there this morning accompanied by a talkative and pleasant French sergeant, and had a grand view over the nearer scenery. We ought to have looked up the valley of the Isère to Mont Blanc, but there the clouds were envious and would not let us see him. This afternoon I had a strolling climb in another direction, and was equally repaid : a great wall of mountain behind me throwing the near fore-ground into shadow, while beyond, a line of sunlight lay on the green plain, and the city, and the white craggy citadel, and then on the green range of slopes immediately bounding the valley, and the purple curtain of snowy Alps, of which the tops were confused with the great masses of white sun-lit cloud ; the contrast being striking and beautiful, between the white of the clouds, soft and like swan's down, and the hard pure white of the patches of snow, seen at intervals through the breaks in the clouds.

GRANDE CHARTREUSE, 16th May 1862.

I should like to write to you from this, one of the most remarkable places I have ever been in. The road to it, along the side of a torrent, the Guier Mort, is most magnifi-cent ; but I am going to write to you my first impressions of a real monastery. It lies on the steep slope of the moun-tain, with great wall-like precipices rising above it almost all

round : where there are not rocks there are woods—all is still
as can be.   The first sight of monastic life was a lay brother
in his white gown and hood of the Carthusian order, harness-
ing two horses to a carriage of some excursionists.   I went
and rang at the bell, and was admitted by a smiling, pleasant
lad in a blouse, to whom I expressed my wish to see the
convent.   I was conducted by him to an anteroom or
parlour, where, when we entered, was an old priest on his
knees at a *prie-dieu*, before a statue of Nôtre Dame, with S.
Bruno, the founder, bending before her.   He got up when
we came in, and sat down.   My guide knocked at the door
of the Père Coadjuteur, who is the receiver-general of
strangers.   The rule of the house is absolute silence for all
the brethren, but this rule does not apply to him.   The
door was not opened for a while, as he was engaged, but the
lad, in asking me to wait a little while, spoke in whispers,
and we all sat down in silence.   The room was hung round
with a few prints of the life of S. Bruno, with a crucifix over
the fireplace.

At last the Père came out with another monk, with whom
he had been doing some business ; they bowed to each other
in taking leave, in the most solemn fashion, but with French
grace and courtesy.   The dress is all white, coarse white
cloth, with a cowl and a curious strip down the back.   The
Coadjuteur asked my business, and I asked leave to sleep
here to-night : they give hospitality to all comers, but of
course you are expected to pay for it.   So, after a few compliments and bows, I was conducted to the waiting-room of
the strangers—the Hall of the Province of France—a stone-
paved hall, with numerous chairs and two or three tables,
where we are to dine. . . . In this hall the silence was not
so complete ; two garçons, laying the table, chattered as if

they were in a *salle-à-manger*. Presently a white monk in a beard came in and asked me whether I would dine by myself or with the other strangers : he further brought me a *petit verre* of a famous elixir which they are famous for making here—recommending it after my walk. This was the Frère Benoît, as my guide, the lad who let me in, confidentially informed me.

There is a stern, dreary look about everything, all very simple—chairs, tables, walls, windows, ceilings—but all in good order, and they make you welcome. It is a regular showplace in the fine weather; a curious mixture of the showplace and a monastic rule of the severest kind. We dined in the strangers' hall, five of us—three Frenchmen and two Englishmen, and spoke French to one another. They gave us a fair dinner of *maigre* fare. The Frenchmen discoursed largely on the *tristesse* of the monastic life, and criticised the cuisine : the Englishmen ate and made no remarks. At nine o'clock we found our way to our cells—very clean, brick-floored, but rude in the furniture. I must go to bed, for I am to be called at midnight, to be present at the night service of the monastery.

. . . I was called at a quarter before twelve, and ushered into a gallery at the end of a longish vaulted chapel, at the end of which burned the lamp before the Sacrament, and into which were gliding white figures with lanterns and candles. They took their places, and the service began,—chanting in a slow, simple manner : where they knew the particular part of it by heart the lights were put out—at best they only gave enough light to read by. It was certainly very solemn to think of these psalms breaking the utter silence of the rocks and forests, and to think of this having been done, almost without interruption in nearly the same manner, and on the same spot, for eight hundred years ; and that every night of one's life these men get up at midnight to chant them. The office was from twelve till two, when they glided out again, and I went to bed till six.

Now I am preparing for an ascent to the Grand Som, the highest peak near the convent. In the afternoon I mean to make my way back to Grenoble.

PARIS, 27th May 1862.

One thing which strikes me in this place, in the grand public buildings, is the free way in which the people use them. At the Louvre, for instance, with all its grandeur and magnificence, and so well soigné besides—there are stone seats all round, which are generally occupied by the men in blouses and the women in caps ; and all about them are the children of these people playing about the courts, just as they play about the dirty alleys here or in London. The multitude certainly has its full and fair share, not by favour, but as an understood and familiar enjoyment, of the outside at least, of the beauty of this great city.

I walked out this evening by the banks of the Seine, all carefully and beautifully built up in quays and landing-places, with the river itself so clear and calm—to the Champ de Mars, a great review ground, where many strange things were done in the Revolution and Napoleonic days. Then I crossed the river, and came home by the Champs Elysées, a quarter, half trees and alleys, half buildings—dwelling-houses, and also tea gardens and dancing places, which, as far as I can make out, are the common resort of respectable people and unrespectable. But the scene, in walking through it, is utterly unlike anything we have in England. Lights in all directions among the trees, lines of light marking rows of houses, isolated lights at corners and cross roads, figures of lights, crowns, lyres, inscriptions, pyramids, where the different gardens, and concert places, and cafés, display their attractions; and in the midst of these stationary lights are the innumerable lights—white, red, green, and blue—of all the cabs, and carriages, and omnibuses, which are passing to and fro, as thick as in Piccadilly at three o'clock. Then you come to the Place de la Concorde, where the obelisk and the statues, and the outlines of the adjoining buildings are lifted up in the clear air; and there you have the glitter, dimly seen, and the whish and splash of the fountains. . . . The strange thing is to think of what ground all these pleasure-seekers are treading on. There, in that Place de la Concorde, all so gay and beautiful, one can put one's foot exactly on the spot where stood the guillotine of Louis XVI.; and there, on the other side of the obelisk, is that whence Marie Antoinette might have looked along the avenue of horse-chestnuts up to the central Pavillon of the Tuileries, one October morning, for the last time. And there, besides, perished between two and three thousand persons. Yet it all looks so smiling, and given up to the fine arts and gaiety.

PARIS, 30*th May* 1862.

The rain has begun and it has been showery all day, with intervals of sunshine. So I have been at the galleries for the most part. This evening, in the intervals of the showers, I strolled up to the place where Louis XVI. and Marie Antoinette were buried after their execution. It was then an out-of-the-way cemetery attached to the parish of the Madeleine, and there they were thrown in anyhow, and, I believe, quicklime thrown over the bodies. The place was afterwards, it is said, bought by a royalist, who turned it into an orchard, by way of turning away any suspicions; but he kept note of where the bodies were laid. Then at the Restoration, what was to be found was removed to St. Denis, and the ground purchased, and a Chapelle Expiatoire built on it. It is somehow one of the gloomiest places I remember seeing ; surrounded by dead walls or high houses, with just a border of ivy running round the ground ; and then a ponderously heavy building, a sort of cloister and chapel, enclosing the old burying-place, with great iron posts and iron chains fencing it round, and the arches of the cloisters as deep and heavy as they could be made. No doubt it was not meant to have all this gloomy look ; but if any one had planned to convey all the melancholy and hopeless ideas connected with the fall of the old monarchy in the Place de la Concorde by embodying them in a dismal and dreary monument, he could not have succeeded better than Louis XVIII. has done in this case. One street that I pass continually is the street down which the carts passed to the place of execution ; and the street leading to the Chapelle Expiatoire is the one up which the carts with the bodies must have come. And now all is so different, and yet all is marked with the tokens and suggestive memorials of what was done then. The people you meet are the grandchildren—and some the children—of those who died and suffered those things.

PARIS, *Ascension Day*, 1862.

Ascension Day is a great holiday, greater than any ordinary Sunday, and all Paris is on its legs pleasure-hunting. There is full service at Mr. Gurney's chapel as on Sundays, which adds to the confusion in which one gets as to the day, as if it was Sunday and not Sunday. I went to the 8.30 early Communion ; then I meant to spend the middle of the day between the Invalides and the Jardin des Plantes ; but when I went to the Invalides, where the tomb of Napoleon is, Thursday being one of the days for seeing it,

I found that as it was Ascension Day there was a grand
military Mass at noon, at which the Governor, Marshal
Somebody, and no end of military grandees, were present.
This would take some time, and there was besides such a
crowd of holiday-makers, that one of the soldiers I spoke to
advised me to come another day, when I could see things
more quietly. The military Mass was curious. The Governor
and his suite were escorted to the church by a number of
the Invalides, old battered fellows in long great-coats and
caps, holding drawn swords. In the church there was a long
double line of these same old veterans, holding pikes with
tricoloured flags ; and up this lane the Governor marched
to his seat, the drummers beating furiously in the church,
and the soldiers all keeping their hats or caps on, and the
word of command being given as vigorously as on parade.
When the Governor was seated, and the veterans, who look
very like Chelsea pensioners, had grounded their pikes and
flags, the service began—all the music being performed by
the military band, the drums being very prominent. The
priest at the altar seemed lost in the military array ; and
certainly all the religious part of the ceremony was completely
obscured by the braying and thumping of the military music.
It seemed to create a good deal of interest in the crowd which
flocked into the church. Along each side of the walls hung
a long array of flags taken in battle, in all stages of decay,
faintly waving with the light air currents. Among them I
noticed two or three English, one apparently a ship's ensign.
There were many Spanish, and doubtless, though I could
not make out more than one or two, a number of Austrian.
I was rather amused with the glee with which one or two
of the groups of holiday-makers, who had come to look at
the church, singled out the big English ensign.

To the Rev. C. M. Church.

PARIS, 1st June 1862.

I have spent to-day at Meaux, Bossuet's see and burial-place ; it is about 1½ hour from Paris on the Strasburg line. The road to it is rather pretty. It soon strikes the Marne, and follows it to Meaux. The Marne flows first (going from Paris) through fine grass fields with lines of poplars, very rich, and almost rank in vegetation ; and then by wooded heights, looking something like wild Nunehams. At one reach of the river there was a pretty sailing-boat, cleanly and sharply built, and fairly cutter-rigged, only with sails cut too broad aloft, beating up the river to a fine bridge, and looking very Isis like. The road also passes through a very pretty bit of woodland, with walks cut through it, part of the confiscated Orleans property, now to be sold in building lots for *petites maisons de campagne*, which abound on the line. The approach to Meaux is pleasing ; the cathedral stands on high ground, and with its remaining west tower and high roof dominates over the town. The church is internally very good, far better than one expected of a cathedral of which Bossuet had been bishop, for somehow there seems a fitness that it should be a grand renaissance or Louis XIV. sort of building. But, on the contrary, it is a singularly pure and beautiful geometrical decorated church ; within two feet as high inside as Nôtre Dame ; with a number of round columnar piers, of the transition between Romanesque and pointed, and with the main features of the tracery and mouldings, as I said, of a very beautiful geometrical kind. The middle aisle is broad, and there are two side aisles on each side, besides the lateral chapels between the wide buttresses. It looks very tidy and clean, without looking

new, of the hue of the stone of Winchester ; and there are
remarkably few altars in it. . . . The wainscotting of the
choir is of the age of Bossuet, and the bishop's throne ; and
what is still more interesting, the pulpit is the one in which
he preached ; it has the date of 1621 on it, before his time.
It is really not much larger than our Whatley pulpit, which
it resembles in general design, except that it has an angel
with a trumpet on the sounding board. They say that his
grave was not disturbed at the Revolution. There is a
modern monument, something of the Cyril Jackson style,
put up in 1820. But, on the whole, there is the cathedral
much as it was when he presided in it. The bishop's palace
is close by, enclosed by the old town walls, with their round
bastions, beneath which is a boulevard on the site of the old
town ditch. I went into the gardens, pretty, with pleached
alleys running round flower-beds and kitchen garden ; but
the interesting part is on the old city rampart. Here
Bossuet built himself a study and a bedchamber, which have
been put in order, and are probably much like what they
were in his day, wainscotted and parquetted. This is on
one of the round bastions ; while along the curtain beyond
is a yew-tree walk, clipped and thick, with little windows
cut in it, like a wall of green, in which, it is said (and I think
also reported by his nephew or editor), that he used to walk
and meditate, and harangue to a train of followers. The
place altogether is very taking, most tranquil, and up on the
wall most retired ; and there is an air of neatness and ease
about the town, or at least this quarter of it, which is very
pleasing. The contrast is wonderful to Paris ; I can hardly
believe myself back again this evening. . . .—Yours affectionately,   R. W. CHURCH.

To Dr. Asa Gray.

WHATLEY, 19th January 1864.

DEAR DR. GRAY—It was very kind of you to give me part of your Christmas Day. It is always a great pleasure to me to see your handwriting.

. . . I congratulate you on your prospect of getting a permanent habitation and ownership for your collections.[1] It must be something like the feeling of having at last well and happily bestowed a favourite child in marriage. There is nothing sadder, I think, in any kind of collecting, than the feeling of uncertainty as to what will become of things on which we have spent our love as well as our money and pains. In such things as favourite books, which one knows by look and feel, and which bear the marks of our converse with them in disfiguring pencil marks and notes, it is really quite painful to think into whose indifferent and unworthy hands they may have to come. And of course this must be much more the case, where a collection has something of a unique character, and is intrinsically precious. So I can quite feel that you must have a weight off your mind in being able to look forward to your plants and books remaining as you have known them, and placed them—together and in a place where they will not lose their interest, and where your gift of them will always be remembered with peculiar interest.

. . . So you have heard of my small piece of ambition,[2] and ambition disappointed. It was a curious little adventure while it was going on. In my private heart I am very glad

[1] A herbarium and botanical library which Dr. Gray had presented to Harvard University.
[2] The Professorship of Ecclesiastical History at Oxford.

that I had not to leave this place, where I have taken fast
root; and a very good man has been appointed. But some
friends, who had a good right to expect their recommendations attended to, were disappointed; and for their sakes I
am sorry. It was Lord.Shaftesbury against Gladstone; and
Lord Shaftesbury for the time had Lord Palmerston's ear;
and besides, he had to object that in the old days of the
Oxford Movement I had been a great friend of Newman's.
However, I am quite satisfied. . . .—Ever yours very
sincerely,   R. W. CHURCH.

Kingsley's attack on Newman, which drew from the
latter his *Apologia*, was an occasion to rouse all the
old affectionate loyalty of Mr. Newman's friends. From
this time, down to Cardinal Newman's death in 1890,
the correspondence was resumed on the old footing of
intimacy and freedom.

To THE REV. W. J. COPELAND.

WHATLEY, 26*th April* 1864.

DEAR COPELAND—I heard yesterday from Newman,
asking me to look over sheets, which of course I will gladly
do. It must be very painful for him to have to go over all
this ground again. I cannot help wishing that he had
spared himself, or at any rate that he had left Kingsley
alone, and said what was to be said without mixing it up
with his quarrel with Kingsley. But he knows better than
I do what best becomes him.

The truth is, he has a hard task before him. . . . When
the whole question comes to be opened afresh, as to what
people who don't agree with Newman are to think of the
legitimacy of the position which he took up, while coming

round to be what they so shrink from and dislike, it will be
a hard matter to make explanations which will satisfy even
candid ones among them.   There is nothing so trying and
so hard in the world as the position of a man who is changing his views, and doing so with due time, and deliberation,
and caution.   The more careful and conscientious and
hesitating he is, the more people insist on flinging charges
of dishonesty and inconsistency against him.   If Newman's
Apologia to the British public succeeds in bringing them
round to judge him fairly, he will have accomplished a
remarkable feat.   He can do it if any man can ; but he runs
a risk.   You see how the row has brought out a man like
* * * to have his shy.   The public and the personal questions are so intermixed, that every one who is afraid of Rome,
or dislikes it, will think himself bound to pronounce against
Newman.   But he must go on, and we must help him as
well as we can.—Ever yours affectionately,   R. W. C.

TO THE REV. J. B. MOZLEY.

WHATLEY, 3rd *February* 1865.

DEAR MOZLEY—Thank you for your brother's account.
How very well he does it.   He brings out so well the points
of Stanley's manner : his rhetorical skill, his aggressive and
defiant pluck, his desperate determination to claim everything and everybody with life in them as on his side.   And
then, after all, what *is* his side ?   What is this nineteenth-
century religion for which all things have been preparing,
and to which all good things, past and present, are sub-
servient and bear witness ?

I saw him in town last week ; we went and drank five-
o'clock tea with him, and found him in great force.   He

showed us over the Deanery, and had his historical anecdotes
for each hole and corner. His wife is very pleasant, and
nothing can be better apparently than the *ménage*. But he
seems to me in the position of a prophet and leader, full of
eagerness and enthusiasm and brilliant talent, all heightened
by success—but without a creed to preach. I suppose he
would say that testifying for liberty and the love of truth
and tolerance is a sufficient creed. But at any rate it can be
only to intellectual people, and the world in general is not of
that sort.

I wish I could come and talk with you about your
subject,[1] and then hear you. I don't think you need fear
that your subject is one of which all that has to be said has
already been said. Stanley's insensibility to the immeasur-
able difference that miracle or no miracle makes in our ideas
of religion has always struck me as the most singular mark
of his want of depth. The course would be worth preaching,
if only to impress on people's minds how much turns on
miracle. I should like to have other talks with you also,
e.g. this Final Appeal Court business, about which I cannot
satisfy myself at all. I do not like clerical judges ; and if
there is to be a creed at all, this legal way of dealing with
theology reduces it to an absurdity.

13th June 1865.

I could not get up to Oxford at the time when I thought
of going. I suppose that you have done your work for the
University, and will soon be addressing the general public·
When do you publish ?

I was in London for a couple of days last week at Rogers',
and met Newman, who was staying there. He had come
for Manning's consecration. It was the first time I had seen

---

[1] *Bampton Lectures* for 1865.

him for twenty years nearly. He was very little changed in look or general manner or way of talking, except that he seemed almost stronger in body. He was in good spirits, very hearty, and talked very freely about all sorts of things ; reminding us every now and then that he was across the border, but without embarrassment, and without any attempt to flaunt anything in our faces. It was a much more easy meeting than I could have supposed possible. We seemed to fall into the old ways of talking. He talked about Manning, and about his own position, and his differences of views about education. He thought Manning had certainly plans, but no one knew what they were ; it was clear, however, that Newman did not much expect them to be what he would lay most stress upon. He spoke of the difficulty of getting interest or money for anything but immediate objects ; the poor, or the training of priests ; while literature, and higher education, and the education of the laity, no one cared much about or thought worth efforts. He spoke of his own school at Birmingham, and of the effect of its example in making the other schools, even the Jesuit schools, less Continental in their ways and more English, as in trusting boys and giving up *espionnage.* The effect was as if he was working his own way, and giving up the general course of affairs to Manning and those who went with the current.

Are you going to be at home all the summer ?—Ever yours affectionately, R. W. C.

The frequent interchange of letters between himself and Dr. Gray had added to the interest with which Mr. Church had followed the varying fortunes of the civil war in America. At its conclusion he writes to Dr. Gray :—

To Dr. Asa Gray.

WHATLEY, 1*st* *November* 1865.

Your letter has been on my conscience for a long while.
I hope that, though the reply to it has been so long in
coming, you will not think that the delay has been owing
to any indifference on my part to the great subject of interest
of which it was full. Astonishing as the war was all through,
the most astonishing part of the whole has been the abrupt-
ness with which it has ended, and the rapidity with which
everything tended to settle down into peace. You have very
difficult questions before you. But, undoubtedly, you have
shown a power of meeting the great trials of a nation that
seems to me new in history. I hope with all my heart that
as you have begun so you will go on. Slavery is destroyed.
I cannot say that, beforehand, I should have said that this
was the way in which it had best be destroyed. But the
thing is done, and I earnestly trust that its consequences may
be controlled in the right direction.

Now that the actual excitement of the struggle is over,
the interest in American affairs is growing less in the newspapers. But any one who has a conception of what history
means must feel, not only that the revolution through which
you have so wonderfully passed is without any parallel in
the story of the world, but that the spectacle of the reconstruction of a nation is going on before us in even a more
astonishing form than when Washington and Hamilton first
laid the foundations of the Union. I only wish I had leisure,
knowledge, and opportunities to enable me to follow and
understand what, I feel, is the most marvellous political
phenomenon of the times I have lived in.

As you see, we have lost Palmerston. While he lived

there was a tacit understanding that no internal battles of
consequence were to be fought or great issues raised. He
was like a great-grandpapa to the English political world,
whose age was to be respected, and whose vivacity, spirit,
and tact saved him from the fate of old men. Now he is
gone, and no one knows what is coming. I am a Conservative by instinct and feeling ; but there is at once a negative-
ness and barrenness, and also a fierceness, about the soi-disant
Conservative party which is not pleasant or hopeful. I
cannot imagine that they can ever govern unless things are
greatly changed. The great interest is to see how Gladstone
will comport himself. It is an awful time for him. The
" heart of all Israel is towards him." He is very great and
very noble. He has been the one man who has done any
effective work in Government lately. But he is hated as
much as, or more than he is loved. He is fierce sometimes,
and wrathful, and easily irritated ; he wants knowledge of
men, and speaks rashly. And I look on with some trembling
to see what will come of this his first attempt to lead the
Commons, and prove himself fit to lead England.

Did you meet two friends of mine who were lately in
America, Goldwin Smith and James Fraser ?

Will you give my kind remembrances to Mrs. Gray.—
Yours very faithfully,   R. W. CHURCH.

Mr. Keble's death took place in April 1866, and
Mr. Church was one of the numerous gathering of
friends, new and old, which met at Hursley for his
funeral. Many memories were wakened by such a
return, of old days at Winchester with Dr. Moberly,
and at St. Cross with his stepfather's family, as well as
of visits to Hursley itself.

To the Rev. W. J. Copeland.

WHATLEY, *7th April* 1866.

I thought that perhaps I might see you yesterday at Hursley, but I was not surprised not to see you. It was more like a festival than anything else, though there was black and white about. But the sun and the fresh keen air, and the flowers just coming out, and the beauty of the place and the church, and the completeness of that which had come to its last stage here, put all the ordinary thoughts of sorrow, not aside, but in a distinctly subordinate place. There were some seventy or eighty people, I should think, at the eight o'clock celebration, with *him* in the midst of us, once more in his chancel, and before the altar. At the service and funeral itself the church was crowded, and Rogers, Dean Hook, and I were glad to get a school children's bench in the corner. Yet it was a strange gathering. There was a meeting of old currents and new. Besides the people *I* used to think of with Keble, there was a crowd of younger men, who no doubt have as much right in him as we have, in their way—Mackonochie, Lowder, and that sort. Excellent good fellows, but who, one could not help being conscious, looked upon us as rather *dark* people, who don't grow beards, and do other proper things.

Peter Young's account of the end was touching. He thought that the anxiety about Mrs. Keble some three weeks ago had overstrained him ; and when she began to rally, then it began to tell on him. Thursday fortnight he got up earlier than usual, and by mistake took a cold bath, which should have been a warm one. In the course of the morning, while reading the service to Mrs. Keble, he felt unwell, and at last fainted. He came to himself again, and the doctors thought it a bilious attack, but it got worse. He began to wander ; and then came erysipelas in the head. On Monday, for the last time, he was removed from Mrs. Keble's room, and she never saw him again. He thought, when he was removed, that he was being taken to church, and knelt down and said the Lord's Prayer. All the time of his wandering, from which, I understand, when once it began he never recovered, he was uttering fragments of prayers and hymns ; and the last words heard from him were a verse of a Latin hymn. At last he became entirely unconscious, till 1 A.M. on Thursday week. They were anxious about the effect on Mrs. Keble of the tidings. Her sister took a crucifixion, which had been at the foot of his bed, and placed it at the bottom of hers, and then she knew that he was gone, and she burst out into deep thanks. But she was so ill that it seemed probable that both would be buried together. But it was not to be, though she is between life and death, and cannot be here much longer. It is an end which could not have been expected, that she should have been spared the trouble of leaving him.

Pusey was there, but I am afraid very poorly, and not able to come to the funeral itself. But I did not see many faces that I knew, though the crowd was so great.—Ever yours affectionately,   R. W. C.

Mr. Church's first sight of Switzerland dates from the autumn of 1866. From this time, until his power of walking began to fail, no pleasure and refreshment equalled that given by his yearly holiday in the Alps. Writing to Dr. Newman a few years later he says : " Do you know the Alps *near ?* I never did till two or three years ago ; and now I feel crazy about them."

To the Rev. C. M. Church.

NEUFCHATEL, 13th September 1866.

We left Paris last night—slept through the old dull
Bourgogne, and woke up with the morning light just before
Pontarlier. The night and morning were as beautiful as each
could be, and served the remarkable railroad and its scenery
well. The look down over the broad plain of Burgundy to
the Côte d'Or, with the valley below, was very fine with the
first sun just striking it. I was surprised at the uplands on
the top, sometimes looking like the wild parts of a park,
sometimes like Mendip and Dartmoor. The gorge with the
Fort de Joux is really fine,—something like Cheddar, with
a fort on the top. And the descent on Neufchatel through
the defile is wonderful as a bit of mere railway travelling,
and exceedingly beautiful besides. The *trajet* was diversified
with a painful spectacle. The village of Travers, near this,
from which the valley takes its name, had caught fire in the
night, and when we passed it had been nearly entirely
destroyed ; eighty or ninety houses gone, and smoking, with
a *bise* blowing up the valley ; the fields and roads about
strewn with the household furniture saved, and the people,
by the pile of things, homeless. Only two or three houses
seemed to have escaped. All the country side filled the
train to go to help or to see, and they told us that the people
would be lodged by the neighbouring villages. There were
some old people at the station who seemed crazy and out of
their senses with the blow. They had engines and plenty
of water. The popular view is that it is incendiarism, as
such fires have been abundant lately. I should think very
hot weather, shingle roofs, and an odd spark or two from
chimneys, was sufficient to account for it. But we saw one

P

fellow in custody, followed by a mob, who, no doubt, assumed his guilt. It was a sad sight coming on a *voyage de plaisir*.

We stayed here to-day, tempted by the beautiful, and, to both of us, perfectly new scene : a cloudless sky, a fresh breeze capping the waves of the lake, and making it look as much like sea as Southampton Water ; and beyond, ghostly, yet cut clear, as if out of the very substance of the sky, the Jungfrau and her brethren in front, and the dim snows of Mont Blanc far away. The first sight of the Bernese Alps, far above a long trailing belt of clouds, and up where no one expected to see them, was positively startling. You know them, but I had never seen them, or any true Alps before ; and certainly they are perfectly unlike anything of the mountain sort I ever saw. We have spent the day looking at them changing as the sun moved on. To-morrow we go to look for lodgings at St. Cergues.

PARIS, 21*st September* 1866.

We stayed at St. Cergues till Monday the 18th. The view was glorious all day long, and there were delightful fir-woods to wander through, with bright green glades, and the cattle, with their bells, making them full of pleasant sound. It was mere lazy holiday-making, looking on and doing nothing, and from time to time going up to the Observatoire Restaurant, perched on its rock, where we made great friends with M. Amat, the keeper of it, a character in his way, who has been put in a book : an odd mixture,—a perfect gentleman, and a Boniface who piques himself on his cuisine ; a humorous sort of recluse, who in the summer carries on the restaurant trade, as much for the amusement of seeing people, and having his *causeries* with them, as for the profit of the thing (though no doubt he does very well) ; and who, in winter, if he does not go to his native Bayonne, spends it on the top of his rock all alone, rising early and going to bed late, reading and writing, in the midst of the snow. It came out that he had early had a great loss,— "une fille de dix-huit ans," but whether daughter or lady-love we did not like to ask ; and now, he says, "je vis de mes souvenirs et de mon avenir." Altogether, though you never can help suspecting a Frenchman, especially in a strange position, he gave one the idea of a man who was not acting, though he liked to put himself *en évidence,* where he thought he would be appreciated, and he plainly likes to be considered, as he is called in a book by one of his friends, "Le philosophe du Jura." He certainly added to the diversion of being at St. Cergues, and probably tempted us to stay : we spent our Sunday there.

. . . From St. Cergues we went to Geneva, which really is very striking : and the rushing of the Rhone below the bridges is glorious. Tuesday we steamered up the lake to Villeneuve, and back to Lausanne. The day, like all our days, was fine and bright, but with mist or thick air about the hills ; but the vaporous gorge, with its varied lines of hills one behind another, like the scenes of a theatre, was, in its way, as grand as any clearer sight of the mountain features could have been. Lausanne is a striking place, with a great modern viaduct connecting an old and new town, and with a very mediæval series of steep wooden steps, under a wooden covering, leading up the side of the hill, to a fine simple thirteenth-century cathedral, which presides over the town. . . .—Yours affectionately,   R. W. C.

Mr. Church's love of the country, which had been

strengthening steadily as the years went by, was acknowledged now with little to qualify it. " There are only two things which I regret in the life I lead here," he writes to James Mozley ; " one is that I never have the chance of good music, such as one gets in London ; the other that it is so difficult to see the world, and I am getting older and older, and such a number of things not seen that I should like to see."

The following letter with its bright glimpse into the home life at Whatley has its part in adding to the completeness of the picture :—

To Dr. Asa Gray.

Whatley, 17th January 1868.

My dear Dr. Gray—The sight of your handwriting gave me a twinge of conscience ; but one of the evils of getting old is, with me, an increasing hardness about my manifold neglects in the matter of letter-writing. But I did feel that you had given me a lesson. I should be indeed sorry to lose the pleasure of corresponding with you, and I cannot help feeling the visible tendencies of my laziness. I can hardly plead hard work, yet somehow I don't find time for things as I used. I suppose that unconsciously " strength faileth " where outwardly all seems the same. For though I am past fifty, I have never fairly got out of the feeling that I am a mere boy. This, with other reasons, would always be an objection with me to being made a bishop.

In all these troubled times, the years, with us, have gone forward very peacefully. There are changes. My boy has grown up into a public school youngster, and has won his place on the foundation at Winchester ; an odd mixture of childishness and cleverness, idleness and interest in work, affection and petulance. He is a curious instance to me of how a boy, of apparently feeble health, works through rough-ness, and seems to thrive and improve under it. I remember the time when I thought it absolutely impossible that he could ever stand school life ; but, step by step, he has gone on, and now is always better at school than at home, though at Winchester the life is rather of a military hardness. Then there are three little girls, still of that delightful age when they have not come to dream of young ladyhood, while they have all the interest of life and quickness, which only mere children have for their dolls. They are companions not the less pleasant and interesting, from the totally different order of ideas in which they move, and the original points of view from which they see things. And so we have been going on. From year to year we see great changes ; but when the changes come about no eye can see. At this moment the whole party, with the boy at the head, are in the shrubbery, showing the effect on his mind of a recent course of Cooper's novels ; and energetically following his lead, while he makes them " be Indians " for him—Mohawks, Delawares, and Shawnees—and they have been pursuing on the war-path, tomahawking and whooping, and displaying the scalps they have taken, all the afternoon.

I was very sorry to hear your news about Mr. Loring. I heard his name from Fraser. And Fraser is a man who would fully prize him. There is a peculiar beauty and tenderness about the relation of a father and daughter, when it takes its full proportions ; I don't know anything like it, and I wonder sometimes that it is so rare. In Mrs. Gray's weak health the loss must be a trying blow. May I send her my most kind remembrances, and the assurance how much she has our sympathy.

Perhaps you have heard that you are likely to have Goldwin Smith to·settle, it is supposed, permanently among you. He had a terrible blow in his father's death. And perhaps that has contributed to make England distasteful to him. I think he has given us up too soon. So much nobleness and elevation are a loss to any society, and we can hardly spare him. But I think that he has latterly been carried away by extremes both of indignation and sympathy; though I must say that such a political year as last year is some excuse for any man.—Yours very sincerely,

R. W. CHURCH.

To THE REV. J. B. MOZLEY.

WHATLEY, 21*st January* 1868.

Do you ever look over old letters? Or perhaps, like a wise man, you do not let them accumulate. I have suddenly discovered that I have great heaps remaining from the old days of Tractarian warfare. I have begun looking over them, to sift at least, and burn largely. One's feelings are very mingled. I can hardly say that I feel quite satisfied or glorious; but there is a mixture of approval too. But those wonderful strings of names appended to protests and memorials are very queer, when one thinks of what Oxford has got to now.

11*th February* 1868.

I spent two or three days in London last week with Rogers. I did two things. I went over the Abbey with Stanley, who was good enough to give us a morning. He is a very good guide, and has it all on his fingers' ends. It certainly is a very impressive place. There is a sort of effect of being in a dream, and meeting all sorts of strange people, from Edward the Confessor to Thackeray, really brought close to you in actual existence, and yet only present by tokens and signs of the most heterogeneous kind. And we had a fine day, and the Abbey itself was very noble.

The other thing was a lecture of Tyndall's at the Royal Institution. It was said not to be one of his best ; but his experiments were curious, and neat, and uniformly successful. But all the time I could not help a kind of sense of the insolence of the man, such as he appeared to be, claiming to bring all truth within what he called science. There was hardheadedness, originality, and sometimes a touch of imagination. But there seemed to be also a hard and hopeless onesidedness, as if nothing in the world would open his eyes to the whole domain of soul and spirit close about him, and without which he would not be talking or devising wonderful experiments.—Ever yours affectionately,

R. W. C.

To Dr. Asa Gray.

WHATLEY, 11th December 1868.

MY DEAR DR. GRAY—I received your note from Hyères, which revived some very strong longings of old date. I was in that country in 1847, about the same time of year, and, to my sorrow, I have never seen it again. I wish you had seen Arles and Orange, where there is a wonderful Roman theatre, with the great scene wall still standing ; and the Pont du Gard. But it is unkind to awaken fruitless regrets.

. . . Well, you will ere this have heard of the issue of the great election fight, which sent so many heroes to Hades, and caused such wounds and wrath. Dizzy acted wisely in throwing up the game when it was no longer any

use carrying it on ; and he retires with the glory, such as it
is, of having done what no other man in England could have
done.   For the first time a Quaker becomes the " Right
Honourable," and sits in the Council, only making an affir-
mation instead of an oath.   For the first time the Irish Lord
Chancellor is a Roman Catholic—and I suppose, though it is
shockingly uncharitable to say so—a great lawyer—Roundell
Palmer, with the English Lord Chancellorship not only within
his grasp, but actually by the voice of the profession and the
country inviting and begging him to take it, has resolutely
foregone the great prize, because he thinks the proposed Irish
measure, which his party are to carry, deficient in complete
justice.   The change has, as yet, made little difference to the
world at large.   But we have a Ministry, of newer blood,
and more detached from the old routine, than any within
living memory.   The House of Commons, on the other hand,
seems made up of much the same materials, and Gladstone
will have a tough job to keep it in order.   There never was
a man so genuinely admired for the qualities which deserve
admiration—his earnestness, his deep popular sympathies,
his unflinching courage—and there never was a man more
deeply hated, both for his good points and for undeniable
defects and failings.   But they love him much less in the
House than they do out of doors.

I beg your pardon for being so political when I am writing
to be read within view of the Pyramids.   I will forward the
Times on the chance when there is anything worth seeing.
There is a curious, and, as far as I remember, rather novel
bit of popular enthusiasm in the "handshaking" at Windsor
Station of Gladstone and Bright, in a number which gives
the account of the swearing in of the Ministers.—Ever yours
affectionately,   R. W. CHURCH.

To Sir Frederic Rogers.

WHATLEY, *7th January* 1869.

MY DEAR ROGERS—I had on Tuesday a very kind note
from Gladstone, offering me a vacant Canonry at Worcester.
When I began writing on the Irish Church last year, I made
up my mind that possibly something of the kind might
ensue; and that, going against the general Church feeling,
and in favour of a policy which was sure to bring its leaders
into power, I should have to give some proof that I had not
been writing for the good things which such writing might
bring me. It is a question like the old Roman Catholic
Emancipation contest; and I felt that it might be difficult
to take anything when Gladstone should be in power. But
the great kindness of his note shook me. The Canonry
itself, though an inviting one, would not have much affected
me; but he put the offer in terms which made it hard to
say no.

But I came back to my first resolution. There was,
indeed, nothing to change it, except the feeling of gratitude
for the way in which the offer was made. But on the other
hand, the last few years seem to me to have so brought back
the old spirit of preferment-seeking among the clergy, and
especially the Conservative and moderate High Church clergy
—for of course the Ritualists have no chance—and infidel
writers, like those in the *Pall Mall*, are avowedly counting so
confidently on the self-seeking and ambitious habits of the
clergy—that it seemed to me more important, even towards
the success of Gladstone's own policy, that it should seem
possible that High Churchmen should support it disinterest-
edly, than that I should become a slightly bigger man as
Canon of Worcester. I think I am more alive than I was to

the call to accept responsibilities;—I don't know, perhaps not:—but there was something in the feeling of the old Tractarian days which, as far as I remember, quenched the thought of preferment. I found it hard to bear the idea of being held up as an example of the lucky High Churchman, who managed just at the right moment to pronounce in favour of what two-thirds of his brethren consider an anti-Church policy in Ireland.

So I said no ; never, I think, with greater regret ; not for the thing refused, but for the refusal itself, and the impossibility of explaining it to him. I send you Gladstone's letter : please return it. Curiously, the last appointed Canon of Worcester was Wynter of St. John's, my old V.-C. when I was proctor, and chairman of various anti-Gladstonian Election Committees, appointed by Lord Derby.—Ever yours affectionately,   R. W. C.

To DR. ASA GRAY.

WHATLEY, 5th April 1869.

The newspapers will have told you how the world goes on. The great parliamentary question of the Irish Church is, I suppose, settled. If it were possible to make the change less violent and rough, one would almost wish for a more powerful opposition. But this is hopeless, and therefore I do not regret that the matter should be settled decisively. There will be a great deal of hardship and some wrong ; and the immediate effect will probably be imperceptible in reconciling Ireland to her elder sister. But it is not an easy thing for a nation to clean its hands, and I am willing to make much allowance for the probable imperfections and clumsinesses of the process.

We are here much as we were : reading, parochialising, and so forth. We have our village concert to-morrow evening. I hope it will do my wife's untiring work with her singers some credit. I am just reading an interesting book, Lecky's *History of European Morals*,—a book of much reading and candour, but which does not reach my ideal standard of either. It is an old commonplace, unfortunately too true, that theologians and apologists colour and soften ; but I must add that the propensity is not a bit less apparent in philosophical historians, though they are often just as well intentioned. I have come, too, on two volumes from · your side of the water, Lowell's volume with his *Commemoration Ode.* Lowell seems to me the most perfect exponent in poetry, of the sense of national greatness, of any one that I know. The other book is *Hans Breitmann*, who, detestable as he often is, has real genius in the queer line he has chosen. He has caught strong hold of the *Spectator.*

We are beginning to amuse ourselves with Alpine plans. Our present thought is to spend the end of June and July round Monte Rosa as a centre, chiefly on the Italian side. But it is still some while to that. . . .—Ever yours affectionately, R. W. CHURCH.

The appointment of Dr. Temple to the see of Exeter woke afresh the outcry that had been provoked by *Essays and Reviews*, to which he had been one of the contributors :—

TO DR. ASA GRAY.

WHATLEY, *5th November* 1869.

The outcry against Temple is, I think, most unjust, and in its violence very discreditable. It is the direct result of the extravagant measures which were taken years ago against the *Essays and Reviews*.   People then got committed, in Convocation and elsewhere, to a false position against it, and now they are obliged, in consistency, to shriek at the very name of it.   Temple, as you say, is certainly not in the same boat even with Stanley.   He is a man of strong, masculine earnestness, sympathising with the masses ; and alive to, and perhaps even frightened by, the powerlessness of speculation to meet the difficulties of mankind in general. I believe he will make one of our best bishops.   But the agitation, I think, threatens to be very mischievous.   We have not so many great names on the religious side, that we can afford to see a man like Pusey, who is a man after all to rank with religious leaders of a high mark in all ages, casting away all the lessons of a lifetime, and countenancing the worst violence of a zealot like * * *   We shall smart for all this.   Mere disestablishment will be the least of the mischiefs.   Seeing a man learned and religious as Pusey is, so blindly unjust and intemperate, is a heavy blow against that which is more dear to Pusey than life. . . .—Ever yours affectionately,   R. W. CHURCH.

To THE REV. C. M. CHURCH.

WHATLEY, *9th November* 1869.

DEAR CHARLES—Everything went off right at Windsor, and the Queen was not too tired with Saturday to come to service. . . . I had a pleasant stroll with the Dean in the private grounds, and a good deal of interesting talk.   He is a capital host, and sets you at ease at once ; and the house is a pleasant one.

. . . I feel like a boy home for the holidays.   I have got something to do for Macmillan, and then comes the Christmas Ordination, which is a bore. But I hope I have done with sermons for a good while. I will send you the Westminster one[1] in a few days. I was requested to leave the Windsor one behind again.—Ever yours affectionately,   R. W. C.

The year spent by Dr. and Mrs. Gray in Europe, during which they had found time to pay a visit to Whatley, and for a few weeks were together with Mr. and Mrs. Church in Switzerland, had added new strength to the friendship between them.

To Dr. Asa Gray.

Whatley, 24th December 1869.

MY DEAR FRIEND—First, we must wish you joy on having got over your voyage, though I am afraid that it must have been a disagreeable kind of dream for you. . . . Next, as this is Christmas Eve, we must wish you a very happy, and even merry, Christmas.   It is strange to think that you are gone. You had seemed so near us for so long—for even in Egypt there was the looking forward to seeing you—that it needs an effort to remember that you are really across the Atlantic, for some time at least.

We are all well : holidays have begun, and brought back with them my boy from Winchester College ; a queer creature, with weak frame and languid health, and quick brain and tongue, whose interests are divided between his classical work, his fossils, and, in summer, his cricket.   Just now at home the geological rage is at its height ; every corner and every

---

[1] Preached at the consecration of Dr. Moberly as Bishop of Salisbury, in Westminster Abbey, on St. Simon and St. Jude's day, 1869.

chair is covered with precious Terebratulæ and Rhynconellæ, which, if any one approaches (and it is hard in our little house not to approach them if one moves), he flies out in wrathful fear and distress, and objects to any one being touched. What the housemaid does under the circumstances I cannot imagine, except give herself a conscientious holiday from all dusting and scrubbing ; and meanwhile the house looks like a place where people had scraped their muddy boots on every chair and table. But I am assured that the apparent mud is most valuable and interesting, full of wonderful remains, which are waiting their turn to be assorted, and classified, and ticketed. And everybody pays deference ; especially the young gentleman's sisters, in whose eyes, very properly, he is a great hero. It is very amusing, and the eagerness is satisfactory. . . .

You see I go off rambling, while the Œcumenical Council is sitting, and the world is agape to know whether it will decree personal infallibility, and what is to become of Bishop Dupanloup and his companions ; and while here, Bishop Temple has been consecrated, and, by our folly and childish exaggeration of what we don't like, a very serious beginning of division has been established in the English Church. Temple was unbending, and would not give place to subjection, no, not for an hour : perhaps he was right, but though the opposition to him was unscrupulous and unmeasured, he ought to have understood that he had given, and by his own admission, some ground for distrust to a great mass of the body in which he was to bear high office ; and explanations might, I think, have been given, both in charity and in wisdom, without any compromise of liberty. However, all is over now, and we have an energetic, high-souled, and, I believe, most religious bishop ; but it is a grave fact that four Bishops recorded their formal protests at the last moment against his consecration, and four more, not formally, expressed their dissent. The Archbishop, whom we saw so well at Westminster, has had a formidable paralytic attack, and, I should think, would never be fit for work again. Temple was consecrated by a commission of Bishops.

I have been doing work as examiner at Salisbury, for the candidates for orders. And now I feel myself quite comfortable at home again, looking forward to next summer's run in Switzerland. . . .—Ever yours affectionately,

R. W. CHURCH.

To THE REV. J. B. MOZLEY.

WHATLEY, 29*th January* 1870.

MY DEAR MOZLEY—The times are curious, and I wish I could have a talk with you. But I see no chance of getting a week just now. I am just come back from spending a day at Fraser's. He had been down to Manchester, and was pleased at his reception. He is sent there as an Educationist, which seems to be the thing Manchester is full of: and I suppose he knows a good deal about that, and can take a line upon it with some weight. . . . Fraser's letters of congratulation have been many and warm. His great love and reverence for Hamilton are a drag upon his liberalism. I should think his rule would be a firm and also a generous one. The Provost's notes were very characteristic ; Nestor-like precepts, and stories about the failures and successes of other bishops, and nicely qualified courtesies to Fraser himself. Fraser is a good deal subdued by the change ; and also much amused at the tremendous reversal which his costume has to go through, and the extraordinary measurings

of the Episcopal tailors, and the strange apparatus which
they display before him, and tell him that he must have.
Moberly is flourishing at Salisbury. I was there for the
Christmas Ordination, and found him brisker and in better
health than I have seen him for many years. The open air
work suits him ; and I believe that he does his confirmations,
etc., very well. The palace in summer time must be one of
the most charming places in England.

What a wonderful affair this Roman Council is getting !
It seems to me almost the most crowning even ░░ the age,
and one which no one could have imagined poss ░░. And
I suppose it really would not have happened but for Manning
and Ward. I never could have guessed that it would have
precipitated, like a chemical reagent, all this mass of recal-
citrant independence, which is not Protestantism, nor even
Gallicanism, but simply secret hatred, and contempt, and
indignation at the Roman Court and its tricks and humbug.
One's old feelings towards Heads of Houses, Symons and Co.,
make one partly understand how fellows like Dupanloup are
dealt with, and how they don't like it. There is a good deal
of Nemesis in it, for all their past flatteries and unctuous
rhetoric about Rome and the Pope. I should think that at
Rome they could not have anticipated all this fuss, or they
would have done without the Council, which they quite well
might have done. But now I don't see how they can help
passing the personal infallibility. Not to do it, or to evade
it, would simply be to show themselves beaten by internal
disunion. They had better risk schism, which I don't expect,
however, than that. It may cost them a great deal in the
next generation, but I doubt whether they care for that.
The world is full of warnings to people that they may be
taken at their word, and that they had better measure their

statements, and not talk big ; but the position of the French bishops is one of the most remarkable ones.—Ever yours affectionately,   R. W. CHURCH.

To DR. ASA GRAY.

WHATLEY, 4th February 1870.

MY DEAR FRIEND—I suppose by this time that you and Mrs. Gray must almost have forgotten that this time last year you were in Egypt, and that only a few months ago we were all lying on the turf, counting the flowers on the Riffelberg. I hope that both of you find that you have brought back a good fund to draw upon in the winter, and for work.

You will have heard before now of Fraser's elevation. I knew that it was coming sooner or later. But if a place could have been looked out for him to suit him, it would have been hard to find a better place than Manchester. He is a man of large sympathies and fixed opinions of his own ; ever since I knew him, independent and able to resist the currents from different sides which have swept across clerical opinion during his time ; but always winning not only respect but affection from people with whom he has been associated, and who are as widely separated from one another as the late Bishop Hamilton of Salisbury and Mr. Liddon are from Mr. Lingen and the authorities at the Privy Council office. His manner has something of the offhandedness of a boy, and with his large knowledge and practical shrewdness there is a curious boyish simplicity about him. But he knows his work, and his heart is in it, and I hope a good deal from him at Manchester. But no doubt he will come on trying times.

I think, sometimes, that we are nearer than we know to

a great break-up. The difficulty is beginning to be more visible every day, of reconciling a Church with great privileges with the general set of modern policy; of combining a National Church with a Church having the *raison d'être* of a religious society, believing in a definite religion, and teaching it. Generosity, consciousness of our ignorance and liability to prejudice, and honest tolerance, may keep things together for a time ; but tolerance is apt to take the form of mere indifference or absence of convictions ; consciousness of ignorance requires more knowledge than most people have ; and generosity sometimes is merely making free with what other people value and you don't care for, and what calls itself by that name is often a very questionable quality. So, one of these days, I expect that we shall find ourselves put into the position of having to choose between making the Church coextensive with what can be called the religion of the whole nation or giving up our present position. I think it will be an evil thing for the present generation at least when that time comes ; for certainly no machinery, that I can see, could take the present place of the Church in the country districts ; and with all their innumerable short-comings, the English clergy, as a whole, have worked well and hard for the poor and helpless, who would be badly off without them. But no doubt the time must come. But I wish we could wait at least till there was less fierceness like that called forth by Temple's appointment ; till Churchmen were more large-minded, and Dissent less vulgar and bigoted. People are so committed on all sides to hastily professed views and old parties, that there will be a great many false positions if the break-up comes, and the bitterness will be aggravated by people reproaching one another with incon-sistency and unfaithfulness to their principles. It is like the Roman infallibility tangle. People there have been talking rhetoric for ages, beyond their real thought, and now that they are taken at their word they are all in confusion. But I suppose it is a long time off before people learn the danger of talking beyond their meaning.

1st March 1870.

Here is a regular wet afternoon, and as there is no going out, and perhaps I may not always have time for letter-writing, I shall devote part of it to you. . . .

I stayed with Fraser some three weeks ago. I have not heard that he is consecrated; but he is looked upon as a great acquisition, especially just now, with the Education question before Parliament. The two great bills have been well received in England,—not, of course, in Ireland,—and ministers, I hear, are in high spirits, though of course they are not out of the wood yet. But certainly no man we have ever had has matched Gladstone in the grasp and daring, combined with thorough detailed knowledge of his great legislative constructions. Doubtless there are powers stronger than he. But we have not known what a really strong minister is in all the time between him and Pitt. Peel was very powerful, from his very caution, combined with thorough political integrity; but he had not genius and boldness. Gladstone's weak point is what is most amiable in him, his strong vein of sentiment. It is the spring of what is noblest about his impulses; but it is a perilous quality too.

WHATLEY, *25th May* 1870.

MY DEAR FRIEND—I have been suffering the pains of a bad conscience and shame for some time past, when my eye caught your last letter lying unanswered on my study table; but you probably don't know how a little extra work brings, not fatigue, but a fit of wanton idleness, with its vain self-deceits and excuses. But I really was going to write this week even if I had not been wakened up by Mrs. Gray's reminder to my wife. I can suppose all that she tells one of your hard work just now. Flowers will not wait even for professors ; and I suppose that the throng of them comes in with a rush with you even more than with us. We are most beautiful just now. The year has been backward, very dry lately, and north winds. The rain has not yet come, but the green has, and the sun, and astonishing boundless light, φῶς ἄσπετον, which seems to make the visible world, even in day, so much greater than it seems in winter ; and one goes about thinking of bits from all the poets one can remember, to give some touches of the wonder and glory, which become greater, to my mind, every year one lives. But you see I am going mad.

I am afraid that we must do without Switzerland this year. I have got to look after the rebuilding of our church, and I do not much like to be away. So one of my years of walking in the mountains must be given up : perhaps to be a little made up for by an autumn run in Normandy and the north of France.

. . . The year has not been very excited ; but it is marked in my calendar as a very important one. The debates on the Education Bill have made it clear that the position of the Church of England, whether disestablished or not, will soon undergo a great change. Forster's Education Bill was meant to be studiously impartial in its dealing with religious teaching. Its effect would have been to leave everybody free ; but where there was no preponderating religious tendency in the direction of non-conformity, as is generally the case in the country, there the Church, from legal position, tradition, usage, and because the parson was the person on whom the expense and trouble of schools had long fallen, would have an advantage, because there was really no rival influence. But this has stirred the antagonism of the Nonconformists generally, and they have thrown themselves on the secular, and really the unbelieving side, rather than let the Church get an additional hold on the country. I am sorry for it. I should not be for an Established Church in a country like this, if all was to begin *de novo*. But with our history, habits, and conditions of life, what damages the Church, damages the best chances of simple, unsectarian religion. It would be a long time before any system could grow up to take the place of our parish churches and superintendence in country places.

Have you seen a striking essay by Matthew Arnold, "St. Paul and Protestantism"?—Ever yours affectionately,

R. W. CHURCH.

To SIR FREDERIC ROGERS.

WHATLEY, *3rd July* 1870.

MY DEAR ROGERS—I have not had time to tell you about Newman's visit, which was duly chronicled in the local papers. It was very pleasant. He was very well and happy, walking and even running, though it was that very hot weather. I took him to Longleat, and you know how he lets himself go when he enjoys being out in the air on a fine day, and looking at what he thinks beautiful ; and Marston and Longleat looked their best for him. He made himself quite at home with Helen and the children ; with the children he compared notes about children's books, which has ended in their sending him, and his very heartily accepting, one of their books of nonsense, *Alice's Adventures in*

Wonderland, which he did not know, and they thought he ought to. He talked very freely and a great deal ; neither seeking nor avoiding subjects, but taking everything as it turned up, and becoming very animated at times. It was curious to learn, what of course is very natural, only it does not occur to outsiders, that there are degrees, and considerable ones, in the "Infallibilist" party ; and that the passing of the Definition, in the shape in which it is likely to be passed, is looked on by some of them as almost a failure, to be deplored and to be wretched about, as not going far enough. He is anxious about the future of his school at Birmingham. I should gather from what he said that the Jesuits pick up the most promising of the converts from us. I must stop.—Ever yours affectionately,   R. W. C.

The progress and fortunes of the Franco-Prussian war were filling all minds through the autumn and winter of 1870. He writes to his brother and to Dr. Gray :—

To THE REV. C. M. CHURCH.

WHATLEY, *6th September* 1870.

DEAR CHARLES— . . . Well—1848 if not 1792 is back again, and in a very ugly form. It is scarcely credible. I cannot think of the parallel of such a fall, so rapid and so great. It shakes one very uncomfortably out of those tacit assumptions of immunity from the disasters of less favoured nations, in which I, at least, catch myself commonly dwelling. I remember at Salisbury during the Assize week, the very acute Judge Willes being perfectly scornful, as at a piece of ignorant and idiotic wantonness, at the suggestion of any real struggle at the beginning of the war ; the French,

it was as clear as anything could be, would begin with their
irresistible rush ; and it was only a question how the
Germans in the end would recover themselves and per-
severe.

Now, I suppose, a different sort of struggle will begin.
The Colviles are safely back ; the Horners are expected.
They were at Mayence on Saturday, and Horner sent me an
"extra-blatt" with the news just come in, "Napoleon hat
capitulirt." They will come through Belgium and Holland.
—Ever yours affectionately,   R. W. C.

To Dr. Asa Gray.

Whatley, 13th September 1870.

What have been your thoughts during this wonderful two
months ? What is one to think ? How is one to judge ?
What is one to wish ? My own feelings and opinions go
through half a dozen variations in the course of the day, and
the end is,—I feel beat. It is so easy to condemn French
insolence, to rejoice over so signal a vengeance, to admire
German thoroughness and devotion, to be enthusiastic over
military skill and success such as the world seems never to
have seen the like of ; but it is as easy to see that ever since
Count Bismarck guided Germany, Germany, if triumphant
and mighty, has caught the audacity and unscrupulousness of
the Prussia of Frederick the Great ; that she has taken to
picking quarrels, that her policy has been provocative and
disquieting, that this very war with France, of which undoubtedly French folly and wickedness gave the signal, is
the very thing to serve the Prussian statesmen's end—the
welding together, by a bloody and successful struggle, North
and South Germany. With all my wishes for a grand and

united Vaterland, the means which, it seems to me, have been
deliberately chosen to bring it about are simply hateful ; as
hateful as Napoleon's *coup d'état* and demoralising despotism,
which have succeeded for nearly twenty years in making
France the first nation of Europe.   I believe that the law
of retributive justice is for Germany as well as for France,
and that from one, as from the other, it will wait to claim
its due.

But was ever such a downfall seen as the Empire's ?   One
has to go back to the Old Testament prophets to find words
to express one's feelings.   You must be reminded of Sher-
man's piercing and disclosing the hollowness of the South.
It was time that it should end, for it was false and base,
though so much that is pleasant and charming in France is
gone with it for our generation.   But it looks as if France
needed to be purified and braced, and that the only way was
by going through the depths of adversity.   If Frenchmen
have any stuff in them, and I cannot doubt it, the trials and
sacrifices and humiliations of this astonishing war ought to
make them more manly and more modest.   They are too
grand a race, with all their faults, to be missed out of the
civilised world.   But if ever a nation seemed on the point of
hopeless ruin, it is France just now.

The very air seems full of wonders.   You will have heard
of our famous turret ship, *Captain*, going down in three
minutes, in a mere common squall, with five hundred of the
best blood and the best skill of the navy in her.   And to-day
the Italian troops are to march on Rome, to finish up the
great Roman drama of the year, and put the finishing touch
to the decree of Papal Infallibility. . . .

I was very much obliged for the Memoir of Mr. Loring.
I still often wish that I could come out and know some of

those good people of yours by seeing them at home. Perhaps it will come about some day, unless our poor old world is going to be driven into a new course, and the cycle which began at the end of the last century is going to begin again. It is your turn now to look on at the wonderful vicissitudes of fate.—Ever yours affectionately,   R. W. CHURCH.

During the leisure of this year Mr. Church had been engaged in transforming his two essays on Anselm, which had originally appeared in the *British Critic*, into a volume of Macmillan's *Sunday Library*.

To THE REV. J. B. MOZLEY.

WHATLEY, 29*th October* 1870.

Doing *Anselm* a second time was rather tiresome work. The getting it up was almost as troublesome as the first time, without the zest of a new subject. But I am glad I have done it, because I think the character deserves it. What you say is so true, not merely about the many sides of the character, so much beyond what was to be expected in his time and position, but about the kind of "elegance" that there is about him, with an entire unconsciousness of the idea of grace or elegance at all. He almost answers to Matt. Arnold's requirements of "sweetness and light," in the free way in which he lets his thought return upon itself, and play about common subjects and received words and formulas.

I wish you would follow out your thought about the great men who have been checks to their own side and party. I suppose the position of some of the freer thinking High Churchmen of the seventeenth century, like John Hales, was something of the kind. I did not know it of

T. Scott.   I should think that things could be quoted of
Wesley of the same kind, which have been swept away in
the great current of popular Methodism.

Another matter to occupy thought and time during
1870 was the restoration of the little village church.
Within the first few years of his coming to Whatley,
Mr. Church had at his own cost restored the chancel
of the church, and at length he was to see the completion of the work.   A touch of affection was stirred
for what was to pass away, ugly and homely as it was.
"I felt," he wrote at Christmas to Miss Colvile, an
absent parishioner, "that we were taking leaving of the
church as it is and has been since I have been here;
and the last meeting, even with the horrid old pews,
which we have been accustomed to so long, has something touching in it.   'On ne se détache jamais sans
douleur,' Pascal says—even from the church decorations
of old William Shore.   Next Christmas I hope we shall
look better."

To Dr. Asa Gray.

Whatley, 31st October 1870.

My dear Friend—Here is your letter just come, and I
have an uncomfortable misgiving that I already owe you for
two.   I hope I may be mistaken.   But I have been in such
a whirl of brick and mortar thoughts of late, that I have
quite lost count of my friends' letters, and of everything but
the daily telegrams from France.   This will tell you that I
am not yet out of my church building troubles, but we hope
to be out on Thursday next, 3rd November. . . . We hope
to get the Bishop of Salisbury to do us a good turn, and

come and preach at our opening. I wish you could see our little old church with its new face. It is still plain and quiet, as it ought to be, but with a little more care about forms and shapes, and about goodness of material. I know you feel interest about such things, as when you had the Herbarium in hand, and you will sympathise with the anxieties and fuss of a brother builder. The work has kept us here all the summer. It will be a thing to remember that it was contemporaneous with the downfall of the French Empire.

As you say, it is one astonishing solution succeeding another. War seems all of a sudden to have assumed the dimensions of scientific conquest, and almost to rival it in precision of foresight and work. It is rather corrupting, I think, to see such military success without the counter-check of a really national cause, such as you had in your war. Surely it will be a revival in Europe of the war fever of Napoleon and Frederick the Great. Poor France ! my feelings go backwards and forwards ; how terribly appropriate is the chastisement for her special offences, insolent meddling, and incredible recklessness about veracity ; and then, how piteous the sight is of a nation like France, so full of all that is charming and kindly and good, fairly going to pieces, not knowing how to give in even if she wished it. It is a terrible commentary on the effect on the tone and fibre of a nation of a rule like that of the Imperial Court. I should feel more sympathy with Germany, if it was only a question of its being welded together. It has a right to be one ; it has a right to all the power which it would have as one ; and if it could really be a powerful confederation like yours, I for one should not envy it, or argue that any one had a right, from ideas of " balance of power," to hinder or embarrass it. But I cannot get quit of the belief that German unity,

at present, means simply the predominance of a great military
monarchy at Berlin, animated by the spirit of a feudal caste
which looks on soldiership and war as the highest and most
honourable of human occupations. Bismarck has turned the
German longing for nationality and unity into the weapon
of Prussia, just as the elder Napoleon turned the revolutionary spirit of France into an engine for a conquering
despotism. And this abates much of my sympathy for
German success, though I think that, putting scruples apart,
both German feeling and German soldiership are the most
complete and masterly display of the qualities which lead
nations to greatness that the world has seen. . . .

I sent you *Anselm*, which I hope you have got by this
time. I am glad you met Tom Hughes. He is a man who
may do good to both of us on each side of the water by his
manly honesty and enthusiasm for truth and right.

Thank you much for the seeds of the *Passiflorae*. I hope
I shall have some work with them. You see Darwin's new
book is coming soon. Our kindest remembrances to Mrs.
Gray ; and I do not give up the hope of crossing the continent and seeing the Wellingtonias.—Ever yours affectionately,

R. W. Church.

The following letter describes a confirmation at
Portland Convict Prison at which Mr. Church, as
chaplain to the Bishop of Salisbury, was present :—

To his Wife.

Weymouth, *4th December* 1870.

We have had a capital day ; very cold, but bright and
sunny and successful. We drove off to Portland about nine ;
the views were fine, with the broken sunlight striking on the

Chesil beach. At the prison we were received by the governor, admiral, chaplains, etc., and processed into the chapel between *blocks* of convicts. They are dressed in whitey brown jackets and breeches, blue stockings, and shoes. There were some 1200 or 1300 in chapel, a great cruciform hall, cut up into separate partitions for groups of two or three hundred. The group who were to be confirmed sat in front of the altar ; there were about sixty on this occasion, rather more than last year. There was Morning Prayer, and the ante-Communion service, the canticles being chanted, and two or three hymns. The general behaviour was most orderly and quiet ; of course each group was under the guard of some six or eight warders, raised above them, and watching them. Those who were nearest to us, and who were to be confirmed, were more than orderly ; they were, as far as one could see, really attentive in the service and at the sermon. The singing was very impressive coming from such a body of male voices, and such voices. I never shall forget the way in which, in the *Te Deum*, they sang very solemnly and slowly, " We believe that Thou shalt come to be our Judge." The Bishop's address to the men after confirmation (he confirmed them one by one) was as good as I can conceive for the occasion—manly, earnest, delicately sympathetic, straight from man to man ; and if one could judge from looks—and they were very natural—it was *felt*. It was a day more to be remembered than most.

Then we lunched on board the *Boscawen* training ship, and looked at the ironclads ; and I struck up an alliance with the first lieutenant, who asked me to come off to-morrow to go on board some of the big ships. The confirmation on the *Boscawen* is to be to-morrow at one o'clock.—Ever yours affectionately,   R. W. C.

To Sir Frederic Rogers.

Whatley, 16th January 1871.

My dear Rogers —I share your indignation in part; but it is with me so balanced by another current of indignation, that I hardly know which of the two is my real feeling. I go backwards and forwards from one to the other. With your wrath against the strange and scandalous lying with which the French have tried to help out their shortcomings I go with all my heart. That a whole nation, or at least all speaking in its name, should have suddenly disclosed such a rooted habit of falsehood and imposture, is a terrible bit of the modern natural history of man. One used to think Carlyle's account of Barrère's *Vengeur* a little over-coloured. But Barrère has been beaten by Gambetta. His trust in lying is fatal to his character ; for though I think a great many things may be done and suffered in such a cause and conflict, gross systematic lying is not one of them.

But I think there is a good deal to be said for French obstinacy, and hoping against hope. I think that now the Loire army is at an end, as I suppose it is, the end of hope is come. But up to this point I think the French chances, though poor, were not worthless, and were such as to make continued resistance to be naturally felt the most sacred of political duties by a Frenchman.

I think peace ought to have been made after Sedan, and it was the fault of Paris and its leaders that it was not made. But it was not only, nor I think mainly, their fault that it was not made. We must not say that France would not confess itself beaten. It was abundantly willing to do so. It had received the most cruel punishment and humiliation that any great nation has received, without being actually

ruined, like Prussia after Jena ; this surely was part of the
penalty of the war, and in spite of the "not one stone of
our fortresses," other penalties and humiliations might have
been got, if negotiations could have been *bonâ fide* set
going. But the Prussians would not make peace easy ; they
determined to have the additional revenge of marching to
Paris, and they were possessed with that fatal delusion about
drawing the teeth of their enemy. And so, to their great
surprise and against their calculations, Paris held out, and
the war went on. And I think it would have gone on with
us, if after a great naval disaster the terms of peace had
been the surrender of Ireland ; and we should have been
willing to suffer as much as France before we accepted those
terms.

You see my disgust at French lying and vapouring and
vanity, abominable and astonishing as it is, is mixed with
another feeling, of which I feel it difficult to express the
strength. I have not words to express my admiration at the
unequalled intellectual greatness of the Prussian success ;
its preparations, its magnificent uninterrupted march, its
absolute unchequered triumph. It beats Napoleon hollow,
for it depends so much less on imposture, and so much more
on long, underground, patient headwork. But I also have not
words to express my fear and detestation of the morality and
political spirit and temper which has been the mainspring of
this great achievement of human intellect. It seems to me the
revival of the military barbarism of the kings and nobles of
the old times, with all the appliances of modern knowledge
to help them, and make them more horribly proud, arrogant,
relentless in their will, contemptuous of right in their
means, unmeasured in their claims. The French wickedness,
their conceit and lies and chattering insolence, seem to me

almost childish by the side of the deliberate pride of force
of which the German nature is so capable, and which seems
to me to have disclosed itself in such proportions since
Bismarck and William of Prussia became its masters, and
have taught it its strength.   What it may be is seen in the
obstinate and insolent persistence in the cry about our want
of neutrality, when the Americans are allowed to go on ex-
porting arms a hundred-fold, without a word being said, without the Germans choosing to see and believe that they do it.

I am rambling.   I entirely give up Gambetta as a
charlatan and mischief-making busybody.   I admit that if
France could not conquer without him it had better have
submitted to its fate.   But I could not say so much without
at the same time saying that I cannot condemn in the same
way the policy itself of resistance, even at Paris, barring the
lies (though I hope Trochu did not know of Chanzy's defeat
when he wrote his proclamation).   I think,—granting war
at all,—that there are occasions, as in the struggle of the
Dutch against Spain, when disasters are a possession worth
having for a nation, almost as valuable as successes.   They
are measures and standards of national temper, endurance,
and self-devotion ; and till the case is desperate, which I
think it is only just becoming, it seems to me that the
French are justified in resisting, and that great allowance
must be made for men in such straits.   The miserable thing
is that there is no trace in them of that " jugement héroïque,
dont le principal usage est de distinguer l'extraordinaire de
l'impossible."   And it may be that people who have not
that power of seeing " le point de la possibilité " ought to
renounce a conflict which they ought to feel themselves
unable to direct. . . .—Ever yours affectionately,

R. W. CHURCH.

In 1871 changes were preparing both for himself and his friends. Bishop Fraser had gone to Manchester in the previous year, and in January following, Dr. Mozley accepted the Regius Professorship of Theology in Oxford. Mr. Church in writing to his brother, and after commenting with great satisfaction upon the appointment, continues :—

WHATLEY, 30th January 1871.

Mozley, I take it, will not *draw*. But no one of any mind can mistake about his originality, subtlety, and grasp of his subject. He inspires respect even if he fails to convince, with antagonists like Tyndall and the secularists of the *National Reformer*. . . . But it is very curious to go back in remembrance twenty-five or thirty years ago, and think of what Mozley and his prospects were then ; a man whom a few people, such as Newman, or old Dr. Routh, recognised as a man of singular powers, but whom, with his slow ways and fastidious choice of thoughts and words, the general opinion held very cheap ; who tumbled into a *third* like his brother Tom ; who vainly knocked at the door for fellowships, till Routh gave him one at Magdalen, and who used to be thought of as a kind of waiter upon Pusey's charity for lodging and work. But Newman and Routh were right in their judgment.

In August his own time had come. The Deanery of St. Paul's, vacant by the death of Dean Mansel in July, was offered him by Mr. Gladstone, and after long hesitation on his part, and much pressure from his friends was finally accepted by him.

R

To Dr. Newman.

WHATLEY, 25th August 1871.

MY DEAR NEWMAN — It was settled on Wednesday. Gladstone would not let me off. Whether I was weak, and a coward in yielding, I cannot tell. I only know that every day makes me feel the change more immediately bitter, and more formidable for the future. I hope I may have a few weeks' respite. I should like very much to see you if I can, and if I may.

Much has been said about coveting great place, and much about shirking responsibilities. I think that there is still something wanting to be said about the doctrine of the son of Sirach, about a man "trusting his own soul," and about there being no man living "more faithful unto him than it." "For a man's mind is sometimes wont to tell him more than seven watchmen, who sit above in a high tower" (Eccles. xxxii. 23; xxxvii. 13, 14). This quaint phrase runs much in my mind.—Ever yours affectionately,   R. W. CHURCH.

A nearer view brought upon him, as a heavy burden, the sense both of the responsibilities of his new office and the character which his work was to assume. "I have been up to survey St. Paul's, staying with Liddon," he writes to Dr. Mozley.

WHATLEY, 31st August 1871.

It is clear that what I am to come in for is very tough practical business, and that I am not to be as other Deans have been. It is to set St. Paul's in order, as the great English cathedral, before the eyes of the country. I mean that this is what Gladstone has in view, and what Liddon, Gregory, and partially Lightfoot expect of their Dean. I

have three things before me : (1) To make a bargain with
the Ecclesiastical Commission about the whole future
revenues of St. Paul's, and get from them what will be
necessary for the works and wants, material and other, of
the *reformed* cathedral. (2) To carry on the architectural
restoration, for which a quarter of a million is the sum
demanded. (3) To fight and reduce to order a refractory and
difficult staff of singing men, etc., strong in their charters
and inherited abuses. I don't mean that all this is to be
done single-handed, but the responsibility will fall on the
Dean.

                        WHATLEY, 16*th September* 1871.

I am in the thick of papers left by Mansel about the
arrangement with the Ecclesiastical Commissioners, which is
the first thing I shall have to take part in. St. Paul's
cannot get on, especially with all the grand plans afoot,
without large revenues ; and the Commission, besides other
things, probably doubt what guarantee they have that if
we get it, we shall spend it rightly, so we shall probably
be cut close. But they ought to be liberal. I have to go to
Gregory at Lambeth about this next week. . . .—Yours
affectionately,   R. W. C.

The parting came at length. What it cost him to
give up the quiet happiness which had grown up round
the nineteen years of his life at Whatley may best be
told in his own words. They are words which also tell
the sorrowful apprehension with which he drew near
to his great tasks in London. That apprehension,
deliberate and serious as it was, was falsified in large
part as his work went forward. But the record of such
heart-sinkings in the presence of heavy responsibilities

and demands, has a value that is enhanced rather than cancelled by the happiness which afterwards corrected it—a value so plain as to warrant perhaps the insertion of the following letter in its completeness :—

To Dr. Asa Gray.

WHATLEY, 10*th October* 1871.

My dear Friend—I am ashamed of myself that your letter should come before I had written to you. But my necessary letter-writing has been more than usual of late, and at last my delays and puttings off have found me out. Mrs. Church indeed wrote to Mrs. Gray. But you ought not to have heard of a change in which you have taken such interest from any one but myself. And I suppose you heard it from the papers before my wife's note came.

It is now nearly two months since the first step was made, and this day week, the 17th, I am to be installed. And now what shall I say to you, after having had these two months to cool from the first surprise, and to face quietly and reasonably what is before me for the rest of my life ?

Pardon me, my dear friend, if I do not write as you would wish me to write. I mean, and I hope I shall be able, with God's help, to do and to bear the duties and the accidents of my new state. And though I feel it is a shame to damp the satisfaction—in some it is the joy—of my dear friends, at what they believe to be what is good both for me and for God's Church, yet there are some who will like even more to know the truth of what I think and feel about it ; and you are one, even above all my friends in England, to whom I can speak with the belief that from your distance

and your point of view, you can, even more than they, allow
for and understand the way I look at things. I wish I
could say I was reconciled to what is to be. But I am
not; and I cannot expect to be. I have made a great
mistake, the mistake of not knowing how to say *no* to warm
and pressing instances from people whom I respected, when
my own judgment was really quite clear the other way.
This comes on me more and more strongly every day. It
may perhaps be more or less forgotten in the whirl of
business. But in these quiet intervening days before
business begins, when I have heard all that is to be said,
and have thought much and anxiously about the whole
matter, that is the conclusion which remains. I am sure it
is but the too true one. I have made a great mistake in
exchanging this peaceful life, where I could work calmly
and at my leisure, for that tangle and whirlpool of ecclesiastical politics in which so few people see their way, or are
strong enough to meet temptations which are subtler, and
keener, and of a worse order than those of politics.

I know that this is idle and vain talking; you shall not
have any more of it after this. But you will not mind my
telling you, once for all, before this treadmill work begins,
how happy my life has been these nineteen years, what
blessings I have enjoyed in the sense of liberty, in being
able to worship and serve away from the strife of tongues,
in the perpetual delight of the beauty of nature all round,
of sun, and air, and green fields and flowers, in the kindness
of friends in high estate and still more in low, in the deep
and growing affection at home, every year becoming richer
and more charming.

I have not valued them, I have not used them, as I
ought. I dare say it is very good, perhaps necessary, for

me that they should be taken away. But it is very bitter
to take leave of them, and know that they will never come
again as they have been. And if I believed that the sacrifice
was for an end which would compensate for it, and required
it, I should be more content. But it is a sacrifice *en pure
perte.* The place—one of hard business administration,
organisation, management of a troublesome and powerful
staff, of representation and speech-making, of reform of old
and strong abuses—is not fit for me, nor I for it. What I
could do, I shall have neither time nor strength for longer;
what I shall have to do, I have neither aptitude nor experience for. It used to be a place of literary leisure; and so
it was under Milman. But times are changed. What is
required now is that St. Paul's should waken up from its
long slumber, and show what use it is of, and how it can
justify its existence as the great central church of London.
The end and purpose is a great and right one; but the
detail of weary official work, which such a reform involves,
few can guess. And for this, and for all this going right,
with energy, with good sense, with due power of finding and
using resources, I am to make myself responsible. Indeed,
this is not my line.

In truth I cannot but look at my going to London as an
experiment. I should not be surprised if I did not stay
there a year. I have not the least notion how far I
can bear the huge change from the country, with its fresh
air and simple ways of life, to the gloomy atmosphere (and
the Deanery is like a prison, shut up between high walls),
and big dinners, and late hours of London. My health may
break up, and then I shall go—but if I stay, it really is
more possible than it was, that I may find my way across
the sea to you. That would be very pleasant. . . .

I must finish. Remember us both most affectionately to Mrs. Gray. I hope, tell her, to see her and you again ; but I don't care much to show her the gloomy magnificence under which my work is to be done for the future. I wish I could send you, perhaps I may, a photograph of our little church here, which we have just put to rights, and in which it is a pleasure to say our prayers ;—and now it has to be left.—Ever yours affectionately, R. W. Church.

Your next letter had better be addressed, Deanery, St. Paul's, London.

PART III

THE letters greeting the Dean's appointment to St.
Paul's are very different in tone from the one which
closes the record of his Whatley life. His friends felt
nothing of the doubt with which he himself was
oppressed; St. Paul's seemed to them the very place
fitted for him. From Dean Stanley, who eight years
before had left Oxford for the Deanery at Westminster,
came a characteristic note of welcome. "If together,"
he wrote, "we cannot do something for London, may
the malison of St. Peter and St. Paul fall upon us."
And from Mr. Gladstone, in reply to Sir Richard
Church, who from Athens had written to express his
pleasure at his nephew's appointment, come words as
confident—"You can hardly be more pleased than I
am that we have at length drawn forth your nephew
from his retirement, and induced him to assume a
position more conformable to his powers and his deserts.
Quæsitam meritis sume superbiam. It has been by merit
and service only that he has reached his high position;

but that, being what he is, he should also be your
nephew, is to me a source of additional satisfaction."

Once at St. Paul's, as the preceding letters have
shown, the Dean found his work awaiting him. The
task of fitting St. Paul's to become a centre of spiritual
life and influence in London, and of enabling it by
measures of administrative reorganisation and reform
to meet the changed conditions and heavier demands
of cathedral work, was no light or easy one ; and it was
to such a task that the Dean with the Chapter, of which
he was the head, had at once to set themselves. The
Dean's letters refer but seldom to this part of his work
at St. Paul's, although for many years it continued to be
the closest and most responsible occupation of his daily
life. Something of its special character, as well as of
the wider aspects of his influence in London, may be
learnt from the sketch which follows, by Canon Scott
Holland, who during the later years of the Dean's life
was intimately associated with him alike as friend and
colleague.

"Even as undergraduates at Oxford in 1871, we
could feel the dramatic force of the stroke by which
Mr. Gladstone transferred Richard W. Church from the
secrecy of his Somersetshire retreat to the heart of
London.

"Oxford memories are, indeed, apt to be very short
when once a man has dropped out of his place there.
How can it be otherwise with generations that come
and are gone within a four-years' span ?

"But the remembrance, the tradition of 'Church of Oriel' was still fresh with us. His name was knit into the old Tractarian story; it mingled with the records of J. H. Newman, whose personality still exercised over us that intimate fascination which was so peculiarly his own. Everything that belonged to that historic movement had about it something heroic and imperishable. And we were well aware, therefore, of what might be found in that Whatley Rectory; and we knew that, in certain fields of critical history, there was one hidden there to whom we should look for a supreme judgment; and we debated what was the work which he was probably employed in perfecting. And now and again we trooped to St. Mary's, eager to see the hero of the Proctorial Veto in 1845; and we listened with deepened interest to the preacher, as we noted, with the naïve surprise of young men, the many faces among the congregation of dons whom it was very rare to see at a University sermon. We began to recognise that strange consent, in later days so unique, which made men of every type and party, whatever their quarrels or differences, somehow, always, accept 'Church of Oriel.' Round every other name there was hot debate, attack and defence, challenge and counter-challenge. But no one ever discussed the worth or the authority of this name; it was an established matter, about which there was no division of opinion.

"So we saw, so we learned. And when, therefore, Mr. Gladstone made it his most earnest and urgent business to get Church to the Deanery of St. Paul's on the first opportunity that offered, we only felt that he had done what Oxford looked to him to do. We entered eagerly into his convictions and hopes. There was intense interest in the sudden appointment, but no surprise.

"There was only one person of those who knew anything whatever of the situation, who had any doubt or difficulty about the matter. That was Church himself. We have seen, in his letter to Dr. Asa Gray, how his detestation of personal prominence, his ingrained reserve, his self-depreciation, his horror of all loud and brawling life, combined with his deep love of quiet work among the poor, and his passion for all that was peaceful and restrained in the 'tender grace' of a country home, to make him offer to this proposal a strenuous resistance which only yielded under extreme pressure, and which protested to the last against its own submission. When, years after, he had been engaged in an attempt to induce Dr. Liddon to consider the question of a bishopric, I remember well the amused smile with which he told me how, as he listened to Liddon's fervid arguments against any such offer being made him, he could not help recalling the way in which that very same fervour had disposed of the very same arguments when he himself had used them to Liddon as his own reason for declining the Deanery.

" What it cost him to leave Whatley, those only know who, taking into account his extreme avoidance of every form of personal expression in public, have

read, in his first volume of *Village Sermons*, his farewell
to the peasant-folk whom he loved so dearly—a farewell
which echoes the refrain of that most pathetic of all
farewells in English literature, uttered once in Littlemore Church and ringing for ever in the ears of all who
had ever loved John Henry Newman.

"And, again, what it cost him to face the storm and
stress of roaring London, those only can tell who saw
his misery during his first year in St. Paul's Churchyard.
Misery is not too strong a word to express the recoil of
his whole manhood from all that was involved in the
position of a great Church dignitary, thrust into prominence at every turn, encompassed with petty pomps, and
forced into a multitude of public affairs.

"And indeed the task that met him was one that
would sharply strain the fine and nervous organisation
of a scholar.   It was the task of proving that St. Paul's
Cathedral could justify its position as the central house
of worship for the Church in London.   Hitherto it had
been a magnificent architectural monument, waiting, in
dignified renown, for the discovery of its activities.   Its
main bulk lay practically idle, except for special occasions such as the festival of the charity children, or on
great public functions such as the burial of a hero.   At
all other times, over the length and breadth of its large
area, cold, naked, and unoccupied, mooning sight-seers
roamed at large.   Its daily services had always been
hidden away in the choir, behind the thick organ screen
against which Wren had so vehemently protested.   There,
in seclusion, a tiny body of cultivated musicians sang to

a sprinkled remnant of worshippers. Everything was
done on the smallest scale, and much was mean and
slovenly to the last degree. The attendance of the
Chapter, and of the cathedral staff, was reduced to a
minimum. There was little attempt at discipline or at
dignity in the conduct of the daily services. An elo-
quent preacher could, of course, make a difference at St.
Paul's as well as elsewhere, and no one would wish to
forget the stir caused by the beauty and the nobility of
sermons like those of Henry Melvill. For him the small
space of the choir, which alone could be used, would be
thronged. But any such momentary stir came and
went with the preacher. It had no relation to the
cathedral as such; it had no bearing upon its corporate
worship, nor did it affect its ordinary existence, except
for the one afternoon service on the Sundays when this
or that preacher was in residence. For the rest of the
week, the cathedral droned on as usual.

"Two main efforts had, indeed, been made to correct
this state of things, both during the chieftaincy of the
great student and poet, Dean Milman. First, under
the insistent pressure of Bishop Tait, special services
had been begun under the dome on Sunday evenings
during a certain portion of each year. The terrors that
obstructed the original introduction of these services in
1858 had been dispelled, and though they still figured
as acts of supererogation, carried along under temporary
arrangements for choir and congregation, they had proved
to what use the full space of the cathedral might be put.

"Secondly, an appeal had been set moving by Dean

Milman on behalf of the decoration of the church, without which its bare walls, discoloured by mouldering distemper, were bound to chill the heart out of the worship offered there, and to invite irreverence or uncomeliness. Through the effort thus made, in 1860, an effective touch of gilding was introduced into the roof of the choir, and into the great arches and drum of the dome ; and a beginning was made with the mosaics in the dome spandrils. The Dean, by his book on the cathedral, had eloquently expressed the need of splendid decorative treatment. Here, again, as in the dome services, the movement was prophetic. It directed attention on what had to be done ; it gave practical evidence of its possibility ; it prepared the way for a fuller achievement.

"The task then had been set for the new generation. Its two departments were marked out in the broad : (1) the whole cathedral must be used from end to end for public worship ; and (2) the whole cathedral must be endowed with the living warmth which should belong to a house of prayer and praise, into which men might freely enter, and where, as they entered, they could not but pronounce, 'This is none other than the House of God ; and this is the Gate of Heaven.'

"The task was set : now to carry it out. To do so, on an adequate and intelligent scale, involved a recon- struction of the cathedral organisation from end to end. The staff, the fabric, the funds, the statutes—all these were, as they stood, ridiculously unequal to the work to be taken in hand.

"For what was it that was required? First, it was essential that the worship carried on in the central church of London should be continuous as the life which it was needed to sanctify. It must be an ever-present fact, accompanying with its regular successions the human movement that surged around it. Morning, noon, and evening there it must be, unfailing, un- flagging: not intermittently filling a pause on Sundays, but felt as an incessant pressure throughout the thronging occupation of the week. Men, when they turned in at the doors, must find it continually happening; they must be able to find its succour with regularity and security; they must be sure that it will be there when they want it.

"And, secondly, the worship must not only have the mark of continuity, but also that of dignity and grace. It must uplift something of an ideal; it must be honour- able, seemly, reverent; it must show that there is a per- fection to be sought in these matters; and that here, in the Church's cathedral, men are putting their very best into the acts by which they hold communion with their God and Saviour. There must be no sign of carelessness, or of meanness, or of sordid sloth, or of indifference. It must be clear that love has thought it worth while to pay that close attention to the details which betokens its affectionate delight in what it is about.

"And, above all, the central Eucharistic Act of the Church's Communion with God must occupy the house which was built to enshrine it. It must fill its due place. It must be always at hand, to be found by all who may desire it. It must open each day with its sanction. It must be brought out of the corner in which it has hitherto lurked—the privilege of a secluded knot who have it all to themselves at the obscure end of a Sunday morning service. It must show itself as the culminating moment of public worship, to which the varied gifts of music and art, by which men heighten their devotion, contribute their finest and fullest ministrations.

"Again, this worship, continuous and honourable, must be also on a large scale; it must cover the ground allotted to it. The typical cathedral service in England is far too much inclined to shut itself up in a nook, and there delicately pipe to a ring of select experts. At St. Paul's, with its Palladian spaciousness, with its unbroken vistas; at St. Paul's, set upon the central platform in the midst of enormous populations,—it was essential that the appeal should be wide-winged; its music must be full-voiced, powerful, abundant; it should reach to all parts of the building; it must be capable of drawing multitudes under its spell.

"Once more, it must not only be large in range, but also given freely. There should be no limitation of the use of the cathedral by the suggestion of payment, or of reserved or appropriated seats; there should be no challenging vergers, no obstruction to free movement, no inquiries, no suspicions, no exclusions, no shaking of the money-bag. The opportunity of worship must be open to all, without stint. Everything must be done to emphasise the invitation, 'Ho, every one that thirsteth, come ye to the waters, and he that hath no money:

come ye, buy and eat ; yea, come, buy wine and milk without money, and without price.' The endowments of art, the enrichments of music, the dignity of worship, —these should be offered at their very best, as the free inheritance of all who should go out and come in, be they rich or poor, known or unknown.

" And, lastly, the cathedral must be brought into sensitive touch with the multitudinous forms of Diocesan life. The day of sterile isolation must pass away, during which the Church in London had hardly been aware, so far as its practical work went, whether it had a cathedral or not. It is true that London Diocesan organisation was at that date singularly backward ; but that was all the more reason why the need of a central hearth should be satisfied. The Church, in its parochial activities, was intensely alive ; and the rise in parochial activity had forced Churchmen to feel the necessity of large united gatherings at which the swarms of scattered workers, who were bound by the tie of a common cause, should look each other in the face, and be enheartened by the glow of a felt fellowship. Missions, committees, guilds, leagues, societies, associations,—all these, in their manifold varieties, should find opportunity for union, in corporate acts of worship, before the one altar, under the mothering dome.

" It was, indeed, an inspiring task to realise in its completeness. But what would it not ask, at every turn, of him who was to head it? What breaches would have to be driven into ingrained habits ! What collisions with vested interests and obstructive traditions, and solid

S

blocks of resistant sloth! What rough and ready treatment would be required in dealing with those immemorial
conditions which made advance impossible, and with
characters and men who were without the faculty to
understand what was now to be required of them! Such
a transformation as we have sketched can only be lightly
taken in hand by those who are thick-skinned enough
to disregard the insulting degradation that inevitably
belongs to conflicts with angry fellow-men. To the new
Dean, resolute and dauntless as was his nature, such
personal incidents had in them the cruelty of torture.

"On the other hand, tough as was the nature of the
work in hand, there was much to set against its severity.
For he had arrived at the Deanery at the most favourable moment that could possibly be imagined. The
conditions vital to the impending change had all been
prepared with curious felicity. The whole of the Chapter
who had grown up under the older régime had died
within three years, and the new men were simply waiting for the opportunity to begin. They were alive to
all the rising demands which the quickened Church life
must make on a cathedral; they possessed among them
a brilliant combination of the very gifts which could
enable them to respond to those demands. Gregory
had been appointed by Lord Beaconsfield in 1868;
Liddon by Mr. Gladstone in 1869; Lightfoot by the
same judgment in 1870. Already the movement of a
new activity was astir. The crowds which came to
Liddon's sermons had carried the ordinary Sunday
service out of the choir into the dome; and, once there,

it never went back. The rearrangement of the whole choir was under consideration and experiment. Lectures and services in the chapter-house for city men were being schemed. The committee for the decoration of the cathedral, which had stagnated, had been revived. And, moreover, a decisive step had been taken towards grappling with the preliminary problem which was bound to precede all serious reform. For the reconstruction of a cathedral, as of every other institution, depends, for its possibility, on finance. St. Paul's could never be in a position to realise these wide public obligations until it had reorganised its resources with a distinct regard to the functions that it was required to fulfil. This involved coming to terms with the Ecclesiastical Commissioners as to the redistribution of ancient endowments. That inevitable act had been delayed and delayed. And the delay, however much it may have been due to sluggishness or to the temper of sheer obstruction, had, at least, permitted it so to happen that when, at last, the late hour struck, the period for distrusting, decrying, starving the cathedrals had passed, and men were capable of apprehending, with a larger intelligence, the splendid uses, so vital and so imperative, which these great homes of the Catholic Church could alone fulfil. When, therefore, during the short reign of Dean Mansel, the resolution to strike a bargain with the Commissioners was arrived at, Canon Gregory, to whom, as treasurer, the work of fighting for terms fell, had gone into the fray possessed of a distinct and complete conception of the work that a cathedral might do,

and of the funds that would be necessary to its achievement. He had planned out this work on a large scale,
with the conviction that whatever the Metropolitan
Cathedral attempted to do should be done with nobility
and distinction. With this plan before him he demanded
a staff, an equipment, a plant, a stock of corporate resources, adequate to the intention. These, instead of
being pinched down to the lowest level of efficiency,
must be enlarged and enriched beyond their present
scope to meet the strain of multiplied services, and of
a church continuously open and in use. The Commissioners were impressed with the practical reality of the
treasurer's design, and recognised that his large demands
were all regulated by a strict eye to business. They
became content to entrust the cathedral with the funds
that such a scheme necessitated. The actual settlement
of the scheme, in all its details, occupied most of the
first years of the new Dean's rule. It involved a complete revision of each and every department of the
cathedral staff. But it was an immense gain for him
that the preliminaries were through and that all was in
train by the time that he arrived, and that he inherited
a treasurer keen to press on with a work already in hand
and intimately congenial.

"The financial condition, then, was already singularly favourable, and it was the same with the spiritual
revival. The personal factor, by which the claim of St.
Paul's to become once more a wide spiritual home for
London could make itself heard and felt over the hearts
of large multitudes, was to be found in the preaching of

Dr. Liddon. That voice reached far and wide. It fixed the attention of the whole city on what was going forward in its midst. It kindled the imagination, so that the big world outside was prepared for great things. It compelled men to treat seriously what was done. No one could suppose that the changes in the services and ritual at St. Paul's were superficial or formal or of small account, so long as that voice rang on, like a trumpet, telling of righteousness and temperance and judgment, preaching ever and always, with personal passion of belief, Jesus Christ and Him crucified. It is impossible to exaggerate the value of Liddon's presence for these twenty years at St. Paul's, in the way of making acceptable and justifiable to reasonable men the type of worship which was to be asserted under the leadership which now made it practicable. And it was of unspeakable importance, therefore, that Liddon should have been what he was to the new Dean. Not only were they in absolute accord on the practical aims which they were bent on making good, but Liddon placed also at the Dean's service an enthusiastic veneration for one who was, for him, the ideal of that perfected and chastened Christian character which Tractarianism, in its highest mood, had fostered. Chivalrous loyalty belonged to the innermost fibre of Liddon's nature ; and all of it was freely offered to him whom he was delighted to accept as his chief. There was nothing which he would not submit to the Dean's verdict. His delicate sensitiveness would be ever on the *qui-vive* to interpret and to ratify the Dean's judgment. There was no one in England, except Dr. Pusey himself, to whose authority he could more joyfully and entirely surrender himself.

"Gregory and Liddon, then, were already in action, and all their activity was at the immediate disposal of their new head. To them had just been added Lightfoot, with his unrivalled reputation as a critical scholar, his glowing ardour of speech, his robust sense of equity, his delightful geniality. There could never be any difficulty in securing his co-operation in anything that made for the effective utilisation of the great church; and the united force of such a body carried along with it the kindly courtesy of Bishop Claughton, who had just been appointed to the Archdeacon's stall. Thus the Dean found himself in the rare position of heading a Chapter which was prepared to act with practical unanimity. It was not as is so usual in cathedral bodies, an odd assortment of stray goods, a collection of contradictory specimens, each of which had been specially selected in order to neutralise the others. It was a corporate body that was animated by a single purpose, and possessed of sufficient coherence to prosecute this purpose with some consistency and continuity of will. It was ready and able to act together in its integrity, so that it might create a regularity in the life and the worship associated with the cathedral, such as would survive the monthly succession of canons in residence. These might come and go; but the tone, the atmosphere, the type, of which each, during office, was the responsible guardian, would abide unchanged now that the sequence of liturgical actions and ordered services, carefully considered and fixed by a united Chapter, could be laid out on authoritative lines and secured against the whims and freaks of individualism. It was to this unity of purpose and mind that Dr. Liddon continually attributed all that the Chapter succeeded in achieving at St. Paul's; and this unity, as he was never tired of asserting, became a practical fact through the incomparable authority that resided in the character of the Dean. He was so entirely free from all suspicion of personal motives; so obviously single-minded; so direct, and real, and true; so incapable of selfishness, or smallness of any kind, — that it became possible for the Chapter to go decisively forward in a fixed direction, without losing the confidence of those outside or the harmony of those within.

"It is needless to enter into the details of the labour thrown upon the Dean during this reconstruction of the cathedral organisation. It took years to work through the whole scheme; it involved new statutes, new men, new buildings. It left upon him the memory of sharp anxieties and rough personal conflicts, to which he could hardly bear to refer in later days, and then only with ominous shudders.

"But, on the other hand, I never had known the measure of his thankfulness for what had been done until, at the close of his life, before one of his last departures for abroad, when he thought himself dying, he took me apart and charged me, with the utmost solemnity and with something like vehemence, to see to it that no memorial of any kind or shape should be placed of him in the cathedral; he could hardly desire even that his name should be recorded on its walls; it was enough, he said, for him, and more than enough, that he should have been permitted to be associated with such a momentous work of revival.

"It should be said, and said with emphasis, that all through this critical time the Bishop of London bravely supported all the changes which, as visitor, he was required to sanction. Without this consistent and favourable support all the thoroughness of the reform would have been lost.

"It is impossible to single out points in which the Dean's initiative can be directly detected. Indeed, a marked initiative would not be in his manner. He would not formulate proposals, nor frame a policy. That would be wholly unlike him. Rather, within the Chapter, as without in his relations to the Church at large, he stood as a judicial conscience, up to the standard of which all must be brought. If it was a matter of liturgical order or devotional rule, Liddon would be set to frame a scheme; if it was a bit of financial or administrative business, Gregory would make his proposal. But, always, there was a judgment to face which would be anticipated by each as they worked at this task. Every plan must be such as would satisfy the sensitive and delicate estimate of right or wrong which was so pre-eminently characteristic of the Dean. It was impossible to bring before him anything shabby, or ungainly, or raw, or unseemly, or careless. His presence held in it a capacity for rebuke which acted as a perpetual check that prevented such lapses occurring. No one could venture on taking the Dean lightly. Anything done under his eye had, perforce, to be done at the best level that the conditions permitted. It was in this way that his influence, without formally initiating, was felt at every turn, and permeated every portion of the action that was taken to render the cathedral effective. It was always there, to be taken into very serious account. It made incessant demands that things should be done in the best possible way. His approval was recognised, at once, as conveying sanction—as disposing of doubts and hesitations. His dissatisfaction was a final objection ; the matter must drop. All this would happen almost in silence ; certainly, without much argument. He had but to show how he stood, and every one recognised the result without question or debate. It was as if a verdict went out from him by sheer necessity of nature—that inevitable verdict which is the note of spiritual mastery and of disciplined excellence. I never met any one with whom this effect was so instinctive and so vital ; and it was all the more striking because of the noticeable absence of all the pedantries of self-assertion. No one could abhor with a more profound abhorrence than he the priggish pose of the moral censor. His vivid humour, his intense reality, his pure naturalness—all these made any such personal assumption of superiority inconceivable to him. No temper could possibly be more remote from him than this. He never even suggested it by anything that he did or said. Yet, in spite of his instinct of self-efface-

ment, in spite of his elastic sympathies, in spite of his
quiet gentleness, in spite of his innate reserve, the fine-
ness of his judgment told instantaneously, like the keen
edge of a knife. No one could be with him and not feel
himself put to proof under scrutiny that forbade trifling
and broke up disguise. He might be most tender, most
affectionate; but, for all that, you knew still that you
were moving under the eye of a judge whose verdict
was a matter that neither you nor any one else could
afford to ignore.

"It is well to dwell on this, because herein lay the
final secret of the impression he produced; yet only
those who came into personal contact with him could
be thoroughly aware of it. And this has led to a
popular conception of him which omits his cardinal
characteristic. People knew of him as the quiet, refined scholar of exquisite taste. They heard of his
humility, his self-abnegation, his shrinking from pub-
licity, his avoidance of high position, his love of retirement, his unworldly simplicity. They saw, perhaps,
a slight, thin figure glide in and out of St. Paul's, or
slip low down to kneel on the floor in the Dean's stall.
At a distance, in the big place, it was hard to distinguish any marked feature in the small head and
spare face. He seldom appeared at any public gathering or platform. If he went about, he was, from his
slightness of physique, as well as from his habit of
withdrawal, easily unnoticed. And the result was that
he was regarded with the honour given to some shy
recluse, some delicate student, devout, lowly, perhaps

timid, who wrote beautiful books, and who was dearly
loved in private by those who knew him, and whose
intimacy with J. H. Newman or Mr. Gladstone was a
witness to his personal charm as a man of exceptional
culture.

"Now this impression, however natural, is ridiculously inadequate, just because it fails to convey a hint
of the primary quality which constituted the special
power of his personality. That quality was judgment.
He possessed judgment: that is what we should begin
by saying of him, if any one asked why we thought
him so great. No one in England could be counted
upon to give so high and fine and sane and robust a
decision on matters brought before him. He gained
this judicial authority by a rare combination of the
special qualities which constitute right judgment. His
touch on a subject was singularly true : he had strangely
few infirmities, or prejudices, or lapses ; he had all the
felicitous instincts of an intelligence thoroughly trained
and in hand ; and, above all, he brought into play a
conscience—a conscience peculiarly manly, firm, courageous, severe.

"Here, in the direction of conscience, lay the central
impulse of his life. It might show itself, as it obviously
did, in the field of scholarship, as an instrument of
literary criticism ; or, again, it might make his study of
Lord Bacon a perfect type of the method in which a
moral verdict can be delivered through the impartial
medium of history. But this was not all. It was in
keen exercise over all the life of conduct, social, political,

moral. It impelled him to fix his deepest intellectual
interest on the study of conduct and character in nations
and races; and, again, on the application of the Christian code of ethics to modern society. It made him
passionately alive to all that was going forward in
Church and State, where he was intensely sensitive to
the awful seriousness of the moral issues at stake.
The daily affairs of politics and diplomacy were for
him the active scene on which good or evil worked out
their immemorial war; and he watched on at the conflict with the solemn zeal of a prophet, in whose eyes
God's. honour was engaged. It was this which explains
the heat of his words at a time like that of the Bulgarian
massacres. The decision to be taken at that hour by
England was felt by him to be charged with all the
momentous significance that would belong to a personal
choice between right and wrong. At such a public
crisis, as in many a private one, a fire of moral indignation would suddenly reveal itself in him which startled
the ordinary man. We are used to such passion over
personal wrongs; there it gives us no surprise. But a
flame of righteous anger that has no trace of personal
injury in it, and that leaps up at the sight of public
wrong because it is wrong, and for no other reason—
this is rare indeed. And it was all the more startling,
as it sprang from one so' associated with courteous
gentleness as the Dean. Yet there it was. No one
could mistake it. It was the pure, white anger of an
outraged conscience. When once you had caught sight
of it you never forgot it. It was recognised as the

typical expression of his personality. I have known
people who have said that it was the only human experience which gave them a clue to what was meant by
the paradox of St. John, 'the wrath of the Lamb.'
Certainly, I can imagine no one whose rebuke would
be more terrible to undergo. One or two occasions on
which I saw him deal with a committed offence remain
imprinted on my imagination with unparalleled vividness. His condemnation was a punishment in itself
at which one trembled. Certainly, the minor officials
of the cathedral, whose contact with him was chiefly
through matters of discipline, found him strangely full
of awe.

"Not that his natural temper forbade lightness and
gaiety ; far from it. He was playful ; he delighted in
domestic fun, and dearly loved a bit of humour. He
was quick, frank, elastic. But there was at the base
of his character a strain of austerity. You felt it in
the innermost fibres of his being. There was the old
Tractarian instinct of self-repression ; there was its
hatred of all that bordered on display, its aloofness
from all that tended towards popularity or worldly
success. There was the deep undertone of one who
had passed through the fire, who had survived the
tremendous hour. The strain of the great convulsion
of 1845 which 'strewed wrecks on every coast' had
told on none more than on him. And its stamp was
still upon him—the stamp of an austerity which over-
awed the men of a younger day, and made them seem
of a weaker build and blood. Perhaps, again, no one

can steep his soul in the work of Dante, as he did,
without winning from it some touch of severe uncarth-
liness. Certainly he had the outlook of a warrior—not
as one who loved the temper of a fight, which indeed
he loathed, but as one who had been through it, and
had known the strain and weight of the foe, and was
aware of all that yet might be again. There was a
sense in him of one holding a fort against grim odds,
which survived out of the perilous days, and which
kept him on the watch lest the attack should swing
back his way. This used to surprise our lighter-hearted
generation, who had grown up since the terror of the
storm. 'The old war-horse was out to-day,' I used to
say when the Dean had shaken his head with an
upward look of grave defiance, as at some threatening
onset that he foresaw bearing down. The war-horse!
Yes! That was again and again the picture that rose
in my mind as the slight figure drew itself together,
and the eyes flashed. There would be no flinching in
him when the trumpet began to blow; that was clear,
as his mouth grew stern. After all, behind all the
smiling veils, this world (one felt) is an arena in which
the battle of the Lord goes forward. We shall not get
through without a tussle, a fierce bout. Evil is strong,
and may come in like a flood; and in the great day
of Armageddon he at least would not be found unready
or unarmed.

"Thus he had won out of an older past, which was
to us as an heroic epic, the spirit of the Christian
soldier warring for the right. But, on the other hand,

of all that elder race, he was the one who most intimately followed on with the new movements and the
fresh temper. He was absolutely in touch with the
younger men. No brick walls blocked them out, or
brought them into abrupt arrest. He did not encounter
them with a challenge of suspicion, or hold them off at
arm's length. He felt what was going forward; he
believed in its worth; he took it seriously. Right to
his very last years, he caught the spirit that was abroad,
and was sensitive to its necessary differences from
earlier types. Thus the younger men could come to
him with their vague and crude aspirations, unafraid
and unchilled. They were sure of sympathetic consideration—of a judgment that viewed their case from
inside. They felt that he saw with their eyes; and,
with that assurance, they could freely yield to his
authority, which it was a delight to recognise. There
was no one at all of the great heroes of the older
struggles who came so close to them; and this was of
vital significance during the crucial years, when the
currents set moving by the Tractarian impulse were
beginning to work out new grooves and receive fresh
tributaries. Such changes must happen; and they are
hardest to effect or to tolerate where the original effort
has been most heroic. And the Tractarian struggle had
been strangely heroic. It had been played by great
men, at a great crisis, on a great stage. It had fascinat-
ing personalities and dramatic movements, and undying
memories. And the Dean had been in the very heart
of all that was most touching and most famous. Yet

he was never imprisoned within the tragic attraction of that epoch in which he had played so high a part. So it was that, little as he himself would find it to his taste to enter into the battle over rubrics and cere- monies, he recognised the necessity that threw the stress of the fight upon those points, when once the theological movement had passed out of the Oxford quadrangles to the streets of crowded cities. His name, as much as any, forced those in authority to recognise that it was no affair of millinery or external ritual which they were labouring to repress. He was found, at each crisis, ready to verify the connection between the struggle for a larger doctrine and the struggle for a richer ritual. Nor only that; but when this stage of the conflict too was passing, and the position had been secured, and lawful liberty was greater, and, in consequence, the older movement was turned to other tasks, and took fresh interests, and began to be busy with the problems of contemporary thought, and with the new anxieties of Biblical criticism, he still would not hold himself back from those who had moved on to the new ground; but justified the necessity for the advance, perilous though it seemed to him; and not only corrected and guarded, but also appreciated and encouraged the effort that was being made to assimilate the fresh material of know- ledge. It is difficult to exaggerate his influence in re- conciliation and in control at a juncture when old bonds were stretched near to breaking. He stood between the old and the young, procuring the entire confidence of each, with an authority over both that was unique.

"Austerity and sympathy! These, fused into one, constituted him the type of moral judgment. By these he took his noticeable place as a standard conscience by which men tested their motives and their aims. That was his work in his study at St. Paul's. That was what made him the counsellor in all emergencies, public or private. 'What does the Dean say?' That was one of the necessary questions at each crisis. So it was that Mr. Gladstone turned to him as to no one else for advice on Church affairs, for a verdict on men and books. So it was that he could be anxious to see him placed in the highest seat of authoritative government in the Church of England. That desire was not merely a tribute to a refined scholar; it was the recognition of a force of moral judgment which had in it the authority essential for rule and leadership. Such was the Dean, and as such there was quite a peculiar felicity in his being planted for nineteen years at St. Paul's, just where all who needed could find him; just where he could lay his finger, with apt readiness, on the right or the wrong; just where he could be outside the actual hubbub, yet close at hand to those engaged in the thick of it. And it was an especial joy during his closing years, when bodily infirmities withdrew him, of sad necessity, from most of the administration business, and when his acute conscience was driving him, with an almost morbid anxiety, to mutter continually 'resignation,' to recognise that there, in his study, enclosed though he might be, he was still playing the part which it was his peculiar prerogative to fill. He was still actively justifying his

T

office; for still men sought in him the judgment, the conscience, which they found nowhere else in so authoritative or pure a form.

"I have ventured to labour this point, for, alas! this eminent characteristic of the Dean is one that disappears wholly at his withdrawal by death. The books which he wrote can still bear witness to his intellectual refinement and his scholarly insight. Every one can turn to them and feel the influence of their delicate style. His letters will reveal something of his personal charm, which brought him throughout his whole career such singular devotion from all who knew him. But there is nothing to tell of what he was as a living voice of moral authority, as a presence that put men and things to spiritual proof. Yet this is exactly what made his position at St. Paul's so noticeable. And it is only by keeping this clearly in view that the reading of the letters will give any measure of his personal significance.

"'There was such moral beauty about Church that they could not help taking him.' So Mark Pattison records, when speaking of the Oriel Fellowship which he himself failed to get, in that strange autobiographical fragment, in which he seems to have set himself to record the worst both of himself and of every one else. Amid all its sour pages, in which each high reputation appears distorted and discoloured, it is striking how at this one name, Richard Church of Oriel, the book suddenly and always softens into tenderness. 'Moral beauty!' That is the note struck by the Dean's life. And its effect was irresistible. As in Pattison's *Memoir*,

so through all the storm and stress of fifty years, in
which passions ran high and conflicts were hot and
blind, and slander and malice and uncharitableness plied
their evil trade round each prominent chief, there was
one name, and one name only, that never moved wicked
tongues or kindled anger; one name that always, and
from all, won unquestioned honour, and was beyond
dispute or challenge, beyond spite and hatred; one
name against which lay no suspicion, and which held by
an unbroken spell the favourable and affectionate attention of the rival controversialists.   It was that of
Richard William Church.   Yet he took a very strong
side. He spoke very strong words. He took an active
part in the very hottest part of the battlefield. Still,
the note of honour and of peace prevailed wherever he
was; and it did so, surely, through the power of this
'moral beauty' which won from Mark Pattison his
solitary touch of unqualified admiration.   His career is
a proof that there can be an unworldliness, a spiritual
temper, so true and so untainted, that it need not be
afraid though all men speak well of it. All men spoke
well of Church.   And he could afford it.   That is
the highest moral praise that can be given a man. And
that it should have been so does honour to the world
that gave him honour.   We are always engaged in
abusing the world for its admiration of glittering and
superficial brilliancies, or of strength that is unscrupulous
in its audacity; while it ignores the deeper powers that
hide themselves in modesty and quietness.   No doubt,
the world too often justifies our abuse; but, at least, let

us recall that it gave itself the lie in its treatment of
Richard Church. Never did any one more resolutely,
and almost morbidly, resist anything that could bring
him into notice or win popularity. Never was any one
more determinedly bent on holding himself withdrawn,
in hidden shadows, reserved and alone. Never was
there any one to whom it was more hateful, or more
impossible, to do anything for effect. And the gifts,
moreover, which this self-repression held withdrawn
were of a type that could make their full appeal only to
the few—to those who would appreciate the flavour of
fine and fastidious excellence. They were just of the
order which one would well expect to escape the judgment of the 'world's coarse thumb and finger.' Even
his sermons, into which he was careful to put his best
work, and which possessed for those who had ears to
hear such incomparable charm, were not calculated to
reach the multitude. There were no physical effects to
aid the impression. The voice, though pure-toned, was
far from strong; and in delivery he held fast to the
earlier traditions so characteristic of Newman and the
Tractarian chiefs. Gesture, action, were all rigidly
discarded; and the voice retained its even measured
monotone throughout. Again, he hardly ever preached
on public occasions except where his duties compelled
him; and this meant, in general, his rare sermons as
Dean, and still rarer, as University preacher. He never
would let himself go out to meet the general attention.

"Thus both his gifts and he himself fought against
public recognition. And it might well have seemed

that he would have succeeded in retaining the seclusion
that he desired. Yet the special significance of his life
is that he totally failed in this. To very few men in
his generation was it given to win such wide and un-
stinted recognition. Dragged out of his hidden rectory
to the Deanery of St. Paul's, and planted down in
London's central roar, he was accepted by one and all
with an unquestioned and unqualified completeness, as
bringing honour and weight to the post which he held.
We, at the cathedral, went about our work with the
consciousness that the dignity of a great name was
behind us—a name which did not merely win the admiration and love of those who knew him, but which
had a hold upon the imagination of the large world outside. This man, upon whom the world had no power,
told upon the world from which he abstained. Devoid
of the very taint of ambition, he obtained a singular
authority which was accepted without cavil or debate.
Such an authority was a witness to the force and beauty
of high moral character. It testified to the supremacy
which belongs, of right and of necessity, to conscience.
His special gifts would, under all conditions, have played
a marked part; but they do not account for the impressive sway exercised over such multitudes by his
personality. This it was which was so unexpected;
this it was which it was given him to wield, in spite of
himself. To have reached that position without ever
having made an enemy, without a quarrel, without a
mistake, without a doubt, is a tribute not only to the
character of him who so achieved, but also to the latent

goodness of a world which had the eye to recognise what it possessed. Amid all the miseries of misunderstanding and entanglements which beset great reputations, it enheartens us all to be made to acknowledge that men, after all, can welcome with frank and generous freedom the power of high rectitude and the beauty of goodness. No concessions need be made to the exigencies of practical life. No slanders or suspicions need, of necessity, encompass the path of those who would hold themselves pure. It is possible for a man to pass through the world, upholding a severe standard which warns and checks and menaces, and yet so to do this as to touch and draw out the best that there is in each, and to win every one's goodwill. It is possible for a man to keep clear of all animosities and bitterness, and to be in favour with all men, and yet never to swerve from the line of duty or to submit to the taint of a compromise. It is possible, for it was done by Richard William Church. Therefore it is that his memory is so fragrant and his name so full of good cheer. This earth is proved by him to be a better place than we ourselves had thought it. We look out at it with kinder eyes. We have a larger trust in the power of righteousness, not only to endure, but to conquer and to charm. We can tread our path with a better heart now that we see that even here, amid the tangle and the tumult, 'the path of the just is as a shining light.'"

The letters of the first year at St. Paul's give little beyond a hurried outline of the life to which the Dean had to accustom himself. "We have got into our new house somehow," he writes in the beginning of December 1871 to his brother :—

I had my first celebration in St. Paul's this morning ; the first time in the North Chapel at 8 A.M. ; and my first sermon at the 10.30 service. I found that I could be partially at least heard. At any rate I shall not feel afraid of the Dome when I am in ordinary strength. In the after-noon Liddon preached, the first time I ever heard him. He is very wonderful both in voice and words. . . . Lots of work cut out for me of all kinds. Gregory is of cast iron.

And a week later :—

I have lots to tell, but not much time for telling. Liddon's " Conference " on Tuesday was a remarkable occa-sion. He spoke for an hour to some seventeen hundred young clerks and shopmen. In the evening we met a party of swells at Stanley's—Duc de Broglie, Lord Lyttleton, Roundell Palmer, Capes and others ; and yesterday I had my first city dinner with the Worshipful Company of Cloth-workers, ate my first turtle, and made my first speech. It is an odd mixture of intense bore and flashes of amusement. . . . I have no time, no thoughts, and I have not opened a book for a fortnight except in church.   ·

9th December 1871.

Only a line to say that we are alive in spite of cold and fog, and whirl of all sorts. We are waiting anxiously for bulletins which come in continually from Sandringham.[1] Up to noon to-day there was slight improvement. But we were watching all night last night, waiting for the announce-ment which is sent from the Mansion-house to the Dean, on which the great bell begins to toll.

---

[1] During the illness of the Prince of Wales.

The Thanksgiving service for the recovery of the Prince of Wales was held in St. Paul's on the 27th of February of the following year, and was the Dean's first official experience of a great public ceremony.

To THE REV. C. M. CHURCH.

DEANERY, ST. PAUL'S, *7th March* 1872.

DEAR CHARLES—I am alive, which is the most interesting fact I have to communicate at present. I don't think I ever was so tired in all my life as last Sunday evening. However, all went well, in spite of various anxieties on the part of the police authorities, which did not make one's task lighter ; and now all I have to endure is the grumbles of people who did not get tickets, and who think that it was my business to prevent them getting squeezed when they found themselves in a crowd. This is the first letter that I have written during the last three weeks, which has not been more or less on business. I assure you I have been corresponding with very great persons,—Archbishops, Prime Ministers, Home Secretaries, and Lord Chamberlains—all, I was amused to find, just as if they were my oldest acquaintances. It is odd how soon one gets into the official trick, and writes without being afraid of their grandeur.

I must send this off. Good-bye. I hope you are all well.—Ever yours affectionately,   R. W. C.

To THE REV. C. M. CHURCH.

WINDSOR CASTLE, 13*th April* 1872.

MY DEAR CHARLES—I have had to come here to preach, and this time an additional bit of experience has come on

me, as I was summoned to stay at the big place instead of
the Deanery. There was an amusing degree of uncertainty
about the whole thing ; first, whether I was to go to the
Castle ; then, if being there, I was to dine with the Household or in the highest room : the questions were finally
settled so as to enlarge my ideas to the full extent. Gladstone is here, so that there was a bit of historical interest
in being at a dinner with H.M. and her Minister. It was
very solemn, but not solemn as I expected : people talked
and even laughed, but not loud. After dinner there was a
circle made round the room, and the Queen went round and
talked a little with each set.

. . . Gladstone has migrated to the Deanery, and I am
going to meet him there at dinner. It has been a beautiful
day, and we have been strolling through the park, which is
almost in its perfect charm ; a want of fulness of leaf, but,
on the other hand, the most exquisite first green.—Ever
yours affectionately,   R. W. CHURCH.

To DR. ASA GRAY.

LONDON, 7th November 1872.

MY DEAR FRIEND—Your letter gave me a qualm of
conscience. When did I write to you last ? I am sure I
cannot tell, but I am afraid a long time ago. But I won't
waste time in apologies. For once in my life I find in
reality what it is to be not master of one's time. Thank
you very much for the account of your trans-continental
expedition. It must indeed have been an experience for
which not even Egypt could have given you points of comparison. The pleasure of recognising *alive*, plants of which
you had been telling the history, and ruling the classifica-
tions, though only through their dead specimens, must have

been one which not many people could share with you, and
is one which I almost envy most among the pleasures of your
tour.   It must have been like finding friends in a strange
land, and something more.

We have not much of a story to tell.   Last July we
escaped from one of the hottest and most thundery summers
remembered in London to the snows.   We took our eldest
girl with us, and she proved a capital walker and good
companion, and later my boy joined us.

We went first to the Oberland—Lauterbrunnen, Mürren,
Grindelwald, Rosenlaui—where we had some fine weather,
and pleasant walks, with moderate climbing.   Mürren is
charming ; it is perched up high, with a magnificent perspective view of the Jungfrau group, and an awful-looking
depth of valley between it and the great mountains.   Then
we crossed the Gemmi, and got to the southern valleys running from the Rhone up to the great mountains dividing
Switzerland and Italy ; the valleys parallel with the Zermatt
valley, Evolena and Zinal, places which brought you back
to our remembrance, for it was from thence that we came
when we met you at the Riffel and Zermatt.   They are
charming places in fine weather, and we had some beautiful
days with some very bad ones.   Still it was holiday, and we
were well, and Mrs. Church walked bravely, and the children
scrambled up and found abundant edelweiss, and we were
altogether happy.   But holidays come to an end, and we
came back without misfortune.   And now London work has
fairly begun.

I am afraid we neither of us like this life better than we
did.   There is much going on which is interesting, and one
is thrown across people whom one is glad to know.   But
the worst is that there is neither time nor chances to know

them to much purpose. Among all the changes of my life
the one which comes home to me as most of a change is,
that having been used all my life to have one friend at
least, to whom I could go and talk over any matter that
turned up, now, in all London I have not one. Numbers
of friends with whom I am intimate and confidential on
this or that *public* matter ; but literally not one to whom I
could go and talk about things in general, or what specially
interested myself. Of course it is the fate of a new-comer,
beginning London life late, and I am not complaining, only
it is so odd and strange in feeling. On the other hand, I
meet endless people whom it is only possible to meet in
London—only it is tantalising to see so little of them.

St. Paul's is a big ship to command. I hope things are
mending a little in it, but there is much to be done, and
much to fight about, which is not much in my line. But I
must be satisfied if I leave it a little, only, better than I
found it. I hope I may do that.

. . . Our best love to Mrs. Gray. My boy is just gone
to Oxford, to New College, and will, I hope, do well.—Ever
yours affectionately,   R. W. CHURCH.

To DR. ASA GRAY.

DEANERY, ST. PAUL'S, 22*nd November* 1872.

MY DEAR FRIEND— . . . We are just in our gloomiest
part of the London year ; a portion which the great city
companies of London try to enliven with marvellous banquets
in their various halls. I was at one last night. They are
sights to see, for the halls, and plate, and dinner, and crowds
of diners, and all the odd customs which are kept up in
them. These companies are the lineal heirs of the old trade

guilds of London ; there are some sixty or seventy of them, great and small, but the small ones are not much heard of. The great ones—Fishmongers, Grocers, Mercers, Merchant-Taylors, Salters, etc.—are political powers, and possess huge revenues. Well, I hope that you will come over soon, that you may see us in our present odd manner of life. But I won't promise, if you delay long, that you will find us here. —Yours ever affectionately,   R. W. CHURCH.

To Dr. Asa Gray.

DEANERY, ST. PAUL's, 25th July 1873.

MY DEAR FRIEND— . . . We are just now under the influence of a great shock, which was felt through the country last Monday at the news of Bishop Wilberforce's death.[1] He was a man of great mark, and now that he is gone, people admit this more freely than they did.   He took such a leading part, that of course he came into violent collision with great numbers ; and he was so abounding in resources of all kinds, that it was easy to say that he was too clever in all ways.   But the truth is that he was a statesman, and a statesman's ways in great religious divisions are liable to offend people of strong, simple, perhaps one-sided, religious ideas.   He was, I believe, a thoroughly sincere man, with a very lofty and large idea of the religious aims to which he devoted his life.   He was a man of very large sympathies, of untiring interest in all that interested mankind—too extensive, per-haps, in his interests for any deep and accurate knowledge—a very strong, bold, and earnest man.   Of all men of his time he comes next to Gladstone as a man of inexhaustible powers of

---

[1] The death of Bishop Wilberforce had taken place by a fall from his horse.

work. Gladstone was much attached to him, and feels his loss greatly. There was a great nobility of nature about him. He was a man for the poorest and least educated rustics, just as much as for London churches and London drawing-rooms, and was as genuine in his intercourse with the humble and poor as with those who responded to his own brilliant cleverness. He is buried to-day in a little country churchyard in Sussex, where he wished to lie, as his wife's grave is there. It was wished to bury him at Westminster, but his own desire was respected. . . . —Yours affectionately,

R. W. CHURCH.

The two following letters contain the expression of the Dean's personal feeling towards two of the subjects of the day, which were being fiercely debated in Convocation as well as in public meetings in different parts of the country during 1873. The debates on Confession in Convocation led at length to a Declaration on Confession,[1] drawn up and signed by Dr. Pusey and some thirty members of the High Church party. To this Declaration the following letter from the Dean to Dr. Pusey refers :—

To DR. PUSEY.

DEANERY, ST. PAUL'S, 11th November 1873.

MY DEAR DR. PUSEY—I have to thank you most sincerely for having been so kind as, in the midst of all that you have to do, to write to me yourself.

. . . The Declaration sets forth nothing but what I hold

---

[1] A Declaration on Confession and Absolution, as set forth by the Church of England. See *Guardian*, 10th December 1873, p. 1589.

to be true.   But for myself, I have a strong objection to collective Declarations of this kind, except in cases of the last extremity.   I regret and dislike most deeply such utterances as those of the Bishop of Gloucester.   But I cannot help thinking that they have been provoked, though not justified, by extreme statements on the other side—statements which, if tenable, are fatal to the position of the Church of England. In a Declaration like this, people do not read or weigh the expressions, but only the heading and the names.   And they form false conclusions from both.   And there is the risk, which we saw verified in the case of the 483, of men, after signing, backing out on alleged misunderstandings.   I cannot help thinking that a calm and grave statement from yourself of what is contained in the Declaration, full as it would be of the cautious and considerate spirit necessary in dealing with such a difficult subject as confession, would weigh much more with English people than a Declaration however signed.

For myself, I should always be ready to maintain the liberty which, it seems to me, the English Church gives on both sides.   I am most thankful to those who, like yourself, have turned our attention to this great and once neglected remedy and medicine for many sinful souls.   But, however inconsistent I may be called, I cannot go beyond liberty.   I cannot seem to be on the side of those who, if not in formal statement, yet practically, press for more.

I hope that you will forgive me if I have written too freely.—With great respect and gratitude, yours ever,

R. W. CHURCH.

Another Declaration[1] to which the Dean's name is

---

[1] See *Guardian*, 20th May 1874, p. 626.

attached appeared in May of the next year, after the introduction of the Public Worship measure, and urged the danger of enforcing a rigid uniformity in the conduct of Divine worship, especially in the matter of the Eastward position, and the wearing at fitting times of a "distinctive Eucharistic dress."

To PRECENTOR VENABLES.

DEANERY, ST. PAUL'S, 26th May 1874.

MY DEAR SIR—The Declaration was in the first instance intended for a limited number of clergy, whose names, it was supposed, would carry some weight. But there has been such a strong wish to sign it expressed by many others, that a notice will be given in the papers this week, saying where names may be sent to in order to be appended to the Declaration. Any names sent to me shall be added to it.

I cannot be surprised at the opposite criticisms on the Declaration. Doubtless they are just, from each person's point of view; but the fault is in the odd and anomalous state in which the whole matter to which it relates is found to be.

My own feeling is much like yours about such things as vestments. I understand the frame of mind which, partly out of special reverence for our highest service, partly out of regard to what I suppose was early, if not the earliest usage, makes men wish for them. But for myself, I should feel very uncomfortable if I had to wear them; and, indeed, I have never seen a specimen except the cope which our Bishop wears once a year at the ordination on Trinity Sunday. I wish the congregation could have some constitutional voice in the matter. The difficulty is how to give it them. No doubt there *is* clerical despotism ; but, I am assured, it is an evil not confined to Ritualists. It would be a curious study to investigate the various forms of despotism under which, especially, country parishes groan. A large place must be kept for female despotism.—Yours very faithfully,   R. W. CHURCH.

These letters mark the new responsibilities which the Dean's position at St. Paul's now brought upon him. They serve also to lead up to the critical period in ecclesiastical affairs which was brought about by the passing of the Public Worship Regulation Act in the summer of 1874,—an Act passed "at the dictates," to use Dr. Liddon's words, "of an unreasoning panic, and with much apparent disregard of the historical structure and spiritual independence of the Church of England." [1]

Hitherto, at any rate since the changes of 1845, the Dean had been, to use his own words, little more than an "outsider" to the main current of vigorous and practical Church life which had received and carried on the inspiration and principles of the Tractarian Move-ment. At Whatley, although always an attentive observer of its fortunes, his life, with its parochial duties and constant literary occupation, had afforded few oppor-tunities for any regular intercourse with the leaders of the High Church party ; and of the younger men into whose hands the later development of the Movement had fallen he knew but little, as was shown in the letter of the 7th April 1866, which describes the meeting of

---

[1] See preface to *Thoughts on Present Church Troubles*, p. viii.

old currents and new at Mr. Keble's funeral. It was not until he came to St. Paul's that he was in any way brought into personal relationship with the ritualist party, and then his appreciation of their work could not hinder a sense of much that was provoking and extravagant in their teaching. "I feel," he wrote to Dr. Pusey in 1873, "that some of these younger men, whom I cannot go along with, are so very much my superiors, and beyond my criticism, in their devotion and earnestness. But I dread to think what the end may be from self-will and ὕβρις, where otherwise, in spite of everything, there seems more hope than I can see anywhere else."

But notwithstanding the feeling expressed by these words, the aim of the Public Worship Act, of "putting down ritualism" by means of prosecutions and imprisonments, offended at once his historic instinct and his sense of justice, and his letters show that his opposition to such a policy was resolute and uncompromising. "The truth is, in a battle you must fight," were words of his, and they give the clue to the position he now took up. With all his hatred of controversy, and the fierce temper and rough methods of controversy, he did not hesitate, in the long conflict which ensued, to take his place on the side of those who urged patience and toleration and measures of impartial treatment towards the members of an unpopular and suspected party.

In April 1874, the Public Worship Regulation Act was introduced into the House of Lords by the Archbishop of Canterbury, and in August it passed in the

House of Commons. How critical the occasion had become, and how serious was the strain during the passage of the bill, may be gathered from some outspoken words of the Dean's, written in the freedom of a private letter to his brother :—

DEANERY, ST. PAUL'S, *July* 1874.

You have chosen wisely. You would only have found here oppressive heat, and people out of temper, and the beginnings of a Church breaking up from the impatience and folly of governors and governed. The Church of England, at the beginning of the year, stood for the strongest and most hopeful Church in Christendom, with much excess and folly in it, as in all human things that have life, but growing into the only work for which a Church ought to live,—reclaiming, consoling, binding up, teaching men to worship and rejoice in the unseen Goodness and Glory. The ignorance of some, the pride of others, the suspicious injustice of even wise and good men, have brought things to a pass, when those who for fifty years have been steadily disbelieving in a break-up, have come to look at it face to face.

Writing on the 30th of July to Sir Frederic Rogers— or as he had now become, Lord Blachford—he adds :—

The bill you see is through. Blakesley told me that the House was "frenzied," and that if it had been proposed to cut off the hands of all offending clergymen, they would have carried it. It is too early really to decide on the practical meaning of all this. We shall see in the course of the autumn. But every one must feel it to be very grave.

A year had yet to elapse before the practical working of the measure could be tested. But when once it had

passed into law there were many among moderate High
Churchmen, to whom the growth of ritualism had been
always distasteful, who urged acquiescence in its enforcement. Such was the view taken by Lord Blachford, to
whom many of the letters which follow on Church
matters are addressed. Some words in a letter from
the Dean, written immediately after the passing of the
bill, reveal the difference which was already beginning
to arise in their judgment. "I quite enter into your
point of view," the Dean writes, "though it is not quite
my own. If it were a mere question of keeping order
and restraining absurdity, I should go along with you
quite. But unfortunately there are strong and irrecon-
cilable parties, and there is a Church Association, rich
and organised, and a strong popular current of feeling,
partly reasonable, partly ignorant, but anyhow formidable
and not very discriminating. It may cool down, but I
shall be surprised if it is allowed to do so."

Other letters follow, which illustrate this difference
of opinion even more distinctly.

To LORD BLACHFORD.

DEANERY, ST. PAUL'S, 7th December 1874.

MY DEAR BLACHFORD—I have looked over your review.[1]
In all that you *say* I think I quite agree, notably in the warning against effeminacy and excess. But I think that I should
have given Hope more credit for sharing in this feeling, and
wishing to check it. It seems to me that this is a time when

---

[1] A review of *Worship in the Church of England*, by A. J. Beresford
Hope.—*Guardian*, 9th December 1874.

ritual is taking a shape which may be permanent, and that there is a chance, which never was before, of settling the outline and principle of an intelligent, appropriate, expressive, outward form or shape of worship, *within the lines* of the Prayer-Book, fairly interpreted. Of course I mean according to the ideas of worship which belong to the movement. And it is from this belief that Hope writes, without imposing what he accounts fit and proportionate ritual on those whose divergences from his idea of doctrine are, in fact, sanctioned and allowed in the Church. I don't think he wants an excessive and ornate, much less a fiddling and fussy ritual; but, as there is no escaping the subject, whether you care for it or no, he wants it careful, appropriate, and, where the place calls for it, grand,—as good and suitable as it can be. In fact, he writes as much against the Ritualists as against the Puritans.—Ever yours affectionately,   R. W. C.

To the Same.

DEANERY, ST. PAUL'S, 11*th January* 1875.

My dear Blachford—The Christmas Pantomime in Spain is a more promising one than usual. I suppose this is what they have been driving at there for some time, and probably they have got what they wanted, after their sickening with the Intransigentes. I suppose it will make Spain a piece on the chessboard once more, and on the anti-Bismarck side.

Gladstone was here yesterday, lunching with us. He is still boiling with anti-Vatican wrath. . . . He corresponds with Döllinger, and is getting very much interested in the religious (and, I suppose, also the political) prospects of his party; and he wants the *Guardian* to have a special place for German ecclesiastical affairs. Certainly Stephen's augury about Gladstone, that he was deficient in combativeness, is one of the most whimsical bad shots that I know.

I had a curious interview with another great man the other day. The Archbishop asked Liddon and me to come over to Addington and have a " free talk " with him about Church matters. The invitation arose out of a talk with Lake, who reported its substance to the Archbishop. We went, and found him very civil and courteous, and though he talked the most, he let us have our say. Nothing much came of it ; but it was a good thing to have seen one another, and talked quietly by the fire in his study. His point was—no legislation : nothing to bring things before Parliament, which does not want to meddle ; but trust the new court, and make it as good a court as you can. He disclaimed all designs against the "great historical High Church party, as represented by Bishop Andrewes," and went as near as he properly could to a sort of apology for the strength of his language in his speeches last session. I could not help wishing that he had had the talk last year. He had also seen the week before a number (some twelve) of High Church clergy to whom he had talked in the same line —conciliatory—and allowing them to state their points, and wishing to meet them. But as to what is to be done, it is not so easy to see ; and except his own disposition for peace, there was not much to be gathered from what he said.— Ever yours affectionately,   R. W. C.

The following letters are examples of a kind of corre- spondence in which, as his influence made itself more widely felt, the Dean became more and more frequently engaged. The letters themselves will be found to indicate the nature of the questions to which they are a reply :—

To *   *   * *.

DEANERY, ST. PAUL'S, *3rd March* 1875.

MY DEAR MR. * * * —You are right in suggesting that I have not much time for answering, as they ought to be answered, such hard questions as yours. I wish I had, for they are very interesting ones. I can only write first thoughts, which you must take for what they are worth.

The *fact* of what is meant by original sin is as mysterious and inexplicable as the origin of evil, but it is obviously as much a fact. There is a fault and vice in the *race*, which, given time, as surely develops into actual sin, as our physical constitution, given at birth, does into sickness and physical death. It is of this inherited tendency to sin in our nature, looked upon in the abstract and without reference to concrete cases, that I suppose the Article[1] speaks. How can we suppose that such a nature looks in God's eyes, according to the standard of perfect righteousness which we also suppose to be God's standard and law. Does it satisfy that standard ? Can He look with neutrality on its divergence from His perfect standard ? What is His moral judgment of it as a subject for moral judgment ?

What He may do to cure it, to pardon it, to make allowances for it, in known or unknown ways, is another matter, about which His known attributes of mercy alone may reassure us, but the question is—How does He look upon this fact of our nature *in itself*, that without exception it has this strong efficacious germ of evil within it, of which He sees all the possibilities and all the consequences ? Can He

---

[1] The ninth of the Thirty-nine Articles, *Of Original or Birth Sin.*

look on it, even in germ, with complacency or indifference? Must He not judge it and condemn it as *in itself*, because evil, deserving condemnation? I cannot see what other answer can be given but one, and this is what the Article says.

But all this settles nothing about the actual case of unbaptized infants, any more than the general necessity of believing the Gospel settles anything as to the actual case of heathens who have never heard of the Gospel. If, without fear, we leave them to the merciful dispensations, unrevealed to us, of Him who is their Father, though they do not know Him, much more may we leave infants who have never exercised will or reason. But in both cases we are obliged by facts and Scripture to acknowledge sinfulness and sin. In Christians, and those who may know of the Gospel, this is cured, relieved, taken away, by known means which He has given us. In those who, by no fault of their own, are out of His family and Church, we cannot doubt, both from what we know of Him, and from what He has told us, that He will provide what is necessary. But still *there* is the sinfulness and the sin; and as sin, *quâ* sin, we can only suppose that He looks on it with displeasure and condemns it.

I don't see that the Article, which is only treating of sin and sinfulness, and not of its remedy or God's love, does more than express what must be God's judgment on all sin, even in germ. How He deals with it is a separate matter.

I must leave this hurried scrawl to your kind consideration.—Yours faithfully, R. W. CHURCH.

To the Same.

DEANERY, ST. PAUL'S, *6th March* 1875.

MY DEAR MR. * * * —What I meant was, that owing
to the imperfection of our faculties of conception and expression, almost all abstract truths are only parts of the truth, and
require to be limited or supplemented by other unexpressed
assumptions and supposed truths, to be true in fact and
reality.   You must allow for friction in practical mechanics;
and *real* points and lines have other qualities from *geometrical*
ones.   Yet we lay down our mechanical laws and geometrical
propositions.

So I take it, in a quasi-scientific statement, like that of
the Article.   It states an abstract truth which, to be made
really and fully true, has to be completed or limited by other
known and supposed truths.   The Article considers—What
does human nature, *as such*, with its universal fatal taint,
and its tendency to evil, *deserve* of the perfect righteousness
of God ?   Not what must A B, with all his circumstances
and personal qualities, etc., *look for in fact* at God's hands.
The best man confesses himself, and truly, a miserable sinner;
but it would be strange to apply the bare naked idea of a
miserable sinner to some good man whom we love and
reverence.

Geocentric and heliocentric motions and aspects are different, yet are both portions of the same fact looked at from
different positions.

The statement in the Article seems to me parallel, in its
unqualified breadth, to our Lord's words, " Except a man be
born again he cannot see the kingdom of God."   Why cannot
he, except there is in every man something which incurs
God's displeasure ?   And must we not believe that that some-

thing is taken away by a *new birth*, in all who are saved, either by the means of grace which we know, or by others unknown to us.—Yours faithfully, R. W. CHURCH.

A foreign holiday brought with it even more than ordinary refreshment, after the fatigues and anxieties of the previous year. For the first time for many years, the Dean, as the following letter shows, had allowed himself to be tempted beyond the range of his much-loved Swiss valleys :—

TO HIS WIFE.

LUGANO, *25th July* 1875.

Yes, really not gone after all—the cause why is remarkable. We meant to start about eleven for Como, and to have been there by this time. But we thought it our duty first to see one of the lions of Lugano, a great fresco Crucifixion by Luini. I happened to go first before breakfast, and it struck me at once as a really wonderful picture. I went home to breakfast, and after breakfast G. came with me to examine it. I think his verdict agrees with mine. It is a great wall picture on the east wall of the nave, as (I think) at Varallo ; high up, with a front plane of some fifty life-size figures. Behind were two other planes, the upper and most distant containing the Agony and the Ascension ; the second distance, just above the heads of the foreground persons, four scenes—the Purple Robe, the Bearing the Cross, the Entombment, and the Risen Lord meeting St. Thomas. The two sides answered to one another, as preparation and result of the great foreground scene, which they did not the least disturb, either in colour or grouping. Then came the fore-

ground full of animation—suffering, quarrelling, perplexed
observation, satisfied hate, sympathy, indifference, curiosity,
passionate devotion, conviction forced in spite of all the
strangeness of the event. The haters were on the side of the
impenitent malefactor, the lovers and adorers and respecters
on the side of the penitent one. But though the symmetry
was evident when you studied it, there was nothing to strike
the eye till you looked and thought. Then out of and far
above this talking, watching, quarrelling, hating, sorrowing
crowd, rose high, much higher than in ordinary Crucifixions,
three tall crosses, with three corpses on them, just dead; and
they rose far above all that is of the earth, its strugglings and
ignorance and passions, into the dark violet air, where all
was still, even the company of angels above, who were
watching and weeping in silence. The feature of the picture is these three very tall crosses, lifting their dead from
the earth to the invisible world, and the company of the
silent angels; and seeming, without saying so, to connect
what had happened in the sight and by the deed of men
with what happened in the presence of the angels. This
seems to me the idea of the picture; but this is nothing.
As soon as we came to look at it through glasses (it was a
beautifully bright morning) every detail, every group, every
face, showed such unfailing feeling on the painter's part for
the whole, such exquisite ideas of beauty, such nobleness,
such intense and yet most guarded and moderated passion,
such power under control, such respect—if I may so say—
for the expression of the deepest and most awful feelings,
that I am silly enough to say that I cannot recall a grander
picture of the kind, or many grander of any kind. Of course
the well-known Luini face came in often, but let it; I never
knew what a beautiful face it was till I saw it in this church.

Well, the long and short of the story is that I was fascinated, and thought eleven a great deal too early to leave Lugano. I had not seen for long a picture which so much interested me. So I made interest with G. to stay and have my leisure to look at it.—Ever yours affectionately,   R. W. C.

To LORD BLACHFORD.

DEANERY, ST. PAUL'S, *8th May* 1876.

MY DEAR BLACHFORD— . . . We have just been having an interesting military *funzione*—receiving the old colours of the 77th Regiment to be hung up in the cathedral. They were (*i.e.* the colours) in the Crimea, where the 77th were the first considerable body of English who came in contact with the Russians on the morning of Inkermann, and knocked back one of Simonoff's columns in a wonderful way, according to Kinglake. They came some two hundred, laid their old colours on the altar, and then took them to the place where they are to be fixed ; and then all defiled before them, the band playing " Auld lang syne," and the colonel giving a parting kiss to the flags as he delivered them to me.

A few words written at the end of the year recall the strength of feeling at the time of the Bulgarian atrocities and before the Russo-Turkish war :—

12th December 1876.

Everybody is very savage with everybody about Turks and Russians. I think I never remember such an awkward time for meeting people (until you know you are on the same side), except at the height of the Tractarian row.

Divergences of opinion on Church matters were

scarcely likely to grow less marked as ritual prosecutions continued. Lord Blachford, the Dean's most constant and intimate correspondent, had written strongly in condemnation of the ritualist position, and the following letters express the Dean's sense of the divergence, and his unchanged judgment on the course which was being taken :—

To Lord Blachford.

Deanery, St. Paul's, 5th January 1877.

My dear Blachford—I have no difficulty in agreeing with you about the indefensibleness of Mr. Tooth's position; not, though, on the point of the oath ; I having no liking for violent measures—perhaps because I am disposed to be cowardly.

Nor have I difficulty in agreeing about the fact of acceptance by the Church of State interference and control. I am ready to admit it from the very first. I am sufficiently prone to scepticism to doubt all absolute theories as to right on either side. It has always been a matter of arrangement according to circumstances, and the force which each side had.

But, as you know, I cannot understand how it can be thought that this is really the whole of the question. Besides the matter of obedience to courts as interpreters of law, comes the question why the courts were created, how they have interpreted the law, what is the policy which the governors of the Church have thought it necessary to pursue in respect to a party or a set of opinions in the Church, and which has dictated recent legislation, of which the results are now coming on. And here, I am afraid, we look at things from different points of view. You are more likely to be right than I am in all this tangle. But whether I can make good my view or not—which is a question of mental force—I have thought, and tried to think, a great deal about it. And I can only see in the legal decisions, and in the measures which have brought forth their results in the present crisis, a misuse of law such as has before now been known in history, and a policy of injustice towards an unpopular party, which has, I think, as much to say for itself as any other in the Church, which has done good service to the Church, and which, provoking as it has often been, has had more than parties in English controversy usually have to provoke them. I could condemn Mr. Tooth as heartily as you do; but then I must have condemned even more strongly greater men than Mr. Tooth.

I am afraid that we must be content in this matter to be on opposite tacks. I know quite well what your object is, to abate and rebuke extravagance, and to keep us together. And I shall be very glad if what you say is effective for what we both have at heart, the good of the English Church. But as I said, I cannot quite see things as you do. And to say the truth, I do not at present see the way out of the mistakes that have been made on all sides. If it were not that the English Church has survived as great difficulties before, I should think that matters were very serious just now.

I have written this before I could look at your article which came this morning. I have not read it, and I think that on the whole I had better not. I do not belong to the English Church Union, and have always been rather afraid of it. But it must be remembered that such associations are familiar to English parties, and exist on both sides ; and the rôle of the E.C.U. has been, as far as I know, mainly a defensive one. But if you can make them cautious and reasonable it will be a great gain. I do not doubt they need it.—Ever yours affectionately,   R. W. C.

To the Same.

Deanery, St Paul's, 12th January 1877.

Dear Blachford—With the tone of your last article I quite agree, and with the reminder in it of the gravity of the question. But I think there is a further point—not only how much the Church has accepted, but how much she is to accept.

And further, supposing that there is great danger in accepting, how she is to resist accepting or prevent it. And this is to me a very difficult question. . . . It is idle in the present state of opinion to think of changing laws without mischief, for you cannot do it without breaking up the compromise under which the Church has gone on since the Reformation. No one can doubt what a legislative settlement of the dispute would be at present. It would be Hanoverians legislating for Jacobites.

I am inclined to agree with you about the desirableness of questioning all oaths.[1] Though I think that an oath ought not to be pressed against men except on very clear ground. I remember the way in which in the early days we were twitted at Oxford with breaking our oaths, and how the Provost once came down on me with the oath about obeying the "consuetudines" of the college, when we were agitating about a change in the way of giving college testimonials.— Ever yours affectionately,   R. W. C.

---

[1] See Article in *Guardian*, 3rd January 1877, p. 9.

Writing to his brother, who was now Canon of Wells, and who had written regretting the loss of frequent intercourse, which the distance now between them, and the ties of work, entailed, he says :—

To CANON CHURCH.

DEANERY, ST. PAUL'S, 16th February 1877.

DEAR CHARLES—Yes, it is a long time. One gets eaten up with cares, and talks, and committees, and sermons, and finally does nothing of what one ought to do. I think the only thing that has struck one is the quiet which pervades all things. The debate was dull. Midhat's head over heels was like a sphinx's riddle, very odd and amusing no doubt, but really too puzzling as to what it might lead to, to elicit either jokes or prophecies. The *Pall Mall* does not know what to make of things ; it suggests the thought of a serious split in the Cabinet and of a Beaconsfield *contra mundum*. But no one can tell. I am going to dine quietly with Gladstone to-morrow, and perhaps may gather something. But I expect to come away as wise as I shall go. I doubt if he knows himself what he is going in for ; he is ignorant of two main elements—what will Russia do, and what will the English public do. I believe myself that Russia means war ; but it is only a guess.

The Church world is as quiet as the political—with Tooth still in prison, with Bodington coming on before Lord Penzance on the 20th, and the judgment [1] not to come out till after Easter, and everybody rather anxious as to what " other people " will do, so anxious that nobody asks or talks, except

---

[1] The Judgment of the Judicial Committee of the Privy Council on the Folkestone Ritual case.

to sympathisers, either for or against Mr. Tooth, who appears behind his bars this week in *Vanity Fair* with a rather friendly notice.

Wilkinson has been preaching to large gatherings at our midday short service this week. Knox Little, if he is well enough, goes on next week. The Bishop of Manchester was here yesterday, full of the success of his mission time, and telling touching things of his talks with the theatrical folks. —Ever yours affectionately,   R. W. C.

To the Dean of Durham.

Deanery, St. Paul's, *29th March* 1877.

My dear Lake—Thank you for your note—for the freedom with which you have spoken, which was, of course, what was invited in sending you the paper [1]—and for your kindly frankness to myself.

I am quite aware of the objections that may be urged against such a paper—they are as thick as blackberries ; and so far from its being a " Panacea," I should have very little hope that it, or anything else, is in time to do any good, except that there is the experience of the last thirty or forty years to encourage us. I am a most unwilling convert to the demand for any present legislation. But I should like you, or any one else, to show us what better prospect there is by any other course. The first step to disestablishment was taken when the Archbishop called in the aid of Parliament to put down disputes that ought to have been left to time and patience, and wise influence, to settle. My own

[1] An Address presented to the Archbishops and Bishops, 7th April 1877 ; followed by an explanatory letter from the Dean. See *Guardian*, 8th April and 2nd May, pp. 438 and 602.

fear is that it is too late to undo the mischief. I don't expect much from the paper ; but, at any rate, it enables people to state their position.

Let the Ritualists have common justice in such a Church as ours, and not the Mackonochie and Purchas judgments expressed by Lord Penzance, on the motion of outsiders and the Church Association, and then it will be time to call on moderate people to protest against them. But I will never be a party to screwing up the Church extra tightly in one particular point, and leaving it as loose as it is in others which are as grave. I certainly do think that we have great cause to complain of the way in which law has been administered among us. I don't know what rumours you have heard about the forthcoming judgment. But those which I have heard are not comfortable, though I do not trust any of them. But the thing is, that I am afraid it is too late to take out the sting of former proceedings.

. . . You cannot be more afraid of disestablishment than I am. But I am sure of this, that the Archbishop's trust in such Church law as now goes under the name, and his forcing on men's minds, by a policy of coercion, how much Parliament, as it is, may claim to do with the internal interests of the Church, will not help to avert it. That it may be averted by any sacrifice except of justice and honour, I pray day and night.—Ever yours,

R. W. CHURCH.

The consecration of Dr. Benson as the first Bishop of Truro took place in St. Paul's, on St. Mark's Day, 1877, and was in many ways a memorable day. It was one of the first occasions in St. Paul's, when a great religious ceremony was carried out with all the order and beauty of

x

a perfected musical service. To the Dean, as the following letter shows, it was further marked by the step
which had been made in a private friendship :—

TO THE BISHOP OF TRURO.

DEANERY, ST. PAUL'S, 16th May 1877.

MY DEAR BISHOP OF TRURO—It is difficult to answer fittingly a letter like yours. But you will take the will for the
deed, and believe that with the humility with which I ought,
I do most heartily respond to its undeserved and overflowing kindness. It is a long time since such a passage as that
connected with your consecration has happened in my life.
I had no right to such happiness, in seeing you and knowing you, and in such a bright, unclouded day as that when
we were allowed to welcome you, and when I was allowed
so to take leave of you, and wish you Godspeed on your
great undertaking. St. Paul's, I think, was worthy to be
the scene of such a beginning, and of the remarkable company assembled in it. But it was your kindness which has
given me so much place in that day. It has made a mark
in my birthdays.

I am sure that what was so begun must prosper. I suppose that the courage and the brightness which shone forth
on that day must have its trials. But the day was an
earnest that the idea and presage of Lightfoot's sermon would
be fulfilled. I hope you may be permitted to add in Cornwall another to the many victories which the revived English
Church has achieved, and which, in spite of disasters and
menacing troubles, make it the most glorious Church in
Christendom.—Ever yours affectionately,

R. W. CHURCH.

The words of hopeful anticipation with which the foregoing letter closes are the more noteworthy, when the circumstances under which they were written are recalled. In many ways, as previous letters have shown, the moment was one of grave anxiety. Mr. Tooth was still in prison in Holloway Gaol; the Privy Council decision on the Ridsdale Case had just been given; further prosecutions under the Public Worship Act were spoken of as possible and even probable. To one in the Dean's position it was becoming a practical question whether the time had not come to throw up place and position in protest against the further continuance of such a condition of things.

"I wish I could have a talk with your people," he writes to the Warden of Keble, "who more represent my way of looking at things than some of our hot and despairing spirits here. But the perplexity is great. . . . And yet"—and the words recall the little outburst of proud confidence contained in his letter to the Bishop of Truro, written a day or so before—"there is no more glorious Church in Christendom than this inconsistent English Church, nor one which has shown such wonderful proofs of Christian life."

In the two letters that follow, to the same correspondent, the Dean enters at greater length into the question of his personal position, and the action which the circumstances of the moment might demand from him.

To the Warden of Keble.

DEANERY, ST. PAUL'S, 18*th May* 1877.   .

My DEAR TALBOT—I think that your note demands from me something like an attempt to say what I feel in this matter.

Nothing that has happened has shaken, and I do not think that anything of the same sort could shake my belief in the present English Church. It has defects and anomalies in plenty, but so has every Church that I know of, or that I ever heard of. And there is in it a vigour, a power of recovery, and an increasing value for what is good and true, which I see nowhere else. But it is a question what individuals ought to do when, either in a Church or a nation, they seem to see a policy deliberately followed by those who happen to have power which appears to them to be unjust, encroaching, and unconstitutional. If they have no special position they can grumble, protest, and wait, hoping for better things. But if they are in a place of honour and emolument, where yet they can do nothing, and where they are under the temptation of silence and compliance from private motives, submission and waiting are not so clear duties. If they cannot hinder mischief, they may at least resign.

I cannot help believing that the course of government lately in the English Church is such a policy as I have described. The Bishops, frightened by a movement which they have not tried to understand or govern, have encouraged appeals to law. The law courts have roughly attempted to maintain existing usage. The Archbishop has aggravated the mischief by stirring up the country by a measure intended to facilitate the operation of this judge-made law, while he steadily discountenances any attempt to control it by the only constitutional organ of legislation left to the Church. And the end is, that, while all sorts of liberties are allowed to parties in the Church which the public opinion of the hour sanctions, a tight screw is put on one unpopular one, and a grotesquely one-sided and stiff conformity to minute legal interpretations of rubrics is enforced by penalties, and is preached and paraded as the crucial test of loyalty to the Church and honest obedience to the law.

To me this seems to be unjust, unconstitutional, and oppressive. It is certainly exasperating and impolitic. But the only way in which I can show that I am in earnest in so thinking and speaking, is by quitting the high position which I hold.

You will believe, that though I never wished to come here, it is a serious thing to give up, and begin again to find something by which to help my family. That is one thing to hold one back. Another is, that I most earnestly desire to do nothing to shake confidence in the English Church itself. I don't believe in disestablishment : I can see in it nothing but the present victory of mischief in the Church and in the nation. And any man's move, even a simple resignation, under these circumstances, gives a shake. And I am in great perplexity as to what I ought to do, remembering that the Church never gains by what looks like inconsistency and weak compliance by her ministers who have a considerable stake to lose.—Ever yours affectionately, R. W. CHURCH.

To THE WARDEN OF KEBLE.

DEANERY, ST. PAUL'S, 23rd *May* 1877.

MY DEAR TALBOT—I don't know how to thank you for the way in which you have taken my note, and for all the undeserved confidence you have shown to me. All you say is most weighty. Public interests, such as those of the English Church, must be put before private feelings, and up to a certain point a man is bound to sacrifice his character and reputation—everything but his truth and honour—to public interests. But then comes the large question of public interests, and what they involve.

The Church is threatened by many things. But certainly not the least fatal mischief will be the continuance of this system of vexatious and worrying prosecutions and appeals to law. If they cannot be stopped there really will be only one remedy, and that is something that will clear the air, even at the cost of some present sacrifice and trouble to the Church. With all the terrible losses of 1845, I am not sure that without them we should have done as well as we have. They awed people, and made them think ; and gave time for the latent strength of the Church to grow quietly. No losses now could equal those, nor could they be in the same direction ; and the Church is infinitely stronger. What we want is to frighten Ritualists out of self-will and extravagance, and the people in power from worrying Ritualists. I believe both sides, going on in a dogged, helpless conventionalism, want a lesson. It might carry some Ritualists off their legs ; but it would convince the Archbishop—what he does not believe—that men, who are not Ritualists, are in earnest, and will not stand his policy. —Yours affectionately,   R. W. CHURCH.

To Canon Church.

Deanery, St. Paul's, 22nd May 1877.

Dear Charles—I hope you have a brighter Whitsun-
tide than we have. It has turned cold and gloomy again.
We are all dismal and uncomfortable ourselves. No one
knows what is coming from this judgment, or what anybody
ought to do. Things are quiet so far. But I suppose that
the Association will soon make its move, and Mr. Tooth will
do something wonderful, and then the row will begin. If
people can be let alone there is a chance of peace ; but I
fear they will not. There are rumours that Randall is to
be attacked. It is not easy to know what to say or do.

. . . I am going with Stanley to-morrow to see old Lord
Stratford de Redcliffe. I wonder what he will say.—The
public rows are diversified with little private duels between
Liddon and Archdeacon Allen about the use of the pulpit
at St. Paul's. And, meanwhile, the great war is quietly
preparing in the East, and perhaps a rebound of it in the
West. We may see some strange things this summer. I
am sorry that Gladstone is gone to Birmingham. The
Liberal party may be reconstituted, but I greatly fear the
price.

8th June 1877.

My visit to the great Elchi was very interesting. He
hoped that the General's papers would be published, and
said that he thought he had sent me some. Did he send
any to you ? I am not sure that he did not take me for
you. He told stories about the destruction of the Janissaries,
and the way in which he had taught Sultan Mahmoud and
Reschid Pasha (whom he thought the ablest Turk he had
known) their business. The old lion plainly liked to fight

his battles over again. He was wrapped up in dressing-gown, etc., but his face was fresh, and his eye as keen as a hawk's. He is past ninety. Did you see Stanley's lines on his birthday ? We have Midhat for our neighbour at the Royal Hotel, Blackfriars. He dined with Lord Stratford and discoursed to him about the constitution. Lord S. plainly thinks things looking ill. He has a feeling for the Turks, that he might whip them, being, as they are, very naughty boys, but that no one else ought to. . . .—Ever yours affectionately,   R. W. C.

To Dr. Asa Gray.

20*th June* 1877.

My dear Friend—I received the other day a volume of sermons, Dr. Walker's, which Mrs. Gray was kind enough to send me. Will you thank her very much for remembering me, and thinking that they would interest me. They do much. There is a masculine, nervous strength about them, which is less common now than it used to be ; a grip of the subject and idea, which brings out what it is and means, closing with it like a wrestler, and not fencing with it. His direct, forcible style brings home to one the loss in our modern writing of that vigorous, unadorned manner of writing, which people, spoilt by modern fashions of writing round and round a thing, and playing a sort of sheet-lightning over it, are apt to call bald. To me this is always very refreshing. The best writing of the last century is of this kind ; and it is a relief to find oneself face to face with serious and weighty thoughts, without being distracted by ornament and illustration, perhaps questionable, certainly that one can do without. The sermons seem to me a fine example of real, solid, and original thoughts, severely, and therefore impressively, put into words.

. . . I should like to talk to you about our home affairs. We are passing through a state of confusion, political and ecclesiastical, that may pass away, but may lead to serious changes. People are foolish, and wise people become foolish in their ways of opposing folly, and drive on the foolish people further ; and so things end in something like a persecution of unpopular parties. And we have only just escaped, if we have escaped, a war, on behalf of these hopeless Turks, in one of our crazy panics about Russia and India. The world is wise ; but it is very apt to be wise after, not before, the event. Give our best remembrances and love to Mrs. Gray, and do arrange soon to come our way.—Ever yours affectionately, R. W. CHURCH.

To LORD BLACHFORD.

WELLS, 6th October 1877.

MY DEAR BLACHFORD—I have not yet had time to read more than Greg's paper in the new Symposium. I always read anything of his on moral or religious questions. It is like reading Lucretius or Horace, in the reality of the pathetic strain in which he writes. Other people, even * * * , cannot shake off what Christianity has planted in their blood, even if they deny it with all the violence in the world. They are unconscious believers in better things to come, and can no more help it than they can help thinking in English. But Greg always seems to me really to look on life as they did who had never heard of revealed religion. There is a genuine feeling about life, as without any knowledge beyond the mere auguries of nature. And the profound melancholy

of it is expressed in words, the beauty and tenderness
of which have rarely been equalled. Do you know the
"Enigmas of Life ?" . . .—Ever yours affectionately,

R. W. CHURCH.

From 1876 to 1878, the Dean was for the second
time appointed select preacher at Oxford. A sermon
preached during the course, "Responsibility for our
Belief," occasioned the letters which follow. The
sermon, after dwelling upon the character which responsibility for belief assumes, had gone on to speak of the
hope for those who, seeking honestly, were "feeling
after God," though they had not yet attained to an
intellectual acceptance of the Christian creed. The
Dean's correspondent, who was at the time personally
unknown to him, urged that the same hope ought to
apply to the case of the multitude of lives which, to all
appearance, seem spent and wasted in sin and misery.
The Dean's answer, together with a letter written a year
later to the Principal of Hertford College, are placed
together, in order better to preserve the thread of connection which their subject suggests.

To * * * *.

DEANERY, ST. PAUL'S, 23rd November 1877.

MY DEAR SIR—There is, it seems to me, a wide difference
between earnest seeking with purpose and sincerity, and the
shortcomings and failure of the moral nature, however
occasioned. The one has the distinct promise that seeking
shall find. Whatever one says of the millions of publicans

and sinners, or the "six score thousand persons that cannot discern between their right hand and their left," must rest on other promises. There, it seems to me that we are between the certainties of God's justice, mercy, and love, on the one hand ; and on the other, our own absolute and hopeless ignorance as to how He deals, and will deal, with these millions, both in and out of Christendom, as to whom the first difficulty that presents itself is,—why they were born for such inevitable lives, and, apparently, certain moral failure ? I say apparently, because none but He who knows, in each concrete case, the light given, and the real movements of the will, can know what the failure really is. Scripture, which tells us the doom not only of deliberate sin, but of sinful trifling and carelessness in those who know, or might have known, is silent about these masses of mankind, who, so far as we can see, are without what we have.

It seems to me that the difference in the condition of the *will*, about which, in the case I mentioned, we do know something, and about which, in the case you put, we know nothing, allows us to speak with a confidence in one case which would be out of place in the other. We want, and need to speak with confidence in one case, to encourage men to seek. In the other case we ask, "Are there few that be saved ?" to give ease to our anxious sympathies about those whose case we can but—and well may—leave in the hands of the all-Holy and all-Merciful.

Of the publicans and sinners I do not doubt that many will see and know Him *there*, who did not know Him *here*. But I cannot tell who they are. I only know that now, as far as I can see, they are going against His will. I do not know, for He has not said a word to tell me, what He will do with them. Man's destiny stops not with the grave.

There may be discipline for character and will beyond it. But I cannot speak of it, for I know nothing of it. I only know the discipline which goes on here, and which we are told is so eventful. I have, on the one hand, all the hopes which spring out of God's infinite perfection. I have, to check the speculations of anxious human sympathy, the certainty of my own ignorance—ignorance, the depth of which I cannot measure or comprehend ; and further, the very awful fact of the difficulty with which character and will undergo a change when once they are fixed and confirmed.

You see that I can sympathise with your anxieties of thought ; their effect on me is to make me feel how hard it is to speak soberly and fittingly about those things on the other side of the veil. We cannot know or even guess at them now. We shall know something about them soon.— Yours faithfully,   R. W. Church.

To the Same.

Mells, 5th December 1877.

My dear Sir—Thank you for your note. I think it is important in reference to this matter to bear in mind that, in speaking of sin and sinners, we are apt to take as our type of sin one particular class of sin, the sins of the " publican and the harlot." It is natural that revolting, ruinous, and flagrant as they are, they should *represent* sin to our mind. Yet there are sins more malignant, and more difficult to conceive cured. I can conceive many of these poor creatures, whom the world speaks of as " lost," blindly " seeking after God." It is difficult to me to conceive this of those who, with full knowledge and all advantages, prey on human happiness in one way or another—the selfish seekers of their own interest and pleasure,[1] like the man—I forget his name —Mr. Grand something, in *Daniel Deronda*.

May it not be as to the truth of this question, and the relation between God's mercy and justice at last, that, as in the case of many other truths, we are "not yet able to bear it." When one thinks of how the will is able to deceive and delude itself, I can quite believe that it is not safe for us to be told.—I hope some time I may have the pleasure of meeting you.—Yours faithfully, R. W. Church.

To the Principal of Hertford.

11th November 1878.

My dear Principal—I am afraid I have nothing more to say than I said in the sermon,[2] which is, as you say, an expression of ignorance. Indeed, my own feeling about the whole subject is, that the wisest thing men can do is to cultivate diligently a sense of their own hopeless ignorance, and to have the courage to say "I cannot tell."

What Eternity is I cannot conceive, certainly not *a parte ante*, and really not *in præsenti* or *a parte post*. There is one great term of the discussion involved in darkness! Then, as to the purpose of God's creation, who shall venture to be peremptory about its necessary purpose and conclusion, when he has the fact of evil staring him in the face. The fact of

---

[1] "It seems to me," the Dean writes in another letter, "that people get into the way of identifying sin with one kind of sin—the sin of the outcasts—and forget the sins of *character*, of the Pharisees, and of the wicked, wise conspirators against human good and happiness, who are eminently the Bible type of the sinners who have everything to fear."

[2] "Sin and Judgment," preached during the Dean's course as select preacher, 1876-1878, and published in the volume of University Sermons, entitled *Human Life and its Conditions*.

evil is to me quite as great a crux as even eternal punishment ; and even eternal punishment thought of, not for such
as you and me, who know so much, and perhaps have so
much on their consciences, but for the millions upon millions
who have not known their right hand from their left, and to
whom life has had no opportunity of good, or respite from
evil. The common topic against eternal punishment, "Could
any man of ordinary feeling appoint it ? and if not, how
could God ?" is quite as strong about evil. How can we
imagine ourselves, supposing we had omnipotence or omni-
science, enduring to bring into being such unintermitting
masses of misery and sin ? The difficulty of finally dealing
with evil is to me a far less difficulty than that of evil itself.
The ordinary language about eternal punishment seems to
me simply to forget the fact of the equal difficulty of evil.
Two difficulties do not make one solution ; but at least they
ought to teach patience and guarded language.

On the other hand, Scripture, though awfully plain-
spoken and stern, seems to me very *general* in its language
on this matter. I heard a sermon yesterday in the same
sense as * * *'s, and though it was forcible in its Scripture
proofs, I can only say it simply worried and almost exasper-
ated me, because it assumed all through that we knew the
exact definite purport of the Scripture terms used, and that
they were used in exact correspondence with our own on
the same subject. I doubt the assumption, and if I am
asked "What is the use of the Scripture language ?" my
answer is that the general aim intended, viz. the certain and
terrible punishment of sin, may be attained without satisfying definite questions about *how*, and *how long*, and *what
next.*

I have no doubt that we have not yet reached the true

and complete method of Scripture exegesis, and that a great
deal remains to be done by sober and reverential inquiry, in
distinguishing between its definite and precise language
("the Word was God") and its vague or incidental or unqualified language ("hate his father and mother," "shall
not come out till he has paid the uttermost farthing"). But
I shrink much from speculating on the human knowledge
of our blessed Lord, or the limitations—and they may have
been great—which He was pleased to impose on Himself,
when He "emptied Himself," and became as one of us. I
have never been satisfied with the ordinary explanations of
the text you quote, St. Matt. xxiv. 36. They seem simply
to explain it away as much as any Unitarian gloss of St.
John i. 1. To me it means that He who was to judge the
world, who knew what was in man, and more, who alone
knew the Father, was at that time content to have that hour
hidden from Him—did not choose to be above the angels in
knowing it—as He was afterwards content to be forsaken of
the Father. But the whole is perfectly inconceivable to my
mind, and I could not base any general theory of His
knowledge on it.—I think it is very likely that we do not
understand the meaning of much that is said in Scripture ;—
its sense, and the end and purport for which *at the time* it
was said. But it would perplex me much to think that He
was imperfect or ignorant in what He *did* say, whether we
understood Him or not.

I am afraid I have not written what is worth your
reading. But really all I have to say amounts to this—that
I feel that a sense of ignorance, which it is impossible to
over-estimate, ought to play a much larger part in our discussions on the future than it usually does.—Ever yours,

R. W. CHURCH.

To Dr. Asa Gray.

DEANERY, St. Paul's, 28th January 1878.

My dear Friend— . . . Well, the "Suave mari magno" is on your side of the world now. I don't know how it will end. But our policy under Dizzy has just brought us within an inch of a war, which, if it had begun, might well not have left us what we are. They are at it at this moment in the House of Commons, discussing the ministerial demand for an extra war vote of six millions. I suppose they will get it. We hope that now the immediate danger of war is passed. But a great part of the nation is very mad to uphold the Turks ; and we are not out of the wood. And I have been for some days thinking of the humiliation for an English citizen of seeing his country committed to an unnecessary and unjust war, and to one of the greatest crimes of our generation.

I hope soon to meet Sir J. Hooker, and hear about your adventures. He is, I hope, coming to dine with us, and, you know, he is good company. He was in St. Paul's only yesterday, but I could not catch him. I should like to look forward to the prospect, three years hence, of a scour across America. But, somehow, one of my superstitions all my life has been, not a shrinking, but an incapacity to realise being alive and well so long forward as three years. I have come, nevertheless, to the ripe age of sixty-three. But to add three years to that seems an inconceivable thing. However, I will look forward ; and I hope, too, to seeing you here. I should like to show you St. Paul's, more than I should have done five years ago.—Ever yours affectionately,

R. W. CHURCH.

Dr. Mozley's death, after long failure of health, had taken place in the beginning of 1878. In the letter which follows reference is made to an article which Lord Blachford was preparing on two volumes of historical essays which had been republished since Dr. Mozley's death :—

To Lord Blachford.

ZERMATT, 30*th August* 1878.

My DEAR BLACHFORD— . . . I am so very glad that you are going to do J. B. M. I wish I could have some talk about it, because thoughts are beaten out in talking which lie still when one is writing. It would be interesting to trace the maturing of his affluence and richness of ideas and words, from the almost dithyrambic bursts in Strafford, to the more regulated magnificence of his later rhetoric. He was a bit of a despiser when he did not like or understand. . . . It kept him from doing a justice which he could well afford to do to things which he was opposing; and so really weakens argument, because ignoring what his opponents might think their best points. He never seemed to me to feel the force of an opposite argument, till it was really beginning to tell on his own views, and to modify or change them. I hope I shall have a chance of talking about this when I get back.

Thank you for Newman's letter.[1] How very curious

---

[1] THE ORATORY, 22*nd July* 1878.

My DEAR BLACHFORD—I am glad you are so much pleased with P. and A. I thought you would be, though, of course, such a book is, or must be, fairly open to many criticisms. But you are merciful. I find that Amadeus took his quotation from Virgil from the motto to the Paper on Instinct in Addison's *Spectator,* not having his Virgil that he should be dazzled, and what a curious bit of English feeling : "it opens such a view of England, great in the deeds of their forefathers . . . and not degenerate," etc. Fancy any of the Romans writing so ; e.g. Ward, with his heathen mock-virtue of patriotism. I should think that N. was almost the unique cross between a true Briton of the proud school of Chatham and Burke, and the enthusiastic, devout, fervid Roman Catholic. But then the irresistible sense of the grotesqueness of the business finds its place too. It is one of the most characteristic little notes of his that I have seen for a long time. It is odd, too, the touch about " hypocrisy," which he does not see.

I am reading Proteus.[1] It is very interesting, but Proteus seems to me to be weak. I feel sometimes an in-clination both to give a shove—" My dear fellow can't you put your case better," and also to let fly at his assumptions. It never seems to occur to him to clear to his own mind

with him. The *Guardian* throws out the guess that perhaps it was not a real correspondence—but I know the parties, and each would have liked to alter what he had written, but they thought it would take from the life of the discussion if they did so—but surely the outlines of P.'s life, with the Jesuits at Constantinople, and with the Redemptorists at Clapham, are too boldly drawn to be fictions. Nor would a Catholic writer of fiction make his opponent a Catholic.

As to Disraeli's firework, I confess I am much dazzled with it, and wish it well. It is a grand idea that of hugging from love the Turk to death, instead of the Russian bear, which, as a poem or romance, finds a weak part in my imagination. And then it opens such a view of England, great in the deeds of their forefathers, showing that they are not degenerate sons, but rising with the occasion in fulfilment of the "Tu ne cede malis, sed contra audentior ito." And then it is so laughably clever a move, in a grave diplo-matic congress—and then it opens such wonderful views of the future, that I am overcome by it. Nor do I see the hypocrisy you speak of.—Ever yours affectionately,   JOHN H. NEWMAN.

[1] *Proteus and Amadeus ; a Correspondence*, edited by Aubrey de Vere.

what he means by that wonderful and mysterious "matter," which could be "unconsciously just," and "wise," and "creative"; and why not also "unconsciously generous, and compassionate, and affectionate," etc. etc. But I am only half through it. . . .—Ever yours affectionately,

R. W. C.

To the Same.

Deanery, St. Paul's, 4th November 1878.

My dear Blachford—I have just got out of the bustle of the bells.[1] The excitement they caused was really curious. Though notices had appeared in the papers that there was to be nothing unusual in the service of the day, the people were determined to believe that there would something happen which they could see by coming to church. And we were besieged for tickets as if for a great musical service. Of course many came to hear the bells open; but this hardly accounted for the crowd in the church, which was full from end to end. However, they had the sight of the procession which went through the nave, and disappeared at one of the doors on its way to the belfry. It was very good of the Bishop to climb up all the steps to the ringing loft, where we all assembled, and had the service I showed you. It was a striking sight in its way. The chamber was filled with the choir in surplices, and, mounted on their ringing boxes, the twelve or thirteen "college youths," stalwart fellows in their shirt sleeves, grasping their ropes, and standing still and silent like statues. There was something odd about the scene, which suggested somehow a scaffold and execution.

---

[1] A peal of twelve bells had been hung in the south-west tower of the cathedral; they were rung for the first time on All Saints' Day, 1878.

Then, when the service was over, the Bishop, or his chaplain for him, gave the word, *Go*. And then they began slowly and gently pulling, and we heard the sounds above. When the people in the Churchyard heard it they gave a great cheer ; and they hung about the place all the evening. The crowds were delighted with them in spite of Mr. Haweis. The *Times* could not leave us alone. However, it has brought out the Bishop of London on our side.

There is an odd impression of want of confidence about ; —"what a mess," is the sort of typical phrase you hear about you. But nobody knows anything. Paul told me that he heard from the Abbé Martin in Paris that J. H. N. is to be a Cardinal, if he lives till Easter.

. . . I am going to dine at the "Literary" to-night, where I may see Sir James Colvile, and possibly the new earl. Kindest remembrances at Blachford and Moor Cross. —Ever yours affectionately,   R. W. C.

In the beginning of 1879, the vacant Bishopric of Durham was offered to, and in the result was accepted by Dr. Lightfoot.

To the Bishop of Truro.

DEANERY, ST. PAUL'S, 23rd *January* 1879.

My DEAR BISHOP OF TRURO—First, I must thank you for the cathedral book—for the work itself, for republishing it, and for the inscription with which my copy has come to me.

And next, for writing to me about this most anxious matter, which touches us both so deeply, and not us only, but greater things. I admit that it is hard for me to be fair. The thought of losing him is dreadful. And I know that I have a character of being a coward in these things. And all that you urge is of the greatest weight ; and you have put the side which Westcott (*e.g.*) takes with the greatest force, when you urge the value of his "spirit of counsel" in the high councils of the Church. It is a point which, as I expected he would, the Archbishop urged when Lightfoot saw him yesterday ; and with good reason, though he frightened Lightfoot by expressing anxiety as to who there would be to take *his own place* if he were removed, and opening further prospects of tremendous responsibility. And I am worldly enough, too, to feel a great rising of heart at the recognition, with such, and not inadequate honour, of the first scholar of the English Church.

But yet, even for that, I do look with distress at the breaking off just now of the career which he has deliberately designed for himself, which he is fulfilling so nobly and so usefully, and in which he leaves no successor ; none, I mean, of the same rare and commanding powers. For he is not only full of knowledge, he is able to make knowledge *live*. He is able to animate it with the sense of its connection with the needs and hopes of present modern life. And at Cambridge, I take it, he is showing a crowd of men, who are to take our places, how this is to be done. To be the foremost teacher of Christian learning at Cambridge at such a time as this is to hold a critical post, which is, in its way, alone and without its fellow, even in the highest places of the Church.

It is true, as you say, that counsel is wanted, and fresh thought and independent ideas of a Bishop's leadership, not after custom and the world, but after the greatness of his real calling. And if he goes I shall most hopefully console myself by thinking what we have in him of all this. But I have ventured to plead for the interests, not so much of knowledge, but of study, and for the value in such days as ours of a life professedly devoted to these ends, contented to fulfil them with the enthusiasm, the conscientiousness, the unselfish independence with which all great ends must be followed. As the epistle of this week says, there are "gifts differing according to the grace given unto us." I am sure you will pardon me for attaching the greatest value to those gifts which we have seen and been so thankful for in him, and for being dismayed at having to exchange them for others, excellent as they may be.

This, as far as I know I can trust myself, is the one ground of my judgment on the subject, my strong and increasing sense of the value of the life which he has deliberately chosen, and to which he has, as far as he might, dedicated himself ; its value as a work for the Great Master and the great purpose ; its value, especially, considering how few men can, or have the right to choose it for their vocation, from want of the combination of gifts which it demands. Will you forgive me for thinking of standing between yourself and such a colleague in your great tasks ? And yet, I am sure that at least you sympathise with my value for what he is, even if you see reason to wish that now at length he may exchange it for the great honours proposed to him, and carry his singular excellences of mind and character to a new sphere.

I don't know how he will decide : to-morrow, I suppose, he will settle. He is still torn and perplexed. But if he goes to Durham, Bishop Butler will have a successor worthy of him, in the combination of innocence, simplicity, and

pure nobleness of thought and purpose, with intellectual
forces which make his fellows wonder and admire.

But oh dear! if he leaves St. Paul's. And yet the day
must come, somehow. He is gone to the Athenæum to have
a talk with Lake. Stanley of course urges Durham.
Vaughan was not well enough to see him.—Ever yours
affectionately,   R. W. CHURCH.

The following letter to an old college friend sufficiently suggests by its contents the questions to which
it was a reply. Other letters will be found later in the
volume, written to Lady Welby herself, the originator
of the correspondence :—

To THE REV. PHILIP MULES.

, DEANERY, ST. PAUL'S, 8th March 1879.

MY DEAR MULES—I am very sorry to have been so tardy
in replying to your note. But just now, besides the ordinary
business of the day, I am fighting with some proof-sheets,
and can hardly keep my head above water.

I am very much honoured by your friend's wish to know
any thoughts of mine on the subject of her perplexity. But
she makes it embarrassing when she makes the condition that
she "must not have vagueness and platitude." For the
subject has been before the minds of men, along with many
others as perplexing, ever since they began to think. I do
not see where any novelty about it is to come from. Without knowledge, it is difficult not to be vague, and without
discovery and the possibility of discovery, difficult to avoid
platitudes. I am afraid that nothing that I ever thought
about the matter would bear the test.

As far as I understand the difficulty it is this : How could our Lord *really* have sympathised in *all* human pain, when He could not, by supposition, have known that which gives it its worst sting—its apparent uselessness and its helplessness ? Well, I can only say that I cannot form the faintest conception how, in the actual depths of that Divine suffering nature, all human pain was borne, and shared, and understood. I can only see it from the outside. I see the suffering ; I am told, on His authority, what it means and involves. I can, if I like, and as has often been done, go on and make a theory *how* He bore our sins, and *how* He gained their forgiveness, and *how* He took away the sins of the world. But I own that the longer I live the more my mind recoils from such efforts. It seems to me so idle, so, in the very nature of our condition, hopeless, just in proportion as one seems to grasp more really the true nature of all that went on beyond the visible sight of the Cross, all that was in Him who was God and man, whose capacities and inner life human experience cannot reach or reflect. But one of the thoughts which pass sometimes through our minds about the sufferings of the Cross, is, what *could* be the necessity of such suffering? What *was* the use of it? How, with infinite power, could not its ends have been otherwise attained? Why need He have suffered ? Why could not the Father save Him from that hour? Did that thought, in the limitations and "emptying" (Phil. ii. 7) of the Passion, pass through His mind too ?

But I suppose that, after all, the real difficulty is not about Him, but ourselves. Why pain at all ? I can only say that the very attempt to give an answer, that the very thought of an answer *by us* being conceivable, seems to me one which a reasonable being in our circumstances ought not to entertain. It seems to me one of those questions which can only be expressed by such a figure as a fly trying to get through a glass window, or a human being jumping into space ; that is, it is almost impossible to express the futility of it. It is obvious that it is part of a wider subject, that it could not be answered *by itself*, that we should need to know a great many other things to have the power of answering. And what is the use of asking what we cannot know ? Why we are what we are ;—how what was not came into being ; —what is the present life, the mode of action, the presence of the Divine Being ;—what is eternity ;—what is going on in the fixed stars ?—It is one of those questions about our present condition of which, if we choose, we may ask any number, with the same chance of an answer. Why is Nature, being so perfect, yet so imperfect ? Why of all the countless faces which I meet as I walk down the Strand, are the enormous majority failures—deflections from the type of beauty *possible* to them ? Why are there poisons, and what is the use of poisonous beasts ? For a snake, a bee, a wasp, don't want their poisons to take their food. Or to take what to me is as much the crux of our condition as pain—the relation of the sexes, the passion of love ; how strange, how extravagant, how irrationally powerful over all the world, how at the root of the best things of life, how at the root of its very worst ? Strange, ambiguous, perplexing lot for creatures made in the image of God.

Of course this is only Butler again ; it is only vagueness and platitude. Every one knows it. But not only I cannot get beyond it, but I cannot imagine any one doing so. And then it comes to the old story : here are facts and phenomena on both sides, some leading to belief, some to unbelief ; and we human creatures, with our affections, our hopes and wishes and our wills, stand, as it were, solicited by either set of facts. The facts which witness to the goodness and the love of God are clear and undeniable ; they are not got rid of by the presence and certainty of other facts, which seem of an opposite kind ; only the coexistence of the two contraries is perplexing. And then comes the question which shall have the decisive governing influence on wills and lives ? You must, by the necessity of your existence, trust one set of appearances ; which will you trust ? Our Lord came among us not to clear up the perplexity, but to show us which side to take.

The paper you sent me speaks of the deteriorating effect of pain. I most entirely recognise the accuracy of the observation. It is one of the most terrible features of suffering. But then it must be remembered that anything, not only pain, may be deteriorating—either by fault of the will, if health and faculties are unimpaired, or, as is, we hope, often the case in illness, by failure of that physical organisation through which the will acted soundly and loyally when the man was in health. And how terribly deteriorating is the effect sometimes, not merely of success, but of a simply quiet, undisturbed life. We are poor creatures, and yet we have in us the making of heroes and saints.

You see I have rambled on into sermonising. I hope your friend will forgive me ; and remember that I do not pretend to fulfil her conditions, though I thoroughly sympathise with the frame of mind which imposes them.

I do not know Hinton's book, but I quite agree that the sufferings of the inferior animals are almost the most difficult part of the subject. Their condition, generally, gives me vertigo when I think of it.—Yours ever,

R. W. CHURCH.

The transition is an abrupt one from this letter to the two which follow it, which recall memories of Basle and Constance, where part of the summer holidays of 1879 had been passed. But brief though they are, they are too characteristic to be omitted.

To the Warden of Keble.

Deanery, St. Paul's, 21st August 1879.

My dear Warden— . . . I forget what you know of my proceedings in the last fortnight abroad. The feature of them was a closer acquaintance with Basle—its minster, its towers, and its Holbeins. There the memory of the Council is shadowy; it was a feeble affair after Constance. But the interest of Basle is about Erasmus, and his printer Froben, and his painter Holbein, and his friend and executor Boniface Amerbach, the collector of all the Holbein relics which enrich the museum, and his great rival Œcolampadius, the Zwinglian reformer ; and all the tombs and epitaphs in the cloisters of the men with famous names, Buxtorfs, and Burckhardts, and Wettsteins, and Bauhins, and Meyers, and Schweighäusers, etc., scholars and professors of the brilliant days of Basle. I have been reading about Erasmus since, and with great interest. He is a man whom it is impossible to admire, and yet, in such a time of turmoil, violence, and breaking up of foundations, one cannot but have sympathy for his perplexities, and wonder for his bright and keen intellect, his indefatigable laboriousness, and his singular good sense. But he was selfish, insincere, and mean-spirited. —Ever yours, R. W. Church.

To the Same.

DEANERY, ST. PAUL'S, 10*th October* 1879.

My DEAR WARDEN—Thank you very much for remembering the Lay Sermon. I am very glad to have it.
I must look at Milman's account of the Council [of
Constance]: I only know Lenfant's. I am sure that it is
a turning-point worth knowing about. Of course there was
an immense lot of rubbish about it; and the mischief had
gone so deep into the Church and society, that none but
strong men and strong measures, and further, real knowledge,
could have seriously turned things right. But there were
good men there, like Gerson, who burned, and Huss, who
was burned; and Hallam, who probably was more of a statesman than the foreigners. But it was not to be. They got
rid of the schism, and John XXIII., and they got back at
once to their old Popes and ways, Colonnas and Piccolominis,
and so on to Borgias and Riarios and Della Roveres. Even
if they had had a stronger prophet than Gerson, I suppose
he would not have prevailed any more than Elijah did, or
Isaiah, or Jeremiah. I sometimes wonder what Savonarola
would have done if he had been at Constance or even Basle.
I suppose they would have burnt him all the same; but
with that popular power, which Gerson wanted, he might
have done something;—hardly, perhaps, among Germans.

I do not know when I can come and see you. I came
back all well from Devonshire, and two or three days in
town bring me back at once to what I was before I went
away.—Ever yours,   R. W. CHURCH.

To   *   *   *   *.

DEANERY, ST. PAUL'S, *9th March* 1880.

MY DEAR SIR—You have asked me a hard question, and one on which, after all, each man's experience is perhaps his best guide. My own belief is that it is not *books* (like Spenser and Shakespeare at least) which do mischief, but *companions*. If children can be kept from evil companionship, I believe that for the most part they pass through books with shut eyes and entire unconsciousness. I assume that the atmosphere of the book is wholesome, and the general interest high and attractive. I am quite sure that I used, as a boy, to read the old *Arabian Nights* without a suspicion of what is only too obvious to grown people, simply carried away by the excitement and wonder of the story. And so I am sure that children whom I know have read Shakespeare, and come to know it well.

If children learn nothing from companions and servants, I believe they will learn little or nothing from books. But of course when, and if, their eyes are opened, then danger begins. But my own belief is that, speaking generally, it is not one of great magnitude, if children have been well and Christianly trained, if their sense of duty has been kept strong, and their natural instincts of purity, modesty, and shame at evil and coarseness, have been fostered. There is all this on the side of good against the promptings of evil, and still more of curiosity ; and besides, in the case of great writers, there is their greatness and nobleness, and height of feeling and thought, throwing into, and keeping in the background what is bad. This it is which makes the difference between Shakespeare and the other Elizabethan dramatists. If this were not so, reading would be a dangerous

gift. The dangers from books are not so much for children
as for grown-up people—perhaps even the older they get.—
Yours faithfully,   R. W. CHURCH.

To LORD BLACHFORD.

DEANERY, ST. PAUL'S, 30*th March* 1880.

MY DEAR BLACHFORD—I was at a crush at Tennyson's
last night. It seemed to me that the room was throbbing
with Anti-Gladstonianism. Tennyson began by asking me
whether I was a great admirer of Diz.—Well, he said, he
was not either—he was always a Liberal ; but really the way
in which * * * was going on, also * * * was quite intolerable ; and then he spoke of the Austrian business very
bitterly.

Then I came across Spedding—(what a haranguer—a good
one—he is). He went on in the same way, only more
temperately and evenly than the poet, without jerks. He
said that his sympathies had been all his life with the
Liberal party (he still read his *Daily News*), but that as
things are, he could not now wish them to come into power.
He did not see what they could do, or how they could
improve things.—Then Gladstone. He ought to have held
a position quite unique in England by this time, and have
been the most powerful person among us, with a capacity
for benefiting the country which no one for years had had,
and no one else could have ; something analogous to that
of the Duke of Wellington, only higher, in proportion to
his larger political experience and larger sympathies : that of
a moderator above all parties. . . . He thought that after
all, things had gone well under this Government. He did
not think there was much in the cries raised against them :

"Imperialism," for instance. He suggested that it was one of Dizzy's dodges and amusements from time to time to throw out a phrase "to be worried," like "scientific frontier," and "ascendancy," and "unconstitutional"—knowing that he had the thing all right. It was a frank despair of the Liberal cause from an old Liberal.

Then Stanley was very brisk—he had just been writing to a French friend, that he was at war with "les Clericaux, les Medicaux (*i.e.* the Westminster Hospital doctors), et les Radicaux." The whole scene gave me a sense of the wave of Conservatism which is sweeping over us, and of the intense disgust at Gladstone among the "thinkers." Spedding said that Adam, the Whip, is very confident.

The City of London Conservatives have placed their claim on the sole ground of the foreign policy of the Government. No doubt they know best what will tell in the City; but it is surprising. But it clears my view, and I shall vote for the three candidates who do *not* represent approval of this foreign policy.—Ever yours affectionately,

R. W. C.

The ecclesiastical history of 1880 is full of the perplexities and troubles brought about by the ritual litigation which had grown up since the passing of the Public Worship Regulation Act. The Clewer and Mackonochie suits exhibit under one aspect the course and character assumed by such prosecutions; another and more painful side was shown in the cases of Mr. Dale of St. Vedast, in the City of London, of Mr. Enraght of Holy Trinity, Bordesley,—and after a short delay, caused by some technical point in the procedure, —of Mr. Green of St. John's, Miles Platting, where

the refusal to recognise that "civil courts, imposed
upon the Church by Parliament, and never accepted by
the Church herself, acting freely and in her corporate
capacity, ought to govern the conscience and conduct of
English clergymen,"[1] had at length brought about the
penalty of imprisonment for contempt of court. Distress
and indignation grew more widespread and fierce, when
it was seen to what extremities such enforcement of
the law in ritual prosecutions might lead; and the
letters, memorials, and protests of the year all combine
to show how acutely critical the situation had become.
"It is much easier," writes the Dean to a correspondent
at the close of the year, "to see how much amiss things
are than to mend them."

Things that have got into confusion by our fault or
negligence cannot be set right at will. But I think that
we have had a warning where danger lies, and we must see
to it as well as we can. . . . It seems to me that an *immediate*
want is the restoration of peace by putting an end to all
this law business, with its imprisonments and deprivations,
and a willingness on the part of the Bishops to stand forward
as the upholders of fair liberty; and a reasonable and
generous toleration of differences, even strong differences of
ritual. If they cannot see their way to this, they must
make up their minds to seeing men who are not Ritualists
refusing to share any longer the dishonour of an administration so partial and unjust.

And next we must see how we can best indicate and

---

[1] See letter from Dr. Liddon. *Guardian*, 24th November 1880,
p. 1628.

secure, according to the present needs of our time, the spiritual character of our Church. It is not easy, but we must try.

. . . I hardly think the time has come for any meeting, and I am not the person to take the lead in a meeting. It may be necessary, but it is a dangerous instrument; and if it saved the Athanasian creed, it had, I fear, something to do with passing the Public Worship Act. It infuriated the House of Commons. But the more and the more earnestly the opinions and feelings of the clergy are brought home to the knowledge of our authorities in Church or State the better.

Two letters to Canon Carter of Clewer carry on the subject to the further consideration of the remedies to be sought for to put an end to this state of things :—

To Canon Carter.

Deanery, St. Paul's, 23rd December 1880.

My dear Mr. Carter—I ought to have thanked you before for your most interesting note. I think I entirely agree, and I am sorry for it, with your view of matters—that is, I see no exit at present. If the Archbishop was so alarmed as to realise to himself the state of things, he might help us. But the newspapers and the clubs and people like * * * tell him that he is all right, that he has the "people of England" at his back, and none but a few malcontents and dreamers to deal with. With all his shrewdness he does not know the English clergy ; and I cannot help fearing that if any of us approached him, he would only think of putting us into difficulties, which it is

Z

easy enough to do, both as to what we go for, and as to how far we are agreed ; and would send us away, satisfied himself that we are very unpractical people.

I think that we ought, if we can, to make up our minds what to propose.   There are two distinct dangers—(1) The rooting out true Church doctrines and liberty by a policy of persecution which has been going on for the last fifteen years.   (2) The gradual confusion of the limits of civil and spiritual authority by the way in which courts have been constituted, and have acted in recent judicial arrangements and proceedings.   The first is the most crying and immediate danger, but I don't think it is the most formidable.

I am content myself to leave the Privy Council where it is, so that it is purely a secular court, deciding Church causes only as it decided the Guibert case from Canada.   But we want a spiritual court of appeal besides, on doctrine and discipline, and I don't see what we can have but one of Bishops, either representative or as a body, according to Liddon's [1] proposal.   Of course any one can see the risk. But what else can we propose on principle ?   And an appeal from it can only lie either to the Synod of the Church of England or to —— ? the day when there shall be a free council.

At any rate I should be willing to take this as my proposal ; and further, that the lower courts, arches, etc., should be formally and avowedly courts acting in the name and by the delegation of the spiritual authorities.   I think the mere discussion of such suggestions would at least help to arrest that increasing confusion between Parliamentary and Church authority which is gaining ground.

---

[1] See Preface to Liddon's *Thoughts on Present Church Troubles.*

But, first of all, unless the Bishops will be reasonable and stop this deliberate policy of hunting us out, it is no good to talk of anything else. If they will be reasonable, then it will be time to call upon a good many people to remember what a bishop's authority is. But the distrust of them is so great that every one is afraid of committing himself to any understanding about submission to their authority or advice. I am glad to see that Dean Lake has ventilated the perilous question of touching the Public Worship Regulation Act,[1] though I can hardly hope that either that or the Privy Council judgments will easily be reformed. Things are in such a ticklish state politically that I doubt whether Gladstone would get Parliament to look at things fairly.

But I hope that some of our friends will measure their words and not say rash things. There is time on our side, and growing Church feeling and power. We must not throw away our chances.

I agree with you that we cannot go on for ever resisting the courts, whatever they may be.—Yours very faithfully,

R. W. CHURCH.

To the Same.

Deanery, St. Paul's, 28th December 1880.

My dear Mr. Carter—I am very glad that you are going to see the Archbishop. It is very good of you to go.

The pressing thing is to get some peace and toleration—toleration, not precarious and depending on people's tempers, but acknowledged as wise, if not as just, by the Bishops.

But I think he ought to be made to see that the Public Worship Act and its consequences have not left things as

---

[1] In a letter to the *Times*. See *Guardian*, 29th December 1880.

they were, and that he ought, in the interests of the body of which he is the Primate, to do something to make clear the spiritual authority of the Church. We don't want to affront Parliament or judges ; and if the Bishops would only sympathise with us, and condescend to learn as we have to learn, I, for one, should be content to submit to their rulings. But we cannot go on letting the world think that we acquiesce in the idea that we are merely an "Act of Parliament" Church.

It is curious, the most insulting letters which my production has brought me are from Roman Catholics, gnashing their teeth at our claim to be a real spiritual body.

I saw a letter of the Archbishop's to Lake, expressing full approval of Lake's letter. This is hopeful. But we must be cautious. If he is in earnest, the Convocation resolutions may be a fair basis ; but they will probably want reconsidering in some points.—Yours very faithfully,

R. W. CHURCH.

The "production" of which the previous letter speaks was a letter to the *Times*, entitled "The Established Church." The letter itself runs as follows :—

To the Editor of the *Times*.

16*th December* 1880.

Sir—The "short and easy method" of dealing with the Ritualists—I mean in argument—is, that English clergymen are ministers of an Established Church, and are, therefore, as much bound to submit to all that Parliament orders as any other public functionaries—to submit or to resign ; and by an Established Church, as used in this argument, is sometimes expressly signified in words, but always implied, whether people see what they mean or not, a State Church, deriving all its rights, duties, and powers from Parliament; for unless this were so, the inference would not hold. If the Church be supposed to have an existence and powers of its own, besides what the State gives it,—and however closely joined with the State, to be something which the State, though it may claim to regulate, can neither create nor destroy,—then the debate is open whether the conditions of union and co-operation have been observed on either side. Whether the Ritualist contention, in particular, is right or wrong is another matter.

If this proposition is true, that an Established Church is what Parliament makes it, or allows it to be, and nothing more, then everything easily follows. People may well express surprise at clergymen pleading conscience for disobeying courts of justice. "Mutinous ecclesiastics" and "bad citizens" are too light terms of condemnation for those who defy the law of England, and throw all the social order into confusion which they are especially sworn and paid to maintain.

But if this is a true account of the Church of England, and the old constitutional theory of a union of Church and State, recognised as well as violated in a thousand transactions of our history, be a figment, then other consequences too will follow. It will follow that all that is found in the books of our greatest masters of religious teaching, in all Churches and sects, about the nature of the Christian Church, is ranting nonsense. It will follow that the Ritualists are indeed rebels, perhaps more inexcusable than any who are troubling the Queen's peace in Ireland. But it will also follow that the English Church is not what religious men of

all schools, Churchmen and Nonconformists, believe a Church
to be. It will follow, that such a claim as Mr. Voysey—for
whose honesty and courage I have a high respect—expresses
in the subjoined advertisement, is a legitimate one :—"The
Rev. Charles Voysey, speaking for himself, and in no way
pledging other members of the Theistic Church, desires to
make it known that he retains his Holy Orders in the Church
of England, and personally upholds the present relations
between the Church and State, as by law established. He
approves only some of the doctrines of the Church, which,
having been ratified by Parliament, can by Parliament be
annulled, and he looks forward to a second Reformation by
which the Church of England may be made truly national."
I think it will follow that three-fourths of the English clergy,
if they are the men I take them to be, will say that such a
State Church was not the Church which they believed themselves to be serving and defending, or a Church which it
would be possible for them to accept.—Your obedient servant,

R. W. CHURCH.

But the public conscience could not for an indefinite
time stand the sight of hard-working and exemplary
clergymen imprisoned for refusing to submit to a court
whose jurisdiction they felt bound to deny, whilst
irregularity in directions opposite to that in which they
were said to have strayed went notoriously unpunished,
and even unrebuked. Before long such one-sided rigour
provoked a reaction of sympathy; and the more hopeful
tone which may be detected in the Dean's letter to the
Bishop of Salisbury,—who in a pastoral letter to his
diocese, had urged "as the first and greatest need" for
the moment, the exercise of a "larger and larger-hearted

tolerance,"—suggests that there were already signs of
a turn in the tide of misunderstanding and condemnation :—

To THE BISHOP OF SALISBURY.

DEANERY, ST. PAUL'S, *13th January* 1881.

MY DEAR UNCLE GEORGE—May I send you my most
hearty thanks for your admirable letter. Oh ! if all our
Bishops would deal with things as wisely and reasonably,
we should not be in the trouble in which we find ourselves.
It is a brave and true statement. Is it not worth while
sending it to the *Times?* It will be mocked at, but it will
be read by people who do not see the *Guardian.*

The Archbishop has received our memorial very kindly,
referring us to his letter to Mr. Wilkinson, and promising to
bring the subject of the Memorial before the Bishops. He
has been very friendly in his communications with me and
other people. He had Mr. Carter down at Addington, and
they got on together delightfully. These troubles will not
have been in vain if they impress on us all the necessity of
trust in one another, patience and charitable desire to understand one another ; if they help to turn the hearts of the
fathers to the children, and the children to the fathers.
Meanwhile, the immediate danger is great on all sides, and
the remedies more easy to wish for than to find.—Ever yours
affectionately, R. W. C.

To THE REV. W. J. COPELAND.

DEANERY, ST. PAUL'S, *30th January* 1881.

MY DEAR COPELAND—Many thanks for your letter. It
has been a worrying and anxious winter. One never knows
how ticklish things are ; but they are ticklish. I have been

surprised at the extent to which indignation and alarm have penetrated among the clergy. I am quite sure that if any man with a name had put forth a strong declaration, undertaking under no circumstances to recognise Lord Penzance or the rulings of the Privy Council, it would at once have attracted more, and more enthusiastic signatures than our paper.[1] There was a time three weeks ago when lifting a finger would almost have been a signal for revolt. People sign our paper for want of something stronger. At least that is my own impression. Our paper has averted that : whether we have been wise I don't know. I don't suppose we shall have much thanks for it. And what is worse, I don't see what is to come of it. I suppose that we shall have some reform of Convocation to stop our mouths. I should never be surprised if there was some sort of Royal Commission ; and probably no Bishop just now will be forward to employ Lord Penzance, except to scold and preach to drunken parsons. But the courts will remain intact for the present ; and probably the Archbishop's alarm will pass away as time goes on. He will try to keep things quiet, but no reform of the courts while he and Thomson are in office. We shall very likely have the cry of "the Mass" sprung on us, and that will cause a diversion, like the "Confessional" some years ago.

I have written something in the *Nineteenth Century* for February, and I have sent you a reprint of an old *Christian Remembrancer* article.[2]—Ever yours affectionately,

R. W. C.

---

[1] An Address, signed by more than 2000 clergy, to the Archbishop of Canterbury, urging "toleration and forbearance in dealing with questions of ritual."

[2] *The Relation between Church and State*, reprinted from the *Christian Remembrancer*, 1850.

The Dean's practical experience as a parish priest comes out in the following letter of criticism on Mr. Albert Grey's Church Boards Bill of 1881 :—

To G. W. Russell, Esq., M.P.

DEANERY, St. Paul's, 2nd April 1881.

My dear Sir—I am very much obliged to you for the copy of the Church Boards Bill.

It certainly ought to be quite well understood that this is not a small matter. Section 10 of the bill, if it becomes law, would make a revolution in the Church hardly less than those made in the time of the Commonwealth. And such a change, if Parliament thinks fit to make it, ought not, I think, to be made in the disguise of an innocent little bill for controlling the despotism of incumbents, and making things work better in parishes.

(1) It transfers the spiritual and religious work of the incumbent, for which he is responsible to the Bishop and to the law of "this Church and Realm," to a new body. There is nothing, except perhaps the language of sermons, which is not covered by the words "management of any matter of an ecclesiastical nature, affecting the general interests of the parish, which has. heretofore been managed by the incumbent"; e.g. the interpretation of the Prayer-Book.

(2) It transfers to the same body the rights and duties belonging to the churchwardens, or the incumbent and churchwardens together.

(3) And it transfers these matters, including so much of the deepest religious interest, matters belonging to the inner religious sphere of the Church, matters of duty and conscience, on which, as all the world sees, convictions and feelings are

so strong among serious Church people, to whom ?   Not to
the communicant members of the Church—not to the
ordinary congregations—but to a body which does not
profess to be even Christian : a body erected by ratepayers
or parish voters.   It creates the Presbyterian organisation in
every parish, *minus* the requirement that the lay elders
should be either Churchmen or Christians.

I am certainly not afraid of lay influence, counsel, or
agency in a parish.   I do not much mind, what nevertheless
is often as practically mischievous as it is in principle anomalous, the "people's churchwarden" being a Nonconformist.
I think any wise clergyman in a large parish would try and
gather round him a body of lay councillors, co-operating with
and advising him.   But to transfer ecclesiastical, and therefore, in part at least, religious affairs to the hands of professedly non-Christian bodies, to say nothing of ignorance or
avowed and perhaps conscientious hostility to the Church,
would be, on the part of Churchmen, to commit suicide— to
throw up the claim of the Church to be able to teach the
people for whom churches were built and parishes formed.

I say nothing of the practical mischiefs which, it seems
obvious, are likely to follow.

We have heard a good deal lately of the dangers of Con-
gregationalism.   This, of course, would double the tendency by removing the Bishop to a further distance from
influence on what goes on in a parish.   If incumbents have
been troublesome to deal with, a Church Board would be
infinitely more so ; its little finger would be thicker than the
parson's loins.

Unless both incumbent and Board were very wise people,
they would almost inevitably fall into habits of jealousy and
antagonism.   The incumbent would feel that he had masters

put over him, and the Board would be watching for encroachments to resist or repress.

Then when you think of the ordinary composition of
large parishes, the opportunity would be irresistible to
persons hostile either to the Church or the incumbent to
interfere to his annoyance, and possibly to his hindrance :
to appeal to the large class of those who care nothing about
religion for an exercise of power over things that others *do*
care for.

Add to this the fluctuating nature of this body to whom
so much is entrusted ; it is making the religious customs
and observances of a parish depend on the accidents of an
Easter vestry.

These alone are serious objections, but my real objection
is much more serious. Churchmen believe the Church to
be a religious society as much so as a Congregational body, as
much so as the Roman Catholic body. It has also become
in England an Established Church ; but it has not therefore
ceased to be a religious society, with principles and laws of
its own. We have inherited an anomalous state of things,
in which the logical inconsistencies show the traces of our
keen and repeated struggles ; but, like other Englishmen,
we put up with many anomalies which have come down
to us.

But this bill goes on the principle—

(1) That ratepayers, whatever their creed, are the persons
entitled by the law to settle what (subject to law) shall
be the administration of the Church services in each parish,
in all the numberless details which make the difference
between a good and bad parish. And (2) that henceforth
their authority is to override that of the incumbent, and be
its substitute. If I know anything of the English clergy,

they will not submit to this ; because they will say, and say truly, that it is ostentatiously placing Church administration in the wrong hands, and not merely in lay hands, but in non-Christian hands. No one would seriously make such a proposal to any professedly religious body in existence. And if it is made by Parliament to the English clergy, and the large body of lay people who agree with them, it can have, I think, but one result. It would be impossible for them to accept it.

I have put down a few things that occurred to me on reading the bill, and I am very grateful to you for allowing me to say so much to you. I shall be at home all next week if you should have anything about which you may wish to ask me.—Yours faithfully,   R. W. CHURCH.

To LORD BLACHFORD.

DEANERY, ST. PAUL'S, 6th April 1881.

MY DEAR BLACHFORD—I dined with Gladstone yesterday, and I am bound to contradict the suggestion that, outwardly, he shows the smallest sign of impaired strength. He had been talking on Monday about the Budget, had sat up that night till one or two, had been busy all day, and in the House at question time, and till it was counted out ; but there he was at dinner, as full of talk on every subject, trade, agricultural depression, down to handwriting, and the comparison of quills and steel pens, with all the old eagerness and vigour. There were Duke of Argyll, Bright, Evelyn Ashley, Andrew Clark—just a scratch party picked up in the House ; but of course these were lively gentlemen, and Gladstone was the liveliest. He is not going to drop just yet, whatever else he may do, and whatever the *Pall Mall* may think of his " tired face."

7th April 1881.

Many thanks for your news about the Commission,[1] which, except in one point, was news to me.

I have asked to be excused. I cannot stand these long sittings—they kill me. The disagreeable alternative is that I shall probably have, in my old age, to be once more examined. But I prefer the sharp agony of that (and I would rather have a lot of teeth out) to the endless sitting. And I could do no good either. I hope something may come of it with all my heart. . . .

I forgot to tell you of Gladstone's enthusiastic eulogy of the *Guardian* to Bright, Evelyn Ashley, and Agnew the picture dealer, who had only faintly heard of it. It was, he said, far the best weekly account of news to be found, in selection and arrangement. It was this point which he dwelt upon. A person reading it could, except for immediate use, quite dispense with the daily papers. The news department was quite admirable.—Ever yours affectionately, R. W. C.

To THE SAME.

DEANERY, ST. PAUL'S, *26th April* 1881.

MY DEAR BLACHFORD—Certainly I hardly expected such an outburst of allegiance to Lord Beaconsfield.[2] I remember the first thing that ever made me aware that he had popularity out of his party was the cheering, not very great, but still very distinct, as he came out of St. Paul's on the day of Thanksgiving for the Prince of Wales. Of course he was then in opposition, but there was a contrast between his

---

[1] A Royal Commission appointed to inquire into the Constitution and Working of Ecclesiastical Courts.
[2] Lord Beaconsfield's death had taken place the 19th April 1881.

reception and Gladstone's, which was not at all warm, if I remember. Of course this was in the City; but I have always thought of it as the beginning of his rise in popular favour. To-day everything shows as much mourning as it can, public buildings and the police ship in the river with flags half mast, and the blinds of the clubs drawn down; and the *St. James's Gazette* exultant at the amount of enthusiastic feeling "which even his warmest admirers did not expect." It is an uncomfortable sign of what he has done to enchant and mystify the political morality of the country, at least in the south. I suppose there was something tender about him, as the correspondent in to-day's *Times* makes out; and one feels staggered at finding the apparent affection so great. I feel as, I suppose, some good Protestants feel puzzled about Newman's popularity.

. . . But it is all very wonderful. And there is poor Gladstone with his terrible Irish Land Bill, and colleagues who cannot speak for him, and apparently making blunders himself. All the world expected him to say a few words about Dizzy last night, which was a natural occasion, and he need not have said much. Now, he puts off a fortnight, when he must make a studied panegyric, and, meanwhile, gets the credit of an intentional slight yesterday. I am afraid hard times are in store for him. . . .—Yours affectionately,   R. W. C.

The news of Dean Stanley's death, in July 1881, reached the Dean while he was on a yachting cruise in the Irish Channel. "Stanley's death is a great shock," he wrote to his son; "he did not seem like a man to die early—though after all he was sixty-six; but he seemed so young and fresh. It is another man gone of my own generation. . . . I cannot think who will go to Westminster. . . . But it will not be Stanley, with his faults and his excellences." In a letter written after his return from the funeral in Westminster Abbey, the Dean enters more fully upon the same subject :—

To THE WARDEN OF KEBLE.

YACHT *SIBYL*, PORTLAND ROADS, 31st *July* 1881.

MY DEAR WARDEN—Your letter found us rocking and rolling here, with a half gale from the south-west, well sheltered, but with all pendulous things gently swaying and making one sleepy. We have had various fortunes from Holyhead, but in spite of some evil hours to some of us we have been very happy ; and most of us are looking forward with regret to our parting with the *Sibyl* and her rough company.

You have asked me a hard thing. Stanley was a man of my own generation, and he was always very kind to me in spite of our very opposite sides. I think his generosity came out to *me ;* for, of course, he must have utterly disliked both the company I kept and my general line. And this was a bar to any very free intercourse ; but up to a certain point he was ever forward in his friendliness, and I was astonished the other day at the heap of small characteristic notes of his which have collected in my boxes and bundles. And Stanley, when disposed to be friendly, was very delightful and attractive. And I think that what made him so was not his brilliancy and resource and knowledge, but the sense that he was sincerely longing to be in sympathy with every one for whom he could feel respect. It was the basis of a very grand character ; but Stanley had intellectual defects,

like his physical defects as to music, or smell, or colour, or
capacity for mathematical ideas, which crippled his capacity
for the sympathy he wished to spread all round him.   One
of these defects is indicated in what his critics say of his
aversion to metaphysics and dogmatic statements.   They
were to his mind like the glass which the fly walks on and
cannot penetrate : when he came to them his mind " would
not bite."   Another defect seemed to me always his incapacity for the spiritual and unearthly side of religion ; the
side which is so strong in the people whom he opposed,
Newman and Keble, and, in a lower way, the Evangelicals ;
the elevations and aspiration after Divine affections, and
longings after God, which, whether genuine or alloyed, are
above the historic and dramatic plane which was so congenial to him.   These were two enormous disqualifications
to a religious teacher ; and there were others.   Among
them a certain freely indulged contempt for what he did not
like, and a disposition to hunt down and find faults where
he did not love people, especially where he did not think
them quite true, as in the case of Newman and S. Wilberforce.

. . . If his had been a deeper mind, seeing below and
through the history which so fascinated him, he would have
been a High Churchman, or, it may be, a Roman Catholic.
And, indeed, if he had chanced to live before instead of
after the Oxford Movement, he would have been in advance
of his time in warmth and sympathy for the party, and
have been reckoned, like Scott and Wordsworth, as a fore-
runner of the great religious revival.   But coming after it,
and seeing the vast prominence of its theological over its
poetical and historical side, he was repelled from it ; and
seeing further, that it was likely to grow and become

powerful, his repulsion developed into systematic opposition and hostility. But with all his faults, I feel it a great sorrow to have had him all my life ranged on the opposite side, always ranged against the people and the things which I most cared for. For if he did not understand the spiritual side of religion he did thoroughly understand the greatness and the breadth of the moral side of it; the value of the great virtues, justice, veracity, courage, and their essential connection with the Christian type of character. He was a very earnest preacher of religious morality, though he was blind to some important parts of it, and was driven by his religious partizanship to exaggerate some other parts—as in his grotesque and vehement efforts to claim admiration for the eighteenth-century type of religion, and indignation at criticisms upon it.

I think Vaughan's picture is true as far as it goes, but it does not take in the great faults and gaps in the intellectual and religious character, the conspicuous blanks and incapacities which marred it, and which, I should think, he must be conscious of, though it was not the time to dwell on them; and of course Vaughan sympathised with a public line which you and I think a mischievous one. It seems to me that his influence was a very mixed one, depressing as well as elevating, raising the standard of religious ideas and work, and also confusing and thwarting very much in detail; and it is difficult just yet to estimate fairly how much he told in each opposite direction. I hardly remember any one whom it was so easy both to praise truly and condemn truly, according to the side of him you looked at.

Well, I have rambled, but I am writing in the yacht saloon, with much talk round me. . . .—Ever yours,

R. W. CHURCH.

2 A

To Dr. Asa Gray.

DEANERY, St. Paul's, 16th December 1881.

My dear Friend—Thank you for your tidings of your safe arrival. Considering what we have heard of the weather in the Atlantic I am glad that you went when you did, and that Mrs. Gray got through it so bravely.

I had Mr. Lowell's most kind invitation,[1] and took some time to think about it, and see if it could be managed for me to accept it. But I could not, without great danger of its ending in a fiasco. I am busy and rather worried just now. Our whole cathedral constitution is going under the harrow of a Commission, which wants to improve cathedrals but does not quite know how, and which therefore may make some great mistakes. Then there is another Commission, on which I have to give evidence, about nothing less than the fundamental relations of Church and State, as established at the Reformation and modified by subsequent events. It is a ticklish business. Probably it will end in nothing. But circumstances might make it come to a great deal ; and it gives us something to think and to read about. Then I have to preach as select preacher at Oxford, which also gives me something to do. So I cannot quite reckon on my time, and do not fall easily into the mood of preparing lectures fit for your audience, and worth going across to you to deliver. But I am deeply sensible of the kindness of the invitation and of the great honour offered me. Love from all to Mrs. Gray.—Yours affectionately,   R. W. Church.

During his yearly holiday in the spring of 1882, the Dean made his way for the first time to Rome.

[1] An invitation to give a course of Lowell Lectures at ~~Cambridge~~ *Boston,* Massachusetts.

To LORD BLACHFORD.

HOTEL QUIRINAL, ROME, 27*th April* 1882.

MY DEAR BLACHFORD— . . . It is hopeless to talk about Rome. My inclination was not strong to come here, and when I got here, and it was before my eyes in all its rugged picturesqueness, all my feeling was one almost of hatred to the place. It seemed such a mixture of all incompatible things — ruins and magnificence, waste and civilisation, tumbledown squalidness and untidiness, and stateliness and grandeur, such as one has never seen elsewhere ; an anti-religious world and an ostentatiously religious world, really *as* worldly, and also an undeniably magnificent organisation of high religion quite unique. It was a real worry and vexation to have it all forced on one's thoughts and sight at every step, in every view one had, and every inscription or name that came across one. I can only say that my feeling the first day was of hatred such as I never felt to London or Paris. I had the feeling that it is the one city in the world, besides Jerusalem, on which we *know* that God's eye is fixed, and that He has some purpose or other about it—one can hardly tell whether of good or evil. A good deal of His purpose is visible—and what of the rest ? I cannot tell you how this kind of uncertainty about what the real meaning of the whole thing was tormented and vexed me.

Well, one gets accustomed to things, and I am more at home ; but I never felt so strange to any place I was ever in. My first stroll was to the Pincian, where we had a fine afternoon, a brass military band, and troops of young seminarists with all sorts of sashes—green, red, violet—taking the air. Our first visit was to the Sistine, the Stanze, and the Loggie. The Sistine is oppressive ; the ceiling of course wonderful when you can see it. The Loggie are charming; but the three Stanze (Incendio, Segnatura, and Eliodoro) seem to me the perfection of all that painting can do. Everything, principal and accessory, walls and ceilings and pavement, all make these three rooms things which I never expected to see. We have been there twice: St. Peter's I have just seen, and as yet with a certain disappointment: S. Paolo fuore le Mura with great wonder and admiration, though it is but the new and not the old. Still the new work is so grand and good. S. Maria Maggiore is very fine: St. John Lateran an utter disappointment, it is so horribly modernised—and they are at work at worse mischief still—but most wonderful in its desolate situation. S. Clemente we have just seen, but not to advantage.—Ever yours affectionately,   . R. W. C.

Oh, how I wish you were here—though probably you don't.

To the Same.

Rome, 2nd May 1882.

My dear Blachford—We have now been in Rome a week. It has been fine weather, and only very hot in the middle of the day, and in the sun. It is a wonderful place. I don't care much about the ruins, though they are awful in their magnitude. But these old churches, with their old columns and pavements, are most delightful. I walked out this morning at seven to S. Agnese in the Via Nomentana. It was deliciously cool and soft, scents from acacias and roses constantly coming in whiffs from the gardens or wayside alleys, and the blue hills rising out of a light mist that hung over the Campagna. And there were the larks and nightingales singing all the way. Do you know the church? The foundation of it goes up to Constantine and Constantine's daughter Constantia, with a beautiful fifth or sixth century mosaic in the east apse, and columns, the spoils of the heathen, in two orders, one the main row of columns, and above them a gallery with lighter ones ; but both beautiful. You go down to it by a kind of slope ; and on each side of the wall are inscriptions, mostly Christian, from the neighbouring catacombs. There were three persons in church, where a mass was going on (I must say very reverently)— myself and two *contadini*. In the midst of it entered two more women with a huge shepherd's dog, which walked about the church with the utmost quietness and gravity, looking into all the corners just as if he was a tourist. It was all so inexpressibly odd—the morning freshness and solitude, the charm of the place, and this queer intruder of whom no one took any notice.

We went the other day to Tre Fontane, where the Trappists declare that they have conquered malaria by planting eucalyptus, and they are allowed on this ground to remain by the Government, which recognises them as a "Société Agricole Civile." I am bringing you some eucalyptus seeds to experiment upon.—Oh, the museums, and the portrait busts of emperors, and statues such as I never saw before, and all the infinite variety of detail which seems to bring early Rome, both imperial and Christian, so very close to one ! . . .—Ever yours affectionately,

R. W. C.

But even amid the wonders of Rome, the Dean's thoughts were constantly recurring to the anxieties and troubles of the time in Ireland. "Rome is indeed wonderful," he writes to the Warden of Keble—

"more wonderful than I was prepared for. I did not expect to like it, and I don't like it yet. But every step one takes and every sight one sees, forces upon one, in spite of ancient desolations and modern prettinesses, what an awful place one is in. But even here," he adds, with a foreboding only too quickly and surely to be justified, "Ireland haunts me day and night."

A week later came the news of the murder of Lord Frederick Cavendish and Mr. Bourke in the Phœnix Park, Dublin.

To the Warden of Keble.

PERUGIA, 9th May 1882.

My dear Talbot—I must write a line with my wife's. What a horrible light on Irish caving in, and on Forster's warnings! It is too dreadful to think of. Of course, we have only the telegrams as given in Italian newspapers, without even their comments. But I shudder to think of all that this Irish answer to Gladstone's attempt to conciliate will bring forth, both in Ireland and in England. I have tried hard to believe that he has been right. But it seems to me that he is blind to Irish insolence and Irish keen sense of their winning game. How can he or any one forget Parnell's words, quoted by Gibson ; and if so, what is the good of an apparent truce ?

I wish you could say to all your dear people, how this has made us think of them all night long since we heard it. It has come like a black cloud on our bright days here. We are going to Assisi to-day. There was truth in St. Francis' view of the world, though not the whole truth.

We stay here till over Wednesday, then to Siena, getting to Florence on Saturday. If you could give us a line about how they all are, and what is the outlook, I should be grateful.—Ever yours affectionately, R. W. C.

To CANON CHURCH.

FLORENCE, 17th May 1882.

DEAR CHARLES—We have had a very pleasant time here. The weather has been most kind, neither too hot nor too cold, nor monotonously bright, and Florence certainly has looked like a city for holidays, as Charles V. said. There is something about it which is to me more attractive than any of the great places where we have been—Genoa, Perugia, Siena, Rome. It is certainly most beautiful. I suppose the harmony of everything, the characteristic buildings, the river, the hills round about, and the unconscious association with all the wonderful works of art and beauty in it, give it this, to me, unique character. There is nothing rude, nothing coarse, nothing obtrusively ruinous or decayed. All is venerable, yet all seems fresh. It is hard work to see all that it has to show us. The Uffizi are tremendous, merely as a walk. Then the churches, S. Maria Novella, S. Croce, S. Marco, need hours of looking, if one is really to enjoy their wall-painting.

I have been round this afternoon to look at the Villa Torregiani, and the Casa Annalena.[1] The latter appears to have gone back to its original destination, and is become once more a religious house for ladies. It surprised me by looking so low. I thought there had been a higher storey,

---

[1] The Dean's early home in Florence.

besides the mezzanino and first floor. But it must be a very
nice house.

. . . It is almost uncomfortable to be having such
pleasure while such miseries and dangers are going on at
home. But one of the things which these dreadful horrors
have brought out is, that English people are equal, at least
morally, to their position. No Roman or Florentine lady
ever said a more heroic thing, than what Lady Frederick
Cavendish said to Gladstone the first time she saw him after
the news had come : " Uncle William, you did right to send
him to Ireland." We have heard a good deal about her and
her people from Talbot and Liddon. I wish I could think
that her prayer is likely to come to pass—that his death
may help to bring peace to Ireland. It is plain that the
Parnell and Dillon set are at the mercy of the Irreconcilables,
more extreme and thorough-going than even they, and who
will destroy them if they show the slightest sign of relenting,
or accepting any terms from England, but unconditional
surrender. Say what they will, Parnell and his friends
have brought about the state of temper which makes Ireland
ungovernable, and they and we must accept the fact. Good-
bye—love to all.--Ever yours affectionately,   R. W. C.

To the Warden of Keble.

Deanery, St. Paul's, 26th August 1882.

My dear Warden—Thank you so much for writing,
and for letting us see that most interesting bit about Ireland.
The change of manner between the older and newer generation is very significant ; and also the deepened nationalism
produced by increased schooling. The more I think of it
the more hopeless the prospect becomes. I cannot see how

we can ever reconcile them, or how we can possibly let them
go. But I am afraid I can see easily how, not under very
impossible circumstances, their blind hatred may bring about
something which will indeed be the vengeance of the years
that are past on England. It is the only part of our system
where the attempt to govern justly and reasonably seems to
fail. I should like very much to see the continuation of
your letters. I have not read anything so instructive for a
long while.

We are still here, with the children so happy and making
us so happy, that if I were a Greek I should fear Nemesis.
They all thank you most heartily for your remembrance of
them, but are all astonished that you have not found out *La
petite Fadette* before. It is a favourite of old Whatley days
with them. I think Mr. Horner gave it them.

Freddy is not yet back. He went from Grindelwald to
Zermatt, only to encounter the news of another terrible
accident—poor Mr. Gabbett and his two guides on the Dent
Blanche, which F. had come to Zermatt with Melchior
Anderegg to climb—the one peak he meant to allow himself.
Instead, he had to help at the funeral of the Englishman
and the guides. All this has been a great shock to him.
Please remember us most kindly to your wife, and if it may
be, to Lady Frederick.—Ever yours affectionately,

R. W. C.

To the Rev. George S. Barrett.

Deanery, St. Paul's, *13th October* 1882.

My dear Mr. Barrett—Thank you very much for
sending me your sermon.[1] May I say that with the positive

---

[1] " The Influence of Dr. Pusey on the Religious Faith and Life of
the Nation."

side of it I heartily sympathise ; that it is in the negative
side of it that I find myself in disagreement.   Our points of
view are necessarily very different.   But I gladly thank you
for the more than candour, the generous appreciation of men
once thought worthy to be insulted by every scoffer, to whom
I feel that I owe, as you do to Mr. Dale, the best of all that I
am, and almost my own soul also.   And there is throughout
that respect for what you disagree with and condemn, and
that deep and genuine feeling of great unities, even under
our grave and important differences, which is the most
reassuring sign that really a time may be " within measur-
able distance" when even our most serious controversies,
even our great and apparently hopeless controversy with
Rome, may be carried on as if in the presence and under the
full knowledge and judgment of the Lord of truth and
charity.   I do not expect that controversy will ever cease ;
but I do think that the time may be hoped for when a
controversialist will think it his first duty, at the cost of
losing many effective weapons, to put himself as far as he
can in his opponent's position, and understand what he
understands, and feel what he feels.

Such a sermon as yours seems to me such a sign of
promise.—Yours very faithfully,   R. W. Church.

The foregoing letter suggests the fitting place at
which to introduce the following personal recollections [1]
of the Dean, by Dr. Barrett, the President of the Congregational Union in 1894.   The friendship which had
grown up between the Dean and Dr. Barrett had won
much of its sincerity and freedom and its wide range of

[1] The recollections are, in part, reprinted, by the kind permission
of the Editor of the *British Weekly*, from an article written by Dr.
Barrett in December 1890.

sympathy from the frank acknowledgment on either side of differences as well as of agreement. There are words in recognition of this in the preceding letter, and they are met by the touching words with which Dr. Barrett concludes his recollections :—" Although," he writes, " the Dean's ecclesiastical position was necessarily far removed from that which Nonconformists occupy, yet it may be permitted to a Nonconformist to lay this poor wreath of reverence and affection on the grave of one of the purest and saintliest men he has ever known."

The recollections themselves continue as follows :— " My own acquaintance with the Dean began many years ago at Zermatt, and I recall even at this distance of time the delight he took in the ever-changing wonder and glory of mountain and cloud and snow, and the inexpressible elevation of character that marked all his ordinary intercourse. Indeed, I think it was this latter feature that most impressed one whenever I met him in later years. He had some of the finest gifts of the purely literary man ; he had a culture so large and rich as to seem almost faultless in its perfection ; he had the eye and the ear of the poet even if he had not the poet's tongue ; but it was none of these things which made the deepest impression on those who knew him. It was the rare elevation of his whole nature, the spiritual atmosphere in which he lived, the far-off look that you caught at times in his gaze, that told you his deepest life was lived in God. He brought to all subjects he touched the ripest and fullest knowledge, and he could use, as his essays abundantly testify, the most delicate and penetrating criticism in literary discussion; he could disentangle as with a master's hand, and then seize the threads of the great movements in European history, alike in secular and ecclesiastical affairs; but there was something in him even rarer and more precious than these great gifts. There was the personality of the man himself, his humbleness, his sweetness, his devoutness—above all, the sense of the majesty and mystery of God that brooded over his heart and life.

"Of his published works this is not the place to speak. I content myself with saying that in the opinion of no mean judges they will rank with the finest literature of the Victorian era. The first reading of *The Gifts of Civilisation*,—perhaps the greatest and most characteristic of the Dean's writings,—which were lectures delivered in St. Paul's Cathedral, and of the sermons prefixed to these lectures, which were preached before the University of Oxford, has formed an era in the intellectual life of many men; and, some years ago, one of the greatest of living preachers amongst the Congregationalists, and himself one of the ablest theologians of this age, told me there was one sermon in that volume he had already read through six times.

"Only once was it my privilege to hear the Dean preach in St. Paul's. It was on a Whit Sunday, and I recall even now the spare figure, almost insignificant in its stature, standing in the pulpit; the upward look, then the quiet reading of the text, 'Grieve not the Spirit,' and then the whole vast congregation subdued into breathless attention, not by the spell of a great

orator, but by the wonderful spiritual power of the
man, as the first sentence of the sermon fell on their
ears—'Grieve not—pain not—pain not the Spirit of
God.—Then we may pain God.' I have more than once
ventured to suggest to the late Dean the publication of
a volume of sermons which should comprise some of
those which he had preached at St. Paul's, and as Select
Preacher at Oxford, and which as yet have had no more
enduring record than the columns of a newspaper.[1]

". . . In politics I believe the Dean was always a
Liberal, although he lived far enough removed from
the conflicts and littleness of party strife. He owed
his appointment at St. Paul's to Mr. Gladstone, who,
on the death of Dean Mansel in 1871, offered the
Deanery of St. Paul's to Mr. Church, then the rector of
an obscure country parish in the south of England;
and he never lost his admiration for the intellectual and
moral greatness of Mr. Gladstone's character, although
he diverged from him on the question of Home Rule for
Ireland. One incident I may mention as an evidence of
the Dean's estimate of Mr. Gladstone. During Mr.
Gladstone's last tenure of office as Prime Minister a
clergyman, whose only opportunity of knowing Mr.
Gladstone had been through the not too trustworthy
descriptions of hostile critics, happened to say in the
presence of the Dean that he believed Mr. Gladstone

---

[1] "Since the death of the Dean this has been done in a volume
entitled *Cathedral and University Sermons;* together with two
volumes of *Village Sermons*, remarkable as a revelation of the union
of profoundly spiritual thought with the utmost simplicity of expression."

was a thoroughly insincere man. The Dean was sitting
in his chair when the remark was made, but he instantly
rose, his face even paler than it usually was, and he
said, evidently with the strongest suppression of personal feeling : 'Insincere! Sir, I tell you that to my
knowledge Mr. Gladstone goes from communion with
God to the great affairs of State.' It was high testimony
to be given to any man, but highest of all when we
remember who gave it."

The continuous series of letters begins again with
a characteristic letter to Dr. Gray, whose services to
botany, as after years of laborious industry they were
drawing to a close, roused in the Dean a sense of
admiring envy :—

To Dr. Asa Gray.

Deanery, St. Paul's, 31st October 1882.

My dear Friend— . . . I shall be glad to hear that, at
last, the " Compositæ "[1] have begun their march. But what
a thing to be envied, to have put them in due order, and
marshalled them as an army of your own. I should like to
have done one good hard long piece of work—I don't mean
like that, but something like that—have edited some great
book, or had to do with a Dictionary like Littré's, or written
a treatise on history, as the French say, de longue haleine.
The pleasure of finishing is with me mainly confined to
finishing a longish sermon, or an article or essay, or small
book. But it makes me understand how you must feel
about your " Compositæ."

---

[1] See Letters of Dr. Asa Gray, vol. ii. p. 747.

I was very sorry to miss Mr. Lowell on his last visit to
London. He called when I was out, and when we went to
look for him two days after he had already left. I am very
sorry to hear of the sorrow which had come on him. I did
not know it when we heard of his being in London.

We are in a lull just now. Egypt and Ireland both hung
up for the present, and Gladstone, of course, very strong. I
cannot help hoping that he has made some impression on
Ireland, though there are plenty of ugly symptoms, and the
ineradicable hatred is still there. But if ever courage, hard
work, and self-sacrificing love of justice deserved success,
Gladstone deserves to improve Ireland. To cure it is beyond
mortal power.

Give all our loves to Mrs. Gray.—Ever yours affectionately,   R. W. Church.

To the Warden of Keble.

Deanery, St. Paul's, 18th December 1882.

My dear Warden— . . . I am particularly glad that
you met Blachford. He has been so much to me, and is so
much in himself, that I don't feel that things are complete if
my friends, who have come on the stage later, do not know
him. He was for much more than people know in the
original development of Newman's mind. We have not
always agreed, and probably do not quite now. But I never
knew so *thorough* a man : high in his own standard, and
true to friendship, even to the breaking point. . . .—Ever
yours affectionately,   R. W. C.

The following letter, written upon the occasion of the
death of Archbishop Tait, and the appointment of the

Bishop of Truro as his successor, carries with it its own
sufficient explanation :—

TO DR. ASA GRAY.

DEANERY, ST. PAUL'S, 31st December 1882.

MY DEAR FRIEND—I do not like to let this year go without a line to you. We were so sorry to hear of your accident.
I hope it is doing well ; but the interruption of work must
be a real trial. I don't know if other people know the odd
feeling which comes across me after an accident of this kind
—that only the *slightest* difference of conditions would have
avoided. It seems so much harder than other troubles, which
have come as it seems in ordinary course.—"If only I had
been there a minute before or a minute after.—If only the
thing had moved a little slower or a little faster," etc. etc.
To have got into a scrape by just a very little seems so
foolish, and also so unnecessary.—I should like to make a
collection of such irrational impulses of indignation against
things and oneself.

You see the newspapers have been taking liberties with
my name. Formal offer there was none, and could not be ;
for I had already on another occasion told my mind to
Gladstone, and said that reasons of health, apart from any
other reasons, made it impossible for me to think of anything, except a retirement altogether from public office. But
Gladstone was very kind, and people round him talked in a
way which accounts for the newspaper gossip. Benson is, I
really believe, the best choice that could have been made in
England. Everything that he has touched he has done well·
He is quiet, and he is enthusiastic, and he is conciliatory,
and he is firm. . . . But of one thing I am quite certain :

that never for hundreds of years has so much honest disinterested pains been taken to fill the Primacy—such inquiry and trouble resolutely followed out to find the really fittest man, apart from every personal and political consideration, as in this case.   Of that I can bear witness.   I hope it may be rewarded by an administration of the great office, conceived of and carried out in a higher spirit than any of us have yet witnessed.—Ever yours affectionately,

R. W. CHURCH.

To THE SAME.

DEANERY, ST. PAUL'S, 3rd April 1883.

MY DEAR FRIEND— . . . I hope that you are quite set up again with full use of your shoulder, in your great wrestle with the "Compositæ."   It is a wonderful family, almost as wonderful in its grim rigour of general plan as the orchids are in their boundless extravagance.   I hope I may see the face of some growing flowers in Italy or Switzerland this year.   I have seen none yet.   I have entangled myself in a little job which I undertook with a light heart, and which I do not relish as I go on.   I promised to write a little book about Bacon in the "Men of Letters" series, edited by J. Morley.   But writing such a book means writing not only about his genius and his books, but about his life ; and the more I read of Bacon, the man and his life, the less I like him.   James Spedding edited his letters, etc., with a running commentary, in which he makes him out to be one of the noblest and purest of men.   I can only read in him one of the poorest and most ungenerous of characters.   But it is a horrid thing to have to connect one's name with what will be called blackening one of the greatest of the benefactors of

2 B

the race.   And I don't know what to do, except to leave the thing alone.   And I am somewhat in tribulation about it.

We are not quite relieved from the dynamite scare.   I don't myself much fear it.   But of course possibilities are undeniable if people will only encounter risks.   Happily the dynamite people don't seem inclined for that.

Kindest remembrances to Mrs. Gray.—Ever yours affectionately,   R. W. CHURCH.

The following spring found the Dean once more in Italy, where each return seemed to waken a renewed power of enjoyment, and an ever keener and more penetrating sense of the beauty and wonder in all he saw :—

TO THE WARDEN OF KEBLE.

FLORENCE, 25th May 1883.

MY DEAR WARDEN—We are just back from a most delightful three days of Dantesque and Fratesque topography.   The Casentino, you know, is the upper valley of the Arno, from its source to where "turning up its nose" at Arezzo (Purg. xiv.) it doubles back on itself round the great ridge of the Prato Magno (Purg. v.), in a north-westerly direction, to Pontasieve and Florence.   The Casentino is a broad green valley, well marked by its bounding mountains, like a Greek Lacedæmon or Argolis, from its head, the Falterona (Purg. xiv.), between the Prato Magno and the Camaldoli range or Giogana, till the enclosing ranges come together at the narrows where you enter it, and the Arno goes out not far from Arezzo.   Three or four little towns perched on hills, with towers and sometimes walls (Bibbiena, Poppi, Pratovecchio, Stia), mark the course of the river and give a distinct character to the valley from whatever side you look at it. But the feature in the view everywhere, in the outline of bounding mountains, is the great hill of St. Francis, where he received the Stigmata —Alvernia or La Verna as they call it here—the sort of Tabor of the Franciscan legend, the " crudo sasso intra Tevere ed Arno " (Par. xi.), which, with its strange form and stern blackness, is in strange contrast with all the mountain outlines round it. The Casentino was long fought for and coveted by Florence, and at last won. Dante knew it well. He was in the great battle of Campaldino, under the walls of Poppi, where the Guelfs overthrew the Ghibellines of Arezzo. He has shown how he remembered it and all the region round in Buonconti's story (Purg. v.), whose body was swept away by the fierce Archiano torrent which comes down from the " Eremo " of Camaldoli into the Arno, in the tempest which followed the battle. Dante delighted in the " green hills and cold brooks " (Inf. xxx.) as much as he hated its inhabitants (Purg. xiv.) I don't know what they were then, but we found them very pleasant now.

Well, to this region we have been, visiting the two great sanctuaries, the Franciscan at La Verna, and Camaldoli, the sanctuary of S. Romoald, with its white Frati and " Sagro Eremo." I must confess that what first determined us was the learning that the landlord of our hotel here had become the proprietor of the disused portion of Camaldoli, which he had turned into a hotel, and was very desirous that we should try. We went by train to Arezzo, then drove from that picturesque and foul place, with its idle gaping crowds, along the prosperous Casentino as far as Bibbiena, not knowing exactly how we were to travel to Camaldoli, as on the ordnance map there were nothing but mule tracks marked, and no " via rotabile." . . . However, we found that a

new carriage road had been made the whole way to Camaldoli, just like a Swiss pass, going along dreary mountain shelves, with tremendous plunges below them. We
saw nothing of the place till, turning a corner, the convent
appeared—rather in a hole, but with such richness and
beauty of spring greenery all round it. After the heat of
the plains it was quite chilly, and called for wraps, indeed
we should all have been better for a fire, but all was very
clean and comfortable. There is still a body of nearly a
score of Frati, who have part of the convent buildings;
picturesque persons, in their white dress and white cloaks,
and large flapping straw hats. The Government has taken
all their vast possessions, but has, I don't know quite how,
allowed the Order to go on and to recruit itself, as far as
they are able to maintain themselves by their own resources,
which are said to be considerable, as they have many friends.
They now lease their buildings from Government on a ten
years' lease, paying no rent ; but they are bound to keep up
the buildings and to spend twenty thousand lire in the ten
years on them. And they are still the big people of the
place, looked upon as ill-treated owners, who will one day
get their own again.

Above the convent is the " Sagro Eremo," the scene of S.
Romoald's visions, and where he passed his life. The religious
life there is more severe than in the convent below, more
distinctly of the hermit sort. One brother, they said, had
been in seclusion for forty-eight years—coming however, I
understood, into choir for the offices. There were fourteen
hermits and four novices. The place is most beautiful ; such
forest walks, such forests of firs, beeches, and chestnuts, such
delicious springs, and such flowers.

From there M. and I made a day to La Verna ; carriage

the whole way, but you change into a lighter carriage at
Bibbiena, for the gradients are tremendously steep between
it and La Verna. We were between four and five hours.
How the fellow drove ! It was Corpus Christi day, and all
the world was making holiday. La Verna, when we got
near it, appeared as a huge mass of columnar sandstone,
falling on all sides in sheer cliffs, and crowned with a forest
of beech and fir. At last we espied a building, attached like
a cage to the rock, but how it was to be got at did not appear.
But of course the way up duly showed itself. Up steep
zigzags, under a fierce sun, we wound up. The first thing
we came to was the "Chapel of the Birds," where the "pictæ
aves" all came to salute St. Francis with "ave." Then we
came through a gateway into an irregular piazza filled with
country people who had come for the great festival, and were
now, after the procession, lounging, eating, gossiping, visiting
the sacred spots, saying their prayers, and interrupting them
to shake hands and have a laugh with their friends. Here
the Franciscans have been let alone, and are quite masters
of the situation. There are ninety of them (twenty-seven
priests), and they collect in alms enough to give food, on an
average, to two hundred travellers and "poveri" a day ;
while on a day like a great festa they "give to eat" to over
a thousand. There was immense bustle, but they gave us
hearty welcome. One Frate was told off to show us all the
wonders ; and, oh dear, how wonderful the whole thing was !
The crowd had got into one sacred place where they had no
business to be. Some were eating, some were saying their
prayers, but our conductor was very angry at their having
got in without leave, and had a great row with one man
whom he tried to send away, and who got into a great rage.
"There were all these people eating and drinking, and these

strangers come to look about, and he only wanted to say an Ave Maria at St. Francis' cross, and they would not let him. But he *would;*" and storming and roaring at our conductor, who was quite unable to restrain him, he rushed into the sacred cavern and knelt before the cross, saying his prayer, and after cutting a bit off for a relic, he came away victorious.

After seeing all the sights and hearing all the miracles, we were taken to the guest-chamber, where they would not let us eat what we had brought with us : no, we must have the hospitality of St. Francis. They gave us a very good, simple dinner ; one friar sat and chatted, another — very quaint and full of humour—played anxious host, taking care that we ate enough, and another brought in the dishes. It was like a picture of Giotto or Benozzo Gozzoli. They were very jolly and nice ; and they and the crowds whom they served at dinner made a tremendous clatter. They were very anxious that we should stay and see the Benediction procession to the chapel of the Stigmata, but we had not time. The crowd were rather scandalised, I think, by the favour they showed us. They let M. go into some place not usually allowed to women, to look at some beautiful Della Robbias. . . .—Ever yours affectionately,   R. W. C.

To the Rev. W. J. Copeland.

Deanery, St. Paul's, 14*th July* 1883.

My dear Copeland—It is a long time since I have heard of you. We are just come back from two months' wanderings among the wonders of the world—Pisa, Florence, Bologna, Ravenna, Venice, Innsbruck, Munich (where we dined with Döllinger), Nuremberg, Cologne. It was very hot, and we came back rather tired, but we are all right again now.

I saw the Cardinal shortly before we started in April. I thought him looking wonderfully well and bright. He has been up to town since. He seemed to me to have shaken off much of the weakness which had hung about him since he was at Rome.

The Royal Commission on Courts have finished their sittings and signed their report. I gather that it will not dare anything very striking. But it will put an end to the Judicial Committee in its present form ; and it will bring together a great deal of important and authentic information and opinion. The hero of it has been Stubbs, who has worked as few men can work, and has won universal admiration and honour. The report does not satisfy him, but he thinks it the best that could be hoped for ; and at any rate his contributions will give it value. . . .—Ever yours affectionately, R. W. CHURCH.

TO DR. ASA GRAY.

DEANERY, ST. PAUL'S, 6th August 1883.

MY DEAR FRIEND— . . . I forget what I told you about our holiday doings ; perhaps I did not tell you at all. But I think you must have heard from some one better than I am. But we had a "golden time," as Bacon would say. Just imagine—and all in warm but not burning sunlight—the Riviera, and Pisa, the sweetest of forlorn old cities, with its pine forest by the sea, such a blue sea, and such fine-cut Carrara mountains. . . . Then Florence, lovely and wonderful as ever, full of new beautiful things, though I have known it so long—the one place I think I never should tire of. Then with the fine railway journey across the Apennines (how you, with your astonishing Colorado railways must look down on such little European performances) to Bologna, the city of doctors, where the showman of the museum made me sit down in Volta's chair, and where Bolognese art, after Florentine, made us very cynical—for it is fine after all. Then a good day at Ravenna, with its basilicas and mosaics, and mighty tomb of the first and last Teutonic king of Italy, Theodoric the Goth. And then Venice—I need not tell you how people enjoy themselves in Venice, when the weather is fine and they are well. But we picked up a number of dropped stitches in a former visit, and made ourselves more at home there, and read Mr. Howell's with much satisfaction. Then we meant to have had a bracing week in the mountains—the Dolomites—which we talk much about in England, and which I had never seen. Bracing, yes, as much as we wished, from cold and wet; but seeing, not much, for, except one day, the mountains were in the clouds. It was so miserable after our Italian warmth and luxury, that we gave up being braced, and rushed off to flat, hot Germany—Innsbruck, Munich, and two old places of the utmost interest and picturesqueness, Ratisbon and Nuremberg. It was hot, and we came back rather panting and washed out, but we have seen something of our little old world this year, and our education has had a little polishing and finishing.

And now I am back to St. Paul's—and Bacon. I must finish him, but I wish I had not taken him. It is unpleasant to take against your subject; and I get driven out of all patience by Spedding's special pleading for him. He seems to me to have done no *work*, to have shown no example of what he calls his method. But his imagination was his great faculty, and all that is most valuable in him is due to the prescient instinctive insight with which he looked on the possibilities of knowledge; the enthusiasm of a seer, not of a philosopher who had measured, and weighed, and compared, and done what Mozley calls the underground work of solid thinking. Galileo, as you say, and Pascal *did* what Bacon talked about without knowing how to do it, and they talked *after* they had touch of the realities of a hunt after physical truth. I believe this may be said now with less *invidia* than of old ; still it is a bore to abate reverence for a great name. After all, he belongs to an age of vast ambitious adventure, which went to sea, little knowing whither it went, and ill provided with knowledge or instrument. His is a sort of poetical inauguration of science, as Shakespeare opens the gate to that complex modern world of ideas and feelings and tendencies, so different from the mediæval or the classical world.

At the conclusion of his task he writes again to Dr. Gray :—

My poor Bacon has gone to the printers. It has been very interesting work to read for it, but now that I have done it, I should like to do it all over again. It is curious to pass within so short a time from the poetical and fanciful science of Bacon to the hard-headed mathematical science of Newton. . . .—Ever yours affectionately,

R. W. CHURCH.

To THE WARDEN OF KEBLE.

BLACHFORD, 25*th August* 1884.

MY DEAR WARDEN— . . . I have been reading the *Journal Intime.*[1] It is full of interest, but an interest which you never can be sure whether, when you turn the page, it will not turn from admiration to repugnance. It is a very

---

[1] *Fragments d'un Journal Intime*, II. F. Amiel.

awful picture, on the whole, of what fine and religious minds
are coming to in the atmosphere of the Continent. It is
a strange state—the hold of an idea without its facts, of
redemption without a redeemer, and the presence of hope
and a kind of faith, with scarcely a shred of comfort except
from the sense of duty. The prominence of the idea of *sin*,
in such a writer, is remarkable. How good he is as a critic,
e.g. Renan.

We have been having wonderful summer days, such as he
describes on 25th August 1871. I am glad you are delighting yourself in the *Paradiso*. That is the true *pierre de
touche* of the student of Dante.—Ever yours affectionately,

R. W. C.

To LORD BLACHFORD.

DEANERY, ST. PAUL'S, *12th September* 1884.

MY DEAR BLACHFORD—We are having it for a few days
like those wonderful summer days at Blachford ; but they
are not quite the same thing, even on the Embankment and
in the parks. Some time or other I shall have to ask you
for a little help—that is, if I go on with my notion of having
my say about the old Oxford days. One thing that I should
try to do is to bring out Froude. Of course his time was
cut short. But it seems to me that so memorable a person
ought to be duly had in remembrance ; and people now
hardly recognise how much he had to do with the first stir.
But of course all my knowledge of him is second-hand, or
gathered from his books. He reminds me of Pascal—his
unflinchingness, his humour, his hatred of humbugs, his
mathematical genius, his mechanical interest (architecture
and the French *Révolutionnaire*[1]), his imagination, his merci-

---

[1] R. Hurrell Froude's *Remains*, i. p. 313.

less self-discipline. I should like to bring all this out, if, as I suppose, it is true.—I don't suppose Pascal would have loved the sea, he would have been "*seek !* "

The death of Bishop Jackson, who had been Bishop of London since 1869, took place at the beginning of the following year :—

To the Same.

Deanery, St. Paul's, *6th January* 1885.

As you will have heard, we have lost our Bishop. To us he is a great loss. To the cathedral, not always agreeing with us, he has been uniformly so kind, so generous, so hearty in recognising anything that seemed likely to be useful. When I think of what other bishops might have been, even good bishops, I cannot say how much I honour his readiness to believe good, his sympathy and goodwill, in spite of his cold manner. And his cold manner has been thawing more and more during his later years. It ended by his being quite affectionate to me and all mine. . . .—Yours affectionately,   R. W. Church

The "dynamite scare," of which a former letter had spoken, had not yet passed away :—

To Lord Blachford.

Deanery, St. Paul's, *27th January* 1885.

My dear Blachford—You see we are living among volcanoes. It is an odd sort of feeling, and curiously devoid of any real alarm, that while we are at service a dynamite

packet may go off. One listens sometimes to see if it will
not. If it did, no doubt the feeling would change. I don't
think myself that they will hurt us unless they can get
nothing else to hurt ; then perhaps they might *do* us rather
than be quite idle. But I think that they would rather
avoid the odium of attacking a religious building, and of
bloodshed, though they do not mind the latter if it cannot
be helped. Only plainly they do not aim at it. The only
thing that gives me any misgiving is that St. Paul's was in
a list of condemned buildings, three of which have come
true—the Bridge, Westminster, and the Tower. And so we
keep our eyes open. I have frantic letters warning me
against black bags being carried into the cathedral. I
believe there is no doubt that the dynamite at Westminster
was carried in a woman's under-garment. But it is disagreeable that none of these fellows can be caught. They have
scored off us this time ;—wrecking the House of Commons,
and specially the Government side of it, must be such a
triumph that I should not wonder if it was too much for
the reserve and silence of some of the gentlemen.

We are waiting anxiously for news from Egypt. It will
be curious if Stewart has boldly left Metammeh on one side,
and struck for the sixth cataract, where the Khartoum
steamers are supposed to be. That would be impossible
against regular troops, but might be possible against Arabs.
—Ever yours affectionately,   R. W. C.

To the Warden of Keble.

Deanery, St. Paul's, 26th February 1885.

My dear Warden—Thank you for letting me see the
enclosed. You will have seen the Archbishop's complaint

echoed in the *Guardian* article.[1] I question whether it is
quite fair to say that it is either the Church Union or the
Church Association who really have prevented any move
towards improvement by legislation, such as suggested by the
Commission. What has been much more serious and
effectual in stopping things is the certainty that most people
feel, probably Mr. Gladstone not the least, that it would be
hopeless to attempt to carry out the recommendations of the
Commission in Parliament. A bill of course might be got
through, but a bill in which the rather nicely - arranged
balance of the report would be rudely and unceremoniously
upset. And then, how should we be better off,—with the
Bishop's veto finally extinguished, and the "supremacy of
the law," and the lawyers well clenched ?

I don't think myself that the "truce of God" did depend
so much on expectation of improvement. It was much more
that men were for the time sick of the thing, and this feeling
had been strengthened by the late Archbishop's last days,
and the effect produced on Bishop Jackson. But of course
these things wear out ; and I daresay it is possible that we
are on the eve of another time of trouble. The Liverpool
affair seems quite unprovoked.

Whoever is guilty about the stoppage of legislation, it is
clear that great people have a great deal of weight, and some
responsibility, in being able to *express opinion* as to the
mischief of needlessly appealing to the courts. They cannot
stop it, but they can judge it.

Matthew's letter is very interesting, and opens up wonderful prospects of a native church. How very pleasant is his
account of the Oxford Mission ; but what does he mean by

---

[1] See *Guardian*, 25th February 1885, p. 297.

their "methods," which he "doubts"? "Not by words of
wisdom" *alone*, certainly not, but by words of wisdom from
men who follow the epistle for this week (2 Cor. vi.), in
which knowledge is one of the instruments. . . .—Ever
yours affectionately,   R. W. C.

Orvieto, with its cathedral and its great series of
frescoes by Luca Signorelli, ranked as the central point
of interest in the holiday of 1885. Yet no Italian
journey was complete without a pause at Florence,
when each return added fresh strength to the Dean's
love of his early home.

To Lord Blachford.

PERUGIA, *29th May* 1885.

MY DEAR BLACHFORD—Well, we have done Orvieto, and
you may envy us. It is worth doing even at the cost of
more inconvenience than we found ; for the inn is very
tolerable, clean, roomy, with civil people ; and the heat,
though great, endurable. We drove from here on Wednesday
—much the best way if you have time (nine hours), for the
drive over the high ridge dividing the valley of the Tiber
and the Chiana is very delightful, passing by several
picturesque villages, once walled and fortified, and rising
through fine oak woods, filled also with scented broom in
full golden flower ; nightingales too, and everything proper
to a mountain road, except water. At the top of the ridge
you look down on the two valleys or plains ; the sides of
the mountain being scored with deep gashes or ravines in
the clayey ground, full of golden broom. You know the
look of Orvieto from the station—just an example of the

"Tot congesta manu præruptis oppida saxis," "Fluminaque antiquos subterlabentia muros."

It took us more than half an hour to drive up (in fierce afternoon heat) to the town. But it was worth the drive. The façade is of the same kind as Siena, but I think more beautiful : the enrichment of the portals and basement more delicate and full—beautiful bas-relief and Cosmato work—a most exquisite rose window in a square, and the three gables ; not so good in outline as Siena, but with much more richness of mosaic and marble colour. Unfortunately the mosaics, which have been restored, are very inferior to the smaller portions of the old work which remain. Still, the whole effect, with the bright afternoon, and later, the evening light upon this great face, is simply superb. Then inside there is a chapel covered with frescoes by Luca Signorelli, which takes rank with any of the great painted chapels which can be named. Every inch of it is covered with fresco, picture, or ornament ; I never saw such pro-fusion of imagination and invention, and all with such perfect self-restrained power and taste. The main subjects are, the End of all Things, the Apocalyptic Woes, Resurrec-tion, Judgment, Heaven, and Hell ; but the remarkable feature is that this is prefaced by the appearance and triumphs of Antichrist. Antichrist is no dreadful monster, but a most grand and dignified figure, with just a faint suggestion of Him of whom he is the rival ; noble in look and form till you look into the face, and then the wickedness discloses itself ; and he is surrounded with groups of the same stateliness or beauty, and with a profusion of rich and beautiful things, but with nothing that openly suggests bad-ness—only worldliness and its temptations, till you look to the background, and there persecutions and bloodshed are going on. But the whole thing is like reading a perfectly original book on a well-known and trite subject. Henceforth Luca Signorelli will be very high in my estimate of painters ; but no picture I ever saw of his gave me any notion of what I should see of his here. . . .—Ever yours affectionately,

R. W. C.

To the Warden of Keble.

Florence, 4*th June* 1885.

My dear Warden— . . . We are lounging here, taking things easy, and enjoying blue sky and pleasant airs. To-day, Corpus Domini, is a great day. We saw the procession in the Duomo, the Archbishop carrying the Host, and a large crowd of people, partly devout, partly curious, and afterwards a great Mass at S. Maria Novella. But the outdoor processions are given up, except those of the Confraternities, in their white dresses and with their banners and crosses, going and coming. It is hard to make out the real state of feeling ; but I should say that the outward look of devotion was gaining, only one cannot see or hear what goes on among the mockers and haters. The clergy seem to have a considerable hold over the young children ; they have singing services and processions, and the children certainly like the hymns, and know them by heart. When the Archbishop left the Duomo this morning the children were all crowding to kiss his hand, both of their own accord, and put forward by their friends.

But they are funny people. At a Mass this morning there was an old fellow who alternately begged and responded. (*Whisper*), " Povero vecchio, caro signore." (*Aloud*), " Et cum spirito tuo." (*Whisper*), " Un po' di limosina." (*Aloud*), " Amen." (*Whisper*), " Per carità." (*Aloud*), " Amen."

(*Whisper*), "La prego per amor di Dio." (*Aloud*), "Amen,"
and so on. They manage to say their prayers and talk at
the same time without any inconvenience ; you need never
fear interrupting them by a question.

We have been prowling over our old grounds. It is
distressing to see what progress the worms (*tarli*) are making
in some of the dear old pictures on wood. The beautiful
Botticelli in the Uffizi is suffering ; the brutes have drilled
their holes in conspicuous places ; I am afraid they are
as aggressive as the Russians at Pendjeh. The only new
acquaintance we have made is a pretty little cloister of the
Scalzi, near S. Marco, painted by Andrea del Sarto. But
there is nothing like the old places. One gets new estimates
of them. I don't think I used to prize the Accademia as
much as it deserves. The big room is full of magnificence,
even more than the Uffizi, though there are special things
in the Uffizi which nothing equals. And then the great
painted chapels—the S. Maria Novella ones, the Carmine,
and S. Croce. And now we have something to match them
with—those at Spello and Orvieto. I get overwhelmed
sometimes with the wonder, and with the little that seems
to have come of it all. . . .—Ever yours affectionately,

R. W. CHURCH.

For some time past, as an earlier letter has shown,
the Dean had had in mind a History of the Oxford
Movement. The following letter shows that the work
was already in progress :—

To the Warden of Keble.

Deanery, St. Paul's, *7th April* 1886.

My dear Warden—I wish I saw some chance of a rush to Bournemouth. But I do not. I am in the thick of work which is not very easy, trying to say what I can about the later development of the Movement, when Ward got hold of the *British Critic* and drove it like Phaeton till it upset, and he was tumbled into matrimony and the Roman Church. It is not easy work, and I want to get at least a first draft off my hands before Easter. But I hope to have a few days at Oxford after Easter, and to find you there, though Bournemouth would be pleasanter.

It is all very dreary and unhappy just now. The G.O.M. persisting in his heroic enterprise in the teeth of everything and everybody, sure that he is right, and apparently sure that he knows best the conditions of success. I cannot conceive how it will all end. But, whether he is right or not, there is something to me unspeakably pathetic in his solitude.

. . . And if he goes, I am sure I shall not like the conjunction of Lord Hartington and Chamberlain better. Perhaps he is right, and the *via salutis* may open out of the thick of disaster. But I can't see it; and for the second time in my life I have to try as well as I can to unite unabated admiration with the impossibility of moral or intellectual agreement.

Well, I dare say you have heard that we had three days of the Cardinal. He was so bright, so kind, so affectionate; very old and soon tired, but also soon refreshed with a pause of rest, and making fun of his old age. "You know I could not do an addition sum." Anyhow, he was quite alive to all that is passing round him, though cautious and reticent, as he should be. But the old smile and twinkle of the eye, and bright, meaning εἰρωνεία, are all still there, and all seemed to belong to the old days.

So W. Forster is gone . . . Gladstone's little speech was touching, considering how they had parted.

Aubrey Moore is giving us very good lectures. Fred must be getting near the coast of Greece, about Sphacteria and Pylos. He ought to be at Athens to-morrow. He got on very well up to Marseilles.—Ever yours affectionately,

R. W. C.

The writing of the final chapter of *The Oxford Movement*, with its narrative of defeat and seeming failure, had opened up memories of the dark days of 1845 and 1846.

To the Warden of Keble.

Deanery, St. Paul's, 11*th* *November* 1886.

My dear Warden—Thank you for your kind note, and, as ever, kind and generous interest in what I sent you. I think I can read between the lines, that this bit has disappointed you ; and no wonder. It ought to wind up the climax of the tragedy, and it only shows the languor of defeat, even in remembrance. But I don't know what else there was to tell. We sat glumly at our breakfasts every morning, and then some one came in with news of something disagreeable—some one gone, some one sure to go.

The good Heads ate and drank, and only cared in an obscure sort of way for these things. When an impudent and troublesome imposture is at last blown up, the impostors —and it was not they who went, but we who stayed, who were voted impostors—keep "coy," and say little. We read, we worked at articles for the *Christian Remembrancer* and *Guardian,—et voilà tout.* The only two "facts" of the time were that Pusey and Keble did not move, and that James Mozley showed that there was one strong mind and soul still left in Oxford. All the rest were the recurring tales, each more sickening than the other, of the "goings over;" stories, often incredible, of the break-up of character for the moment ; mixtures of tragic pathos with broad farce, of real self-sacrifice with determined indulgence in the pleasure of satisfying one mastering craving ; of blundering trickery and a conscience like a compass which has lost its magnetism, with undoubted and most serious earnestness.

But I must stop. I am better, but still bad. I am so glad to hear of your mending.—Ever yours affectionately,

R. W. C.

The "truce of God," in ecclesiastical matters, of which the Dean had spoken in a former letter, had been rudely broken in upon by the prosecution of Mr. Bell Cox of St. Margaret's, Liverpool, for ritual offences, and his consequent imprisonment.

To the Archbishop of Canterbury.

Deanery, St. Paul's, *26th May* 1887.

My dear Lord Archbishop—You have always been so kind to me that I venture, asking your indulgence if I am too bold, to write a few words to you about what has greatly disturbed and distressed me—the Bell Cox matter. I do not write to give you the trouble of answering, but because I think you may wish to know what is passing in the minds of persons and classes of many different shades of opinion.

I say at once that I have no remedies to suggest for the unhappy and unexpected state of things into which we have drifted back. I cannot hope much from legislation, even if legislation of any kind were just now more practicable than it seems. My only hope is from the moral weight of the Episcopate being thrown with all its force on the side of toleration and peace. But I will venture to say what particularly touches me in this case, and what seems to me a special danger arising out of it. This Bell Cox case has come home to my sense of justice far more strongly than any of the previous imprisonments. They were in the thick of battle, and of hot blood. This comes after all has cooled down. . . . To me it comes with the sense of almost intolerable wrong, when one sees a quiet man, in full agreement with his congregation, made a victim, in the midst of all the varieties of opinion and practice. . . . For it is too cynical an excuse, as I believe is sometimes made, that a bishop needs some outward move, like a prosecution, to make him obey what he emphatically proclaims to be the law over his own clergy.

What makes me very uneasy is this. The day may come on us, notwithstanding our present respite, when the Church may have to go forth into the wilderness. It will anyhow be a difficult task to keep parties together in her in such a revolution. Low Churchmen, Broad Church, High Churchmen, will all be difficult to manage. But it will make things still more awkward, if there is then any large body of men who are smarting under a strong sense of injustice suffered during the days of establishment. Think how the arguments for Rome would be pressed, and how bitterness of mind gives them force. The one counterpoise to this would be if men could remember that, though the lawyers had been hard upon them, the Episcopate had made its voice heard clearly and powerfully on the side of patience and forbearance and real fairness, against the miserable system of ignoble worrying, which ends in things like the Bell Cox scandal.

Please forgive me if I have spoken more warmly than becomes my place. But I am afraid that I am thought a coward by some of my friends, for not repeating what has been done before, and heading a list of signatures to some public representative. The time for that seems to me past, and it might be greatly misinterpreted. But I do feel as strongly as to the real wrong, and the real danger of such things as we have only just escaped, as any one who wishes to speak strongly in public. It must not be forgotten *before whom* all these things are done ; not only the English Church and people, but Christendom, which means more and more to us every year that we live, as every year brings new and formidable dangers to all religion. And what all see is, that while Mr. Bell Cox goes to prison for having lighted candles, and mixed water with the wine, and refusing to give up such things, dignified clergy of the Church can make open questions of the personality of God, and the fact of the resurrection, and the promise of immortality.

Under our present conditions—necessary conditions as it seems to me, with which I for one do not quarrel—of vast liberty and inevitable compromise, I should be sorry to see even such things put down by courts of law. Their true enemies, their true antidotes, are not judicial sentences, but Christian ideas, not only in discussion, but in life and action ; as long as these ideas can command enthusiasm and self-sacrifice, they will do what arguments cannot do, and much less, force.

. . . Once more, please forgive me. Believe that I am most sensible of all the difficulties which encompass any public action, and most sure of your deep sympathy for all that is just and merciful, and that makes for peace ; and that it is with the sincerest respect and affection that I subscribe myself your very faithful servant,

R. W. CHURCH.

To LORD BLACHFORD.

DEANERY, ST. PAUL'S, 25th June 1887.

MY DEAR BLACHFORD—Well—our drums and trumpets [1] (the latter very fine) banged and blared to great effect, and made Mayor and Aldermen and Common Councilmen "sit up," to their great satisfaction. I flatter myself that our service was not the least properly arranged one, or the least effective. As Stainer says, Handel's *Te Deum* is heavy to modern ears ; and I think it does not touch the tender and pathetic part of the *Te Deum*. But it is wonderfully stately and impressive in its opening. I noticed one thing which perhaps is an over-refinement. The least striking bit is the rendering of the verses concerning the Three Persons—" The Father—Thine honourable, true, and only Son—Also the Holy Ghost the Comforter." It is not dwelt on, but run through—almost rushed through, as if it were only one verse. Well, when Handel wrote was just the time when Queen Caroline, wife of George II., was supposed to be countenancing the people who took the wrong side in the

---

[1] At a service held in St. Paul's on the occasion of the Queen's Jubilee.

great Trinitarian controversy then raging. It would be curious if that influenced a composition which, of course, would be talked about in the court of the hero of Dettingen, 1743.

The Grays are with us, not a bit tired with all their gay doings at Cambridge and Oxford. This evening Dr. Gray is gone off with my wife and F. to a garden party at Dollis Hill, having a great desire to see the G.O.M., and Mrs. Gray and the girls to the Archbishop's party at Lambeth.

I hope your affairs went well. It has, after all, been a wonderful time. I am rather better, but cannot do anything fatiguing without bringing on breathlessness and distress. I was greatly done up with the *funzione* on Thursday.—Ever yours affectionately,   R. W. C.

To the Rev. George Bainton.

Deanery, St. Paul's, 21st September 1887.

Dear Sir—I would gladly help one who writes so kindly as you do, if I could do so. But I have nothing to say. I have never studied style as such ; and I hardly imagine to myself how it is to be studied. It has always seemed to me that thoughts brought their own words, which, of course, had to be considered and sifted; but the root of the expression must be in the thought itself, which, if it was real and worth anything, would suggest the expression.

And except in watching against the temptation of *unreal* and of *fine* words, I do not recognise in myself any special training for style. The great thing in writing is to know what you want and mean to say, and to say it in words that come as near to your meaning as you can get them to come. Of course this is sometimes troublesome, and often in the end unsatisfactory. That is the old and the true rule of writing, because it is based on the effort after reality, and is the counter-charm to laziness and negligence, and to show and make-believe. It involves certain bye-rules against these faults—care and trouble, and satisfying yourself that you have said what you meant ; merciless cutting out of merely fine language and of useless adjectives and adverbs ; care about your verbs in preference to your adjectives. After all, self-restraint and jealousy of what one's self-indulgence or vanity tempts us to is the best rule in writing as in eating. A good writer once said, "Always cut out a passage which you are most proud of."

As you see, I am a bad expounder of the secrets of writing. When I was a boy, and at college, I did a great deal of translating from English into Latin, which is a great discipline in itself. Where one's stock of words came from I cannot tell. But I suppose they come if one reads with care good English. Shakespeare, Wordsworth, Burke, Walter Scott, Defoe (*Robinson Crusoe*), Goldsmith, were, as far as I can remember, the books I used to value, as giving, besides their thoughts, the most delightful and striking ways of saying them. Besides these, I heard and read a good deal of Mr. Newman's preaching; and it is, I am sure, to him that I owe it, if I can write at all simply and with the wish to be real. Of course being accustomed to good models produces insensibly a habit of mind which dislikes and shrinks from what is merely conventional, unmeaning, and "flash."

I am afraid I have not been able to suggest anything that you do not know as well as I do. But, as I said, I have never gone into the analysis [1] of style.—Yours truly,

R. W. CHURCH.

---

[1] Some jottings from an old note-book of the Dean's, in which he has set down some observations on the course and working of his own

To Dr. Asa Gray.

DEANERY, ST. PAUL'S, 26th November 1887.

MY DEAR FRIEND—I have treated you very shabbily. I
did not write to say good-bye to you when you left, and to
beg your pardon for not arranging to have a last sight of
you. Of course I have been meaning to tell you this any
time since then ; and now it has come to November, and it
is not yet done.

We were very glad to hear Mrs. Gray's account of herself
during the voyage. I suppose you are happily and busily at
work, with the pleasant feeling that if winter cuts off our
outdoor's enjoyment, it invites to comfortable employment
within ; and you can stay in and work with a good conscience
because it is too bad to go out.

We have not been quite so fortunate. I had looked
forward with some hope to being able to breast the winter
in London, and to avoid the break-up of home, at least till
some time forward next year. But it won't do. About a
month ago it turned sharp and cold, and my lungs began to
give in, and refuse to do their work. Last week was one of
fat, black fogs, thick with carbonic and sulphurous acids. I
was fairly beaten, and ordered away ignominiously to the
Riviera at once. And so I go : though the last few days

mind, may have an interest when read in connection with the above
letter. "*First thoughts*, fresh thoughts ; *second thoughts*, corrected,
often stiff and formal ones ; *third thoughts*, shy, homely thoughts,
lurking about half ashamed and unconscious in corners of one's mind,
exceptions hardly worth while making, qualifications one only just
glances at or passes over, details seemingly not of due dignity, points
which seem too troublesome to make out and state, or too cumbrous,
often generalisations, at first sight commonplace, but with the real
gist of the matter in them. These third thoughts worth keeping a
close eye upon."

have been milder, and I better. But much the worst is that Fred is more deeply touched than I am ; and I am afraid that Dr. Ogle is seriously anxious about him. He may work through it. There are people who are active and doing effective work with only one lung, or one and a half. But every one does not get off so easily ; and for some time to come he will have to lead the life of an invalid, with an end to all prospects at the bar. He can amuse himself with a certain amount of literary work ; but it is doubtful whether he will be able to do much more than amuse himself ; while a severe cold might at any time be more than he could bear.

We go on Monday to Hyères (he also), where, if we like it, we shall be stationary for some time, perhaps for a couple of months, or even more. This will depend on health, and what Riviera air and sun do for us.

I suppose by this time Darwin's life will have reached you. In spite of that refusal to accept the Hand stretched forth out of the darkness, which saddens so many of the lives of our time, he seems a very attractive and noble person. The utter absence of bigwiggedness, the simplicity and the candour, the genuine delight in taking trouble and giving help, the kindness and brightness, the unworldliness and absence of elation, seem to me very charming. I have only seen the review in the *Times*, but it was full, though it seemed to me a little overstrained for the person who was its subject.

Good-bye, and be happy. All best messages to Mrs. Gray. —Ever yours affectionately, R. W. CHURCH.

With these words the long correspondence closes. Two days after they were written, Dr. Gray was struck down with paralysis at his home in Cambridge, America, and died after a few weeks of lingering illness. And

the letter has a further sad significance. It marks the
end of the varied and delightful converse of thirty-five
years; it tells too of a deeper sorrow which was fast
approaching in the death of the Dean's only son.
Hitherto, whatever had been the pressure from public
anxieties, the home life had been one of singularly
unclouded brightness. Nothing had ever occurred to
break in upon its completeness, and as the years had
advanced, they had brought with them the added happiness of tastes and interests and enjoyments shared in
common. His son had inherited from the Dean much
of his classical and literary taste; and in his good
scholarship, his accurate and fastidious literary instinct,
his keen insight, and simplicity, and exacting love of
truth, there were qualities that carried on the resemblance
of mind and character between father and son. His
little volume, *The Trial and Death of Socrates*, published
in Macmillan's Golden Treasury Series, as well as his
translation—the first that had appeared in English—
of Dante's Latin treatise *De Monarchia*, bear the marks
of scholarly workmanship, such as gave promise of further
excellence and success in the future. For a few weeks
after the foregoing letter was written, the change to the
soft climate and sunshine of the south of France seemed
to allow the hope of a possible rally; but such hope as
there was quickly faded, and in the middle of January,
at Hyères, the end came.

Among the letters of sympathy called forth by such
a sorrow was one from the Archbishop of Canterbury,
which brings out touchingly the proud affection that,

under an appearance of reserve, marked all the son's
thoughts and feelings towards his father. "I think I
have told you," the Archbishop writes, "how he once
made an hour pass so brightly and strangely for me by
a most loving and minute account and analysis of his
father's last sermon—how present it all seemed to him,
and he to feed on it. I thought there are not many
fathers who so preach to any son's heart and mind—
or any one's at all."[1]

[1] It will be forgiven, if to the preceding words is added the testimony of the late Lord Justice Bowen, in whose chambers Mr. Church
had for a time read law as a pupil.

"I should like you to know," he wrote to the Dean, "that he
was appreciated by those outside his own immediate circle. In some
ways he was singularly unlike other pupils I ever had—there was
an element of unworldliness of the highest degree about him—that in
spite of his great ability would always have made it difficult for him
to enjoy the law as a career—and which 'differentiated' him in a
marked way from men of intellectual powers like his own. When
you came to know him well, one felt the attraction of this, and all
that it connoted, the spotlessness of character that went with it ; the
separation in some sense that it entailed from others ; and the refinement and chivalrous simplicity that was so apparent, or rather trans-
parent, in all he did. I should have said, recalling all my association
with him at 1 Brick Court, that it would always have been doubtful
how far the rough ways of a rough profession would not have ended,
in spite of his cleverness and his gifts, in driving him away from it.
There was an innocent preference of simpler and better things that
made one conscious that the law was not his ideal of a profession,
though for your sake I believe he would loyally and thoroughly have
done all that his health permitted to succeed. But a 'lovable' and
simple nature is not overjoyed at the bar, and its excitements and
performances—and I should always have half felt as if he was thrown
away at it—unless he had happened (and chance is really an element
in the calculation) to rise suddenly to the crest of the wave.

"You doubtless know how deep and faithful his devotion was to
his home. I never saw *any one* in whom the 'star' of home shone
so continuously and so brightly. I am satisfied, from what I saw of
him, that you were his first thought,—I mean by you, yourself and
those dear to him,—and that he would always have given up anything
for you.--Yours very sincerely CHARLES BOWEN."

To THE ARCHBISHOP OF CANTERBURY.

HYÈRES, 28th January 1888.

MY DEAR LORD ARCHBISHOP—We are very grateful to you and Mrs. Benson for thinking of us. It has been a dreadful and unexpected blow. Nothing that has ever happened to me in life has been like that moment when we saw that no breath came through his lips. We had hoped till the last two days; just before then there had been a distinct improvement, which surprised the doctor. But he was spared much suffering, though he was very weary and feeble. The end was in peaceful sleep.

For more than forty years death has not come very near us; and now we have been made acquainted with his awful presence among us. We have been hearing much of him by the hearing of the ear; and now our eyes have seen him in our own home, and very close to us. We did not know what is such a common experience; now we do know. Such partings are a very sorrowful part of our condition here.

But it is not to be told how much we have to be thankful for; above all, the sweet, gentle, uncomplaining patience with which he went, day by day, along that weary road to the end. He took us by surprise: there was not a murmur from first to last; and he used to be quick and impatient sometimes in his days of health. But now all was quiet, grateful, obedient affection and self-command. We found indeed, that after all our thirty-three years of him, we did not know him—did not know all that he had been thinking of in past days; did not know how he loved us; did not know, either, how he was valued and loved by the few friends whom he lived with, and how his influence with them had been strong, and for all high and good things. Perhaps we should not have known all this if we had gone before him. He had, more than any one I ever knew, the *child*, the child's irony and reserve, joined to the *man* of resolute, independent, truth-loving thought. And all these years he has been slowly ripening, and we could not always understand the process, and at times were even anxious about it. Now we know, as far as this world can know; and it is indeed a thing to bless God for.

Forgive me for so running on ; but a thing like this fills the mind for long. He used to talk of your kindness to him at Zermatt. Zermatt and Athens divided his heart with his home. He was to have spent this winter at Athens. May we ask to be most kindly remembered to Mrs. Benson. —Yours most gratefully and affectionately,

R. W. CHURCH.

To MRS. ASA GRAY.

HYÈRES, *5th February* 1888.

MY DEAR MRS. GRAY—I hope that I am not giving you trouble by writing at this moment, but I do not like to let it pass. I have seen that the end has come. I cannot help feeling that your weeks of waiting have been, for much of them, ours too. So it has been ordered, and if there could be anything that could make his departure more affecting to me, it would be this.

Such a time makes one look back. And surely, I look back with the sense that in his friendship I have had one of the purest and most unmixed blessings in my life. It is so strange too. First, just the chance acquaintance in Oxford, ripening, by his sympathy and by happy events, into most affectionate regard ; never long interrupted, and connected besides with so much that is so delightful to recall: mornings at Zermatt, or lying on the turf at the Riffel among the flowers ; visits at Whatley and Mells, with Mr. Horner with us ; visits at Blachford, and bright conversations between him and Lord Blachford; the arrival of books, or extracts from journals, or essays on Darwin, or scientific biographies —and all the interest which his sympathetic mind seized on. It is all most delightful to remember and to think about ; it is indeed something to be grateful for ; it is something to give body and strength to hope.

But I did not mean to run on. I only write to tell you of our most deep sympathy. And yet, what joy and consolation you must feel in what has been.

All kindest remembrances from us all.—Yours very sincerely,   R. W. Church.

To Lord Blachford.

Cap d'Antibes, 31st March 1888.

My dear Blachford—I hope we shall see you in town. We must be turning homeward after next week. How quickly the first quarter of the year has gone. I wish it had included a week of you here. We have had some uncomfortable weather, but on the whole it has been very pleasant ; deadly quiet, but with one or two acquaintances to remind us of an outside world—an English *propriétaire*, Mr. Wyllie, with a charming place and great friendliness, an old French captain, *au long cours*, Lord Acton, Mrs. Pole Carew.

. . . These French are odd people. In most public matters, it is of course to ignore religion ; but there are just one or two in which it is publicly recognised. The military Mass still holds its ground; but in the navy it seems that it

is necessary to defer still more to the feelings of the sailors,
who are most of them fishermen and men of "*cabotage*," of
whose piety all the churches of the coast contain such ample
memorials in the shape of objects recognising vows made in
moments of danger.   Anyhow, Good Friday is officially
kept on board the fleet, by order of the Maritime Prefect of
Toulon, in the most solemn manner.   At eight o'clock a
gun was fired, and all the flags were set at half-mast, and the
yards and gaffs drooped and sloped, which is the sign of
mourning; and all through yesterday, and till ten this morning, the flag-ship fired a gun every hour.   No work was
done, and especially no washing of clothes allowed.   Then
at ten this morning, Easter Eve, a gun was fired, all the
yards crossed, and flags run up, and a salute of twenty-one
guns fired by the admiral's ship.   And yet they will not
let a Christian put his nose into an infant school if they can
help it. . . .—Ever yours affectionately,

R. W. CHURCH.

From the time of his son's death the Dean withdrew
himself more and more from public life. The thought
of resignation was constantly before his mind, and was
only kept back from more practical expression by his
unwillingness to leave to a successor the burden of a
lawsuit which had been set on foot under the auspices
of the Church Association upon the completion of the
reredos in St. Paul's. There was still the ready and
sympathetic response to the interests and work of others,
as the few detached letters which yet remain to be given
will show; but for himself and for what concerned his
own life the old spring and spirit had in great measure
passed away.

2 D

The following letter, which touches on the literary sympathies of the men of the Oxford Movement, has reference to a letter of the late Master of Balliol to Mr. Wilfred Ward on the subject of the Oxford Movement :—

To WILFRED WARD, Esq.

ETTENHEIM, TORQUAY, 22nd *January* 1889.

I am sorry to hear what you say about Jowett's paper. Of course I quite understand his disliking and despising the Movement as reactionary, unphilosophical, superstitious, and petty. But such statements as that the Tractarians were ignorant of literature, and disparaged it, throws doubts on his power of understanding things. Of whom does he speak ? If he is thinking of the least cultivated and intellectual of the party, it may be true, as it would be of any earnest religious movement which has objects higher than mere study and cultivation of literature. And of course, in the days of the Movement, theology and the interests of moral discipline were paramount to everything, literature included, or politics, or social life, or athletics. But to say that Newman or Keble were ignorant of literature—history, poetry, even novels—or uninterested in it, or encouraged such ignorance in their friends, is too extravagant. The mention of Coleridge and Wordsworth is unfortunate. I should have said they were the poets whom the Movement people thought most of. Tennyson and Browning were too young then. I can say for myself that I was very early a Coleridgian (in poetry) and a Wordsworthian, and I learnt my liking for Coleridge and Wordsworth from three very typical Movement men,— Charles Marriott ; Moberly, once tutor of Balliol, afterwards Bishop of Salisbury ; and F. Faber. Whatever is to be thought of them, they were certainly not ignorant of literature, as literature existed in those days. I used to hear criticisms on Wordsworth's " pantheism," but they were from Evangelical friends.

Poor Tractarians! Jowett attacks them for want of literature, another man for deficiency in Biblical exegesis, another man for want of German philosophy, and ignorance of Kant. It seems that they were expected to exhaust all important subjects in the few years when they were mostly fighting for their lives. It is odd that such a poor lot should have been able to leave such a mark behind them.—Yours very faithfully, R. W. CHURCH.

A new phase in the ritual struggle, to which the Dean's letters for the last fifteen years have so often referred, was begun in the prosecution of the Bishop of Lincoln in 1889 for ritual offences. Such a proceeding was received with disapproval by many who were not High Churchmen. Upon the invitation of the Dean of Peterborough, Dr. Perowne, a Conference was held in the Jerusalem Chamber between members of the High Church and Low Church party for the purpose of considering the present state of Church matters, with special reference to the prosecution of the Bishop of Lincoln. It is to this meeting that the following letter from Dean Church to his son-in-law refers :—

To DR. PAGET.

ETTENHEIM, TORQUAY, 3rd February 1889.

MY DEAR FRANK—I am glad you are going, but I wish Bright was going with you. A great historical authority,

with his facts at command, is like a strong force of movable
artillery in a battle.

It is difficult to see what practical result can come, at least
at once, from your meeting. But I am glad to hear of the
proposal, and I am especially glad that you are going, both
because of what you can say, and because you will have an
opportunity of judging of the men on the other side, which
you could not ordinarily have. . . . Of course the difficulty
on both sides is the strength of their *tails*; it is the difficulty
of all parties, from Corcyra to the Jacobins and the Parnellites.
And the strength of the tails arises from the fear and distrust
of each party towards the other, which makes them unwilling
to lose the support of the tails, even when the main body
dislikes the violence of the tails. And so the fatal circle
goes on.

After touching upon some reported instances of excessive and indefensible advance, the letter continues—

What really shelters [such things] is the practical impunity
which the legal prosecution of innocent and right things has
brought about. Men talk defiantly because law has been so
strained against the Eastward position, and vestments, and
the mixed chalice, that it has broken down under the strain.
Law, strange to say, in England, has actually broken down
under the over-strain. No one cares to observe it, because,
though half a dozen men, perhaps, are made to suffer, no one
feels that it has the authority which law ought to have, as
the real voice of either Church or nation, and it is notoriously
disregarded far and wide by both sides.

The thing that everybody ought to try for is the restoration of the position of law ; law to be used for legitimate
purposes, to put down real mischiefs, not to worry and

disturb things which, in a Church like ours, ought to be left free. The immense majority, not only of English clergymen but of High Churchmen, would be glad to have a rule of law, would be glad to accept the discretion of the Bishops, if they could be only sure that they would meet with sincere and real justice, such as they expect to meet in the civil administration of law. But both law, and, till lately, Episcopal rule, have had such a doubtful record that men find a difficulty in trusting them.

Dean Perowne's side is now the aggressive one, and has been, ever since the breakdown of the Gorham suit. If anything is to be done it is they who must begin. Have they the will or the power to stop these prosecutions? The Bishop of Liverpool surely is as obnoxious to all High Churchmen as the Bishop of Lincoln can be to any Low; yet he has not been attacked, either for his ritual defects or his extravagant pronouncement about the Eucharist. Will they let us have as much "liberty of prophesying" and liberty of worship as the Bishop of Liverpool claims, without legal interference? If they cannot, or will not, or dare not, for fear of * * * and the *Record*, there is nothing to be done.

I send you a note of * * *'s. You see his position. He never can realise (1) that the Ritualists have been unjustly treated, and that this of itself creates the difficulty of restraining and protesting against their excesses, and (2) that the worship of the Church and its forms have necessarily advanced, in a younger generation, far beyond what to an older generation seemed natural and sufficient. Let me know how you fare.—Yours affectionately,   R. W. C.

The letter which follows is in acknowledgment of a

paper read before a clerical society on the question—
"How far is the impression made by *Robert Elsmere*, and
the extent of its circulation, due to any failure on the
part of Christians as teachers?"

To Lady Welby.

Ettenheim, Torquay, 14*th February* 1889.

My dear Lady Welby—Thank you for sending me your
paper.[1] How far your indictment is warranted I do not
know. We all generalise from our own point of view. But
I am quite content to take its warning to myself.

But—apart from scholars and people claiming independence—when the ordinary mass of us have to choose between
speaking of the Bible as the Church has hitherto done, and
the new language of criticism, it is fair to ask, "What *does*
criticism say?" And here it seems to me that while the
questions have been innumerable, and the answers also, the
crop of clear, certain, convincing answers has been a
strangely small one. Nothing seems to me more remarkable
than the contrast in our time between the certainties of
physical science and the contradictory and uncertain results,
the barrenness, as a whole, of criticism applied to the questions which most interest men.

I certainly know no one who is capable of revising the
received belief about the Old and New Testament. This
is a fact to be faced like other facts. Doubtless we are
in the midst of perplexities. They call for courage and
honesty, and they also call for patience, which eminently

---

[1] "An Appeal from a learner to all who teach in the Name of
Christ."

goes with real love of truth. " In patience possess your soul," is a maxim for the intellect as well as for conduct.— Yours very faithfully, R. W. CHURCH.

Among the Dean's papers was found the rough draft of a further letter to Lady Welby on the same subject, which, with added emphasis, enjoins the need of caution and patience :—

ETTENHEIM, TORQUAY, 18th February 1889.

MY DEAR LADY WELBY — Your letter came all right. Thank you for its kindness. But still I am not convinced that the mass of Christian teachers—for of this the question is—have committed a great sin in not plunging into the strife of tongues, in which they are for the most part incompetent to take a useful part, and in which the conclusions arrived at have been so varying and contradictory. It is not dishonest, as it seems to me, for a person to recognise that there are questions which are beyond his force to examine, and which he had better leave alone. A man *ought*, if he is conscious that he cannot deal with them, to leave them alone ; much more abstain from pressing them on others. It may require as much courage to say, I don't know, as to pronounce an opinion ; and much of our trouble comes from incompetent handling on all sides.

Meanwhile the strife of tongues will go on merrily, whether we like it or no. With such cavaliers as your correspondent F., who wants to discuss *Robert Elsmere* at a dinner party, and who feels " creepy " because a father told a daughter that she had better not read it, the war is in no danger of flagging. Polemics are in the air, in novels and newspapers and magazines, and anybody may easily know what is the current question and argument and conclusion.

No one can prevent it, and we know too little to regret it. But I venture to think that we shall find much virtue one day in patience. Patience does not mean inaction, and not talking does not mean not thinking. Without being a sceptic or an agnostic, one may feel that there are questions in the world which never will be answered on this side the grave, perhaps not on the other. It was the saying of an old Greek, in the very dawn of thought, that men would meet with many surprises when they were dead. Perhaps one will be the recollection that when we were here, we thought the ways of Almighty God so easy to argue about.

Nothing that I have said refers to those who have a call to examine and to speak. I only look with alarm on any attempt to press average people to be in a hurry to deal with matters which are too hard for them.

I need your indulgence for this long story, and I am sure I shall have it.—Yours very faithfully, R. W. CHURCH.

For the Dean the time of partings had set in in earnest. Following on his son's loss had come the death of Dr. Gray, and within a year that of Bishop Lightfoot; and he had now to receive the news of the fatal illness of Lord Blachford, his closest and most intimate friend since the days when they were Fellows of Oriel together.

To LORD BLACHFORD.

DEANERY, ST. PAUL'S, 26th September 1889.

MY DEAR BLACHFORD—Thank you very much for writing to me. There are things and times for which there are no words; as when you spoke to me at Blachford about our friendship, and thanked me. What could I say when I remembered the immense difference between your debt and mine, and what life and everything would have been to me without all that you have done for me and been to me— more than I can understand, though it is seldom out of my mind.

It is a thing to be beyond anything thankful for to have had such blessings, and for so long. May God help me to accept the change, and use it as it ought to be used. The thought of what is to take the place of things here is with me all day long since Fred's departure ; but it is with a strange mixture of reality and unreality, and I wish it did me all the good it ought. Books are not satisfactory—at least I have always found it so. It seems to me that there is nothing equal to letting the Psalms fall on one's ears, till at last a verse seems to start into meaning, which it is sure to do in the end. And the Collects are inexhaustible.—Ever yours affectionately, R. W. CHURCH.

To MRS. ASA GRAY.

DEANERY, ST. PAUL'S, 18*th October* 1889.

MY DEAR MRS. GRAY — I have to thank you for two volumes[1] of most interesting reading. Besides the interest of the subjects discussed, there is a special *cachet* in all Dr. Gray's papers, great and small, which is his own, and which seems to me to distinguish him from even his more famous contemporaries. There is the scientific spirit in its best form, imaginative, fearless, cautious, with large horizons, and very attentive and careful to objections and qualifications ; and there is besides, what is so often wanting in scientific

---

[1] *Scientific Papers of Asa Gray*, selected by C. S. Sargent.

writing, the human spirit, always remembering that besides facts and laws, however wonderful or minute, there are souls and characters over against them of as great account as they, in whose mirrors they are reflected, whom they excite and delight, and without whose interest they would be blanks. This combination comes out in his great generalisations, in the bold and yet considerate way in which he deals with Darwin's ideas, and in the notices of so many of his scientific friends, whom we feel that he was interested in as *men*, and not only as scientific inquirers. The sweetness and charity which we remember so well in living converse, is always on the look-out for some pleasant feature in the people of whom he writes, to give kindliness and equity to his judgments.

And what a life of labour it was! I am perfectly aghast at the amount of grinding work of which these papers are the indirect evidence. And it makes one think of one's own loitering life.

I shall always count it among the highest pieces of good fortune in my life—and I have had many—that I was allowed to come across him, and to have the honour and delight of becoming his friend.

Once more, thank you very much for sending me these memorials. The one regret that I have is that Lord Blach-ford, who was so much attracted to him, is now too weak and ill to become acquainted with them. He would have read the history of Sequoia with the greatest interest. But he is slowly fading away—with no pain—but with each week leaving him weaker than the last.—Yours very faithfully,

R. W. Church.

The reference with which the following letter opens

is to the account of a visit paid to Cardinal Newman, in his beautiful and serene old age, at Birmingham :—

TO HIS DAUGHTER.

DEANERY, ST. PAUL'S, *Lord Mayor's Day*, 1889.

DEAR M.—Your letter is an historical document. It may prove to be the last intimate talk that any of us have had with him. That gesture of his, raising his arm, brings back old days as much as anything. The change I should say that old age makes in respect to death is a distinct and remarkable one. Of course at all times of life one may have the quick and keen sense of its possibility, and of what it may be. But in old age, it is like the move to something new and unknown when one moves on a stage in a journey, or leaves home for a new abode—not an abstract thought, but a real *move;* and at last it gets to be the only reality that one has in view, and a reality of a different kind from anything else, because no question of possibility can arise as to the fact of it.

> " All passes with the passing of the days,
> All but great Death—Death the one thing that *is,*
> Which passes not with passing of the days."

I have been reading a most melancholy, but in parts beautiful book, Edwin Arnold's poetisation of Buddhism, *The Light of Asia.* But what a Light !

I send the last report of Blachford. The severing of intercourse, where intercourse was so lively and so continuous, is very sad.—Ever yours affectionately, R. W. C.

Lord Blachford's death took place in November. In his letter acknowledging the words of affectionate sympathy with which Dr. Liddon speaks of such a loss, the Dean touches on the subject of Biblical criticism, to which Dr. Liddon's letter had also referred :—

To Dr. Liddon.

Dover, 28th November 1889.

My dear Liddon—Thank you with all my heart for your kind thoughts of me. There are few separations which could so bring home to me the sense of irreparable loss.

It gives edge to such trials when troubles and anxieties, such as you speak of, are added to them. Ever since I could think at all, I have felt that these anxious and disturbing questions would one day or other be put to us ; and that we were not quite prepared, or preparing, to meet them effectively. To us Church people the general answer was so clear, that it made us think that they wanted no further trouble ; and they have been left outside our sphere of interest, to be dealt with by a cruel and insolent curiosity, utterly reckless of results, and even enjoying the pleasure of affronting religion and religious faith. This was sure to be, from the intellectual and moral conditions of our time ; but it seems to me that our apologetic and counter criticism has let itself be too much governed by the lines of the attack, and that we have not adequately attempted to face things for ourselves and in our own way, in order not merely to refute, but to construct something positive on our own side. That, it seems to me, is the great triumph of Bull's *Defensio* and of your Bamptons, and we want something of the same kind which has not yet been done for the Bible—what it really is—how it came to be—who gave it us. That the difficulties about it have been forced, not on arrogant and conceited "experts," claiming

monopoly of all criticism, but on deep-thinking and devout
Catholic believers like * * *, and have given him trouble,
seems to me to show that there is something unsatisfactory
in the present condition of things—though I am the last
person to know what ought to be done to meet it. All that
I can say for myself is, that for such men my trust is in
patience and sympathy.—Ever yours affectionately,

R. W. CHURCH.

It is almost startling to turn from the last letter, and
from those which immediately precede it, with their
record of partings and of the grave anticipation of death,
to so vigorous a bit of literary criticism as is contained
in the following account of the Dean's experience as a
student of Browning's poetry :—

TO STANLEY WITHERS, ESQ.

DOVER, 9th February 1890.

DEAR SIR—It is as hard to explain how one got to like
Browning, as it would be (to me) to explain why I put
Beethoven above Mozart ; and why I cannot help confessing
Bach to be of a higher order than Handel, though Handel
has written things that seem to me Divine. I can only tell
you my experience. Of course I have known Browning, in
a way, for years ; but I never took to him. I had not
laughed at him, because I instinctively felt that he was a
person to stand in awe of ; and I hold it wrong to laugh
where there are evidences of truth and greatness. But I am
afraid I sometimes smiled at Browningites. Then came the
Ring and the Book, and that, in the first place, satisfied a
longing that I had long had, to have the *same set* of facts told

and dealt with, not as they are in the usual novel or play—
that is, with one side assumed to be the true one—but as
they appear to all manner of different people, each with
their own prejudices and interests, and rules of conduct and
judgment, so as to have a little picture of the world judging
the facts before it ; and next, because I found in it such
piercing insight into human realities of thought and feeling,
into the depths and heights of the soul, such magnanimity,
such pervading sense of the awfulness and certainty of Divine
judgment.   Of course there were things that I did not go
with, but they were as nothing to the great picture of right
and wrong as shown in real men and women.

Then I had young people round me who read, and
loved, and defended Browning, and found in him what
their souls longed for ; and they showed me such poems as
Ben Ezra and *Saul* and the *Death in the Desert*, and *Abt
Vogler ;* and various things from *Men and Women ;* and
Christmas Eve and Easter Day, and *Bishop Blougram*, and
Mr. Sludge the Medium ; and we read the *Englishman in
Italy* at Sorrento.   Oddness was not the word for much of
all this ; the poet was writing, not in a grand robe, but in
his shirt-sleeves, and making faces at you.   But through it
all was the deep sense of truth, lighted up with gleams of
beauty, such as did not belong to any poetry I knew.   So I
thought I would try myself on him in earnest, and I got
Sordello.

Well, it was very hard and difficult—hard in making out
what the story meant, hard in grammar and construction,
hard in the learning exacted from the reader.   But it was
plain that it was written for a reader not afraid of trouble,
and I accepted the condition.   I did take a good deal of
trouble, and read it many times, in many moods, in many

ways, beginning at the end, or the middle, trying on it various theories, reserving what I could not make out, which was much, treasuring what I saw to be purpose, and meaning, and beauty, and insight. And so I began to feel as if the cloud was lifting, and though I do not pretend to know all that was in the poet's mind in writing, I got to feel that I had something, and something worth having. And it was an introduction to the poet's method, to his unflinching view of life, to his ever present sense (in which he is like Shakespeare, and in a lower degree like our modern *Punch*), of how much there is of tragic in the most comic, and of comic in the most tragic. He has dealt too largely, I think, lately, in the presentation of the absurd. I think if I was beginning again I should begin with a serious study of *Paracelsus*, and then the Selections.

Let your friend laugh his will, Browning certainly meant him to laugh, and to look out for any absurdity he could feel. Let him be offended if he will, he will sometimes have the right. But let him try to believe that Browning has a poet's eye, the most comprehensive, the most searching, the most minute, for the truths of our present existence and our future hopes of any of our great names—Tennyson, Wordsworth, Shelley. And let him understand that a man who so thinks and so writes, is not to be understood except by a reader who is not surprised at difficulties, and expects to meet them in such themes as Browning's ; and that a great poet requires trouble-taking readers, and will not open his heart and his treasures to the idle or the scornful.— Yours faithfully, R. W. CHURCH.

The death of Cardinal Newman took place in August 1890 ; and when at last the ending of the long life came, it seemed, in spite of all reasonable expectation, to have about it something of unexpectedness.

To the Dean, in particular, the news came with the sense of a peculiar sorrow. Such a loss sent back his thoughts to Oxford, and to the early days of companionship and work together, whilst it summed up, as it were, and completed in itself, the series of partings which had preceded it. The intercourse between the two friends—whether by correspondence, or by meetings at Whatley, or in London, where the Cardinal came as a guest to the Deanery, or in the Dean's visits to Birmingham—had gone on unbroken since its renewal in 1866. And in spite of the necessary changes which their changed positions had brought about, the friendship preserved to the end its distinct and peculiar character. On Cardinal Newman's side there was still the frank confidence and the reliance on sympathy and counsel which had belonged to the old Oxford days; while by those near the Dean, it was always recognised that *Newman* was a name apart, the symbol, as it were, of a debt too great and a friendship too intimate and complex to bear being lightly spoken of, or subjected to the ordinary measures of praise or blame. Where agreement was not possible, the Dean seldom allowed himself any criticism save that which was implied by silence. "I have not attempted a complete criticism of Newman," he wrote to Lord Acton, to whom he had shown the sheets of his book on the Oxford Movement, "partly because I feel it beyond me, partly because it is so against the grain."

Yet this reserve, whilst it guarded his words, seemed to add fresh force and meaning to them when they came. In the *Oxford Movement*, the portrait may be plainly traced—conveyed as well indirectly and by what is implied, as by the regular course of the narrative, but penetrating and arresting throughout. In an article in the *Guardian*, written after Cardinal Newman's death, the same intimate knowledge suggests a clue to an inner unity of thought and aim that might be traced beneath the outward and contradictory changes of position of which the *Apologia* is the record. The following letter, with its words of affectionate sympathy, will show, under another aspect, something of the way in which the Dean had handed on the knowledge which his long friendship had won for him :—

FROM DR. TALBOT.

THE VICARAGE, LEEDS, *August* 1890.

MY DEAREST DEAN—One word of loving sympathy with you in your great loss. Ah! what worlds of meaning and associations and memory this event must carry with it and bring up for you ; this event of which we have been so long on the edge, and which yet hardly seemed as if it could be. Was there ever a life of more sweetly and gravely solemn power to thrill and touch one? What do we not owe him? and what might have been! It is wonderful to think of him *there!*

I don't know whether you will like me to say it—but it is true that you have done more, so much more, than any one to carry on and convey to us the touch of his special

2 E

spiritual and mental power : that indefinable thing. Forgive me for saying so much—but discipleship to such a master was no ordinary " talent," I suppose ; and it may be welcome to know that many would bear witness (for I know that I am only one of many) of your having used it for them. . . .
—Your very grateful and affectionate,   E. S. T.

To Dr. Talbot.

Deanery, St. Paul's, 15*th August* 1890.

My dear Warden—Most hearty thanks for your letter. Only it does make me feel such a fool to be spoken of in the same breath with him.   It is a sad, dark time, in spite of all that one thinks of and remembers, and all that one sees of warm recognition.   It is much more than mere *extinctus amabitur* feelings, for it has been steadily and intelligently growing, with its side fringe of depreciation and dislike.   But one feels now how unique he was, and how, though he was so retired, his place is felt to be empty, and no one to fill it.   But all this is very dark.   It has been a dismal year for me, though I should have felt it more keenly if I had been younger.   Now one only gets comatose.

I should certainly have gone to the funeral if this bronchitis had not made it impossible.   Frank and Helen are going.   Possibly Mrs. Grundy may snarl.   But at marriages and funerals people are allowed more liberty by that lady.

Once more, my dear Warden, thank you very much for your letter.   One of the greatest of "talents" is having friends.   I wish I had employed mine as it ought to have been employed.—Ever yours affectionately,   R. W. C.

A month later came the news of Dr. Liddon's sudden

death, and with it the last loosening of the ties which still held the Dean to public life. The following letter, commenting on the loss, forms a fitting conclusion to the long and various correspondence of a lifetime :—

To the Rev. George S. Barrett.

Deanery, St. Paul's, 20th September 1890.

My dear Mr. Barrett—Thank you most sincerely for your kindness in writing.

It is hard to believe that Liddon is gone—but he is. How one begins to wonder at and long to know that unknown place where, with our former characters and judgments and likings, we are soon to be as actually as we are here. What will there be to respond and answer to the character we take with us ?

I am very sorry to hear of your anxiety. Please let me know how things go, and how your wife is.—Ever yours,

R. W. Church.

Little more remains to be told of the last months of the Dean's life. The losses of the past few years had been telling slowly but surely on health and vitality. The death of Dr. Liddon, the friend and colleague of nineteen years, had been a further unlooked-for blow, and after it the failure of strength was rapid and without recovery. No one who was present in St. Paul's on the occasion of Dr. Liddon's funeral could have seen unmoved the wasted, fragile figure of the Dean, or have listened, without a sense of its pathos and significance, to his broken and scarcely audible voice as it was heard

2 E 2

for the last time in the cathedral of which he had been
so long the head, in the recital of the sentences of
committal to the grave.

Through the autumn the Dean stayed on in London,
able, in spite of increasing weakness, to carry on something of his accustomed life, working at the proofs of
his book on the Oxford Movement, and still sometimes
to be seen in his stall at the week-day services in the
cathedral.   But the approach of winter fogs warned
him to seek a clearer air, and in the beginning of
November he went to Dover.   At Dover he passed the
last few weeks that remained of life, waiting, as it
seemed to those near him, under the shadow of a great
awe, but with a patience, and gentleness, and simplicity
which knew no failure.   His thoughts turned still to
his favourite books, which he had carried with him,
Homer and Lucretius, Dante and Wordsworth and
Matthew Arnold ; and he still followed with something
of his old keenness of interest the course of public
events.

Throughout its course he had watched with deep
anxiety the trial of the Bishop of Lincoln before the
Archbishop's Court at Lambeth.   " This horrid Lambeth
trial haunts me," he had written a year before to his
son-in-law ; " the only hope I have is that the Archbishop may have sagacity enough and courage enough
to see that the safest course is the boldest, and dare to
revise the Privy Council rulings.   If not, the phrase
'Finis Poloniæ' comes constantly into my head."   The
delivery of the Archbishop's judgment took place in

November, and its character and contents brought the
Dean the last flash of happiness before the end. " It is
the most courageous thing that has come from Lambeth,"
he said, " for the last two hundred years." It seemed
to come to him with a touch of reassurance and confirmation in that steady trust in the English Church,
which would not let itself be overthrown by the disasters of 1845, which had gained for him his years of
happy labour among the poor at Whatley, and which
had held on undismayed through the long conflict that
had marked the years of his work in London at St.
Paul's.

On the 10th of December, early in the morning and
quite quietly, the end came.

The Dean's love of Whatley had led him years before
to choose a spot in the quiet country churchyard there
for his last resting-place. And thither he was carried
from St. Paul's, after the early Communion in the north-
west chapel of the cathedral, where his coffin lay in the
midst, and the later funeral service, with its long procession, and solemn music, and gathering of many friends
and colleagues. And there, in the snow-covered churchyard, beside the chancel of the village church, and amid
the farewell gathering of old friends and parishioners,
he was laid at rest. He had left a strict charge that no
memorial should be raised to him. Only one thing he
had asked ;—that a stone like that which he had chosen
to mark his son's grave at Hyères—and which, though
he was spared the sorrow of knowing it, was also, within
three years' time, to mark the grave of his youngest

daughter there—should mark his own grave at Whatley, and that it should bear upon it the same lines from the *Dies Iræ*—

> Rex tremendæ majestatis
> Qui salvandos salvas gratis,
> Salva me, fons pietatis.
>
> Quærens me sedisti lassus,
> Redemisti crucem passus,
> Tantus labor non sit cassus.

THE following List of the Dean's writings does not include articles or sermons which have not since been reprinted separately :—

CATECHETICAL LECTURES OF ST. CYRIL OF JERUSALEM. Translated by R. W. Church, with a Preface by J. H. Newman. No. II. of the " Library of the Fathers." Rivington, 1838.

LIFE OF ST. WULSTAN. No. V. of "Lives of the English Saints." Toovey, 1844.

ESSAYS AND REVIEWS. Collected from the " British Critic " and " Christian Remembrancer." J. C. Mozley, 1854.

SERMONS PREACHED BEFORE THE UNIVERSITY OF OXFORD. Macmillan, 1868.

FIRST BOOK OF HOOKER's ECCLESIASTICAL POLITY. Edited with an Introductory Essay. Clarendon Press, 1868.

LIFE OF ST. ANSELM. Macmillan, 1870.

CIVILISATION BEFORE CHRISTIANITY. Two Lectures delivered in St. Paul's. 1872.

ON SOME INFLUENCES OF CHRISTIANITY ON NATIONAL CHARACTER. Three Lectures delivered in St. Paul's. 1873.

SACRED POETRY OF EARLY RELIGIONS. The Vedas and the Psalms. Two Lectures delivered in St. Paul's. 1874.

These seven lectures, together with the University Sermons of 1868, have been republished in one volume under the title, THE GIFTS OF CIVILISATION. Macmillan, 1880.

THE BEGINNINGS OF THE MIDDLE AGES. "Epochs of Modern History." Longman, 1877.

ESSAY ON DANTE. Republished, together with a Translation of Dante's Latin Treatise, "De Monarchia," by F. J. Church. Macmillan, 1878.

HUMAN LIFE AND ITS CONDITIONS. Sermons preached before the University of Oxford, together with three Ordination Sermons. Macmillan, 1878.

SPENSER. Macmillan's "Men of Letters" Series. 1879.

BACON.   „   „   „   1884.

THE RELATION BETWEEN CHURCH AND STATE. Republished from the "Christian Remembrancer" of 1850. Walter Smith, 1880.

DISCIPLINE OF THE CHRISTIAN CHARACTER. Macmillan, 1885.

ADVENT SERMONS, 1885. Macmillan, 1886.

HOOKER'S ECCLESIASTICAL POLITY. Edited by Rev. John Keble. Seventh Edition, revised by R. W. Church, Dean of St. Paul's, and Francis Paget, Canon of Christ Church, and Regius Professor of Pastoral Theology. Clarendon Press, 1888.

MISCELLANEOUS WORKS. In Five Volumes. Macmillan, 1888.

THE OXFORD MOVEMENT. Macmillan, 1891.

VILLAGE SERMONS. Macmillan, 1892.

CATHEDRAL AND UNIVERSITY SERMONS. Macmillan, 1892.

VILLAGE SERMONS. Second Series. Macmillan 1894.

INDEX

THE END

Printed by R. & R. Clark, *Edinburgh.*